Silent Wager

Silent Wager

ANITA BUNKLEY

KENSINGTON PUBLISHING CORP.
http://www.kensingtonbooks.com

DAFINA BOOKS are published by

Kensington Publishing Corp.
850 Third Avenue
New York, NY 10022

All Kensington titles, imprints and distributed lines are available at special quantity discounts for bulk purchases for sales promotion, premiums, fund-raising, educational or institutional use.

Special book excerpts or customized printings can also be created to fit specific needs. For details, write or phone the office of the Kensington Special Sales Manager: Kensington Publishing Corp., 850 Third Avenue, New York, NY 10022. Attn. Special Sales Department. Phone: 1-800-221-2647.

Dafina Books and the Dafina logo Reg. U.S. Pat. & TM Off.

ISBN 0-7582-1245-3

First Printing: May 2006
10 9 8 7 6 5 4 3 2 1

Printed in the United States of America

PART ONE

THE FLOOD

CHAPTER 1

8 A.M. August 1, 2001

Pewter gray clouds clutched the Houston skyline, blocking the sun completely. Dark and mean, they stretched from the rooftop of the Enron building to the Fox Television satellite tower far beyond the Galleria. At street level, swirling pools of dark water swamped underpasses and low-lying neighborhoods, forcing morning commuters to abandon their cars and climb onto the hoods of their vehicles to wait for the water to recede. After three soggy days of nonstop rain, the storm showed no signs of easing.

Camille Granville studied the grim tableau from the rain-splattered, third floor window of Vendora, the mansion-turned-supper club that she and her husband, Max, were trying to protect. *Three inches of rain an hour*, she recalled the weather report, drumming her fingers on the windowsill, distressed to see that the sandbags stacked along the southern edge of the property had already been breached. Muddy brown water spewed over the makeshift barrier and slapped hard at the double French doors at the rear of the house. She thought about the ancient hardwood floors downstairs, the heirloom tapestry wall coverings, and the wood carvings done by Max's great-grandfather that embellished the solid oak windowsills and doorframes: All would be ruined, she realized, overcome by a sense of helplessness.

During her forty-two years of living in both Florida and Texas, Camille had experienced hurricanes, floods, and tropical storms before, but none as emotionally devastating as this. While growing up in Bayport, a tiny town on the western coast of the Florida peninsula, she and her sister, Rochelle, had loved to sit at the end of the rickety old pier that connected the Gulf to the front of their house and wait for the approaching storm, unafraid of the fury it was determined to unleash. The furious winds would buffet their faces, whip their clothing tight against their small bodies, and threaten to lift them high into the sky. Remaining on the pier until the first huge drops of rain began to fall had been a wondrous challenge, filled with risk and liberation—a game of waiting that never failed to entertain Camille when dark clouds gathered over the water.

But now, she prayed for the rain to stop and for the water to drain away, as the heavy downpour pounded the aging, urban neighborhood without mercy, peeling shingles off the roofs and slashing limbs from the sturdy pin oaks that had lined the streets for decades.

Narrowing her dark gray eyes at the curtain of water, Camille caught her reflection in the wet pane of glass, and was not happy at what she saw. Mud was streaked across her buff-colored cheeks, her eyelids were puffy from lack of sleep, and her jet-black hair, usually a mass of shiny ringlets, hung in an unruly, ragged ponytail. Quickly, Camille removed the blue scarf that was holding her hair off her neck and shook out her black curls, then used the scrap of fabric to wipe at the grit and perspiration on her face.

Turning from the window, she hurried down the narrow attic stairs and into the wide upstairs hallway, feeling the strain of the last twelve hours in her legs, her arms, and her back. It had been a long, grueling night, and she was beyond tired. Working frantically, she and Max had stripped the lower rooms of everything they could carry upstairs: rugs, chairs, books, perishable supplies, and the numerous gilt-framed paintings of Max's ancestors that had been prominently displayed on the dining room walls. With great difficulty, they had managed to raise the heavy rosewood tables and sideboards onto cement blocks, but not the baby grand piano, which would be sacrificed to the flood if water continued to rise inside the house.

Though it was eight o'clock in the morning, the house was dark. Moving along the hallway, Camille raced past the bedroom where she and Max had spent last night, and glanced fleetingly at the boxes of food, water, and candles she had shoved into the room. They would, most likely, have to spend a second night at the supper club, and with no electricity since late yesterday afternoon Camille had prepared as best she could for the long vigil that lay ahead.

At the top of the grand staircase, Camille leaned over the banister and scanned the muggy rooms below, sighing with relief to see Max come out of the library holding a rare African teak statue and a stack of leather bound books. Water that had been seeping under the front door all night now covered the tops of his boots.

"The sandbags have been breached," she called down to him. "A wave of water is at the back door right now."

"I know. I know," he shouted back, racing up the stairs to dump the statue and the books onto the floor. "We don't have much time. I'm grabbing whatever is easy to carry. The books on the lower shelves and the rugs in the library are gone."

"I'm coming down," Camille decided, falling in behind Max as he turned to head back down the stairs.

"Wait!" he ordered brusquely, reaching out to stop Camille.

She stepped from behind Max and looked down—a long, black snake cut through the muddy water at the foot of the stairs and slithered into the shadows.

"Shit! A snake!" she muttered, watching the reptile disappear, then gripping Max's arm. "Don't go back down there!"

"I have to," he threw back. "Don't worry. That snake is not interested in me. He's looking for higher ground just like everyone else. But you stay put. That back door is gonna cave in any minute."

"Oh, please, be careful," Camille warned, her words spilling out as the sound of breaking glass suddenly echoed through the house.

Immediately, Max took the steps two at a time, plunged back into the floodwaters and sloshed his way toward the source of the noise, dodging broken glass, tree limbs, and garbage that had burst into the room along with a great deal of the bayou. Holding onto abandoned pieces of furniture, he inched his way into the dark recesses of the house.

Camille hugged her arms around her waist and waited, terrified for Max. What other creatures had floated in from the bayou? What additional dangers lurked downstairs? Clasping her hands, she waited for Max to return, wishing she were safe at home, in her clean dry house in the suburbs.

"Both patio doors are shattered and we're taking in water like crazy," Max finally shouted up to her. "Damn. It's a real mess down here. Rats, dead birds, and even a few bullfrogs are swirling around with an awful lot of garbage."

"What? Rats? Dead birds? Max, get back up here, now!" Camille ordered. "You're going to get an infection . . . a disease. You can't . . ."

"Hold on. Hold on," he interrupted in a calmer, more controlled tone. "I've got to try to block this hole and slow the water."

"How? What do you think you can do to stop it?" Camille called back, irritated by her husband's stubborn insistence on trying to fix an unfixable mess.

"Don't know. But I gotta try something." Max tossed back, his voice barely audible now.

Shaking her head, Camille picked up the African statue and the books that Max had dropped and placed them on a credenza, then she sat down on the top step and listened to the sound of rain pummeling the rooftop and Max sloshing around downstairs.

She breathed in the musty humid air, certain she could taste the smelly debris that filled the rooms below. Using her blue scarf, she wiped perspiration from her brow while wondering what Max could possibly do to fix the shattered doors. Ten minutes passed before he emerged once more, looking soggy and extremely irritated. Now, the water was thigh-high, and rising.

"No luck," he reported to Camille, mounting the steps as he spoke. "I tried to cover the doors with some heavy sheets of plastic, but it didn't work. Nothing is going to stop the water now. We'll have to wait this out and hope the rain stops soon."

"I think we should try to leave," Camille decided, more anxious to get out than she had been last night. With the bayou pouring in, and no way to stop it, who knew what problems they might have to face? She studied Max, whose muscled arms were shiny with floodwater and splattered with mud. He was soaking wet from his leather cowboy boots to his blue, short-sleeved knit shirt, and his tattered baseball cap was plastered to his head.

"No, I think we're better off staying put," Max replied, removing his red cap to wring it out. "Might get trapped in high water outside. Besides, I don't want to leave the place vulnerable to looters . . . that could be a problem, you know?"

Though not what Camille wanted to think about, she understood his concern. The neighborhood where Vendora was located had once been a place where wealthy Houstonians lived, but urban flight and city sprawl had forced the area into a downward spiral many years ago. Now, it was not the safest of neighborhoods on a clear, sunny day, and occasional vagrants did roam the streets.

"All right, we'll stay," Camille agreed. "We have drinking water, canned food, and candles. I guess we can stick it out one more night." She paused, and then added, "I'd better call Jaiden. Tell her what's going on and see what's happening at home."

"I'm sure she's fine," Max replied, swinging his head from side to side to work out the tight muscles in his neck. "Kingwood never floods, and it's not raining hard in the suburbs."

"But that could change."

"Maybe, but Jaiden will be fine. She's nineteen years old . . ."

"Eighteen," Camille corrected, concerned about her daughter, whom she had left alone last night. "Not nineteen 'til August."

"Well, she's old enough to manage on her own," Max stated, running a hand over his damp shirt.

"Sometimes I wonder," Camille mumbled, placing two fingers to her lips in a moment of thought before adding, with a slight edge of resignation, "She *thinks* she's an adult. Did you know she's smoking again?"

"Really? But not in her room?" Max replied, clearly unhappy with the news.

"No, I think she got our message about that. But her car smells awful. I had to move it out of the driveway yesterday, and not only did I find cigarette butts in the ashtray, but another speeding ticket stuck under the visor. Her third this year. Texas State is going to cancel our auto insurance if she keeps this up. I don't know what she's thinking."

"That she's grown."

"Then she can pay for her ticket, this time."

"How much is it?"

"Doesn't matter. Max, don't you dare give her a cent toward it. She needs to realize that there are consequences to her actions. You can't keep bailing her out of her messes. She's got money put away that she can use."

"Okay, I'll stay out of it. Anyway, she's leaving for college in a few weeks, and won't have a car on campus, so let's not worry about our insurance right now. But I will talk to her."

"Thank you," Camille said. "She rarely listens to me anymore."

"Well . . . Go ahead and give her a call," Max went on. "Let her know we *have* to stay put, that we're fine and we'll get home as soon as we can."

Max's calm, decisive tone settled the question of what to do next, but left Camille thinking about her only daughter, Jaiden, whose irresponsible behavior had become more than irritating.

Jaiden had given her and Max little trouble while attending Wilton, the exclusive all-girls' school she had graduated from in June. She had been a good student, popular, and actively involved in her teenage social scene, but had never resisted any of Max or Camille's rules—until she became best friends with Nici Donald during her senior year. That was when everything seemed to change for the worse—and during Jaiden's senior year she had been nearly impossible to live with. Attitude about everything.

The sound of rushing water broke into Camille's thoughts and she hurried midway down the stairs, Max at her side. They stopped, jaws dropped open in horror to see a surge of water sweep through the downstairs like a rapidly filling riverbed during a thunderstorm.

"Oh God, Max. It's really coming in. Fast. Look!"

Leaning over the banister, Max assessed the situation. "We've removed or secured all that we can. Nothing to do now but wait it out. When the water recedes, we'll have to get right on the cleanup and try to salvage what is left."

Camille glanced up at Max, whose dark brown face was tight with anxiety.

"Insurance *will* cover this, won't it?" she prompted, trying to find a glimmer of hope in the messy situation.

Max lifted one shoulder in a shrug, and then eased down on the step at the top of the landing, both hands on his knees. "We'll see," was all he said.

Camille remained silent, focusing on her husband of twenty-one years. A big-boned man of forty-six, he spent his days and most evenings at Vendora. His smooth brown face was still unlined and his hair was not yet flecked with gray. The furrows of frown lines on Max's forehead and the grim set of his still-firm jaw told Camille how anxious he was.

With a sigh of resignation, she sat down beside Max, slipped her arm through his, and settled in to keep vigil over the lower rooms of their mansion-turned-supper club on Buffalo Bayou.

How high will the water rise? How long will we be trapped? she silently fretted, massaging her neck while turning Max's comments over in her mind. *He's right about staying. We've put too much into this place to go home and simply hope for the best. We have to fight this through together.* She squeezed his hand, knowing she would always stick by Max. *I left him once,* she reminded herself. *And when I returned, I swore I would never leave him again.*

* * *

One shrill giggle, followed by another, jolted Jaiden from a numbing black sleep. For a moment, she was not sure what she had heard or where she was, but soon her mind cleared and she recognized the voice as that of her best friend, Nici—whose distinctive laughter could not be mistaken.

The room seemed stifling hot, and a fuzzy whirl of disjointed thoughts slipped through Jaiden's mind: The ferocious rainstorm. Nici's arrival. Shot after shot of tequila. Music. Laughter. She licked her dry lips and turned onto her side, silently cursing the dull ache that was drumming at the back of her head. What a night! She needed water. Aspirin. More sleep. But getting up would take too much effort, so she squeezed her eyes tightly shut and tried to force herself back to sleep. When Nici's laughter erupted again, Jaiden sat up and scanned her dimly lit bedroom for the source. Frowning, she flopped over onto her stomach, leaned over the edge of the bed, and studied the mound of rumpled bedspread on the floor. It was moving up and down in a telling rhythmic manner. Jaiden shook her head, remembering: Nici and DeJon. They were still here, and still very much together, it seemed.

Jaiden slid her gaze from the action on her bedroom floor to the open pizza box on her dresser, the beer cans stacked on her desk, and the ashtrays overflowing with stubbed out cigarette butts and partially smoked joints. Black ashes had spilled onto her pale beige carpet, creating a nasty stain. Nici and DeJon's clothes were scattered from the doorway to the moving bedspread, leaving no doubt in Jaiden's mind about what her best friends had done last night and what they were doing right now.

Impulsively, Jaiden rolled onto her back and did a quick self-check, running her hands across her round, soft breasts, her flat stomach and slim hips, relieved to find that her tee shirt and bra were still intact, as were her jeans, her panties, and even one red sandal that was dangling from her right foot by its shiny ankle strap. Sitting up, she peeked over at Kevin, who was lying face-down on the other side of her queen-size bed, hugging a pillow, snoring loudly, and still fully dressed, too.

Thank God, Jaiden sighed, unstrapping the lone red sandal, which she tossed to the floor. *Nothing happened.* She liked Kevin Hamilton a lot, but certainly not enough to do more than let him stick his tongue in her mouth and feel her breasts when they kissed. What a relief! She . . . or Kevin must have passed out before things got out of hand last night. She was not a prude, but she was a virgin—and had no intention of going all the way with Kevin, or anyone else for that matter. She was saving herself for that special man whom she hoped to meet at college. However, Nici and DeJon were different—they were engaged. DeJon had proposed to Nici the night of their senior prom and had put a half-carat round diamond ring on her finger. The two were disgustingly inseparable now.

Jaiden sucked in a long breath, anxious to clear her head, vaguely remembering that her mother had telephoned about 7:00 P.M. last night to say that she and her dad planned to stay at Vendora overnight. Her parents' absence had created the tantalizing opportunity for Jaiden to invite Nici, DeJon, and Kevin over to play pool in her dad's new game room. They had wound up drinking margaritas and watching DVDs on his fifty-two-inch high definition TV and smoking a few joints that DeJon had brought along. After that, Jaiden's grasp on the evening's events faded: her plan to kick it with her friends for a few hours had somehow turned into a full-blown celebration of Nici and DeJon's engagement. Now, she was slightly annoyed with herself for having allowed the impromptu get-together to spin so far out of control. She had better haul ass and get the house cleaned up before her mom and dad got home.

Placing one hand on her nightstand to steady herself, she rubbed sleep from her eyes, checked the clock above her closet door, and then yelled at the mounded bedspread moving on the floor. "Get up, Nici. DeJon! Damn. It's eight o'clock! You two have to help me get this place cleaned up."

Slowly, Nici poked her head from beneath the bedspread, her rust-brown twists clinging to her forehead, covering her half-open eyes. She had a baby doll face with rounded cheeks, small even white teeth, huge dark eyes, and a sweet smile that made her look much more innocent than she was. "Okay. Okay. Chill, Jaiden," Nici mumbled, brushing her feathered twists from her face. "I hear you." Sitting up, she held the bedspread over her naked breasts and cocked her head to one side. "Damn. It's still raining?"

"Yeah," Jaiden confirmed, nodding.

"Well," Nici said, drawing out the word. "No way are your parents getting home anytime soon. Not if it rained all night." She shook her head and then lay back down, advising Jaiden to turn on the TV and check the weather. "See if I'm not right," she added, and then giggled when DeJon reached over and grabbed her around the waist. Nici pulled the bedspread hard, exposing her bedmate's smiling face. DeJon rose up on one elbow and squinted around. "What's going on?" he wanted to know.

"What's going on is the party's over," Jaiden told him. "Come on, DeJon. Get up. I'm in deep shit if you guys don't help me clean up. You know my dad. He'll be plenty pissed if he sees his media room like I know we left it."

DeJon stared dully at Jaiden, then whispered in a hoarse voice, "Okay. Okay." Yawning, he lifted his chin and scratched his neck, but did not budge.

Jaiden narrowed her eyes at her friends. If her mom and dad were to pull into the driveway right now, Jaiden knew she would be in for a serious lecture from her dad, the withering silent treatment from her mom, and most likely face the threat of some major deprivation—like no new laptop to take to college. And since this morning's shopping trip with her free-spending Aunt Rochelle would probably not be happening, her mom might convince her aunt to cancel it altogether. That would never do. No, she couldn't risk missing out on a new wardrobe to take to Brown.

Frowning, Jaiden decided to pull herself together before confronting her friends. Her head was pounding, her throat was raw, and she certainly was not capable of doing much in this condition. *Water. Aspirin. A shower,* she thought, pushing herself up off the bed, heading into the bathroom on shaky legs.

The phone in her parent's bedroom began to ring the moment she reached to turn on the shower. Sighing, she crossed the hall and checked the caller ID, then pursed her lips. Just as she had suspected. The call was coming from her mom's cell phone. Jaiden started to pick up the receiver, then hesitated. Did she really want to talk to her mother right now? Could she manage a coherent conversation before pulling herself together? While contemplating whether or not to answer, the voice mail kicked in and took over the call. Jaiden waited a few moments, and then checked the message:

Hi, Jaiden. Still here. Your dad and I won't be coming home today. Probably have to stay here again tonight. There's about four feet of water downstairs right now and it's still rising. We're stuck upstairs. Electricity is out, but we've got supplies. Call me back as soon as you get up. And do not go out in this weather for any reason. Okay? If Rochelle calls, cancel your shopping trip. No need to take any chances. Bye.

Jaiden was grateful for the reprieve, but not too happy to hear that her shopping trip was off or that Vendora was under water. Her dad must be totally upset. She'd call back as soon as she pulled herself together, but for now she needed silence. She took the phone off the hook, and then made her way back into her bathroom.

After a quick shower, Jaiden pulled her thick brown shoulder-length hair back from her face and anchored it in place with a bright red plastic hair clip. After smoothing moisturizer over her honey-tan face, she slipped into a pair of sweatpants and a tee shirt. Next, she gulped two aspirin and a big glass of water, returned to her bedroom and gave Kevin a hard shake. He grumbled an unintelligible response, shrugged, and then pulled his pillow tighter to his chest.

Damn. This was not going to be easy. Jaiden fumbled among the covers, found the remote control, and then zapped her television on. The weather report was grim:

> "The storm that swept into Houston three days ago has stalled over the downtown area, causing heavy flooding along Buffalo Bayou. Traffic snarls and high water in freeway underpasses have paralyzed the morning commute, and some people are stranded in their cars. Flights out of Hobby Airport have been suspended, but Bush International remains open. Late yesterday afternoon, a woman drowned in the underground parking garage of the Bank of Houston building when the elevator doors opened and floodwaters rushed in. Conditions in the far western and northern suburbs are not as bad."

Jaiden watched the report with dread, aware that Vendora lay at the center of the flooding and that her parents were among those stranded. At least, *she* was safely out of danger in Kingwood, where the huge houses had been built high above the low-lying creeks and bayous that could spill over and cause serious flooding.

Nothing to do but wait this out, Jaiden concluded, pressing the power button to silence the television. She leaned across Kevin, who was still snoring loudly; picked up the half-smoked joint he had placed on top of an empty beer can, and lit it. She inhaled deeply, and then blew a stream of smoke toward the ceiling. Lying back, she slumped against the headboard of her bed, curled her legs beneath her hips and took another hit, *May as well chill out,* she decided, taking Nici's advice as she gazed idly at the droplets of

rain sluicing over the bay window that faced the wooded area behind her home. Listening to the drum of the downpour on the roof
made her headache begin to ease and her anxiety over her parents'
imminent return slipped to the back of her mind. *I've really got all
day to get this place together,* she concluded, plumping up her pillow.

CHAPTER 2

At eight o'clock in the morning, every seat at Gate 18 was taken. Passengers were sipping coffee from Styrofoam cups, munching on sugary doughnuts, and talking on cell phones—passing time until Flight #693 from Las Vegas to Los Angeles was ready to board.

Davis Kepler slouched low in his hard plastic chair with his palms on his knees, his deep brown eyes following the progress of the ground crew as it loaded bags onto the plane that was waiting at the Jetway. He blinked a few times, easing the burning sensation in his eyes and ran a hand over the prickly stubble on his golden tan chin. He was exhausted from his twenty-four-hour marathon gambling session. He had been making quick trips like this to Vegas for several months and they were definitely beginning to take a toll on his thirty-nine-year-old body.

When his cell phone rang, he calmly reached into the inside pocket of his Armani jacket and turned it off without checking the caller ID. He was not in the mood to talk to anyone, and though he felt as if he could drop off to sleep at any moment, he was also buzzed with the flush of success. The cards had been good to him this time, giving up one winning hand after another; not at all like last week when he had returned home with empty pockets and a hell of a hangover.

At seven o'clock yesterday evening, he had arrived at the same gate, gone directly to the Mirage Hotel, sat down at the blackjack table nearest to the bar, and stayed there until one hour ago, tripling the five thousand dollar stake he had converted into chips. Hopefully, this winning streak was going to hold for a while.

Now, he was ready to get on the plane, collapse into his seat, close his eyes, and totally shut down. In less than two hours he would be back in Los Angeles, in his shiny new Lexus, and on his way to Republic Bank to deposit the five thousand dollar stake that had fueled this lucky streak. Then he would go home and put his winnings into the wall safe inside his bedroom closet, where his secret stash was growing.

The gate attendant announced pre-boarding for his flight and everyone got up at once, forming a crowd at the entrance to the Jetway. As eager as any other passenger to be on his way, Davis grabbed his black Coach briefcase and stood, glancing idly at the television set suspended above the boarding area as he waited for the attendant to take his ticket. The CNN National News Update was on: A fiery car crash had shut down ten miles of freeway in Florida. The son of a local politician had been kidnapped in Detroit. A tropical storm had paralyzed a large section of Houston.

At that news, Davis shook his head, thinking: Houston. The word created an immediate flash of memories. How could he ever forget the long, hot, boring summers he had spent in the city while visiting his dad, Davis Sr., when he was a boy? His mother and father had never married, but his mother had made sure that Davis knew who his father was and had insisted he spend two months out of each year with him, too. From the age of five until Davis was a teenager, she faithfully packed five changes of clothing into a small square suitcase as soon as school let out for the summer, pinned a note of identification to Davis's shirt and put him on a plane. The airplane ride had always been the most enjoyable part of Davis's summer, because once he arrived in Houston, his dad would slap him on the back, tell him hello, urge him to eat anything in the refrigerator that he wanted, and then depart for work at the post office, leaving Davis to entertain himself. All day long, he would watch TV, play video games, sit on the porch and read comics or study the strangers passing by, and though he had been forbidden to leave the house, he often rode his rusty bicycle through the neighborhood while his dad was at work.

It had been a carefree time for Davis, whose father often worked a second job after leaving the post office—bartending private parties—so he rarely returned home before Davis was fast asleep. Davis Sr. died twelve years ago, and was buried in a small cemetery on the southeast side of Houston. After the funeral, Davis had never returned to the city on the bayou where his father had lived.

Now, he watched the news coverage with interest, surprised that he recognized many of the landmarks in the flooded area as definitely in the neighborhood where his father had lived. Davis sucked in a short breath when a pink brick, multi-columned house with a flat slate roof flashed onto the screen. He knew the mansion well, and had been inside it many times while his father had bartended lavish parties for the well-to-do black family that owned the property. Davis had fallen asleep on the floor of the cavernous old kitchen more than once while waiting for his dad to finish his work, and had often dreamt of living in such a beautiful place.

Film footage showed the once-elegant mansion sitting in the middle of a swirling pool of muddy water, which was lapping insistently at its windows, doors, and ornate exterior plasterwork. Davis shook his head in dismay as he listened to the reporter describe the disaster and the chaotic situation at Houston's Hobby Airport where stranded passengers were wearily waiting out the storm.

Thank God, I'm not stuck at some airport waiting for floodwaters to go down, Davis thought. He *had* to get back to L.A. today.

Nothing prevented Rochelle Ivors Wyatt Lavoy from going shopping once she planned her excursion. Not a hangover, a bad hair day, an argument with an ex-husband or even a water emergency at her thirty-year-old patio home on the far west side of Houston. So, when she spotted the dark stain on her kitchen ceiling this morning, along with the slow drip of water onto her Mexican tile floor, she had felt as if someone had punched her in the stomach—not because the roof was leaking, but because she would have to deal with it, taking precious time away from her tightly scheduled day.

A quick call to a roofing company confirmed her suspicions: no one would be able to get to her for several days, maybe a week, as emergency crews were swamped with calls for repairs throughout the city. She would have to manage on her own. Undaunted, she covered the floor with a vinyl tablecloth, placed a green plastic container beneath the slow leak, and went off to finish getting dressed. What else was there to do? she told herself. Sit around all day and listen to water drip into a pail? Not hardly. She had more important things to do.

As a personal shopper with a very demanding clientele, Rochelle absolutely hated it when some dreary domestic emergency interrupted her plans. For her, a rainy day was the perfect day to hit the mall; near-empty stores, short checkout lines, fewer shoppers to challenge her for the bargains. Ferreting out exactly what her clients needed, and at prices they were willing to pay, was a challenge that Rochelle absolutely loved, and today, despite the nasty weather, she would carry on, making good on her graduation promise to her niece, Jaiden—the gift of an entire wardrobe for her first year at college.

Where should they go? She checked her watch. It was only eight o'clock, but she wanted to get an early start and be at the mall when the doors opened at nine. Her favorite place to shop, the multilevel Galleria, was definitely out—all streets in that area had been under water for two days. Maybe Willow Creek Mall, she decided, She could head north on I-45, away from the flooding that was devastating the downtown and midtown areas, and hit Neiman's, Saks, and Ann Taylor first, and then try a few of the new boutiques along the frontage roads. The roof repair could definitely wait.

And it better be covered by insurance, Rochelle silently grumbled, stepping into a tight black sheath dress that hugged her plus-sized bosom, nipped her once-narrow waist, and diminished the width of her ample hips. She wore her light brown hair smoothed back and tucked behind her ears in a chic blunt cut that took little care, and her makeup consisted of a quick sweep of cinnamon lip gloss on her full heart-shaped lips and a flicker of bronze blush across the apples of her cheeks. A feather of black mascara around her dark gray eyes and she was ready. Stepping back from the mirror, she pushed out her chest in satisfaction, twisted around to check for panty lines, and then went back into the kitchen to see what was happening with the leak. Only a few drops of water had fallen into the pail.

With a smile, she opened her fake Fendi purse and took out her car keys, making a mental note to dig out her insurance policy when she returned. She had not looked at it in five years, not since the day that the judge had awarded her the patio home as part of her divorce settlement from Howard Lavoy. But, if the leak was not covered by her insurance, Howard would cough up the cash to fix it. She would make sure of that.

Leaving through the door off the kitchen that led directly into her garage, Rochelle got into her ten-year-old black Mercedes and backed out of her driveway, heading toward Kingwood to pick up Jaiden.

CHAPTER 3

Max stared down at the foul, chocolate-colored water that had crept midway up the grand staircase, the smell of the bayou so strong in his nostrils that he could almost taste the gumbo soil at the back of his throat. He tried to visualize what was happening to the hard pine flooring—handcrafted by his great-grandfather—and the thick plastered columns with their elaborately carved bases. Could they withstand this assault and emerge intact once the water drained away and the building dried out? Would the damage be so extensive that he might be out of business altogether? The thought made his stomach tighten in a nervous spasm, though he knew that no matter what the damage might be or how high the cost of repairs, he would devote all of his resources to getting Vendora back in shape in record time: Abandoning the house, the business, and the legacy he planned to leave to his daughter was not an option.

Maxwell Granville grew up in the three-story brick house on Buffalo Bayou, and knew the history of every tree on the property, every piece of furniture inside the house, and could recite the story of how his great-grandfather had won the parcel of land in a seaside gambling den on Galveston Island. Together, his great-grandparents had handcrafted the reddish pink bricks, from the gummy Texas soil, and had built their home with the help of neighbors, friends, and members of their church. The house had a distinctly Italianate appearance, with its flat slate roof, square canopied entry and evenly spaced narrow windows that were framed with white wooden shutters. According to family history, Max's great-grandfather had designed his house to resemble an Italian villa he had once seen on a picture postcard from Tuscany. However, he had tempered the structure's strong Mediterranean façade with charming Southern accents: fluted columns along the front and a colonial-style veranda that wrapped around the entire lower floor and blocked the brutal Texas sun.

At the age of nineteen, Max inherited the house when his parents died of cancer less than six months apart. His brother, Winston, younger by one year, quickly deeded his share of the property over to Max and went off to join the Marines, starting a military career that had kept him out of the country ten months of the year. Though Max's parents had left him an impressive showplace of a home, they had not left him a dime in cash, forcing him to ditch his plans for college and take a job as the produce manager at an upscale specialty food store in River Oaks—where wealthy white Houstonians lived in million dollar mansions.

The pay at the store had been good, the hours flexible, and the position had provided him an opportunity to interact with people who were interesting, influential, and wealthy.

For six years, Max lived the bachelor life in his big Texas villa, which had rocked with music and the laughter of his many male friends who came to play poker and party with him—and the gorgeous women who were always hanging around. Max had shamelessly moved from one woman to another, willingly sharing his massive four-poster bed with quite a few beauties—until he met Camille Ivors, a travel agent to whom he had turned to arrange a getaway vacation to the Bahamas with a curvy, fair-skinned model.

At the travel agency, while talking about airfares, hotel rooms, and sights to see on the island, Max had not been able to stop staring at Camille, whose startling dark gray eyes, soft-spoken manner, and flawless buff-colored skin had drawn him in completely. And while in the Bahamas, where Max and his model-girlfriend swam, dined, danced, and gambled in the Paradise Casino, his thoughts had incessantly strayed back to the pretty travel agent who had arranged the exotic getaway.

Upon his return to Houston, he telephoned Camille and asked her to have dinner with him at a lively Italian bistro. She accepted, and before the wine had been tasted or their fettuccini had been placed on the table, he knew he had fallen in love. The realization had left Max shaken and somewhat defiant: A confirmed bachelor at twenty-five, with a reputation as a risk-taking, freewheeling party-guy, he had not planned on making a commitment to any woman until he hit forty, maybe forty-five.

However, fearing that Camille might slip away, he bought an understated solitaire diamond ring and proposed to her on their second date, praying she would not think he was moving too fast. She had accepted his proposal on the spot, confessing that she admired him for going after what he wanted. They married two months later, and as newlyweds, settled into Max's home.

After the birth of their first and only child, Jaiden, Camille had been the one to suggest that Max leave the grocery business and use his knowledge of upscale party food and beverages to commercialize the family homestead. The prospect of working for himself, with Camille's support, had appealed to Max, so the young couple converted the lower floor of the house into a supper club with an elegant dining room, a dance floor, live entertainment, great food, and a cozy, yet elegant ambiance for the discriminating black clientele in the city. They moved upstairs, transformed one of the walk-in closets into a tiny kitchenette with a small gas stove and dedicated themselves to building a business that rapidly evolved into a highly profitable venture.

Vendora was immediately successful and profitable. Three years ago, Max and Camille had built a custom home in Kingwood, an affluent suburb north of Houston—four thousand square feet of imported Spanish marble and polished oak, with a swimming pool, a media room, and a three-car garage. They owned a getaway cabin at Lake Livingston, forty-five miles north of their home, and Jaiden was set to enter Brown University in the fall. Max generously paid the bills to maintain Camille's mother in a pricey geriatric center in Miami and kept a family membership in the King Crest Country Club. To relax, Max dabbled in horse racing at Sam Houston Park, or drove over to Louisiana to play the slots and blackjack at Lake Paradise Casino, never wagering more than he could afford to lose. And now, he looked forward to indulging in his favorite game of blackjack at the Indian Casino north of Houston which would open in the fall. Max enjoyed nice things and did not balk at paying for the lifestyle he believed that he and his family deserved.

For twenty years, life had been good for Max and Camille—despite a rough patch ten years ago, for which Max took all the blame. However, their marriage had survived the traumatic setback and now rocked along like most others, with the years slipping by while their love for and dependence on each other deepened day by day.

Max turned when he felt Camille at his side and smiled to see that she was holding two mugs of steaming coffee.

"Here," she said, handing one to him.

Max tore his thoughts away from his worries and accepted the white china cup, which had a large gold V on the side. "That old gas stove is a lifesaver."

Camille grinned, arching one brow. "It's all I had to cook on when we lived up here, remember?"

Lowering his eyes in recollection, Max took a sip from his cup. "Oh, yeah. And I have memories of you standing at that stove, teaching Jaiden how to scramble an egg. It's turned out a lot of good meals over the years." He moved closer to Camille, then asked. "Did you talk to Jaiden?"

Camille tucked an unruly black curl behind one ear. "Left her a message. Guess she's still asleep. Or on the Internet. I tried her cell, too, but it's not on."

"She'll be fine," Max stated, moving aside a stack of papers to sit down at one of the round tables that he and Camille had brought upstairs. He propped one elbow on the table, his chin on his fist.

Camille pulled up a chair and settled down beside him. "Try not to worry, Max." Placing her hand over his, she went on, "Don't think the worst. This old place has been through plenty of storms, and once we know what the flood insurance will cover, we can go from there."

"Sure," Max replied, his gnawing apprehension about the future of Vendora trapping more words in his throat. He placed one arm around Camille's shoulders and pulled her closer, resting his head against hers. "I'll make sure we get through this," he promised, nuzzling her neck.

"We always manage, don't we?" Camille replied, reaching up to lock her fingers with his. "Remember when we first opened Vendora and that oak tree fell on the roof and broke out every one of the back windows? Then there was that fire in the indoor barbecue pit that got out of control and scorched the kitchen real good. We recovered from that one, too, didn't we?"

Agreeing, Max inclined his head, and scooted closer, wanting to feel her beside him. He began to relax, quieted by the nearness of her, and for the first time since the storm began, allowed the tension in his upper body to ease. Facing Camille, he brushed her chin with two fingers and studied her luminous dark gray eyes—eyes that had captured his heart twenty-one years ago. Bending close, he kissed her solidly on the lips, hoping she knew how much he needed her and how much her support meant to him at a time like this.

Camille kissed him back, then pulled away and rubbed a finger over his nose, smearing a speck of mud. "I have to say, you taste exactly like you look," she told him, laughter in her eyes.

He swiped at the grit, aware that he was a mess. Neither had showered since early yesterday morning and they both were covered in grimy mud and dust, but it did not bother Max. He loved the taste of Camille, the smell of her, everything about her.

"You don't seem to mind very much," he said with amusement, winking before he kissed her lightly on the cheek. Surprisingly, he was struck with a sudden desire to do more than sit and wait out the storm with his wife. He took a quick sip of coffee, trying to distract his attention from the hardness growing inside his damp jeans. He bit his lip before speaking, wondering if he should get up and walk away or test her interest in a possible distraction, too. He decided to take a chance.

"We could wait out this messy situation in the bedroom," he prompted, his voice soft and hoarse with the growing interest in making love to his wife. In the middle of this crazy storm, with all of the problems they were facing, his craving for Camille was sweeping through him like the water that swept in from the bayou— strong, unexpected, and insistent. He wanted nothing more than to feel her warm, sweet-smelling flesh against his, to bury his face in her curly black hair, and make love to his wife, while putting this god-awful disaster out of his mind for a few wonderful moments.

"Well . . . why not?" Camille whispered, standing. "The bed might be a lot more comfortable than the steps, or these hard old chairs." Adopting a beguiling, expression, she smiled down at Max and extended her hand. "Coming?" she asked, enticing him with a crook of her finger.

Max took Camille's hand and willingly followed her to the comfy, four-poster bed where they first made love as husband and wife.

Rochelle pulled up to the gated entrance to Kingwood Village and pressed the entry code into the keypad. When the heavy iron gates swung back, she headed toward her sister's house, hoping Jaiden was as excited as she was about their upcoming shopping trip. The drive north had been slower than usual, though the rain had eased significantly. However, the highway was slick and spotted with dangerous puddles of water, so she had taken her time.

Jaiden had better be ready to go, Rochelle hoped, not wanting to use her cell phone to check on her niece while she was driving, especially in weather like this. *No need to call*, Rochelle decided, thinking that an unannounced visit might be a good thing, especially since Max and Camille had not been at home last night. Rochelle was no fool. She had been a teenager once, and knew that kids loved nothing more than to be at home alone without their parents around. At forty, she knew what was going on. She kept up with the latest music, the current fashions, and tried to learn the new dances before the latest craze passed. She went out often and had as much fun as possible when the opportunity presented itself— even though the dating scene for a single, mature woman was not exactly pretty: Turning to an ex-husband for an escort meant there would be no hassles or surprises.

Rochelle smiled to herself as she sped along the curved, wet streets of the exclusive subdivision. The perfectly manicured lawns. The Escalades, Jaguars, and Lexus' in the circular driveways. The quiet of it all. Yes, the classy environment suited her sister, Camille, very well. She was a lucky woman. She had a great hunk of a husband who loved her, a beautiful daughter who had graduated from high school with honors, and a custom-built home whose roof was surely not leaking today.

If only I had been so lucky, Rochelle thought. *Three marriages, no children, a bank account that I struggle to keep solvent, a ten-year-old Mercedes, and a paid-for patio home with a leaky roof. That about sums up my life.*

However, she was not as unhappy with her life as she pretended to be: She had a beautiful niece, excellent health, the steadfast support of her latest ex-husband, and Camille as her sister.

Rochelle and Camille had come to Houston from Bayport, Florida, as young women straight out of high school, twenty-five years ago, hoping to find love, wealth, happiness, and an escape from the stifling boredom of their tiny seaside hometown. Camille had immediately found her niche in the travel industry and settled in to start her career, leaving Rochelle to turn her love for shopping into a sporadically lucrative enterprise.

In reality, Rochelle and Camille were half sisters, though few people knew it. They had grown up together in the weathered bungalow with their mutual father, Joseph Ivors, and his wife Annie, who was Camille's natural mother.

While an infant, Rochelle had been abandoned by her natural mother, leaving Camille's mother to decide whether to take her husband's illegitimate child into her home or let the baby go into the county foster care system. Not an easy decision for Annie Ivors to make, but one she had often told Rochelle she never regretted.

Rochelle and Camille had not been told of their father's indiscretion until they were well into their teens, and so had grown up believing that they were blood sisters. Annie Ivors treated both girls as if they had sprung from her womb, and had forgiven her husband's infidelity in order to create a family.

Rochelle had been five years old, and Camille had recently turned seven when Joseph Ivors died. Annie Ivors's mental deterioration began the day after her husband's funeral, and now she resided in a private geriatric center in Florida, spending her twilight years in a fog of broken thoughts and misplaced memories. Rochelle never allowed her adoptive mother to forget how much she loved her. She visited her two times a year and telephoned faithfully once a month, and though Annie no longer knew who Rochelle was, that didn't matter. In her mind, Annie remained the vibrant mother who had loved and nurtured her; the woman who had taught her a very important lesson: Holding grudges over hurtful experiences wasted precious time and ate at the soul, blinding a person to the importance of treating each new day as a chance to start over. More than once, Rochelle had had to remind Camille to put that lesson to the test.

Shaking off thoughts of the past, Rochelle pushed down hard on the accelerator, as if going faster would clear away memories that belonged in the past, and shifted her attention to the upcoming shopping trip with her niece, whom she loved very much.

She and Jaiden were very close, perhaps closer in some ways than mother and daughter. Often, Jaiden would telephone Rochelle when things got rocky at home and beg her to intervene. Invariably, Jaiden would wind up dumping her problems on Rochelle, who gratefully accepted the weight; though in reality, she did little more than listen, knowing better than to take sides in a dispute between her sister and her niece. Jaiden was a good kid who was trying to find her way, and Rochelle thought Camille ought to ease up a bit and give the girl a break—realize how lucky she was to have a beautiful daughter who was still a virgin and not into drugs, boys, or the crazy party scene.

When Jaiden was angry with her mother or having problems with her friends, she called her aunt, and their talks made Rochelle feel needed, trusted, respected, and young. After surviving three cheating husbands and two broken engagements, Rochelle had a lot of experience to draw on when it came to working through testy romantic situations.

Threading her way along the twisting streets in the secluded enclave, she proceeded to Kingway Drive and on to her sister's house; a two-story Country French mini-mansion on a half acre plot, lushly landscaped with soaring pines and tropical foliage. She pulled around to the back of the house, took out her cell phone to let Jaiden know she was outside and ready to go. The line was busy, so she tried Jaiden's cell phone, only to find that it was not on. Probably still in the shower, Rochelle grumbled, pushing her plump frame out of her car. She snapped up her umbrella, and dashed through the light rain to the back door where she let herself in with her key.

When she entered the kitchen, she immediately recognized evidence of a serious party. Shaking her head in a knowing way, she sniffed at one of the glasses on the bar and recognized Max's favorite tequila. Margarita glasses, half-eaten sandwiches, chips and a chocolate cake with large chunks torn out of it languished on the table. What a mess! Jaiden had had quite a party last night. Teenagers! They couldn't help themselves. Unable to stifle a smile, Rochelle recalled having pulled a few similar stunts when she had been left at home alone when she was in high school. However, she had always managed to clean the house up before Annie got home. Camille would throw a fit if she saw this mess in her designer kitchen. Jaiden had some serious cleaning to do before they left the house.

Rochelle checked her Rolex knockoff. Eight thirty-six. She wanted to be at Willow Creek at nine, so Jaiden had better be dressed. They were already running late.

Rochelle headed up the stairs, prepared to find Jaiden finishing her makeup or pulling on her jeans, but halfway up, she paused when a distinctive smell, which she easily recognized, hit her. Quietly, she made her way down the hallway to the partially open door to Jaiden's room, eased the door back and stood in the entrance, both hands on her rounded hips, gray eyes narrowed at her niece, shocked at what she saw.

Two naked brown bodies were twisting around on a rumpled bedspread on the floor, and a young man, fully clothed, was sprawled out on one side of Jaiden's bed. The smell of stale beer and pizza competed with the pungent odor of burning marijuana as Jaiden, sitting with a portable CD player in her lap and headphones over her ears, remained oblivious to it all. She was nodding her head up and down and blowing streams of smoke toward the ceiling.

"What the hell is going on in here?" Rochelle demanded, kicking a pair of white denim slacks out of her way as she stepped into the room.

Jaiden's head snapped up. She gasped aloud, and then hurriedly palmed the lit joint before jumping up from the bed to throw her aunt an incredulous glare. "Aunt Rochelle! Oh, my God! What are you doing here?"

Rochelle was too angry to answer.

CHAPTER 4

Los Angeles, 6:00 P.M.

Davis Kepler parked his car, removed his gold rimmed sunglasses and slipped them into the inside pocket of his navy blazer as soon as he arrived at Romero's. Inside, he paused to allow his eyes to adjust to the dim interior, and then shouldered his way through a group of animated, cigar-smoking men standing at one end of the glistening horseshoe-shaped marble bar that curved into the middle of the club. Davis waved to Rita, the hostess, and gave several customers a friendly high-five. The sounds of ice clinking in glasses, soft rock music, and the lively buzz of conversation mixed with the rich smell of tobacco, creating a subdued, yet highly charged atmosphere. This was his kind of night: The club was packed and money was flowing.

Too bad not more of it is flowing my way, he silently complained, working his way toward his partner, Reet Collins, who was sitting at the far end of the bar.

Friends since their early teens, Davis and Reet had become best friends while living next door to each other in a crowded public housing unit where their single mothers had struggled to make sure that the boys ate at least one decent meal a day. For fun and profit, they soon began hustling stereo equipment, hubcaps, and designer knockoffs from shady sources throughout the streets of South Central Los Angeles, and by the time the boys were in their early twenties, they had moved on to selling more expensive merchandise—dime bags of grass and little white pills—to the party crowd in the frenzied nightclub scene. However, their entrepreneurial adventures came to an abrupt halt when the police busted them during an undercover sting at a topless club on Sunset Boulevard. The judge sentenced twenty-one year-old Davis to three years in state prison, and Reet, who somehow managed to retain a shrewd attorney, walked.

While doing his time in state prison, Davis made up his mind to go straight when he was released, and eventually accepted a job making long-distance deliveries of outdoor furniture for a local freight company. He forced himself to be content with going to work, living in a one-room studio apartment in Compton, and staying away from the bars and pool halls where he knew trouble lurked. However, he never stopped dreaming of being his own boss again.

While Davis led the straight life, Reet continued making shady deals that began to pay off surprisingly well. In time, Reet acquired a reputation in his old neighborhood as a semilegitimate moneyman who was quiet, focused, and very smart. His first serious investment had been in a low-budget film titled *Topaz Queen*, introducing a new actress named Lara Stanton. It was an instant hit and Reet made enough money to invest in a horse-racing track in Florida, a slot machine factory in Las Vegas, and an all-night drive-through steak and eggs eatery in Inglewood. After that, Reet became known as a man with solid connections who was willing to finance risky projects at exorbitant interest rates, and he also became a millionaire. His uncanny ability to get into and out of a project at precisely the right time rarely left him stuck on the losing end.

Three years ago, Reet approached Davis about going in with him to create a wine and cigar bar in a burned-out dry cleaning store that had been gutted and empty since the 1992 riots. Though Davis had only been able to come up with less than one-fourth of his share of the start-up money, Reet had verbally agreed to call him his partner and had covered his shortfall with cash from investors who had been eager to be a part of his venture.

They called the place Romero's and it became an instant hit—a trendy nightspot that attracted a classy, well-heeled crowd. Davis should have been a very happy man: In addition to owning a share of Romero's, no matter how small, he also received a salary that allowed him to live in a gated condominium community and lease a fully loaded Lexus. He had a line of credit at Paul Tremont, a high end men's clothing store on Rodeo Drive, and the sexy actress, Lara

Stanton, was his current lover. He had everything he needed, though his passion for gambling—preferably in Las Vegas—kept his financial status fluctuating between flush with cash and nearly broke

I could use a lot more than what Reet is tossing my way, Davis thought as he moved through the club, which was packed with the usual stellar crowd of wealthy African-American sports figures, actors, businessmen, and corporate types. Davis recognized a high profile sports agent with an Emmy award-winning actress on his arm, and two NBA players huddled at a corner table. It had been this way every night since the place opened, and Romero's was, without a doubt, one of the hottest new gathering spots in L.A.

Davis slipped onto the bar stool next to Reet, whose eyes were riveted on the silent television screen suspended above the bar. Davis signaled to the bartender, who slid a frosty mug of imported beer across the black marble counter.

"Nice crowd tonight," Davis remarked lightly.

Reet swiveled around on his bar stool to survey his establishment. He was a dark-complexioned, slightly built man with a thin mustache and a shaved head. He was wearing a gray pin-striped suit with wide lapels, a black silk shirt that was open at the neck and a heavy gold chain around his right wrist—a diamond-studded Rolex on his left.

"Exactly what I like to see," Reet replied in his deep bass voice, reminding Davis why his childhood friend had been nicknamed Barry-boy, after the sexy singer, Barry White. "Lots of guys in expensive suits, lots of pretty girls . . . a cigar and a drink in everybody's hand." He leveled a serious look on Davis. "If you handle this place right, it can be a real moneymaker for a long time." His dark eyes took in the scene as he fingered the gold chain glittering against his ebony wrist.

"Yeah," Davis agreed. "Things do look good. Very good. *We* got this one right." He hoped Reet caught his emphasis on the word *we*. Davis may have put up a lot less cash than Reet, but the success of the operation hinged almost entirely on Davis's tireless efforts to create the kind of buzz that was bringing a high-class clientele into the club.

"But it's gotta last," Reet interjected, as if to let Davis know that he could not rest on this early success. "Can't live forever off today's receipts. Gotta always worry about tomorrow, you know? Some real important people chipped in to bankroll this baby, and they expect a good return. Right now, we're a novelty kind of place, you know? So, you gotta keep it fresh . . . pump up the word on the street. Keep it live. Understand?"

"Sure. I know what you mean," Davis quickly reassured Reet, though irritated by his remarks.

He had been successfully marketing the club since it opened, and he did not need Reet telling him what to do or how to do it. He had money in Romero's, too, maybe not a full one-half interest, but enough to be treated more like a partner instead of like an advertising man whom Reet could push around and use as his personal flunky. Davis had expected better from Reet, but quickly learned that he had been mistaken. The Reet he had known as a young man was definitely gone.

What had happened to his homeboy? And why hadn't he seen this selfish side of his friend before? he wondered. Currently, Reet made all of the major decisions; kept the books, hired and fired the staff, and seldom discussed the club's finances with Davis. Well, Davis wasn't stupid—he knew the club was making plenty of money and he ought to receive a bigger share. It pissed him off when Reet played the big boss while Davis packed the place every night, and he didn't plan to put up with this shitty arrangement much longer.

"I've got a few things working," Davis went on. "There's a new company that's doing outdoor billboards that play like mini-movies . . . something like music videos, you know? I've set a meeting with them for next week. We could film it here, maybe get some of the regulars to donate their talent, you know? And there's that live broadcast on KTUX that Baby Jam Toms is planning to do from here next Saturday. If you want . . ."

"Great, sounds great," Reet interrupted. "Do whatever you have to. Just keep the place packed and the customers happy."

The undertone of condescension in Reet's low-spoken remark hit Davis like a blunt dagger, leaving him feeling as if he'd been physically assaulted. He had not expected his friend to shove him aside like this. However, he held his tongue, determined not to upset Reet right now. He had plans, too, and he was going to get what he deserved.

"By the way . . . where were you last night?" Reet asked, hunching over his vodka martini.

"Had a quick trip I had to make," Davis answered vaguely.

"Oh? Why didn't you take my calls, huh?"

"My cell was down . . . bad battery or something."

"Fix it. When I need to talk to you, you gotta be available," Reet ordered in a growl that brought his low voice down an octave.

"Sure, sure. Something going on?" Davis asked, thinking that Reet sounded as if he knew exactly what was going on and where Davis had been last night. He picked up his beer and took a leisurely gulp while trying to anticipate Reet's next remark.

"Yeah. What happened with the money? I leave you in charge of closing up and you take off. We got problems." Reet waited, one eyebrow arched high on his domed forehead.

"Problems? What?"

"The deposit was five grand short."

"Five grand? I don't think so. It's all in the bank." Davis adopted a cool tone, frowning as if he had no idea what Reet was talking about.

"Not when I checked," Reet rasped, clearly annoyed by the conversation.

"Oh, that," Davis said, reaching into the inside pocket of his jacket. He removed a Republic Bank deposit slip, which he placed on the bar. "Five thousand was in credit card charges, so I took the slips with me since I had to leave early. Didn't have time to batch them until this morning. It's all there. You musta checked the bank balance before this posted."

Reet glanced warily at the deposit slip, and then muttered, "Yeah, I guess so." He put the piece of paper into his pocket and then returned to watching the silent television.

Davis let out a low sigh of relief. Usually he didn't even tally the bar until two in the morning, but he always batched the charges right away to get the money posted to the account. Yesterday, he'd closed out the cash drawer early, leaving Rita to make the late night deposit, had gone straight to the airport with the club's money and gotten onto his flight to Vegas. Thankfully, he had had a lucky night, had made it back to Los Angeles in time to bank the money, and was over the first hurdle: Reet had bought his explanation. So far, everything was going as planned. He congratulated himself on his story . . . batching the charge slips this morning. Perfect. So what if he'd borrowed a little of Romero's cash for a few hours? Everything was back as it should be. Reet had no reason to squawk.

"That's a real mess," Reet announced to no one in particular, lifting his martini glass toward the muted CNN National News report about the flood situation in Houston.

Eager to move off their conversation about money, Davis stood and braced his back against the bar, studying the newscast that Reet was watching. "Sure is," he agreed in a casual manner, wrapping his slim, golden fingers around his cold beer mug. "I wouldn't want to get caught up in that."

"A lotta businesses are gonna fold behind that kind of flooding." Reet paused, nodding. "But, you know what I say . . . one man's disaster can be another man's opportunity. A lot of those properties are gonna be on the market for peanuts." He picked up the remote control and increased the volume.

Davis followed Reet's gaze up to the news report. "Probably so," he murmured.

"Sure. Great opportunities there," Reet continued. "If you got cash . . ." he gestured at the TV set. "*There's* a good investment."

Narrowing his eyes at the screen, Davis watched the report: A black businessman was talking about the devastation he had suffered during the flood, and he was standing inside the three-story mansion that Davis had recognized earlier. The man referred to the house as a supper club—Vendora—and he was walking through the lower floor, which had been completely swamped at the height of the storm. Water had risen halfway up the grand staircase, and as the camera panned the interior of the historical house, it zoomed in on piles of wet linens, soggy oriental rugs, mud-covered walls, ruined upholstered chairs, and a baby grand piano mired in mud. Tree limbs, garbage, and small dead animals floated in the murky water. Everything was soaking wet and oozing mud. The place was a total disaster.

"Now, that's a place worth saving," Reet cut in, sipping from his martini glass. "A restaurant downstairs and a nightclub with a game room on the second floor. That could be a real nice setup."

Davis tightened his lips as he mulled over Reet's remarks, thinking that his friend might have a point. Though he hated to admit it, Reet did have vision, as well as access to the cash to make his swaggering talk a reality. And that's what Davis wanted. He would still be driving a delivery freight truck, making two hundred dollars a week if Reet hadn't given him an opportunity to go in with him at Romero's. He was grateful, and he planned to buy his one-half share of the business soon in order to become a full partner and get the money and respect that he deserved. His trips to Vegas were key to making that happen.

Reet's voice brought Davis back to the moment when he said, "You know, Davis, Houston's set to have an Indian casino soon . . .

well, it'll be up the road a piece, I think, but people from Houston will drive out there on the weekends. Tons of cash will be floating around. Great city for a smart man to make a lot of money."

"I'll bet so," Davis replied, turning the comment over in his mind. "Something to think about, all right."

CHAPTER 5

The telephone rang the moment Camille entered her back door. She dumped her purse, her bulging appointment book, and a folder containing several travel contracts that she planned to work on over the weekend onto her sleek granite kitchen island and grabbed the phone, hoping it was Max. She'd forgotten to tell him to bring home from Vendora the banquet-sized tablecloths and the large silver serving platters which they would need for tonight's party.

Forty-seven of Max's fraternity brothers and their wives or significant others were expected in less than two hours, and the barbecue from Jason's Grill was due to arrive at any minute. It had been two weeks since the flood, and Vendora remained shuttered, so Camille had expected Max to book a private party room for his fraternity's annual summer barbecue. However, he had refused to even consider such a thing, determined to host his buddies on his own turf and show off his custom-built house—as well as the fifty-two-inch high-definition television he had recently installed in his media room. Wasn't that why they had built such a grand house? he had remarked. To entertain family and friends?

"Hello," Camille said, juggling the telephone as she removed one of her gold button earrings.

"Max Granville, please," a woman asked in a very efficient tone.

"He isn't in. This is Mrs. Granville. Who's calling?" Camille inquired, trying to place the woman's voice, which sounded vaguely familiar.

"Oh, hello Camille . . . this is Julie Stern, Ann Burton's assistant . . . with National Fidelity."

"Oh, yes, Julie," Camille said, relieved that their insurance company had finally called back. Before the floodwaters had even drained completely out of Vendora, Max had contacted Ann Burton, a longtime friend who managed a branch of National Fidelity Insurance. Camille had spoken to Julie on the phone once before.

"Ann is out for a few days, so she left your file with me to follow up," Julie went on.

"Good," Camille replied, remembering when she first met Ann Burton. It had been at a business networking dinner shortly after marrying Max, and she had immediately sensed that the insurance agent and her new husband had been more than friends during his bachelor days. Ann's gently familiar touch on Max's arm, her eye contact with him that lingered a moment too long, and the subtle way she had interspersed references to their longtime acquaintance into the conversation had put Camille on alert. And later, when Camille had jokingly implied that a romantic relationship had once bloomed between Ann Burton and Max, he had become offended, quickly assuring her that nothing of the sort had ever occurred between them. Ann was simply a friend.

When Camille met Max, she had been aware of his reputation as an outrageous flirt who loved the attention of beautiful women. However, once engaged, he had curbed his naturally flirtatious nature and focused all his attention on her.

Now, Camille reached into her planner and took out a pen, then flipped to a note page at the back of the book. "You can give the information to me, Julie. What's the verdict?"

"The roof did suffer some major damage," Julie began, ". . . a lot of missing slates. We'll cover that, along with the property fencing that is down. As for the water damage to the floors, the walls, the wiring, and all the kitchen appliances and furnishings . . ." she paused, ". . . well, it's a shame you decided to let your flood insurance lapse. If you had kept it in force, all of the interior damage, including furnishings, would have been covered."

Camille stopped taking notes and climbed onto a bar stool, her shoulders hunched tensely over the counter. Certain she had not heard correctly, she said, trying not to panic, "What do you mean by lapse?"

"Your flood insurance. We cancelled it in June. We show no payments since last May."

"Your records must be wrong," Camille insisted, not in the mood for a bureaucratic tangle. The water damage to Vendora had been extensive and they had to get the place restored and back into business fast. There was no way she was going to let National Fidelity wiggle out of coughing up the cash to replace the hardwood floors, the intricate woodwork, the wiring, appliances, and furniture that was standing in mud as they spoke. That's what flood insurance was for and they paid enough for it. "Julie, please have Ann double check that," Camille continued, her heart pounding. "There has to be a mistake somewhere in your records."

"I don't think so," Julie drew out her response, as if giving Camille a moment to rethink her request. "Do you have copies of your cancelled checks?"

"The premiums are automatically billed to the company credit card," Camille replied.

"There could be a glitch," Julie said. "Those things do happen . . . and you know, Camille, I'll straighten this out as quickly as possible. Can Max provide us with the credit card billing statements?"

"Of course. I'll have him get back to you as soon as he gets home. I know he has those papers somewhere."

"Okay," Julie replied. "Have Max call me."

"I will," Camille agreed, ending the conversation. She clicked off and closed her eyes, thinking about the implications of the phone call. No flood insurance? Impossible. Max would never take a risk like that and leave Vendora vulnerable. Would he? She stilled her thoughts, worried. He had been edgy and tense since the flood, often refusing to discuss details with her of the timetable for needed repairs. Naturally, she had supposed that his moodiness was due to stress and the burden of straightening out this horrendous situation. But maybe something else was on his mind. Camille crossed both arms on the counter, her chin lifted, and sat very still, praying that Max had not done anything as risky as let their flood insurance lapse.

There had been a time when Max had recklessly roared through life, doing as he pleased, with no one to answer to but himself. He had thrived on taking chances and gambling with fate as long as he got what he wanted. For him, a day at Sam Houston Race Park, a long poker game with his buddies, or a quick trip to Louisiana to play blackjack at Lake Paradise had been his way of relaxing on a Sunday afternoon. Early in their marriage, Camille had tolerated his freewheeling ways, convinced that their marriage was on solid ground and she had nothing to worry about.

She had known what kind of a man Maxwell Granville was

when she met him, and had been attracted to him immediately. He was an exuberant, fun-loving, expansive man who loved a party and pretty women, whom he delighted in showering with attention. At any social gathering he told the funniest jokes, knew the latest dance, and was always the last to leave. He exuded a kind of charisma that created a sense of excitement wherever he went, and Camille knew that was one of the reasons she loved him so much and tolerated his imperfections. However, a shocking incident ten years ago *had* forced Camille to rethink her tolerant attitude toward her husband's playful behavior and she had been forced to act quickly to protect herself.

Now, Camille exhaled slowly, dissolving the memories she rarely allowed to surface. Hurriedly, she gathered her things from the kitchen island and headed upstairs to get ready for the party, girding herself for the long evening ahead. Having partied with most of the invitees over the years, Camille knew what to expect . . . loud music, rowdy laughter, and those same old "back-in-the-days" stories that she had heard too many times to count. She'd much rather climb into bed with a good book, or even her travel contracts, than endure this party tonight, but she knew it was important to Max. At least it would take his mind off Vendora, which remained mud-filled, dank, and empty.

Moving along the upstairs hallway, Camille stopped at Jaiden's bedroom door and knocked, then poked her head inside, hoping Jaiden would be able to help the caterer set up the food as soon as it arrived.

"Hi, Mom," Jaiden said. She was dressed in a pair of red shorts and a loose sheer blouse, and was sitting on the side of her unmade bed, pulling on her sneakers. "Home already? Left the office early, huh?"

Camille entered the room, puzzled. "Where are you getting ready to run off to?"

"Just out."

"Out? Your father's fraternity party is tonight, remember? You're going to help serve the food?"

"Damn," Jaiden remarked, screwing up one corner of her mouth. "I totally forgot. I promised Nici I'd go to the mall with her to look for her wedding shoes."

"Jaiden. Really! Not tonight! Max is counting on you to be here and help."

"Sorry. Can't. Maybe one of his friends can help out, cause Nici's brother has her car, so I gotta drive."

"Oh? Just like that? You've got to go? It doesn't matter what you promised your father?"

"It's not like that, Mom. I forgot. Okay? I'll try to get back early."

"Do that," Camille muttered to Jaiden's back, who was already at the door, her purse over her shoulder.

"Bye," Jaiden tossed out. "I'll really try to get back as soon as I can."

"Right," Camille replied tersely, doubting it very much. Staring after her daughter, Camille balled one hand into a fist and rubbed it into her palm, irritated by the casual way Jaiden was acting. So selfish. What attitude! Max was paying Willie, Vendora's bartender, to serve the drinks, and Jaiden had volunteered two weeks ago to dish up the barbecue, saving them the cost of hiring extra help. At the time, Camille had been pleasantly surprised by Jaiden's offer, believing that she meant what she said.

I ought to call Jaiden on her cell and demand that she come home, Camille thought, but decided against it. If her eighteen-year-old daughter thought so little of the promise she'd made to her father, there was nothing Camille could do to force her to make good on it. Jaiden was an adult now, and adults kept their word without having to be prodded. Obviously, she didn't care.

Camille glanced around her daughter's room, disgusted by the jumble of clothing, CDs, makeup, and magazines that cluttered the place. Even the new outfits that Rochelle had bought Jaiden while she and Max had been stuck at Vendora were heaped haphazardly on a chair. Jaiden's lack of appreciation grated on Camille's nerves. Didn't the girl understand how hard her parents and her aunt worked to give her all these things . . . things that she so casually tossed around?

Yes, Jaiden was an only child, and Camille knew that she and Max had spoiled her by rarely denying her anything she wanted, but they had also been diligent about instilling in her the kinds of moral and personal values that included respect for her parents as well as personal property.

Stepping over to the dresser, she saw a familiar-looking piece of paper crumbled into a ball. After picking it up and smoothing it out, she shook her head in dismay. It was the speeding ticket Camille had seen in Jaiden's car. She saw that the court date had passed five days ago. Well, if Jaiden didn't want to deal with it, she was going to lose her driver's license. Maybe that would be for the best, Camille decided, putting the crumpled ticket back where she had found it.

Looking down, she saw several pairs of shoes heaped beside the bed, and nearby, the corner of an ashtray sticking out from under the bed skirt. She bent down and pulled out a pack of cigarettes and a square glass dish filled with stubbed-out cigarette butts and what Camille recognized as a partially smoked joint. Anger and disappointment came over Camille, and she sat down on Jaiden's bed, wondering what it would take for her daughter to understand how dangerous it was to smoke marijuana, and how damaging cigarette smoke was to her health. This was too serious to ignore.

A few months ago, when Camille had found cigarette butts in the ashtray of Jaiden's car, she had vehemently expressed her displeasure, along with her hope that Jaiden would think hard about the consequences of smoking. At the time, Jaiden had sullenly promised not to smoke again, but now, it seemed, she had gone back on her word. *And more*, Camille sighed, praying this was a phase that would quickly pass; a defiant gesture on Jaiden's part to see how much she could get away with. After all, Jaiden was eighteen years old, and there was little that Camille or Max could do to stop her from smoking whatever she wanted. But in the house? No way.

Camille went into Jaiden's bathroom and flushed the cigarettes and the contents of the dirty ashtray down the toilet. Then she put the ashtray back under the bed, and left the room, pulling the door tightly shut. Their guests would most likely want to tour the house and Jaiden's room was definitely off-limits.

Entering the master bedroom at the end of the hallway, Camille wearily tossed her bag onto the coral satin bedspread and raised the silk Roman shades that covered the huge bay window. She adjusted the sheer under-panels to diffuse the late evening sunlight that streamed into the peach and cream-colored bedroom, then removed her suit, put on her robe and went into her multi-jet shower. She sat down on the ceramic shower seat jutting from the wall and let the water pummel her from all four sides, rinsing away the tension of the day.

What was happening with Jaiden? Growing up meant pulling away, but she was becoming someone whom Camille did not know. Did she think she had no obligations to her parents and only needed to please herself? How was she going to manage once she was living on campus? What would it take to stop this selfish, destructive behavior? Camille shuddered, hoping this difficult transition between high school and college would not last long.

It had better end soon, Camille thought, getting on with her shower. Though her mind was filled with her daughter's surprisingly disrespectful attitude, Ann Burton's assistant's message was not far removed. Camille refused to contemplate the possibility of it being true, because if it was, she and Max had much bigger problems on their hands than managing a willful daughter.

After showering, Camille went to her dressing table and began curling her hair. When she heard the sound of cars pulling into the driveway, she left her dressing room to hurry to the window that provided a view of the large parking area at the rear of the house. She saw that the delivery van from Jason's Grill had arrived with the food, and Max, accompanied by Willie, the bartender from Vendora, pulled in right behind it. A gray Volvo stopped at the end of the driveway. Camille watched as Trent Young, one of Max's oldest friends, got out of his car, accompanied by Vera, his second wife. The couple waved excitedly at Max.

Camille took a deep breath as she watched the reunion, aware that she had no time to waste. She would have to serve the food since Jaiden was not going to be around to help. Her discussion with Max about the flood insurance and what she had discovered under Jaiden's bed would have to wait.

The house rocked with conversation, laughter, and old school music that oozed soulfully from Max's hi-tech sound system. As soon as Max announced that the barbecue was ready, his guests crowded into his large kitchen, where Camille was busily handing out plates of ribs, chicken, potato salad, and beans. Then, plates in hand, everyone headed outside to sit at the round-skirted tables surrounding the lighted pool.

Max put an arm around Camille's waist and gave her a squeeze. "Thanks," he whispered in her ear, giving her cheek a quick kiss. "Sorry you got stuck in the kitchen."

Camille shrugged and set her large serving spoon aside. "No problem. I don't mind helping out, but you need to talk to our daughter about this . . . and a few other things."

"What's happened now?"

"The speeding ticket I told you about . . . I found it on her dresser.

The court date was five days ago and she has done nothing about it. You know what that means. She may lose her license and our auto insurance is going to go up," Camille informed him, deciding not to bring up what else she had found in Jaiden's room. She'd get into that later, after their guests had left.

Max grimaced. "I'll talk to her," he promised.

"*We'll* talk to her," Camille corrected. "About that and other things. And she's got the nerve to pressure us for a new car! She can drive that old Honda until it literally falls apart. A new car! Please! And I don't appreciate the way she skipped out on you tonight. Going to the mall with Nici when I specifically remember her promising to be here is disrespectful, Max. She does exactly as she pleases nowadays, and acts as if we exist only to make her comfortable. Something has to give."

"Okay, okay, we'll talk later," he promised, grabbing a beer from the cooler, then signaling to Trent Young, who was entering the kitchen after having been outside on the patio.

"You'd better," Camille finished, lowering her voice. "Because I'm through talking to her. And her funky attitude has got to go." Camille untied her chef's apron and folded it into a square. "Guess I'm through here. If anyone wants seconds, I think they can serve themselves."

As she was about to step away from the counter, Trent Young waved at her, approached, and slapped Max playfully on the back. "Wonderful party, Max," he said. "And Camille, the food couldn't be better."

"Thank Jason's Grill. Not me," she laughed, shoving her apron into a nearby drawer.

"Well, it's been great. And I appreciate you guys hosting us, but I gotta say I miss the bar at Vendora."

"Don't worry, Trent." Max replied. "We'll be back there for our Christmas party, I guarantee." Then he headed outside with Trent, leaving Camille staring after him. *How in the world does he expect to manage that?* she wondered. Vendora was a shambles, and according to bids from various contractors, the renovation might take as long as four months. Much of the work would have to be done by skilled craftsmen whose talents were in great demand, and the man they had located to do the plaster work would not be available until after Thanksgiving. *Besides that, according to Fidelity's records, we don't even have insurance coverage to pay him,* she recalled, thinking that Max's enthusiastic optimism seemed terribly misplaced.

* * *

At eleven forty-five, Max closed the door behind the last of his guests and sent Camille up to bed while he finished cleaning up the kitchen. The party had been a huge success, and he was glad that he had held the get-together at his home. Humming with satisfaction, he began loading the dishwasher, though he was still unsettled over Jaiden's disappearing act. Camille was right. Jaiden's attitude was entirely unacceptable. He understood that she wanted to help her friend who was getting married, as well as prepare to go off to college. The transition from high school to college might be affecting her more than he had thought it would, but it was all a part of growing up. However, there seemed to be a defiant streak emerging in his daughter that he did not particularly like, though he did believe that she was basically a good kid who would find her way. All that he and Camille had ever asked of Jaiden was that she study hard, choose her friends carefully, and stay out of trouble. So far, she had complied.

He poured the last of the white wine from a half-empty bottle into a glass and sipped it as he continued to scrape dishes and put them in the dishwasher.

Jaiden is deliberately testing Camille, he decided. The two women in his life had had their share of arguments over the years, as most mothers and daughters do—with Rochelle often intervening when things got rocky. But now he could sense a resentment in Jaiden that he had noticed only once before—when he and Camille had separated while going through marital problems.

At that time, when Camille walked out and left Jaiden behind with him, the separation had left his nine-year-old daughter bewildered and upset. It had taken months for him to convince Jaiden that Camille had not deliberately abandoned her, and thank God, things did eventually smooth out. Jaiden grew close to Camille as time passed, but now Max wondered if an incident from so far in the past could affect his daughter now.

Max put the last dish in the dishwasher and reached up to turn out the light above the stove, but he stopped when he heard Jaiden's car pull into the driveway. He waited at the back door until she entered, with the earphones of her personal CD player firmly in place.

"Hi, Dad," Jaiden called out when she saw him, barely glancing his way.

Her casual greeting infuriated Max, who said nothing until she removed her headphones and acknowledged him.

"Why weren't you here tonight?" he started right in, voice firm, eyes steady as he waited to hear what she had to say for herself.

She stared questioningly at him. "What? Didn't Mom tell you? I had to help Nici find her wedding shoes."

"Yes, I heard. So, you decided to go to the mall instead of keeping your promise to me?"

"I told her I forgot about the party. Anyway what's all the fuss about?" Jaiden threw back, giving her father a scowl. "It's not like I've been out drinking all night or doing something really bad."

"But you were supposed to be here . . . and I understand from your mother that you walked off while she was talking to you. Jaiden, please. You know you were deliberately rude to your mother and that is not acceptable."

Jaiden shrugged, not admitting to anything.

Max went on. "First of all, you should have cancelled your plans with Nici as soon as you realized you had another commitment to your family. Your mother worked all day and then had to come home and serve the food tonight. I could have hired a server, but you said you wanted to help me out. Didn't you?"

Jaiden's face fell, and a shadow of remorse flickered in her eyes. "Well, yeah. But, then Nici called and asked me to go with her. I didn't think it would be a big deal if I went. Is that a crime?"

"Not a crime, but pretty selfish. Your obligations to your family come first. Remember that, you hear?"

"Good Lord," Jaiden groaned, rolling her eyes. "I hear you. And you don't have to lecture me all night. Can't we end this?"

"No. This is all about keeping your word. If you promise to do something, then you ought to damn well do it! You are about to go off to college in a few weeks, and I have to trust you to make decisions on your own, including following through on commitments. Letting people down can become a bad habit, and it's the kind of disrespect that I never expected of you, Jaiden."

"Okay, okay," Jaiden grumbled. "I get the message. I apologize." She went to the refrigerator, opened it and removed a tray of left-over barbecue. "Food looks great . . . and I'm starved." She placed some ribs and a piece of chicken on a plate, zapped it in the microwave oven, then settled down at the counter. "This is really good, Dad. And how was the party?"

"Fine," was all that Max could manage. "And before we finish . . .

I understand you did not pay your speeding ticket," he plunged ahead.

Jaiden's head snapped up, eyes squinted in surprise. "I'll pay for it," she immediately volunteered. "I've got it covered."

"You'd better," Max countered, too exasperated to go into that subject. "And if our insurance goes up, you're going to have to kick in on that, too."

"Fine."

Max sighed, hoping these final days with his daughter still at home were not going to deteriorate into a series of arguments and tense conversations that would make life miserable for everyone. Jaiden had grown into a beautiful, intelligent young woman, though he knew she was spoiled and a tad self-centered. However, soon she would be beyond his control, living in a dorm under the rules and regulations of the university, and in reality, never be his little girl again. The thought made him both proud and sad. All he had ever wanted for her was to feel safe, secure, and take responsibility for her behavior. And respect her parents, of course.

Life on a campus like Brown, where she'll have to deal with demanding professors and students from all kinds of backgrounds will cure that, Max thought. "And you need to be nicer to your mother," he finished. "She's got a lot on her now, with Vendora closed and all. Try, okay?"

"Okay, Dad," Jaiden mumbled.

Max studied Jaiden for a moment, certain that she would be fine once she was on her own. After all, he and Camille had prepared her as best they could, sending her to private schools, exposing her to the values, social, and educational experiences that many young people never received. He reached over, touched Jaiden on the chin, and winked at her.

"Good night. I'm going up. Don't eat too much of that," he joked. "I want some leftovers for tomorrow."

Grinning, Jaiden nodded in agreement, her mouth too full to speak.

Max left the kitchen and headed upstairs.

Later, in her room, Jaiden closed and locked her bedroom door, and then sat down on the side of her bed. Why had her dad given her such a hard time? So, she hadn't come home early enough to help out. So what? He had money. He could have hired a server. Besides, she hadn't thought that her dad had taken her offer seriously when she had said she would help him out tonight. What was up with him? Lately, her father had become so damn serious, not at all like his usual happy-go-lucky self. And he was never at home anymore. Always at Vendora, cleaning, fixing, and worrying about getting the place back in shape, and her mom's fuse was so short that Jaiden tried to avoid her altogether. Always nagging her about her room, asking where she was going, or what time she'd get back. Their argument over the cigarette butts in her car ashtray still burned Jaiden up, making her wish sometimes that she could move out, maybe move in with her Aunt Rochelle.

If only they would treat me like an adult and leave me alone, Jaiden wished, uncapping the cold Heineken she had brought up to her room. She took a long swig of her pirated beer, reached under her bed for the ashtray, and then stared at it in disbelief. Empty. She was busted. Somebody had been snooping around in her room and she did not appreciate the intrusion into her private space. Her dad hadn't said anything about the cigarettes, so her mom must have done this.

Jaiden lay down on her back and thought about her options. She could say that DeJon or Kevin must have put the joint there, but that would be admitting that her friends had been smoking pot in her room. She grimaced. The best thing to do was to say nothing, she decided, admit to nothing, and give her mom the silent treatment. What could her mother do to her anyway? Send her to her room?

Jaiden groaned. Everything was getting so complicated. If only she were leaving tomorrow. At least her mom had never found out about the party she had thrown or that Aunt Rochelle had caught her smoking a joint! Jaiden didn't even want to imagine the explosion that would have resulted if her mom, instead of Aunt Rochelle, had come in on her that day.

Thank God, Aunt Rochelle agreed to keep quiet, Jaiden thought with relief, recalling the horrified expression on her aunt's face as she stood in the doorway, her mouth hanging open, eyes wide in shock. Needless to say, her aunt had sternly reprimanded Jaiden for pulling such a stunt. An impromptu party with a little alcohol was not so bad, she had said. But smoking pot and kids having sex on the floor? Not in her sister's house. Jaiden had hurried to clean up the house while begging Rochelle not to tell her mom. Rochelle had blasted her with a strong "You ought to know better" speech that had lasted until they arrived at the mall, but once they hit the stores, her aunt had shut up and zeroed in on her plan of attack, working her way through every boutique and department store in record time. Jaiden had come home with a mother lode of presents.

If Mom pressures me about the joint, I'll just walk out of the room, Jaiden decided, thinking that in two weeks, she'd be gone anyway, out of her parents' house and living in a dormitory with her roommate, Mona, getting started on her new life as an independent woman. She was definitely looking forward to the freedom.

Mona and Jaiden had already e-mailed each other a few times to decide on how to decorate their room. They had settled on a blue and white floral motif, and Mona was buying the bedspreads. Mona was majoring in speech therapy, and was from a city named Essex, in western Pennsylvania—the fourth generation in her family to attend Brown. She had a cousin named Rod who lived in Providence, too—off campus in his own apartment. Mona had e-mailed Jaiden that he threw parties that were the bomb, and was planning one for Mona the first weekend after school started. Jaiden was definitely invited.

After taking another long swallow of her beer, she went to her computer to check her e-mail. A message from Nici popped up.

Nici: *Hey girl. Kevin just called. Totally upset. We talked forever.*

Jaiden: *What'd he say?*

Nici: *That he's real mad. Why don't you want him to write or visit you at Brown? He doesn't understand.*

Jaiden: *What's so hard to understand? I don't want him thinking that I'm his girlfriend, because I'm not. He's been acting so possessive. A drag.*

Nici: *According to him, you are his girlfriend He's crushed that you're breaking off totally.*

Jaiden: *Oh, really? Too bad. What else did he say?*

Nici: *Not much more. Wishes you were going to UT so he could be around you.*

Jaiden: *Yeah. Well, that will never happen. My roommate, Mona, has a cousin who lives off campus and he is throwing a big party right after classes start. I'll probably meet tons of guys—real guys— much cuter and more interesting than Kevin. Things are going to be so different once I leave here, and I do not need baggage like Kevin hanging around.*

Nici: *Started packing?*

Jaiden: *I guess. Can't decide what to take—but I'm definitely taking everything Aunt Rochelle bought me.*
Nici: *You better. Your aunt has great taste.*
Jaiden: *Right: Love to shop with her.*
Nici: *Love her for not telling your mom about our party. That would have been a bummer.*
Jaiden: *Yeah, I know. Gotta go. Later.*

Jaiden flopped down across the foot of her bed and contemplated her upcoming move. After attending a private all-girls high school and struggling to abide by her parents' strict rules, the prospect of going to a coed college eighteen hundred miles away and living on her own, made her giddy with anticipation. She would be able to come and go as she pleased without having to explain her every move to anyone. And if she finished her freshman year with at least a 3.5 grade point average, her dad had promised to buy her a new car—the BMW she wanted so much, even though she wouldn't be able to keep it on campus until her junior year. She planned to study her ass off to make that happen, but she'd definitely make sure she took time out to party, too. After all, she graduated from high school with a 3.88 grade point average and had been inducted into the National Honor Society. How hard could college be?

Camille turned to Max, who was emerging from the master bath, buttoning his pajama top.
"I heard Jaiden come in," she said.
"Yeah. And I had a talk with her. Said she was sorry. Even apologized."
"Right. And you accepted it?"
Max raised one shoulder, as if at a loss to do more. "Guess so. I didn't feel like fighting with her. What good would that do? The party was a success and we managed without her."
"Humph," Camille grunted. "Well, here's some news that you might want to fight about . . . I found a half-smoked joint, along with a pack of cigarettes in an ashtray under her bed."
"Really? Hmm . . . I'm surprised." Max's tone was more serious than before.
"Not good, huh?" Camille prompted.
"No. I don't understand what's going on with her."
"Me neither," Camille agreed. "We've given her everything she's ever wanted . . . probably way too much, and this is how she treats

us. Most high school kids try pot and drink alcohol. But in her room? That is not acceptable. I wish she'd never become friends with Nici. That girl is not a great influence. What do you think?"

Lifting one hand, palm up, Max agreed, "I think you might be right."

"Well, if Nici is at the root of Jaiden's problems, we ought to do something about it."

"Not a good idea, Camille. Interfering will only drive them closer together."

"Nici's father is not in her life, her mother works two jobs . . . never at home. She lets Nici run wild. Not a very stable family situation."

"Don't overreact," Max interjected. "Most kids go through this while in high school. Jaiden simply waited until she finished. She's an adult, really."

"So that makes her attitude and her illegal drug use acceptable?" Camille snapped in disgust.

"What are we gonna do, lock her in her room?" Max countered. "She's let us down and I'm going to let her know that we make the rules and she's got to follow them as long as she's living here."

"Even if she's about to leave home, she's got to change her attitude. Once she is at school, don't think for a minute that our problems with her are over, Max. She has to buckle down and do well or she will have a lot more problems than she has now. All the money it's costing us."

"She'll do fine," Max predicted. "This is an ordinary, teenage phase of rebelliousness. We'll all survive it, I guarantee."

"Let's hope so," Camille replied, removing her robe, preparing to change the subject to the phone call from Fidelity Insurance. Taking a deep breath, she jumped into the next problem, eager to deal with it and see where they stood. "I heard you tell Trent Young that the Alpha Phi Alpha Christmas party will definitely be at Vendora."

"Yep. First Saturday in December, as usual," Max responded in a more upbeat manner.

"Do you really think we can manage it?" Camille inquired, easing into her discussion about the future of Vendora even though she was dead tired and anxious to get some sleep. "Ann Burton's assistant, Julie, called about our insurance claim," she went on, pausing to watch for Max's reaction.

He shot her a questioning expression, both eyebrows raised. "Really? Took her long enough to get back to us. What'd she say?"

"Well, I don't know if this is true or not," Camille hedged, letting her words trail off. "But what she said was not very encouraging."

"What's that mean?" he asked.

"She said we don't have flood insurance. That it was cancelled last June for non-payment," Camille finished, thinking that Max did not appear as baffled as she had thought he might. Her heart sank. Julie must have been telling the truth! "Max, what is going on?"

Max scowled, irritation evident. "Forget about it. I'll talk to Ann again . . . she'll straighten it out." His reply was short and terse. He went to his side of the bed and jerked back the bedspread, clearly dismissing the subject.

"Then it's true?" she pressed.

Max remained silent while giving Camille a blank stare, then muttered, "I said Ann will take care of it. Don't worry."

"*Ann* will straighten it out?" Camille went on. "*How* exactly are you going to get her to do that? Sweet talk her into renewing our policy?" Camille knew her remark was hurtful and uncalled for, but dammit, she did not care. He had better come up with more of an explanation than he had so far.

"Sweet talk Ann? What kind of statement is that?" Max threw back, clearly upset by Camille's implication that he would make a romantic overture toward Ann to get their policy reinstated. "Please, let it go. I'll work it out."

"I want the truth, Max," Camille demanded, trying to control her voice. Jaiden was probably still awake and right down the hall. "Are we covered by flood insurance or not?"

Max punched his king-size pillow hard, avoiding eye contact with Camille. "For a time, no, we weren't covered, but I paid up the back premiums and Ann assured me that Fidelity would reinstate it retroactively. Must have been a glitch."

"A glitch. Oh, my God," Camille groaned. "I don't believe this. How could you have done such a thing, let alone believe that Ann Burton would be able to fix it?"

Max gave an exasperated sigh of his own, and then told Camille, "It just happened. Everything will work out. So, don't worry."

Camille did not want to believe what he was telling her. Who was he trying to fool? "Exactly when did you pay the back premiums and why didn't you at least mention the problem to me?" she asked, forcing a steady voice.

"I paid it last week . . . as soon as I realized what had happened." He slipped between the sheets but sat up in bed with his back pressed against the tufted peach satin headboard, worry tightening his features. "Remember that plumbing situation in the kitchen at Vendora last spring? We had to close for two weeks and it cost us a bundle. Well, after that, I let a few bills slide for a while . . . until the cash flow returned to normal. I planned on taking care of the flood insurance before the cancellation date, but . . ." he shrugged, shaking his head. "I never thought . . ."

Camille strode to his side of the bed and glared down at Max, her lips tight, her gray eyes brimming with tears. She was so angry and disappointed that her whole body was shaking. "You never thought what, Max? That it would never rain? That I'd never find out that you let the insurance lapse? That you secretly contacted your 'friend' Ann, and asked her to fix things for you? Dammit, Max. This is a mess!"

"I know . . . and I'm sorry," he mumbled. "You're right. Really, Camille. I didn't want you to worry."

She turned away from him and went to the window, where she pulled back the sheer curtains and stared out over the dark backyard, desperate to gain control. She was shaking with anger and bewilderment. Could it be that after twenty years of marriage, she still didn't know Max? Or was it that she still could not trust him? Camille focused on the low garden lights that twinkled along the path that led to their gazebo, the place where she liked to sit and enjoy their beautiful home. The water in the fountain under the trailing yellow jasmine cascaded over three tiers of rock to fall into the deep blue swimming pool. She loved her home, her life with Max, and all that they had built together. How dare he jeopardize everything with his reckless, selfish attitude? Angrily, she turned around and faced Max, blurting out what was really on her mind.

"This is not simply about the insurance, you know. It's about trust, and keeping secrets. I thought you had learned your lesson, but apparently not. You'll never change, will you?"

"What are you talking about, Camille?" Max got out of bed and went to stand beside her. "A little glitch with the bills and I dropped the ball. I can take out a loan to repair Vendora and get another flood insurance policy. There's no reason to make more of this than what it is."

"You were thoughtless and selfish, Max," Camille bluntly told him. "Shutting me out. Going behind my back to get Ann Burton to fix your messy situation."

"I didn't think . . ." Max started.

"Think! I know how thoughtless you can be. I learned the hard way, remember?"

"Don't go there, Camille," Max warned softly, placing a hand on her arm. "Please don't compare this to what happened between us. That was a long time ago, and you know I've changed."

When he took her arm and attempted to pull her against him, Camille stiffened, and then edged away. "Please. Your charm will not work on me tonight. I feel completely betrayed."

"There's no need to feel that way," he said in a low, contrite tone.

Moving from the window, she let the sheer curtains fall back over the panes, then turned to face Max. "This is your mess. Literally. You clean it up . . . but you'd better not gamble with our future again."

"I'll take care of everything," he assured her. "The bank will give me a loan. I'll get enough money to fix everything, and at a real low rate."

"Fine. *You* work it out," Camille said through tight lips, infuriated by his oh-so-sure attitude. She went over to the bed, snapped out the light and lay down between the fragrant soft sheets, turning onto her side, her back to Max, who climbed in beside her. Neither spoke again, leaving Camille to struggle in the dark with the flicker of memories that rushed into her mind.

Ten years ago. The woman's sweet voice on the phone. Max's shameful admission that he had indulged in a one-night stand with an old college flame. The shock of his confession. The devastation that followed. She could still see Max's tear-stained face and frightened eyes, when she told him she was leaving. And what hurt most was the dark shadow of Jaiden's face at her bedroom window as she had watched her mother drive away. The image haunted Camille to this day, and she still felt a shiver of guilt whenever she thought of how selfish she had been during that painful time. She had never told Jaiden the truth: that her father had committed adultery and that was why she walked out. She had told Jaiden that she and Max had argued over finances, and left it at that, Why burden her daughter with adult problems, Camille had thought, regretting having left Jaiden behind when she walked out on Max. That had been her biggest mistake.

She had taken refuge at Rochelle's house, where she stayed for ten days, crying, complaining, cursing, and listening to her half-sister's stern prediction that one day she would regret leaving Max. Rochelle had reminded Camille that she had never been one to give up on anything and her commitment to her marriage had to take precedence over pride. Remember what their mother, Annie Ivors, had done? The sacrifice she had made by taking Rochelle into her home to accept her as a daughter, knowing that the infant was her husband's illegitimate child? That ought to serve as an inspiration for Camille to try harder to patch things up at home. Annie had set aside her pride in order to give Rochelle a home, a loving mother, a sister, and a sense of belonging that she never would have found in a series of foster homes. If Annie Ivors could forgive an errant husband in order to hold her family together, so could Camille.

In the end, Camille had not been able to shun her commitment to her marriage and had returned to Max and nine-year-old Jaiden, determined to find a way to go on. Marriage counseling had helped the family heal, though the traumatic incident left its mark on Jaiden, who emerged withdrawn and fearful of being left alone for months afterward. Jaiden's pain haunted Camille as the slow, careful process of forgiveness unfolded. Eventually, she and Max moved past the broken edges of their love, and into the future they envisioned for their family, with him vowing never again to do anything that would place their family at risk. Now, apparently he had.

Camille's thoughts spun out in an uncertain path. What if Max did not get the loan? What if the bank foreclosed on Vendora? They could plunge into that frightening downward spiral that often led to bankruptcy. What about their custom-built home, their cabin at the lake, and how would Jaiden attend an Ivy League university? How would they manage? Their mortgage was a killer, but so far, her salary and commissions from the travel agency were covering it. Barely. And she was not bringing home enough to support the family's current lifestyle. Holding her breath to keep from crying aloud, Camille squeezed her eyes tightly closed. A tear slipped out. She had once vowed never to allow Max to make her cry again, and she had managed to keep that promise for ten long years. She was not about to break down tonight.

"I know our financial situation is not the best right now," Max's words came to her in the dark, intruding on her thoughts. "But hang in there with me, okay? I'll find a way to work this out."

"I hope so," Camille murmured, burrowing into her pillow, desperate to get her mind off the past.

CHAPTER 6

Los Angeles

A short, stocky guard wearing a dark blue uniform and reflective sunglasses stepped in front of the heavily scrolled, black iron gates that protected Monarch Studios from unwanted visitors. He waved Davis to a stop, and without taking his eyes off Davis's gleaming Lexus, approached, clipboard in hand.

"Hello," Davis called out after pressing the button to roll down the window. A blast of late August heat hit him in the face as he reached for his driver's license, even though he knew the guard had recognized him. However, security at the small but active movie lot was tight, so Davis did not mind showing his identification every time he arrived—which was usually two or three times a week.

"Hello, Mr. Kepler," the guard replied, accepting Davis's license. "Good to see you again."

"You too, Al. Well, where's Lara today?" Davis asked as he adjusted his red silk tie and checked his image in the rearview mirror, pleased with his reflection.

I could pass for a movie producer, even a star, he decided, studying his golden tan image. His skin was clear and even; his jaw, angular; and he had a strong upper lip. *As good as any leading man around,* he mused, knowing that he radiated prosperity and success—an impression he labored to maintain. After all, he had convinced Lara Stanton that he was an up-and-coming businessman and a full partner in Romero's who was doing extremely well. She had no idea that he was dependent on Reet for his income and had no say whatsoever in the management of the club.

And she never needs to know, Davis thought, waiting for the guard to let him pass through.

Al handed Davis his license, then made a scribbled note on the chart on his clipboard. "Miss Stanton is on sound stage number six today. It's a closed set, though," he added.

Davis ran his hands over the padded leather steering wheel as he shot a questioning glance at Al. "And?" he prompted. "Are you telling me I can't go in?"

"Oh, no, Mr. Kepler," Al called back, quickly entering his guardhouse to push the button to open the heavy gates. "You're cleared. Just wanted to alert you to what was going on, that's all."

With a curt nod, Davis gunned the motor and sped through the gates, then turned left and headed toward the one-story windowless building at the back of the lot. He knew what the guard had meant: Lara was doing a nude scene today and only those who were absolutely necessary to the shoot would be allowed inside. He grinned to himself: He had seen Lara Stanton nude many times . . . only last night, as a matter of fact. They had dined late at a popular Thai café in Culver City, and then returned to her house in Brentwood where they had spent the better part of an hour seated in her multi-jet Italian marble shower. He could still smell the scent of her lavender soap on the backs of his hands and feel her soft thighs pressed against his. Oh yes, he had seen Lara Stanton naked many times, had admired her luscious honey brown breasts and the shapely curve of her backside from every conceivable angle—but never while she had been in front of a camera.

This ought to be interesting, Davis thought as he pulled into a parking space outside of sound stage number six.

As soon as Roberto Simona shouted, "Cut!", an egg-shaped woman wearing black reading glasses with a yellow pencil tucked behind her right ear hurried onto the set and wrapped a pink satin robe around Lara Stanton's naked body. With one plump arm draped across Lara's shoulders, the wardrobe assistant placed her lips near Lara's ear and whispered eagerly as she escorted Lara from beneath the hot stage lights.

Lara's costar, Guy Fernandes—a well-toned, well-endowed young man with a cinnamon-colored complexion and a bright white smile—strode, naked, from the set and plopped down in a canvas chair next to Roberto's. He crossed his legs and casually commented to his director, "Lara Stanton is something else." He grinned in satisfaction.

"Yes, and you two make a great couple on film," Roberto told Guy, slapping his leading man affectionately on his naked back. With a turn, Roberto focused his attention on Lara, who walked over and touched him on the arm. He took both of her hands in his. "Perfect, Lara. You and Guy have a chemistry that really shines. *Flashfire* is gonna be a hell of a moneymaking movie!" Roberto gave Lara a quick hug, and then said, "Take fifteen, sweetie. The nightclub scene is next."

"Thanks, Roberto," Lara told her director, who was already moving across the busy set to consult with a cameraman. Lara stepped closer to Guy, waved her wardrobe assistant away, and forced herself to focus on Guy's grinning lips instead of the washboard abs and bulging chest muscles that glistened back at her.

"You do that again and you'll be sorry," she hissed, her luminous brown eyes lit with frustration.

Guy shrugged both shoulders, eyes innocently wide. "Do what?" he smirked. "I thought the scene went very well."

"You know exactly what I'm talking about," Lara tossed back, sweeping one hand through her fashionably tangled auburn hair. Her gaze shifted to the lower part of Guy's anatomy. "Keep it under control. This isn't porn. Maybe you're on the wrong set, buddy. You got that? I don't play that way."

"You're paranoid," Guy replied, waving his hand in a dismissive gesture. Leaning forward in his chair, he hissed, "Get over it, Lara. You know you liked it."

With a sharp jerk, Lara raised her right hand, preparing to slap the smug smile off Guy's face, but Roberto intervened and grabbed Lara by the arm. "Please. Not here. Let's cool things down. That was a pretty heavy scene for you two, and we've got more to go. Guy, get outta here. Go put on a robe. Lara, you go relax. We've got a movie to shoot here. Okay?"

In a huff, Lara stomped off toward her dressing room while Guy reluctantly accepted a black silk robe from an assistant. Roberto leaned low over Guy, his face close to the young actor's. "Don't mess over Lara Stanton. She may appear to be all sweet and innocent, but she's a sharp gal. Got some pretty tough guy friends, too. I saw what was happening, but I thought you had talked it over with Lara. Obviously, you hadn't. Spring another surprise like that and this might be your last picture. Keep things under control, you hear?"

From the darkened shadows at the back of the sound stage, Davis had watched the love scene as well as the heated exchange between Lara and Guy, though he had not been able to hear what Lara had hissed at the young actor. Davis's heart was pumping like crazy. Lara should have slapped Guy. Hard.

When Davis first learned who Lara's costar was, he had wondered how it would work out. Guy Fernandes was a twenty-one-year-old actor with a few soft porn movies to his credit who had been selected to star opposite Lara in his first legitimate role: *Flashfire*, an R-rated movie. At thirty-three, Lara was as beautiful as any twenty-year-old, and had built a huge fan base over the years doing sexy, romantic roles featuring strong, no-nonsense women who always got what they went after. Working with a younger man was nothing new for Lara, and most of them were so in awe of her they would never try to pull a stunt like the one Guy had just botched.

That smart-ass, narcissistic punk better be careful, Davis fumed as he cut around the shadowed edges of the bustling sound stage and hurried to Lara's dressing room. After knocking, he waited until she cracked open the door.

"Davis! Thank God. I'm glad to see you," she breathed, pulling back the door, linking one lavender scented arm through his as she held onto him snugly and guided him inside. Before closing the door, Davis kissed her hard, then untangled himself from her arms and sat down in a chair next to Lara's cluttered makeup table. She flashed him one of her movie-star smiles, pushed the door shut, and then resumed repairing her stage makeup, patting bronzer over her burnished brown cheeks.

"Having trouble with Guy?" Davis prompted, hoping Lara wanted to talk about what had happened on the set. Davis was not naive. He knew show business well enough to understand that crazy things were always happening and it was not a good idea to get too uptight if a touchy situation unfolded. If Lara was upset with whatever Guy had done, that was her business, not his, . . . but he wanted to show his concern.

"Nothing I can't handle," Lara replied, giving her cheeks a closer inspection. "He's new. Fresh from porn. I told Roberto he'd have trouble with Guy. We'll see how he works out."

"But you're okay with him?" Davis pressed, wishing she had

enough clout to refuse to work with jerks like Guy Fernandes. "I don't want him making nasty moves on you. I mean it, Lara."

"My, my," Lara replied, gently flicking a fluffy powder brush over the bridge of her nose. "You sound like a jealous husband, Davis. I think I'm flattered."

"Don't be," Davis quickly replied. "I only meant that you deserve to be treated with respect, like the star you are, and he shouldn't take advantage."

Davis could feel perspiration gathering under his arms. *Like a jealous husband? Why did she have to say that?* he thought, tensing. He enjoyed being with her—in and out of bed. They took trips to Vegas, enjoyed nights out on the town in Los Angeles, where they were seated at the best tables in restaurants and were treated with great deference. They attended fabulous parties and rubbed shoulders with heavyweights in the movie industry, including A-list movie stars. This was the life! And he loved it.

Davis knew that Lara was the kind of woman who could get under a man's skin, persuade him to make promises that would suck the life right out of his soul, and Davis was not about to let that happen. However, he did struggle to keep from actually falling for her but he thought about her constantly whenever they were apart; he wondered who she was with and what she was doing, but never let on that she ever crossed his mind. Lara was gorgeous, wealthy, and on her way to becoming a superstar. He had no problem benefiting from an association with her, but he had no intentions of ever marrying Lara, not as long as she could be his good time girl—a beautiful piece of ass that he was lucky to have at his beck and call. Maybe he would move in with Lara, if she asked him to, but that was as much of a commitment as he was willing to make. He wanted no legal entanglement with her, or any other woman for that matter: He had been burned twice before and had no desire to repeat that experience.

His first mistake had been a teenage marriage at the age of sixteen with a "round the corner girl"—the result of a bet he had made, and lost, with Reet and several of his buddies who had dared him to go all the way. The union never should have happened and it lasted seven days—long enough for his mother to find out about what he had done and have the marriage annulled. His second mistake had occurred soon after his release from prison when he had been so desperate for a woman that he had become romantically involved with a reformed prostitute who had given him a lot of attitude and a bad case of the clap. When he dumped her, she pulled a gun and shot at him while he was asleep—luckily, she missed. After that experience, Davis had been careful not to date a woman for more than two or three months, then move on, and he had no use for a clinging, smothering female presence in his life.

Now, Lara laughed, her throaty chuckle coming from deep within her shapely body. "I appreciate your concern, Davis, but I can handle Guy. Remember, I started out modeling lingerie at men's clubs in Reno when I was fifteen years old. I've been fighting off lecherous advances for a hell of a long time. Reet Collins is the only man, I think, who never made a pass at me. Always about business, with him. I was seventeen years old when I met Reet, and when he offered to arrange for me to have a screen test for Roberto Simona, I was the happiest girl around. Happy enough to give him ten percent of my first contract and every contract thereafter. Reet has made a lot of money off me over the years, but he gave me my break in the business, so I have no regrets. "

"And now you're on your way to becoming a true superstar," Davis told her, knowing how much she liked to have her ego stroked.

"Damn straight," she said in a flippant manner. "Artie, my agent, is asking seven figures for me to play the lead in Roberto's next picture, *Daddy's Baby Doll* Hear that, Davis? Honey, I'm about to move onto the A list at last. Seven figures for the lead in a legitimate movie! Believe me, I didn't get where I am by letting other people fight my fights. I can take care of myself . . . and Guy Fernandes. He doesn't know how I operate, but he'll learn soon enough."

"I'm sure he will," Davis conceded.

Lara put down her bronzing brush and turned to Davis. "What do you think?"

He stood, and then moved closer to Lara, scrutinizing her makeup. "Perfect." His eyes locked with hers. Bending down, he kissed her roughly on the lips, pulled back, then returned for a second kiss that was long, deep, and so intense that it left him breathing hard and fully aroused. Davis touched Lara's smeared lipstick with his little finger and murmured, "Well, I think you'll have to redo your lipstick."

Smiling, Lara pulled Davis's face close to hers, covered his mouth with hers and thrust her tongue deep inside, while guiding his hands into the front of her pink satin robe.

Davis welcomed the invitation, caressing Lara's full, warm breasts.

He slid his hands along the sides of her tiny waist, both relieved and pleased to feel her yielding to his touch. With one hand on the rise of her softly rounded buttocks, he led her away from her mirrored makeup table and eased her onto a tan suede sofa in a corner of her dressing room. Lara snuggled down among a scattering of velvet pillows and adopted a smoldering expression, her mascara-covered lashes framing half-closed eyes.

"I can fix my lipstick later . . ." she murmured, sliding her tongue over her glistening red lips. "As well as my hair, my body makeup . . . and my concentration," she giggled seductively, watching for Davis's reaction.

"You sure we've got time for this?" Davis softly taunted as he moved to straddle Lara's satiny torso. With his knees on either side of her and one hand on his designer leather belt, he went on, "You need to prepare for your next scene, don't you? Can't keep Roberto waiting."

"Oh, yes I can," Lara whispered, shedding her robe, exposing every inch of her soft bronze body. She settled her mass of auburn hair atop a large peach-colored velvet pillow, then tossed her robe across the room. "Now, be a dear and lock the door, Davis. I hate interruptions."

CHAPTER 7

Providence, Rhode Island

Laughing, dancing, noisy party people packed Rod Henry's small apartment, and the music was so loud that Jaiden could not understand what he was trying to ask her.

"Excuse me?" she replied, stepping back to make room for a girl wearing a red and white thong bikini to squeeze between her and Mona's cousin. Jaiden glanced briefly at the girl's bare buttocks, which jiggled provocatively as she strutted toward a guy wearing baggy Hawaiian print swim trunks who was standing in a dim corner of the room. Jaiden blinked and turned back to Rod, who was motioning for her to head toward the door that stood open onto the balcony that overlooked the apartment complex courtyard.

The East Coast Indian summer was extremely warm, and Rod's pool party theme had provided an opportunity for many of the girls to wear very short shorts, skimpy halter tops, bikinis, and thong swimsuits. The generous display of skin at the party had surprised Jaiden, who had worn jeans and a sheer, black lace blouse. With her thick brown hair piled on top of her head and filigree chandelier earrings in her ears, she had thought she was dressed perfectly for the casual gathering, but now she wasn't so sure.

I'm probably the only virgin here, too, she thought, watching a confident, sexy, "out there" party girl dance alone in the middle of the room. Dismissing that thought, she pushed through the crowd, which was now gyrating, *en masse*, to the pulsating rap of Dr. Dre and made her way toward Rod.

"Let's go down to the pool." Rod told her as soon as she was at his side.

"Good idea," Jaiden replied, fanning her face, ready for some fresh air. "Be there in a minute." She quickly scanned the room for Mona, who had disappeared shortly after introducing Jaiden to her cousin. Mona was the only person Jaiden actually knew at the party—which consisted of Rod's and Mona's friends, many of whom were upper class students at Brown. To Jaiden, the crowd seemed very mature and rather "edgy"—not at all like the students she had expected to meet on campus. Many of them had multiple body piercings and some were heavily tattooed. Totally different from her friends back home.

The past week had flown by in a blur of new faces, strange buildings, stern professors, and attempts to find her way around in this awesome, exciting place. Last Friday, her parents had safely deposited her on campus at Keeney Hall, and then spent the night at the nearby Holiday Inn before returning to Houston the next morning. Once they had left, Jaiden had felt both relief and apprehension about finally being on her own, but soon found a comfortable place to get acclimated at Faunce House, the student center that was the hub of campus life. There, she spent the morning drinking coffee, smoking cigarettes, and chatting with students, including a fellow Texan, a girl from Fort Worth, who was a second year student. Jaiden quickly adjusted to her newfound independence.

Later that day, back at her dorm room, she had finally met Mona, her roommate, and they had had a blast while unpacking and decorating their room. Buying books, meeting with her counselor, attending classes, and tackling her workload, which was much heavier than she had anticipated, had consumed Jaiden's first week.

But now, it was time to party, and she was definitely ready to have a good time. Before stepping outside with Rod, Jaiden finally spotted Mona—standing with her hands on the shoulders of a gorgeously tall guy who was wearing cutoff jeans and a loose white shirt that was unbuttoned to expose his smooth muscled chest. *He must be Damian*, Jaiden thought, thinking that he looked exactly as Mona had described him.

Mona was model-thin, with chiseled cheekbones, smoky black eyes and wavy dark hair that reached to her waist. Nearly as tall as her companion, she was wearing a sheer miniskirt over her one-piece swimsuit, and was deep in conversation with her boyfriend. Clearly, she had no interest in playing chaperone to her new roomie from Houston. Jaiden was on her own.

Shrugging, Jaiden went out onto the balcony and glanced down, Rod was already crossing the grassy area of the courtyard that led to the pool. She started down the stairs after him, thinking that he walked with a bad boy kind of swagger that she definitely found attractive. He had skin the color of rich caramel, longish brown braids that touched the top of his shoulders, and striking, deep-set eyes that had focused on Jaiden with an intensity that had startled her the moment they had been introduced. Of medium height, he was wearing tight black jeans, black boots with silver buckles at the ankles, and a black, short-sleeved tee shirt that had a fire-breathing dragon on the front and a silver motorcycle on the back. His jeans fit him well enough to accentuate his compact physique, and his muscle shirt allowed him to show off the numerous tattoos on his arms—intricate and mysteriously intriguing. He even had a tattoo of a lightning bolt that snaked up the side of his neck and ended below his right ear. Jaiden had never met anyone with so much body art before.

At the edge of the pool, Rod stopped beside an empty chaise longue—one sufficiently large enough to accommodate two people. He stood with his back toward Jaiden as he gazed into the shimmering blue water, where a few couples were playing around in the swimming pool. Another couple sat on the far edge, their feet dangling in the water, wrapped together in a big beach towel. The sky was dark, but filled with stars, creating a sparkling tableau that stirred Jaiden, who increased her pace to catch up with Rod while sloshing most of her third wine cooler out of its plastic cup.

I've probably drunk too much already, she thought. *But I don't care. I have no curfew tonight, no one to answer to, and nothing to do but party.* It felt wonderful to do as she pleased.

She walked up behind Rod and paused, expecting him to turn toward her and strike up a conversation with the standard kinds of questions that students asked to break the ice: What's your major? Why'd you choose Brown? Having a good time so far? However, he did not speak, but slowly studied her face, and then reached out and touched her gently on the cheek.

At first, Jaiden pulled back, startled by this unexpected move, but then she relaxed, deciding to see where this encounter was headed.

"You're much prettier than Mona described," Rod told her, removing his hand, but not the intensity of his gaze. "Want to sit down?" he offered, gesturing toward the chaise longue.

"Sure," Jaiden agreed, allowing him to hold onto her arm as he eased her down into the chair beside him. Shoulder to shoulder they focused on the blue water and the couple splashing around in the pool.

"I'm glad you came to my party," Rod whispered in her ear, as he eased one arm around her shoulders.

Turning to face him, she answered softly, "Me, too."

When he threaded his fingers through the hair at the nape of her neck, she let out a low sigh. With very little pressure, he turned her head toward him, bringing her face close to his. She did not resist when he brushed his lips over hers, though she clenched one hand into a fist, feeling as if she were melting. Not wanting to be thought a novice at kissing, though she certainly was, Jaiden inched closer and pressed her lips to his.

His kiss was deep, but not demanding, and Jaiden was thrilled when he flicked his tongue lightly over hers. She immediately did the same to him. He responded by placing his free hand at her waist and pulling her even closer.

Jaiden inhaled the clean, lemony scent that came from Rod's hair, skin, and clothing, letting it fill her head and make her slightly dizzy. She held him fast with her lips and moved her tongue in tandem with his, wanting the encounter to last as long as possible.

When he broke off, she gasped and giggled, laughing at her own brazenness as he guided her to her feet and led her to a shadowy clump of trees at the fence that surrounded the courtyard. Standing in the dim shade, he put both of his hands on her back and slid them up and down in a slow, possessive manner that sent tiny waves of heat through Jaiden's body. She began to breathe deeply, determined to remain calm while showing him how experienced she was, though her heart was beating so fast she was sure he must feel it. Jaiden leaned into Rod, parted her lips, and let him know how anxious she was to accept more of Rod's exploration. This was, without a doubt, the first *real* kiss she had ever experienced, making Kevin Hamilton's blundering, lifeless smooches seem totally lame. The kiss lasted until she felt Rod's hardness begin to rise up between them, and the reality of what was happening broke the spell. Stepping away, she fanned her face with her hands and said, "Whew. You do move fast."

"When I see what I like, I go after it," Rod replied, his voice soft, yet strong enough to make his point.

"Oh? And do you always get what you want?" she asked, eager to know more about Rod Henry. Was he a player who kept score? A heartbreaker with no conscience? A casual adventurer who was always on the move?

"No. Not always, but I never stop trying." he confessed, looking down, then smiling up at her.

"And tonight, I'm what you like?" she teased, wondering who his other conquests were.

"Yeah. You could say that," he answered, trailing a finger along one side of her neck and over the buttons at the front of her black lace blouse.

The gesture initiated a flutter in the pit of Jaiden's stomach. "I'm flattered," was all she could manage.

"I'm pleased. Because I definitely want to feel . . . and see . . . a lot more of you."

Now, Jaiden gave a short giggle and eased out of his embrace. "I'll see you around campus, won't I? What's your schedule like?"

Rod was thoughtfully silent while he touched each button, and then lifted his chin as he answered. "No, you won't see me around campus."

"Why?"

"Because I don't go to Brown," he finally admitted with a sheepish grin.

Surprised, Jaiden tilted her head to one side. "Oh? I assumed you did when Mona mentioned that many in her family were alumni, and . . ."

"I dropped out after my sophomore year," he interrupted. "Didn't make the grades, so I enrolled in East Tech Business College so I could stay in Providence. I like it here. "

"What are you studying?"

"I'm taking a class in software development now. My dad was not too happy about my decision at first, but once I convinced him that this kind of computer training will help him in his business, he calmed down and agreed to support me."

"Well, that's good, isn't it?" Jaiden remarked, more intrigued than ever. Rod was like a maverick—an independent spirit who did as he pleased, and was not about to change to please his parents.

"I guess," he said. "You see, my family owns a chain of automotive repair shops in western Pennsylvania and they're doing pretty well. After high school graduation, I wanted to go straight into the business, but my father insisted that I get a degree in business first. So, I entered Brown. Made it through two years as a full-time student, but I hated every minute of it. I know I put forth the minimum effort just to satisfy my dad. My grade point average reflected my lack of interest. So I dropped out."

"Well, I can understand where you're coming from. It's not easy to satisfy some of these professors. I'm kind of worried about making the grades, myself."

"You'll do fine."

"I hope so. My parents would not be as agreeable as yours if I messed up. I'll have to study my ass off to make the grade point average they expect."

"Can't study all the time," Rod commented.

"Right, but you don't know my mom and dad."

"Well, when you need a break from the books, you know where to find me," Rod remarked.

Nodding, Jaiden glanced toward the stairs leading up to Rod's apartment, thinking she ought to go back inside. The kissing, the conversation, the closeness were all great, but how far did she really want to go? Tonight? "Well, give me a call, okay? We can get together sometime." She started to leave.

Rod reached out and touched her on the arm. "Don't go inside yet. Stay a little longer? Please?"

Jaiden studied his face, knowing she ought to go back to the party, gather her wits and get her emotions under control. However, she didn't know a soul inside except Mona, who certainly would not want to be bothered with entertaining her roommate. "Okay. I'll stay. It's too hot in there anyway."

"Good," Rod told her, brushing his fingers up and down the length of her arm. "I like talking to you, Jaiden. And I don't usually talk a lot. You seem different. Not like the other girls in there." He jerked his head toward his brightly lit apartment, which was crowded with partyers who were rocking with the music.

She tensed, but did not move as he slid his hand up her arm, across her shoulder, and onto her chest. But when he began to loosen the buttons on her sheer lace blouse, she stepped to one side, and said, "Whoa," not prepared for what she knew he wanted.

Rod removed his hand and held it up, as if to let her examine his fingers. "Right. Excuse me. I get your message." His voice thick and low. He rubbed his bare arms with both hands and looked down at his boots. "Sorry about that."

While watching him, Jaiden prayed that she had not frightened him off, that he wasn't going to go back inside and take up with one of those half-naked girls in a bikini who would gladly drop her top and let him feel her up. If he walked off and left her standing there, feeling like a complete fool, Jaiden knew she would never see him again. And that was not what she wanted.

"Don't be sorry," she finally mumbled. "I want to stay out here with you and I want to be alone with you. But I'm . . . a bit over-whelmed right now." She searched his face, considering what her next move should be, certain only of one thing—she wanted him, and in a way she had never felt before. But what was she thinking? She had just met him tonight. He was handsome, sexy, and he had told her he liked being with her . . . but he *was* moving awfully fast "Rod, I think you're a nice guy, but . . ."

"A nice guy?" He laughed. "I'm not so sure about that . . ." The words drifted off into the darkness.

For a long moment Jaiden said nothing, then added, "Well . . . *nice* is how Mona described you to me when she was telling me about you, and so far, you haven't disappointed," Jaiden said, struggling to sort out exactly how she felt.

Rod stared at Jaiden, then shrugged and lifted his chin with a short jerk. "Mona *would* say that, but . . . hey, if I've been out of line tonight, say so, okay?" he stated, pulling out a cigarette. He lit it, and drew hard on it, then blew smoke toward the stars, his face to the sky.

Jaiden held her breath, watching him, wanting him to like her. She wondered what else Mona may have told him about her and what he truly thought. Maybe he was testing her, just to see how far she would let him go. "You haven't been out of line," she assured him. "And I'm having a very good time at your party."

"I'm glad, because I'd like to see you again," he admitted in a level tone.

"I'd like that, too," Jaiden confessed.

"All right. Tomorrow is Saturday. No classes, right?"

"Right."

"Wanna go out?" he asked nonchalantly, taking another drag on his cigarette.

"You mean like . . . on a date?"

He grinned at her and inclined his head in affirmation. "Yeah.

Like a real date. I'll pick you up and everything." He touched her on the cheek, his smile widening. "And you don't need to worry. I would never make a girl do anything she didn't want to do. I'm not some kind of a jerk."

Jaiden's nervous laughter broke the tension that had been building since the moment Mona introduced her to Rod. "You're far from being a jerk," she told him, having already decided that one day she would give him what he wanted—and it was going to be beautiful.

Jaiden reached up and removed Rod's cigarette from his hand, took a long drag from it, and then ground it under her heel in the grass. She put her arms around his neck and let him kiss her again.

CHAPTER 8

The house was quiet and Max welcomed the opportunity to tackle the stack of mail on his desk without Camille around, glad that she had decided to spend the day with Rochelle. At his desk, he took out his calculator, pen, and a pad of paper, preparing to create some kind of a budget that would keep him and Camille afloat for a few more weeks.

Money was tighter than it had ever been, and he had to get a handle on their finances soon, or everything they had worked for would be in jeopardy. Flipping the page on his desk calendar to September 1, he grimaced, at the realization that a month had passed since the flood, but he shook off his despair and prepared to dig in, not about to dwell on that disastrous night.

He separated the unopened envelopes into three piles: Junk mail, his and Camille's personal mail, and business-related correspondence—the stack designated Vendora being the thickest. There were utility bills, food and beverage suppliers' invoices; plumbing, woodworking, and electrical repair bills, and an assortment of bids from contractors who wanted the job of restoring his supper club. He tossed the junk mail into the wastebasket, set personal mail to one side, and immediately slit open the envelope from the Bank of Houston that had come today.

He stared in disbelief at the check he pulled out. Several zeros were definitely missing. Max read the accompanying letter quickly, feeling as if he had fallen into a deep black pit. The sinking sensation that swept through him was alarming. What had happened? The loan officer with whom he had worked had assured him that he would be approved for sufficient funds to cover all of the major repairs at Vendora. The check he was holding would not even pay for replastering the kitchen walls, let alone replace all of the appliances. He crushed the depressing letter into a ball and tossed it at the wastebasket, which he missed, then he set the check on his desk and sat back in his chair, thinking. He needed ten times that amount, and he had to get his hands on it soon.

A long delayed surge of panic set in. What had he been thinking, putting all of his faith in the bank? Nearly a month had passed since the night of the flood and he was no closer to reopening his business than on the day that the water drained away. His cash reserves had gone toward professional water removal, debris clearing, and emergency repairs to the damaged windows and doors in order to secure the dark, empty building and keep looters from coming in and stripping away what was left. He had tapped every source of available cash while trying to keep his ten staff members on the payroll, and he had succeeded until last Friday, when he had been forced to let everyone go except Willie, the bartender, a single man who had worked for Max since the day Vendora opened. The only money Max had access to now was Jaiden's college fund, and no way was he going to touch that. Camille's salary was keeping them afloat, but it would not cover their bills much longer.

Camille. Thinking about her made him angry with himself. She was still upset with him, as she should be. He had let their flood insurance lapse. He had set the premium notice aside when the last thing on his mind had been a tropical storm. How could he have predicted that water would sweep in and destroy his business right before his eyes? In addition, Ann Burton had assured him that she would be able to fix his mistake by backdating his premium payment to make the policy coverage retroactive. Why had he trusted her? Apparently, she had not been able to come through and now he was stuck. If the government had declared the flooded area a disaster zone, he would have been eligible for an emergency loan through the Small Business Administration. As it stood now, he was out of luck.

Max studied the check from the bank, contemplating how best to use the money, mentally running through a list of possibilities. Operating a supper club in a historic old house was expensive, and even though Max owned the property outright, he had to pay for liquor licenses, health permits, food, beverages, table linens, live entertainment, taxes, wages, insurance, property management, security, and on and on. The business had grown steadily since the day he opened the doors, and a key aspect of Vendora's popularity had always been its historic ambiance. Simply patching things up in order to throw open the doors would not do.

Max flipped through the pile of bills again, his mind racing, his heart pumping fast as he examined each one. If only he could get his hands on some quick cash, he thought, sitting quietly as a thought came to him, making him stand and pace the room. The longer he thought about his idea, the more intriguing it became. It was risky, but not an impossible solution, and if it worked, he might be able to double, or even triple, the amount of the check.

He glanced at the stainless steel clock on his desk. It was one-thirty in the afternoon. Saturday. The community branch of his bank would close in thirty minutes. Impulsively, Max changed into a pair of slacks and a crisp white shirt, got into his blue Ford truck, and then drove to the bank and cashed the check. Next, he called Camille at Rochelle's and told her he was going out and would be late getting home tonight—he'd been invited to an impromptu birthday party for Trent Young, who was turning fifty this week. Perspiring in anticipation, he swung onto Interstate 10 and headed east toward the Louisiana border . . . and Lake Paradise Casino. Roaring up the highway, Max prayed for a lucky night.

Camille slowly hung up the phone, a wrinkle of concern between her brows. She had hoped that Max would be at home tonight when she returned from Rochelle's because they needed to talk. During the past two weeks, she had been overwhelmed with work at her agency and getting Jaiden settled at Brown. Max had been busy clearing out Vendora, getting estimates for repairs, and juggling their available cash to cover expenses. Now, it was time to talk, and make some hard decisions about their future.

She thought back to the night of the party and the argument that she and Max had had. Ever since, they had barely spoken to each other unless Jaiden had been around, and then they had pretended to get along. She wished she could forgive him for allowing the flood insurance to lapse, but she could not, and she didn't like the way things were going now. Moving around the house like strangers. No hugs, no good night kisses, let alone sex. She felt lonely and depressed and did not know what to do. But how could Max have put them in such a disastrous situation?

Now, rethinking his phone call, Camille felt doubly unsettled.

Max had sounded oddly buoyant and in a rush to get her off the line. A birthday party? She doubted that. He was probably going to Trent Young's house to play poker and drink beer, which he had been doing quite often lately.

"Anything wrong?" Rochelle asked, pouring more iced tea into her glass, and then refilling Camille's.

"No," Camille vaguely replied, looking up at Rochelle. "Max has to go out tonight. Won't be home until late. Guess there's no reason for me to hurry home."

"Good." Rochelle began to clear away the dishes from the late lunch she and Camille had enjoyed. "We can go catch a movie . . . or go shopping?"

Camille laughed. "No more shopping for me. Getting Jaiden ready for college took care of my shopping fix for quite a while. I don't plan to go near a mall for a long time."

"You know that won't last long. Foley's is having their end of summer blowout sale next week. Girl, you know you're gonna be there."

"I don't think so," Camille laughed, not about to confess that her days of spending money on clothes and shoes and purses that she really didn't need were over. She had to be careful. Her paycheck was all that she and Max had right now and there was a stack of unpaid bills on Max's desk at home that needed attention. "With Jaiden in college now, we have to watch our spending," she clarified, hoping Rochelle would let it drop.

"And, now that you and Max have that big house all to yourselves, I guess you're going to be busy doing other things?" Rochelle paused, arching a knowing brow at her sister.

"Right," Camille tossed back sarcastically. "We'll have wild passionate sex in every room of the house, whenever and wherever we please."

"Girl, you said that, not me," Rochelle laughingly tossed back. "But it doesn't sound so bad."

"Please," Camille groaned, though smiling as she reached for the newspaper to begin searching through the movie section. Her eyes roamed over the advertisements for movies, while her mind remained fastened on Rochelle's comment. *It has been too long since we made love,* she admitted, *and I wish things were different.*

After twenty years of marriage, Camille still loved and needed Max, but more than that, she wanted their old life back. Her commitment to her marriage was as strong as the day they married, and she had no plans to let this uneasy coolness that had sprung up between them play itself out much longer.

Lately, Max had been moody, silent, and preoccupied. He had begun to come and go without telling her where he was going or when he would return. She did not like the fact that he was spending so much time with his fraternity brothers, playing poker and drinking beer, and staying out very late. However, with the mood at home so somber, why would he want to stay in? she rationalized, beginning to feel guilty for holding her grudge against him for so long. Sighing, she pushed her worries aside and focused on the newspaper spread out on Rochelle's kitchen table. "What about *The Others*? I like Nicole Kidman." she asked.

"Too scary. Not in the mood."

"*Original Sin*?" Camille prompted.

"Yeah. I heard that it's pretty good," Rochelle decided. "I can take Antonio Banderas anytime."

"Fine. Six-forty-five, then," Camille replied, folding the paper and setting it aside.

"Heard from Jaiden?" Rochelle asked.

"No, she's only been gone two weeks. Give her time to run out of money, then I'll hear from her. You know how she likes to eat out and shop. I hope she's put herself on a budget."

"She'll do fine," Rochelle said. "College is going to be good for her . . . she'll make new friends, have new experiences. Really grow up."

"If she can concentrate on her classes and stop e-mailing and talking to Nici on the phone, she might make it."

"Is Jaiden going to be in Nici's wedding?"

Camille nodded, looking rather wary. "December fourth. Jaiden is Nici's maid of honor, and her dress cost almost as much as the wedding gown. Much too expensive for the kind of ceremony Nici is going to have. I know her mother is a single mom, and I can understand that she wants to give her daughter a wedding to remember, but she ought to be realistic."

"Maybe Nici's mom should have asked me to pull this shindig together," Rochelle said. "I could save her a bundle."

Camille shook her head. "I don't think your taste and Nici's mom's would have meshed. Your idea of what is appropriate and hers are miles apart."

"I know Nici and Jaiden have been friends a while, but don't you think she's a bit immature to be getting married in the first place?"

"Yes, I do. And I can't imagine her and DeJon raising a child," Camille stated. "As far as I'm concerned, this separation from Nici is good for Jaiden. She needs to concentrate on her grades instead of the color of Nici's bridesmaid's dresses and the size of the wedding cake. Thank God, Jaiden hasn't been involved in a serious relationship yet, and now that she's on campus, I'm hoping she'll meet lots of nice young men with great potential, and not rush into any heavy romantic situation right away."

"Hit me," Max said, studying the two cards on the table. Thirteen points. He had no choice but to take a hit, and he prayed for anything but a face card. He had been at the blackjack table for hours, winning, then losing . . . up and down, back and forth, unable to stop the roller coaster ride. However, that was how the game usually went, and that was what kept him at the tables. He hoped his luck would turn on the next hand, because he had everything riding on it.

The stone-faced dealer laid down a queen of hearts. Max cursed under his breath. *That's it*, he thought, pushing back from the table. He went to the bar and asked for a club soda with lime, glad that he had been smart enough to avoid hard liquor tonight. He had a long drive ahead of him and returning home with empty pockets was bad enough.

The bank check was gone. He had drawn all that he could on his ATM card. He thought about Jaiden, away at school and remembered that he had told her he would call tonight. He hadn't taken the time. Well, at least his daughter's college money was still safe. He downed his drink, pushed out the front door, got into his truck and headed home.

The long drive back to Houston gave Max time to think. He was disgusted with himself: He had lied to Camille, forgotten to telephone Jaiden, and had gambled away the last of their available cash. How could he have let things spiral so far out of control? Camille would never forgive him once she found out what he had done tonight. For the first time in his life, Max felt as if he were a complete failure, and he did not intend to get used to the feeling. He would find an investor to help him out of this bind. Selling off a percentage of ownership in Vendora and working with a partner was not what he wanted to do, but what options did he have?

Monday morning, I'll call Paul Cotter. He can help me structure a proposal that will attract the right kind of investor, Max thought, deciding to take his attorney's advice and bring in a partner. *Surely, I can find someone in the business world who is waiting for the deal I have in mind.*

On Sunday morning, Camille waited until Max had finished his second cup of coffee before she eased into the conversation she had rehearsed in her mind until two in the morning, while waiting for Max to come home.

She and Rochelle had ended up going to the late movie and Camille had returned home at eleven-thirty, expecting to find Max there. What she found was a message from Trent Young on their voice mail, asking Max to call him about a tennis date next week. Disturbed by the revelation that Max had lied to her about where he was going last night, she had sat up until one o'clock, waiting to talk to him, but then had given up her vigil and gone to bed. When she heard him enter the driveway, she had feigned sleep, too upset to deal with his deception. But now, they had to talk.

"How'd the party for Trent go?" she queried, keeping her voice as steady as she could. She wanted him to tell her the truth without sensing that she was aware of his lie.

Max set aside the sports pages of the Sunday paper and looked across the breakfast table at Camille. She could see that his eyes were bloodshot and filled with worry. What was going on?

"All right," was all that Max said.

"Who was there?"

"The usual crowd."

"Oh?" Camille replied. "And was Trent surprised?"

"Sure, sure," Max answered, picking up his paper, prepared to end the conversation.

However, Camille was only getting started and was not about to stop until she found out what he had been up to. Angry that he dared dismiss the subject so quickly, she reached over and pulled the newspaper away from Max, tossed it aside and told him, "Funny, Trent called here last night, looking for you. Something about a tennis date?"

Max did not speak.

The guilty expression on his face reminded her of another time when he had failed to deceive her: somber, fearful, and expectant. "So where were you last night?" Camille demanded, so calm she surprised herself. "And why did you lie to me about going to a party for Trent?"

Pushing back his chair, Max got up and walked over to the bay window on the other side of the room, keeping his back to Camille as he stared out into the garden. The silence was awful, but Camille waited it out.

Finally, he turned and began to speak quickly, as if his words had to come out all at once or he would never be able to say them. "Where I went last night is not that important—but what I did is. I took a risk and made a big mistake, Camille. A serious mistake that I can't go into right now because I'm too ashamed. And no . . . there is no other woman involved, if that's what you've been worried about. I would never do that to you again. "

"That's a relief, I think," Camille replied with a smirk, praying that Max was telling the truth.

"You've been so patient with me since everything fell apart after the flood. Your support . . . your paycheck has kept us afloat," he rushed on, frowning. "But now, I have to do something I had hoped I'd never do. I have to fix things for us . . . for our future."

"How, Max? If money is at the root of this problem, then we have to keep the situation in perspective. I love you and I want our marriage to survive this, but you are making it very difficult. You have to be truthful with me. If your secretive behavior and moodiness is going to tear us apart, then maybe we need to rethink your plans for Vendora. Sell it, Max. Get out from under the debt and the pressure. We'll manage somehow. Maybe it's time to let it all go."

"I can't do that. You know what that place means to me. It's my family's legacy, and my legacy to Jaiden. I have to keep it and keep us together."

"We could sell the cabin, then. We haven't been to the lake since last summer," Camille suggested. "Taxes have increased. Maintenance is very expensive. It's a luxury we can do without."

"I'd rather not sell it . . . unless I absolutely have to. Property values around Lake Livingston are skyrocketing. The Alabama-Coushatta Indians are about to get casino gambling, and if that happens, our property will be in a prime location to triple its value. Too good of an investment to let go of right now."

"Well, what about the bank loan? Did it come through?"

Max did not answer right away.

Camille continued to toss out options. "Maybe you ought to call the bank, find out if, or when, the loan will be finalized. Maybe . . ."

"No," Max curtly interrupted. "The check from the bank came, and it's already gone—besides, it would have covered less than a tenth of the renovation costs."

"Then think about selling Vendora, please."

Max cleared his throat, and then went on, "The solution, I have decided, is to sell an interest in the business. That way I can hold onto the property and work my way out of this financial bind."

"You mean, take a partner?"

"Yes. If I can find someone willing to invest in a flood-damaged property with a lot of potential. It may take a while, and there is no guarantee that I'll find a candidate, but the loan officer at the bank did mention that he might be able to help, if I decided to go that route. Paul thinks it's a good idea, and as my attorney and friend, I value his opinion."

Camille got up and went to stand beside Max, then placed her arm around his waist. She knew how difficult his decision must have been and how defeated he felt now. He had always prided himself on not asking for help, of making his livelihood on his own terms. And now he had been forced to admit that he could not go it alone any longer. She could feel the anxiety that clouded his face, and knew how much he needed to hear her tell him that she understood.

"There *is* someone out there," Camille assured Max. "I'm glad you made this decision and if this is what we have to do, then, of course, I'm committed to supporting you, because we can't continue like this. Since the night of your fraternity party, we have barely spoken to each other, and I don't like this feeling of drifting apart."

Max closed both eyes briefly, and pulled Camille closer,

"We've got to get back to where we were before the flood," Camille told him in a hushed voice. "Or we may never make it."

CHAPTER 9

At eleven o'clock on Sunday morning, Jaiden punched in Rod's phone number, her stomach aflutter as she listened to his telephone ringing. Only nine hours had passed since he had brought her back to the dorm, but to Jaiden it seemed forever. What a blast they had had on their first real date. He had arrived on his Suzuki motorcycle at seven o'clock, handed her a helmet, which had crushed Jaiden's carefully styled hair, then helped her onto the back of the bike and taken off, with Jaiden holding on tightly as they zoomed through the streets. Jaiden had never ridden on a motorcycle before and she'd been thrilled by the exhilarating sense of freedom as they sped up the open highway. The wind on her face. The blur of the countryside slipping past. Rod's back against her cheek.

First stop—Twist—a poolroom and tattoo parlor where Rod's best friend, Sid, lived and worked. They had hung around there for a few hours, playing pool, eating nachos, and drinking a lot of Sid's beer. Sid had even allowed Jaiden to watch as he etched a tattoo on a girl's shoulder—a blood red rose with her and her boyfriend's initials on the leaves. The process had intrigued Jaiden, but she had declined Sid's offer to etch a tiny pink heart on the inside of her ankle.

Next, they had ridden over to Myles Lane and spent hours going in and out of the noisy cafés and bars that made up the district where students went on Saturday nights to listen to local musicians and peruse the small studios where local artisans sold their creations. Rod bought her an amber-colored beaded bracelet that she had not taken off since he put it on her wrist.

At one o'clock in the morning, they wound up at Rod's apartment where they had settled down on his brown tweed sofa and watched MTV, doing more kissing than talking. They had really gotten close last night, but not too close—Jaiden had been determined not to let Rod go all the way, though she had let him remove her bra. She was not going to be an easy lay, and she realized that her reluctance to give it up quickly seemed to turn Rod on.

If he likes me enough, he'll wait, she had told herself. But what a kisser! At 2 A.M., he had brought her back to her dormitory, given her his phone number and told her to call him when she woke up. Well, she was up, and ready to talk to him, and prayed that he was waiting to hear from her.

When Rod said Hello, Jaiden's heart lurched, and she had to swallow quickly to clear her throat. "Hi!" she said breathlessly. "It's Jaiden."

"I know. I recognize your voice," Rod replied, his voice sexy and low. "Been thinking about you," he added.

"Really?" Jaiden replied, relieved. "Last night was the bomb. Totally. I had such a . . ." then she stopped talking when call waiting on her cell phone beeped. "Hold on a sec," she told Rod, and then she clicked over to see who it was. It was Nici, rushing on about something related to her wedding buffet.

Nici: *Well, what do you think? Flowers or candles on the tables? Chicken or shrimp puffs?*

Jaiden: *Nici, I can't talk now. Rod's on the line. You know. The guy I e-mailed you about. Gotta go. I'll call you back, okay?*

Nici: *All right. But don't forget. I need your help. I have to decide what kind of corsage I want for DeJon's mother, and . . ."*

Jaiden: *Nici. Please. I'll call you back. Can't mess this up. I will tell you all about him.*

Nici: *You better. And I want details, you hear?*

Jaiden clicked back to Rod, irritated that her time with him had been interrupted, wondering how much she really wanted to tell Nici about Rod. There had been a time when she would have been eager to spill every detail, blow by blow, to her best friend, but not anymore. Everything had changed so quickly, though she had only been on campus for three weeks. An uneasy sense of being pulled in two directions came over Jaiden and she wasn't quite sure what it meant. However, there was one thing she was sure about: Her best friend's wedding plans did not seem that important now.

"Wanna go for a ride?" Rod asked after she clicked back over to him.

"Sure. Where to?"

"Thought we'd head up the coast. Take you out to a special place to meet some of my friends. The weather is great today, but it's not gonna last much longer. Next month, it could be snowing."

"Get outta here. I've never seen snow," Jaiden admitted.

"Yeah? Just wait. You'll see more than you ever wanted to if you stick around here. Anyway, I'll be there in half an hour."

"I'll be ready," Jaiden replied, dismissing the fact that she had planned to spend the afternoon finishing her book report for English and completing two translations for her French II class.

CHAPTER 10

"What do you mean, you don't want my money?" Davis could not believe what Reet had said. One year ago to the day, they had sat down to discuss what a fair price would be if Davis could come up with the money to purchase a true one-half interest in Romero's. And now Reet was throwing this curve at him? "Here it is," Davis said again, extending the pale green check to Reet, who was sitting in his Wilshire Boulevard office behind an expensive chrome and glass desk, both arms calmly folded. "Just like we decided. One hundred-and-sixty-seven thousand dollars. The money I did not have when you asked me to be your partner. And as of today, September 9, 2001, that's what I want to be. A valid fifty-fifty partner."

Reet lifted a hand, as if to say *I don't want to hear it*, then lit a slim cork-tipped cigarette. He inhaled slowly, leaned forward and tapped ashes into an amber glass bowl on his desk. His air of indifference infuriated Davis, who took off his jacket and loosened his tie, as if preparing for a fight. He tossed his jacket over the back of a low-slung black leather chair and stood in front of Reet, waiting for an explanation.

"Interest," Reet finally declared. "Compounds daily. Moreover, I'd say, by now, you owe me about three times the amount of that check. Anyway, I don't want your money."

"Don't want it?" Davis almost laughed, thinking this must be a joke. Why was Reet doing this to him? "Didn't we agree that I could pay you my share of the start-up money and buy a half interest of Romero's?"

"Well, now I disagree," Reet uttered in calm, evenly spoken words. "We never put anything in writing about that, you know."

"So, your word meant nothing? That's what you're saying?"

A slight nod told Davis all he needed to know. "I trusted you, Reet. Maybe I wasn't able to kick in with hard cash in the beginning, but I've put in a lot of work and long hours to make Romero's what it is. I deserve half. Don't ruin it for me now."

"Aw, Davis, what's the big deal? You're making money."

"Not enough," Davis snapped.

"More than you were making driving a truck."

"I want to be a full partner. I've got the right . . ."

"Can't do that," Reet replied. "I like things as they are. Put your check away and stop worrying about paying your share, 'cause it ain't gonna happen." Reet laughed under his breath, seeming to enjoy Davis's distress.

"You know," Davis said grimly, "I can go find myself a business partner elsewhere—one that needs my cash."

"Go ahead. If that's what you want to do . . . but why? Things here are swell."

"Maybe for you," Davis threw out, furious that Reet was shutting him out of ever owning half of Romero's. "This is not what I wanted, Reet. I want to be wealthy, in charge of my own business, like you are, and not hanging onto somebody else's back to make it. This is not fair."

"Fair? Who cares about fair? Nothin' personal, Davis, but I've decided I don't want a partner. Complicates things. Been thinking about franchising this venture, anyway, and Sammy Lee thinks it's best to keep the paperwork simple. You know?"

At the mention of their banker's name, Davis froze. "You've been over to Republic, talking to Sam Lee about franchising? And you never said anything to me?"

Reet smirked, silent.

"I'm supposed to sit around and wait for you to decide when I can make some real money?"

"That's your choice."

Davis clenched his jaw, disgusted with Reet's mockery. There was no way he was going to stick around, do all of the work, suck up to Reet any longer and watch the business grow right out of his hands.

"Then I'm out," he decided, anxious to cut ties with the man he had thought would jump at the chance to keep him around. "And you know what?" Davis went on. "I am not really surprised or even pissed off about the way this is going down. I've known you close to thirty years and I've seen how you operate, but I assumed you would treat me better."

"Never assume that you know all the angles, Davis. You wanna be rich and powerful and in control of your affairs? If so, you've gotta get out there and hustle your balls off. You gotta study the situation, use your head, fight dirty if you have to, and go after what you want. Maybe you got what it takes, I don't know. Go take your chances some place else and I hope you make a go of it 'cause nothin's gonna change here at Romero's unless I say so."

"What about the stake I put up?" Davis asked.

"You want it back?"

"Not really."

"Then, I'll make sure that a share of the profits . . . based on what you did kick in—gets deposited into your account at Republic Bank every month—just like always."

"See that you do," Davis said, forcing his voice not to quiver. With a jerk, he grabbed his jacket, pulled it on, and went to the door.

"What are you gonna do?" Reet wanted to know. He rubbed the top of his bald head as he waited for Davis's reply.

With one hand on the doorknob, Davis turned around and shot Reet a cold, hard stare. "I really don't know," he said flatly, a crack in his voice. "But if I did, I wouldn't tell you."

He left Reet's office, went to the end the hallway and ducked into the men's room, where he splashed cold water on his face, and then wiped it dry with a paper towel. Staring into the mirror, he replayed the conversation he had had with Reet, allowing his anger to ease. At least, he now knew where he stood and he had been smart enough to get out.

Reet can find another flunky to pump up his joint. I'm moving on, Davis vowed. *Balls? I'll show him who's got balls, all right, and the guts to make things happen.*

Leaving the men's room, Davis took the elevator to the ground floor and exited the building through the back door, his shoes slapping dully on the hot asphalt as he crossed the parking lot and headed to his car. Calmly, Davis slid behind the steering wheel of his black Lexus, and then placed his gold-rimmed sunglasses over his eyes. He studied the check that Reet had refused, thinking of the risks he had taken, the sacrifices he had made, and the grueling trips to Vegas he had endured to build up this nest egg. He tore the check into tiny pieces and shoved them into the ashtray. He knew what he was going to do, and hoped he had not waited too long.

Even though it was Saturday night, as soon as Davis got back to his apartment, he put his plan into action. He had never forgotten the story on television about Vendora, the flooded supper club in Houston, or Reet's comment that one man's disaster can be another man's opportunity. He had done some checking and learned that the owner had not yet reopened the establishment, and from what he had been able to find out, was in desperate need of an infusion of cash. Hadn't Davis stood outside that place and dreamed of owning that huge old house one day? If he could turn that place around and make it profitable, he would show Reet who had balls. It was exactly the opportunity he had been waiting for and he'd be able to put some distance between himself and Reet—the best thing to do right now. If he could put together the right deal, he would be able to create the lifestyle he wanted and deserved.

After getting the phone number for Vendora from directory assistance, he called the supper club and was greeted by a recording that informed callers that the establishment was temporarily closed and to call another number to contact the owner, Max Granville. Quickly, Davis jotted down the number at the top of a clean piece of paper, and then he drew a line down the center of the page. On the left side, he listed what he wanted, and on the other side, how much he was willing to pay. It was time to leave Los Angeles and try his luck in a new town, where he could be his own boss. Owning a place like Vendora in a big city like Houston, might be exactly the opportunity he needed. The only person he would miss in L.A. was Lara, and he had no intention of breaking off with her. She would not be happy about his move, but if things worked out as he hoped, he would be in a position to fly back to Los Angeles as often as he wanted—often enough to satisfy her. Besides, she was beginning to take him too much for granted, and nothing irritated Davis more than an emotionally needy woman.

On Monday morning, Davis got up early, drank two cups of coffee, and then telephoned Sam Lee at Republic Bank, the financial officer who handled Romero's account. They chatted briefly about Romero's and how well it was doing, as well as Reet's plans to franchise in the future, with Davis leading Sammy to believe that he and Reet were still on good terms. He told Sammy that franchising Romero's was the only way to go and he anticipated the challenge. In the end, Davis wound up establishing a $250,000 line of credit backed by his interest in Romero's.

Next, Davis placed a call to Max Granville in Houston, and after introducing himself, launched directly into the purpose of his call. He waited nervously when the line went silent for a few seconds while Max digested his proposal, then grinned when Max told him, "I've been hoping for a call like this."

"I spent many summers in Houston as a boy," Davis went on. "On Rose Avenue, where my father lived. He used to bartend parties for your father, I guess."

"Yes, my dad loved to have a good time," Max injected.

"Well, I have not been back to Houston for many years, but I know enough about the property to know that I am very interested in it. So, tell me about its current condition and what you're looking for," Davis finished.

"I need a partner, not simply an investor," Max answered, going on to fill Davis in on the history of his place, the clientele Vendora attracted, and the damage done by the flood. "I have a tight timetable to restore and reopen Vendora, so, you can understand why I need someone right away, with experience running a club who understands the kind of work it takes to satisfy a loyal clientele who enjoys a historical, intimate feel."

"I may be your man," Davis calmly replied, though his heart was pounding with excitement. Becoming a partner would be a start, and in time, he knew he would find a way to own Vendora outright. He thought about his father, who had worked himself into an early grave without ever owning much more than a few changes of clothes and a battered red van. Davis had dreamed so long of making something of his life and now he had a chance.

"When can you fly to Houston so we can discuss the details of a possible deal?" Max asked.

"Tomorrow," Davis answered. "I can get an early flight and be in Houston by noon."

"I'll meet you at the airport," Max said, going on to ask for the details related to Davis's arrival.

CHAPTER 11

8:50 A.M., EST
Tuesday, September 11, 2001

When Professor Jeremy Sands dropped his French book and shouted, "Oh, no!" in a loud, distressed tone, Jaiden's head snapped up from the exam that she had been struggling to get through. Frowning, Professor Sands stared at the note that his assistant had just handed to him, and then hurried to turn on the television in the corner of the classroom.

Puzzled by her usually calm professor's behavior, Jaiden watched him carefully, unable to make sense of his frantic jabbering. A plane crash? In New York? What was he talking about?

She focused on the TV screen, which Professor Sands hurriedly rolled to the front of the room, centering it so that everyone could see what was on. Images of a flaming, smoking, horribly damaged building captured everyone's attention, and newscaster Peter Jennings's careful description told them what was happening in New York. The World Trade Center. A plane had crashed into it. The sight was incredible and impossible to comprehend. A hollow sensation claimed Jaiden, making her body go cold, and then she was suddenly filled with a kind of fright that she had never felt before.

The students began murmuring, speculating about what this meant, forcing Professor Sands to increase the volume. Jaiden got up from her desk and moved closer to the TV, where she stared at the indescribable horror on the screen. Then, the students grew eerily quiet, silenced by the shock of what they were watching, and for the next fifteen minutes, they followed every detail of the spe-

cial news report as the disaster unfolded. Suddenly a second plane
swung into view and plunged deliberately into the South Tower at
the World Trade Center.

Gasps erupted from the group and their excited chatter drowned
out the news reporter's assessment of this second awful crash.

Clearly, this is no accident, Jaiden thought. *It is an attack, and the
terror has just begun.* Jaiden ran back to her desk, grabbed her cell
phone out of her backpack and speed dialed the number to her
mother's office. Suddenly, she needed to talk to her mom.

10:13 A.M. CST

Tears dripped from the corners of Camille's eyes as she gazed in
shock at the small television set in the break room of her travel
agency. Five of the six agents she worked with sat nearby, struggling to muffle their sobs. Not only had the Twin Towers been hit,
but also hundreds, maybe thousands of people, were now trapped
inside or dead.

She had hardly been able to talk to Jaiden, who was in a state of
shock, too. After calming Jaiden down, she had clicked off, promising to call her back. At least her daughter was safe, and hopefully
not in any danger, but who knew what might come next?

The minutes ticked by in grim silence until a newscaster announced that all domestic flights had been grounded by the U.S.
Federal Aviation Administration and all airports were currently in
a lock-down mode. Travel around the world, it seemed, had come
to a virtual halt.

Immediately, the phones at Camille's travel agency began to
ring, shaking her and her co-workers out of their gloomy trance.
Passengers were stranded, many overseas, and it was going to take
a lot of patience and strategizing to get them home. Grateful for a
reason to push the dreadful images of the attack aside, she settled
in for a long day at work.

7:30 A.M. PST

Davis did exactly as the airport security guard ordered: He stood
very still and allowed himself to be thoroughly searched, not about
to even blink. When finally cleared to pass, an agent directed him

into a passenger holding area where frantic cell phone conversations buzzed and people were clustered around two television monitors, hands over their mouths, eyes wide in shock.

Davis elbowed his way up to the TV and listened to the reporter's update on the disaster: Manhattan was almost completely sealed off. The Pentagon had been hit and a large section of it had collapsed. The White House had been evacuated, and a United Airlines flight had crashed in a wooded area of Pennsylvania.

Davis pulled back and hurried over to a nearby flight schedule monitor. The word "CANCELLED" filled the screen. Every flight into and out of LAX was grounded. He was definitely not going to Houston, or anywhere else by plane today. He sat down in the nearest chair, overcome by a mix of emotions that he could hardly sort out. Tears clouded his vision and an awful churning sensation lurched around in his stomach. Terrorists had brought the nation to a standstill and the reality of what was happening was too horrible to digest. In the back of his mind he knew that he was going to be stuck at LAX for a very long time.

PART TWO

VENDORA

CHAPTER 12

Max took a seat opposite Davis at the boardroom table, his attorney, Paul Cotter, to his right. He greeted Davis with a friendly nod, and then accepted the sheaf of legal papers that Paul handed to him, keenly familiar with the details of the agreement. He and Paul had gone over the contract many times, while phoning, faxing, and e-mailing back and forth to Davis in the aftermath of the terrorist attack on the World Trade Center.

During the unsettled days that followed the attack, while the travel industry scrambled to recover, Davis had not been eager to get on a plane, and Max had understood his reluctance. After watching the television reports about the disaster and listening to experts analyze the situation, he had been agreeable to delaying their face-to-face meeting with Davis until now—mid-October.

However, the wait had been difficult. With Vendora still shuttered and the travel agency that Camille worked for doing very little business, his tenuous financial situation had begun to crumble. Bills had piled up and his available cash had dwindled. Unbeknownst to Camille, Max had borrowed against his life insurance policy in order to meet their heavy living expenses, determined to keep his good credit rating intact: It was all he had left, it seemed. Camille would be horrified to learn what he had done, but how could he burden her now? She was under enough stress on her job. After the initial September 11 travel crisis passed, bookings at Blue Horizon Travel had entered a downward spiral, and the agency had been forced to lay off four of its agents, keeping Camille and one other on the payroll. How long before she got the axe, too? he wondered, thankful that Davis Kepler had come through, and would soon ease the money crunch.

Max had warmed to Davis immediately, sensing that he and his new partner would work well together. They were driven by the same kind of entrepreneurial energy that inspired them to take risks that other men might shun. Now, as they entered into the final stage of their partnership agreement, Max was eager to get on with rebuilding his company.

Davis set aside his copy of the agreement, pushed back from the table and threw Max a curve ball that made him sit up straight.

"Now that I've seen the books, inspected the property, and have a better understanding of what you need, I want to purchase a controlling interest in Vendora," Davis stated with calculated assurance.

The declaration caught Max off guard. He had agreed to sell Davis forty-five percent of the business, and the paperwork reflected his offer. "I don't understand . . ." Max prompted, hesitating, giving Davis room to expand on this surprising turn in negotiations.

"Vendora has loyal customers who will return as soon as you reopen the doors," Davis began, speaking in an authoritative tone. "You have been making a fair profit over the years, but not nearly as much as you could have." Davis cleared his throat, and then explained, "You are carrying quite a bit of overhead and there is a lot of waste in your operation. I know how to streamline it, turn things around, and with better, more targeted promotional activities, I can pack the place six nights a week with a younger, bigger-spending crowd. Without drastic changes in your marketing strategy, your bottom line will remain pretty flat."

Davis's comments made Max cringe, and he worried that his potential partner might be playing some kind of a game, trying to weasel out of his verbal commitment.

"Wait a minute," Max tossed back. "Selling you a majority share was never an option. We agreed on your buying forty-five percent and the papers have been drawn up accordingly. Nothing has changed as far as I am concerned." A sense of dread settled over Max. Certainly, he needed an infusion of cash, but not enough to relinquish control of the business he had struggled to build and nurtured to success over the years. As much as he wanted to tell Davis to go back to Los Angeles and forget their deal, he hesitated. Making such a move might prove disastrous.

As if reading Max's thoughts, Paul Cotter jumped in. "How much of a share are you talking about?"

"Sixty percent."

"And you are willing to pay . . . ?" Paul wanted to know.

"The same amount that I offered you for forty-five percent."

"That's impossible," Max interjected coldly.

"I am offering you quite a hunk of cash," Davis tossed back. "Accept it, or we have no deal. Can you afford to continue to go it alone?" he finished, in an offhand manner.

Max pressed his lips together and studied the ceiling for a moment, before shooting a fierce glance at Paul, eyes narrowed in question.

Paul lifted a hand in caution at Max, then turned to Davis and asked, "Why should my client even consider your offer?" His approach was cool and restrained.

"Because without me, he has nothing," Davis said to Paul. "Vendora is in a great location, but it's in need of a total renovation, not simply flood-damage repairs. The place is dated, stodgy, and will not attract the kind of customer that would come out and drop a lot of cash—if they liked what they saw. I love the house. I do have sentimental reasons for wanting to own a part of Vendora, as I told you, but as a supper club it needs to be sleek, yet cozy, nostalgic, yet modern . . . an ambiance that I know how to put together. I did it in L.A. at Romero's, and I pulled in the right crowd."

"But you also walked away," Max reminded him.

"Only because Reet Collins made it clear that I would never be a full partner. He expected me to keep his club full and his bank account flush, and if I go that route again, I want assurances on paper that I'll receive what I'm due. Sixty percent, in my opinion, is fair." He paused, and then added, "And, Max, I don't see any other offers on the table, so unless I can purchase a majority interest, I'm out."

Max thought about Davis's rationalizations for a moment, then turned to Paul, who said, "Davis, would you mind waiting in my office? I need to talk to Max alone."

"No problem," Davis agreed, getting up to go into the next room.

As soon as Davis left the boardroom, Max shifted in his chair to face his attorney.

"Don't overreact," Paul cautioned. "Agreeing to sell sixty percent of Vendora to Davis might be a good move, if we can negotiate on a few points."

"Like what?" Max curtly threw back, irritated by this delay. He had seen this meeting as simply a formality to sign off on a contract that had been thoroughly discussed and fine-tuned over weeks. Now, they were back to square one, it seemed.

"First, you must be given an opportunity to regain your majority ownership. I suggest you request the right to buy back shares if gross profits increase by a certain percentage over a short period of time."

"Such as?"

"Let's say an increase of twenty percent over two years. This gives him ample time to prove his marketing theory, test his strategy, see if it works. If he is successful, you'll both make more money, and you will be able to afford to buy back your controlling interest. You can also request that Davis liquidate the outstanding balances on your bank loans and clear overdue bills. That is very important, Max, because as it stands now, if you don't get some of them paid very soon, you could lose your suppliers and jeopardize your liquor license. Then where will you be? And as Davis pointed out, I don't see any other investors lined up waiting to help you out."

"What you say makes sense," Max reluctantly agreed, though uneasy with the idea of giving up control of Vendora, even for a short two years. He had never thought that such a thing would happen to him, but then, he had never dreamed that his livelihood, his marriage, and his daughter's future, would hang on such a decision either.

"But I don't understand why he's throwing this at me now," Max complained. "He's been in Houston nearly a week, and we've been talking about the deal, the percentages, and the renovation plans the whole time. What prompted this sudden turnaround?"

Paul shrugged. "He's smart. Very smart, Max. He went along with everything you wanted in order to build trust and get you excited about working with him. You have to admit that he knows the business pretty well. He may not have owned one-half of that club in Los Angeles, but he did do a hell of a job making it a success. His revenue projections seem to be attainable, and if he can help you attract a different clientele, as he says, then Vendora might become a much more profitable operation than it has ever been.

Max, if he agrees to the conditions I've suggested, I'd accept his offer."

Max sat quietly and thought about Paul's proposition, knowing his attorney had a point. If he got Davis to accept the deal, it might not only save his business, but also change it into the kind of place that would allow him to think about expanding, even purchasing other properties and opening other clubs.

Paul had checked Davis out thoroughly, even uncovering the fact that Davis had done time in prison while he was a young man. At that news, Max had approached Davis directly.

"Tell me about what happened," Max had asked.

"What's to say?" Davis had replied. "I was twenty years old, and wanted to make money, so I began hustling stuff—some of it not so legal—in the streets and in the clubs. At the time, *what* I sold didn't matter as long as people wanted it and I got paid in cash. But getting busted and doing time were the best things that ever happened to me. The years I spent behind bars gave me a chance to think about my future. I finally grew up and realized that I could put my street-wise merchandising skills to better use. Once my old friend Reet gave me an opportunity to make an honest living. I joined him in establishing his club, Romero's. The place was a success from the day it opened. Now, I want to do the same for a place in which I actually have a pretty sizeable stake, you know?"

As Max had listened to Davis, he realized that a youthful mistake should not create a black mark that lasted forever. What was important was to learn from it. He had done a few things that he regretted, too, and was grateful that Camille had not held them against him. What impressed Max most was the success that Davis had made of himself. He had changed his life by using his enterprising skills to become a legitimate businessman, and been smart enough to amass enough cash to go out on his own. He had the necessary drive and know-how to turn Vendora around.

Max did admire Davis's direct, businesslike approach, and felt as comfortable with Davis as with any of his fraternity brothers. He was lucky to have attracted such a perceptive, compatible business partner.

Last night they had gone out to have a little fun, winding up at the recently opened Alabama-Coushatta Indian Casino where they had tried their luck at the tables. Both had wagered small sums and broken even, and enjoyed the relaxing time very much. On the drive back to town, they had talked about the potential for making money in a city like Houston, chatting easily about their plans for Vendora, reinforcing Max's belief that he and Davis Kepler were meant to be in business together.

Abruptly, Max got up from the table, went to the door of Paul's office, and pulled it open. "Come on in, Davis. Let's talk."

When Paul explained the amended terms of the partnership, Davis pursed his lips in agreement, and then said, "Sounds fair."

"Good," Max replied, handing the stapled stack of papers to Paul, who immediately began making handwritten notations on the contract.

Once Max signed off on the agreement and sold Davis Kepler sixty percent of Vendora, he knew that he would be starting over with a clean financial slate. He could get his family life back. Camille no longer had to worry about whether or not she would have a job tomorrow. At last, he could put this disaster behind him and add a hefty amount of much-needed cash to the business bank account

"It's all set," Paul said, interrupting Max's thoughts. "Anybody got any questions before we sign off on this?"

Davis leaned forward, as if to make sure he had Max's full attention. "None," he said. "I'm very pleased with the terms, as well as my new partner, and I'm anxious to get started on making us a lot of money."

"Then let's do it," Max announced, reaching over to shake Davis's hand.

CHAPTER 13

Lara Stanton surrendered herself to Ricky Rupert's firm and soothing touch as the delicate scent of lavender filled her head and the inside of her spacious master bathroom. She drew in a long, slow breath and pressed her naked body more firmly against her hunky masseur's padded table, wanting nothing more than to lose herself in the magic that Ricky's fingers were working on her tired, overworked body.

"A little higher," she cooed, letting out a satisfied moan when he immediately moved his warm, oily palms deep into the muscles beneath her protruding shoulder blades. "God, that feels good," she murmured, thankful that the day's shoot for *Flashfire*, was finished and she was finally back home. Tomorrow, she would be back on the set at 6 A.M., with four more scenes to do with Guy Fernandes and several close-ups that the director, Roberto Simona, needed. Hopefully, the movie would wrap by the end of the week, and then she'd be desperate for Ricky's services once more.

Flashfire was a sexy action picture that was currently over schedule, over budget, and had not yet been picked up by a distributor. Thornton Woods, the producer, was frantic and had begun showing up on the set, making everyone edgy and unsettled. Roberto was pushing the cast and crew as hard as he dared, requiring twelve- and fifteen-hour workdays, keeping everyone on call. And then there was Guy Fernandes—a total jerk who tried Lara's patience with his off-color jokes, super-size ego, and lack of talent.

During the shooting of *Flashfire*, and as it had been with all nineteen of Lara's B-list, R-rated movies, she showed up prepared to work, gave her all on the set, and then retired to her dressing room between takes. Her private quarters were her sanctuary; off-limits to cast members and crew. The only person Lara allowed inside her dressing room was her romantic interest at the time. And for this movie, it was her golden boy, Davis Kepler.

Hollywood. A man's world, all right, she mused. *Roberto, Guy, Thornton . . . they think they're so damned important. Well, without me, they'd have no movie at all. People will come to the movie theater to see me—my face, my body, my talent.* She closed her eyes, thinking back sixteen years to her first movie, *Topaz Queen,* a low-budget film shot in three weeks. She had worn a tiny grass skirt, a huge white orchid over each breast, and had immediately become the embodiment of perfection for young black men—the sex symbol for whom they had been waiting. That was not to say that men of all races didn't watch her with wide eyes and their mouths hanging open as hard-ons grew in their pants, but to black men, Lara Stanton had become their Marilyn Monroe: Soft, sexy, curvy, and brown. And long over-due, as far as they were concerned.

She loved her status as a black sex symbol, and knew that her commitment, drive, and talent had brought her a long way, but maintaining this illusion of perfection was hard work. At thirty-two, Lara took it seriously.

At fourteen, she had run away from the cement block house in the dusty outskirts of Reno, Nevada, that she shared with her alco-holic mother and verbally abusive stepfather. Finally on her own, she had washed dishes at a diner for a year, until a traveling lin-gerie salesman asked her to model for him at his lunch-hour show in a second-rate hotel. He had paid her fifty dollars and kept his promise to keep his hands to himself, so Lara had stuck with him for the next two years, until Reet Collins invited her to Hollywood to test for *Topaz Queen,* the movie he was financing. From that day on, without family or close friends to lean on, Lara had managed to carve out a niche in the cutthroat movie industry by holding her own in a world where self-absorption and self-preservation ruled. She didn't *need* a man to get what she wanted out of life, or to make her feel complete, but she surely did want Davis Kepler in her fu-ture, and somehow she was going to make it happen.

Now, Ricky gave her buttocks a final, firm squeeze and Lara turned over, demurely holding a small white towel over her pri-vate parts while her full breasts jutted out at her masseur. "Thanks, Ricky," she told him, blowing him a kiss. "Tomorrow night? Same time?"

"You got it," Ricky replied, tearing his eyes away from Lara's bosom to begin packing up his supplies.

After Ricky left, Lara lay back down on the massage table, thinking that a long soak in her hot tub, ideally with Davis, would be the perfect way to finish off her pampering session. But he was out of town, in Houston, closing some big deal that he had refused to discuss with her. What could it be and why in Houston, of all places? she wondered.

A phone call to Reet Collins yesterday had provided little information about Davis's mysterious venture; though Reet had informed her that Davis was no longer working with him at Romero's—having opted to go his own way. However, Reet still considered Davis to be his friend and they had not parted on particularly bad terms. The news had initiated a shiver of insecurity in Lara: Was Davis planning on leaving L.A.? Leaving her? For the rest of the afternoon she had been desperate for a cigarette, something she had not experienced since taking the cure with a hypnotist eighteen months ago. She was well aware that smoking would ruin her skin, foul her clothes, and turn men off, but she still missed her cork-tipped Winstons something awful, especially when she became nervous.

In Lara's opinion, Davis was without a doubt the best lover she had ever had, and she wanted him in her life—permanently. He might not be ready to make that kind of a commitment to her, but she was a patient woman. When Lara wanted something badly enough, she always found a way to get it, and Davis Kepler—handsome, energetic, romantic, and driven—had all the prerequisites she sought in a man.

At thirty-three, and for the first time in her life, she was eager to commit to one man; one whom she could pamper, trust, and be faithful to for the rest of her life. She wanted Davis as her life partner, as the father of the children she hoped she was not too old to bear, and as the head of a normal household. Lara knew the loneliness of growing up without brothers or sisters, and longed for the sense of connection that came with being part of a solid, stable family unit.

Reet Collins had discovered her at seventeen—one month after her mother died in a freak accident on her job at a plastics factory. Lara had concentrated on launching her movie career, filling the unexpected void she had felt after her mother's death with auditions, screen tests, and acting lessons, leaving Lara little time to dwell on the fact that she was virtually alone in the world. As her status as an actress and a black sex symbol had grown, most of the men she dated had only been interested in a physical relationship with her or to be seen with her because of who she was. Now, at thirty-three, she had to think more seriously about the years that stretched ahead—years in which her beauty and her ability to snag youthful movie roles would begin to fade. She wanted to be a wife, a mother, and a part of a family.

Davis Kepler was her answer. In him, she saw her future, but getting him to settle down was not going to be easy. He was a busy businessman, yet a hustler who was constantly on the move. His life was consumed with making deals and making money, and there was nothing wrong with that as long as he made time for her. The only time she felt that she had his full attention was when they were in bed. While making love to Davis, Lara experienced a deep, binding connection that went far beyond the feeling of his skin against hers and the thrill of their mutual climax. During those times, when Davis was tender, patient, and totally focused on pleasing her, which he did to an extent that no other man had done, Lara was in heaven.

I could get him to put a ring on my finger if I had him to myself for a full month, she calculated. *It's all about timing, and it would take careful maneuvering, but isn't that what a good actress is supposed to do?*

The aqua phone on the wall of her aqua-tiled bathroom rang, breaking into her thoughts. She sat up and lazily reached for it, thinking it was probably Roberto with some last minute directive about tomorrow's shoot. However, she was excited to be greeted by Davis's sexy inquiry. "What are you doing?" he murmured in a deep, mysterious tone.

"Lying here naked, thinking of you!" Lara squealed, sitting fully up.

"I'll bet," Davis replied, in a jaunty taunt.

"Really, that's the truth. Ricky just left, after giving me the most wonderful massage, and I was thinking about getting into the hot tub . . . but it's no fun without you."

"Well, hold onto the thought for a while longer, Baby. I'll be back soon."

"You'd better," Lara pouted, pulling her knees to her chest, then hugging her arms around her towel-draped body. "I miss you so much."

"Great to hear your voice, too," Davis replied.

Lara grimaced, nostrils flared. Why couldn't he have told her that he missed her? After all, he'd been gone for nearly two weeks. "How's your mystery deal coming?" she asked, pushing her resentment aside.

"All done. I am now the owner of a fantastic supper club called Vendora. What a deal! It's going to make me a bundle."

"A supper club? In Houston?" she repeated, struggling to maintain a light tone in her voice, less than excited about the news. "Why so far away! Are you going to move there?"

"No, of course not. Don't worry. I can fly back to L.A. so often you won't have time to miss me. Lara, this is *the* opportunity I've been waiting for. I knew it would turn out exactly as I planned. You should see the place . . . well . . . not as it is right now because it's under renovation. But it's going to be a sophisticated Southern showplace once the construction is complete. You think Romero's is high class? Vendora is going to outshine it by a hundred times."

"But when are you coming back to L.A.?" was all Lara wanted to know, hardly interested in his new acquisition. Over the years she had invested quite a bit of her hard-earned money into ventures like the one Davis was describing, including Romero's. Supper clubs, nightclubs, restaurants, and game rooms—they came and went like faddish fashion trends, and her returns went up and down, too. Her last serious investment had been in her house: a five-bedroom, four-bath, gray brick contemporary in Brentwood. It had gold-veined marble throughout the kitchen, a vaulted great room with a fireplace at each end, hardwood floors, and a pool with a hot tub off to one side. She loved her home and had not thought twice about using the entire advance she had received for her next picture, *Daddy's Baby Doll*, to secure the property. Set to start shooting next summer, the picture would bring her salary close to seven figures. If she and Davis married, he would never have to worry about hustling another deal again, but she knew that he had bought this new place, Vendora, for more than an opportunity to make money. He wanted the power and prestige that ownership brought.

"I've got a ton of work to do here, and I need to find a place to stay. I'll be back in L.A. on Wednesday, before Thanksgiving," Davis promised, rushing on to fill her in on his plans. "Time will fly, Doll, believe me. And for Thanksgiving, we'll have dinner at *Le Riche*. The two of us. And we can spend as much time in your hot tub as you want. I'll be yours for a whole week . . . then I have to get back here and . . ."

"A week?" Lara interrupted, already beginning to feel slightly abandoned. "That's all?"

"Baby, I've got a lot on me now. I'm a busy man with a supper club to launch. Grand opening is scheduled for New Year's Eve. This is not like Romero's where Reet carried the debt load and all I had to do was bring in the customers. Vendora is *mine* and it's up to me to make it fly. I promise, when I get there, I'll spend *every* day with you."

"Every day?" she confirmed.

"Of course," Davis quickly agreed. "And every night, too. I'll be totally yours the entire time. We can drive up to Santa Barbara; spend a few nights at Seaside Bungalows. Make a run to Vegas and see a few shows. Do anything you want. How's that sound?"

"Perfect. Exactly what I've been waiting to hear," Lara answered, sinking back on her massage table, smiling.

CHAPTER 14

Mona wandered in from buying a newspaper while Jaiden was finishing her makeup. She stood behind her roommate, a paper cup of coffee in one hand, as she caught Jaiden's eye in the mirror.

"All packed, I see." Mona said, motioning toward the two suitcases that Jaiden had placed by the door.

"Yeah. Just about. Wanted to get the big stuff out of the way. My flight is at eight in the morning and Rod and I are going out, so I don't want to deal with heavy packing when I get back."

Mona shrugged in understanding. "That's a damn early flight."

"Right, but my mom insisted that I get the best-priced ticket I could find, and that was it."

"Did you put in for a taxi? Saturday morning. Thanksgiving break. Might be hard to get one if you wait until morning."

"Already done," Jaiden told her, giving Mona a playful wag of her finger. "No way can I miss that flight. My ticket is nonrefundable and I *will* be on that plane."

"Where are you and Rod going?" Mona inquired, scrutinizing Jaiden over the rim of her paper cup.

"Don't know. Rod said he wanted to ride up the coast. God, he loves his bike!"

"Tell me about it," Mona agreed. "I remember when he got his first motorcycle. He was sixteen. Rode it without stopping for hours and hours. He has never owned a car."

"Really?" Jaiden paused, her mascara brush in midair. "I like his bike, and all, but I gotta have real wheels. You know? My dad promised me a BMW if I make a 3.5 or better."

"Not for Rod. He rarely drives a car, even when he's at home. Only if his mom makes him take her somewhere. And I doubt that he will ever change. At least, it's a gorgeous day to ride, though," Mona said, draining the last of her coffee.

"Yeah, I think it'll be fun."

"I can't believe how fast you and Rod hooked up," Mona observed. "Not that I'm complaining. When I introduced you to my cousin, I never dreamed you two would get wrapped so tight . . . so fast. He really got to you, huh?"

Mona's remark stopped Jaiden in the middle of a brushstroke, and she set her mascara wand aside and focused on her roommate. "Yeah. We clicked right away. I *really* like him, and now, all I think about is being with him. He's fun. Likes to go places, do exciting things. And he's . . . a good guy," Jaiden finished, picking up her blusher to apply a wisp of cinnamon powder over her cheeks.

For the past three months she had been out with Rod nearly every Friday and Saturday night. They went out drinking, for rides on his bike, and to Sid's pool parlor to hang out. She had not slept with him yet, but had been thinking of making that move soon, and was glad that he didn't seem to be in a rush. He knew she was a virgin, and had told her he was fine with waiting until she was ready. Jaiden respected Rod for not pressuring her to have sex, though she had to admit that their heavy petting was coming awfully close.

Mona flopped across the foot of her bed and groaned in mock disgust. "*Good guy,* you said? Well, I'd never use that term to describe him. I'm not saying he's wild or anything. But . . . independent. His own man."

"Yeah, how's that?" Jaiden prompted, hoping that Mona might finally open up about Rod Henry's personal life. She had grown up with him, knew who his former girlfriends were, and was privy to the kinds of details that Jaiden longed to know. Who could be better qualified than his first cousin to fill Jaiden in on Rod?

The day after the party, where Jaiden first met Rod, she had pressed Mona for details about her cousin, but Mona had remained tight-lipped, admitting that she had promised Rod that she would not discuss his personal life, especially his past, with Jaiden. And Mona had kept her word so far, but now, after nearly three months, Jaiden felt it was time for Mona to unzip her lips and dish.

"He's very smart, but he doesn't want people to know it. I think he's afraid of being taken too seriously, so he's always throwing a party or roaring around on his motorcycle to make it look like he's only interested in having a good time. As far as I know, he's never worked too hard at anything, not even at school, and you know he dropped out. The only reason he can stay here in Providence and go to East Tech is because his dad pays the bills. Uncle Donald told him he had to stay in school somewhere or come home and get a job. My uncle promised to pay him a salary as long as he stayed in class. Not even full time. Not a bad setup, if you ask me. So, he takes one course at a time, will probably stay in school forever—as long as the checks keep coming. Why should he worry about getting a degree? He's happy with the way things are."

Some of this was not news to Jaiden, though she did think Rod was more ambitious than Mona described. "And his girlfriends?" she asked nonchalantly, locking eyes in the mirror with Mona. Might as well get all she could while Mona was unloading.

"Girlfriends? Ha! You better ask him about that." A thoughtful expression came over Mona's face as she hesitated, and then went on. "I promised him that subject would remain off limits and I'm gonna keep my word. If he wants to tell you about his past love life, it's up to him . . . I'm not about to go there . . . not with you. He'd kill me if I told you all I know," Mona scooted off the bed, went to their small refrigerator and took out an apple, which she bit into, then flopped back down on her bed.

"Come on, Mona," Jaiden pleaded. "Give me *something* to work with. Rod is the first guy I've ever really liked. I want to know more about him. He never wants to talk about himself and he acts real funky if I joke around and ask him about other girls he dated and things like that."

"Not surprised," Mona said. "He's not one to talk much. Keeps to himself, but he still has a lot of friends. People like him, girls and guys, but they don't *know* him, and that is fine with him . . . if you get my drift. Listen, as far as I know you're the only girl he's dating now, and that's all I can say. Not the way he usually operates, but a good thing for you." Mona walked over to Jaiden and looked down at her. "If I were you, Jaiden, I wouldn't press Rod to talk about himself. Have a good time, enjoy the ride, and see where it goes. And don't let him distract you from the reason you're here. Haven't seen you cracking the books too much lately. You see, going to class and making good grades are not priorities for Rod, but with you, I know it's different."

"No problem," Jaiden agreed, giving her roommate a knowing

glance, waving her away. "I plan to do a lot of catchup reading while I'm home over Thanksgiving."

Jaiden's cell phone rang, interrupting the conversation. Screwing up her mouth in annoyance, she answered.

Jaiden: *Hello.*

Nici: *Jaiden! Girl, we have to talk.*

Jaiden: *Nici, no can do. On my way out. I'll call you later, okay?*

Nici: *No! This is serious. I gotta tell you what happened. Remember, I told you about Della Lee . . .*

Jaiden: *Right. Your cousin who is too fat to fit into her brides-maid's dress. I know. I know. But I really gotta go. We'll talk about it later. I promise. Bye.*

Jaiden clicked off, sighed and stuck her cell phone into her purse, thinking Nici was getting entirely too worked up over Della Lee's expanding waistline. If the girl wanted to look like a blimp walking down the aisle, so what? Nici needed to chill.

I'll be so damn happy when this wedding is over, Jaiden thought, pulling on a pair of stone-faded jeans, a tight black long-sleeved tee shirt and low-cut red leather boots. Deciding not to bother with a purse, she stuffed a ten-dollar bill and her driver's license into her jeans pocket, grabbed her tan suede jacket and told Mona, "See you later."

"Not too late," Mona reminded her, easing off the bed.

Jaiden raced down two flights of stairs and out the front door of Keeney Hall. She waved excitedly at Rod, who was roaring up the street on his gleaming Suzuki. He threw up a cloud of dust when he stopped at the curb, and remained on his idling bike while revving the engine. He was dressed in his standard all-black garb and had a dark green helmet on his head.

"Right on time," Jaiden chirped, accepting the blue and silver helmet he handed to her. She glanced up at her dorm room window and saw Mona standing there, a sly grin on her face. Jaiden gave her roommate an energetic thumbs up, then strapped on her helmet and jumped onto the seat behind Rod. She snuggled closely behind him, braced for the ride, and when he sped away from the curb, she increased her grip, crushing his black tee shirt in her fists. Who knew that college was going to be this much fun?

They zipped along the streets to 195 East, crossed the Seekonk

River and headed out the East Shore Expressway. The rocky coast-line was banked with tall green pines and colorful trees with leaves of vibrant yellow, orange, and red. The late November breeze was cool and dry, and not at all like the humid heavy days that blanketed Houston at this time of year. She loved Rhode Island, with its quaint, old buildings, picturesque streets, and rocky, mysterious coastline. Compared to the flat coastal plains of Texas where she had grown up, this place seemed as exotic and intriguing as a foreign country, and if Jaiden had her way, she'd never go back to Houston to live. However, the Thanksgiving holiday break started tomorrow, and she would be on a plane in the morning, headed home. A whole week without Rod. How was she going to stand it?

The breathtaking ride along the coast ended when Rod turned into a gravel drive and stopped in front of a rustic wood-shingled house. The lawn was blanketed with crisp fallen leaves and a dozen or so motorcycles were parked near the porch, which was wide, shady, and crowded with many of the girls and guys that Jaiden had seen at Rod's party. They were sitting at card tables drinking beer and playing cards while music blared from a boom box, creating a partylike atmosphere.

Rod killed the motorcycle's engine and hopped off, then helped Jaiden down.

"Thirsty?" he asked, removing his helmet, shaking out his braids.

"Very," Jaiden replied, holding her helmet by the strap.

"Good. Go grab us a table and ask Slim for a beer for me. Get whatever you want. I'll be right there. Gotta see somebody first." Then he turned and walked across the leaf-strewn yard in that jerky, cocky strut that took Jaiden back to the first night she met him.

Grinning, she pulled her eyes away from his tight jean-clad rear end and studied the burly, bearded guy who was waiting to talk to Rod. The man was huge, with an ebony complexion and a red hand-kerchief tied across his forehead. His torn blue jeans and weathered leather jacket gave him a rugged, sinister look.

Jaiden watched as Rod greeted the guy with a friendly slap on his shoulder and a complicated handshake. The two laughed, then began to talk in earnest, eventually disappearing behind the house. Shrugging, Jaiden turned toward the porch, stepped into the crowded area and worked her way to a free table next to a girl who was talking loudly on her cell phone.

Right away, a young woman with large white teeth, wearing

blue denim overalls and heavy boots came over and asked, "You with Rod?" She was balancing a small tray with two beers on it in one hand, and seemed perfectly at ease.

Startled, Jaiden blinked, then answered, "Ah, yes. Are you Slim?"

"Yeah. What can I get ya?"

"Rod wants . . ."

"Yeah, his usual. A Coors light with a Jack Daniels chaser. What'll you have?" Slim asked, now sounding a bit impatient.

"Well, I don't know . . ." Jaiden muttered, wishing Rod had not deserted her. She glanced to where he had disappeared and saw no sign of him. Everyone, it seemed, had a beer and a glass of whiskey.

Slim shook her head and chuckled, then leaned down, putting her mouth close to Jaiden's ear. "This is a private home . . . mine, to be exact. It's not a club, though some of my friends seem to think so. You can have anything you want."

"Oh," Jaiden replied. "Like, anything?"

"Sure. I'm not gonna card you."

"Well, I'll have a margarita."

"You got it," Slim replied, turning away as Rod stepped onto the porch and came to sit beside Jaiden.

He took her hand and squeezed it. "See you met Slim. Like the place?" he asked, rubbing his thumb over the back of her hand. Before she could reply, he casually lit up a joint and passed it to her.

Shrugging, Jaiden accepted the offer, took a long drag and then passed it back. "It's interesting," she managed to answer while exhaling and accepting the drink that Slim handed to her.

Rod took a gulp of his beer, then clinked his shot glass of Jack Daniels against Jaiden's margarita. "To a fun-filled afternoon," he toasted.

"Right. A fun afternoon," she agreed, feeling grown up and very sophisticated. Here she was on a Sunday afternoon, far from her parents, having drinks and sharing a joint with a gorgeous guy who liked her and treated her like an adult. Nici would never believe this.

"What time is your flight tomorrow morning?" Rod casually asked, stretching his legs out under the table.

"Eight," Jaiden said, dreading the separation.

"God, that's early. Want me to take you to the airport?"

Jaiden laughed and punched his arm. "Sure. And what about my luggage? I doubt it would fit on the back of your bike."

Rod's eyes crinkled in mischievous glint as he sipped his drink. "Just offering, that's all."

"I wish you were coming home with me," Jaiden said.

Rod moaned, shaking his head. "My old man would never forgive me if I didn't put in an appearance at the big family dinner. Thanksgiving is the one time I absolutely have to go home if I want to stay on my dad's good side. Otherwise, the checks would stop. I go home for Thanksgiving, but on other holidays, I usually stay around here or visit friends."

"What about New Year's Eve?" Jaiden asked, grabbing this rare opportunity to get Rod to talk about his family.

"Some years I go home, some years I don't. Last year I spent it in Florida. Much better weather, you know?"

"You have family in Florida?" Jaiden prompted.

"No. A friend," Rod replied, rather vaguely.

Knowing better than to press him for more details about his friend, Jaiden said, "Maybe you could come to Houston this year. My father's grand reopening of his supper club is going to be on New Year's Eve. You remember. I told you about the flood and everything. It might be fun."

Rod hunched his shoulders in a noncommittal manner and blew a stream of smoke across the table. "We'll see. That's a long way off."

Nodding, Jaiden let the subject drop.

They stayed on the porch for the remainder of the afternoon, drinking, playing cards and listening to music. As the sun moved steadily across the sky Jaiden began to think about her early departure, the packing she still had to do, and the long flight home. She really needed to get back to her dorm.

When the sun had moved low on the horizon and the crisp fall air took on a definite chill, she suggested they leave, but Rod said, "In a few minutes," and then ordered another round of drinks. Slim turned on the outdoor lights that lit up the porch, and everyone stayed where they were. Jaiden let the matter drop. Whatever Rod wanted to do was fine with her.

At nine-thirty, the crowd finally began to thin, and Rod decided it was time to head home. The trip back into town was a blurry windy ride during which Jaiden pressed her face tightly against Rod's back, her head buzzing from too many margaritas and too much marijuana. She did not open her eyes until Rod pulled into the parking space at his apartment complex.

"We're here." he said, shutting down the bike's engine. He stood, removed his helmet and then helped Jaiden off the back seat of his bike. "Wanna come up? I can make a mean margarita, myself," he offered, grinning widely at Jaiden, who gripped his arm and leaned heavily against his shoulder as she struggled to get her bearings.

"You okay?" Rod asked, taking her by the arm.

"Yeah," Jaiden muttered, though she was feeling very shaky. Her head was spinning and everything appeared fuzzy and out of focus. The thought of another drop of tequila passing her lips made her stomach do a quick flip, and she knew she had to get inside fast. "Yeah," she muttered again. "Let's go inside. I can't handle anything else to drink, but I do need to come in . . . but only for a minute. I've got to get back and finish packing."

"No problem," Rod told her, leading her toward the stairs.

Pulling in a deep breath, Jaiden let the cool autumn air fill her lungs and prayed she would not get sick right there on the sidewalk. How embarrassing would that be?

With Rod's assistance, she made it inside, then hurried into his bathroom and threw up. Three times. Once the spate of nausea passed, she weakly swished a gulp of Rod's Listerine around in her mouth, groped her way into his bedroom, slipped out of her jeans and fell across the bed. Quickly, everything went black.

When Jaiden awoke, the sun was shining through the narrow slats in the aluminum mini-blinds that covered Rod's bedroom windows. The apartment was very quiet and she immediately sensed that she was alone. Sitting up, she glanced around and saw a yellow sticky note posted in the center of Rod's dresser mirror: "Gone to get some coffee. Be back in a few. Better reschedule your flight."

She stared at the clock on the dresser in disbelief. Nine-fifteen? It couldn't be! She moved quickly, grabbing her jeans off the floor, desperate to get dressed and gone. She had already missed her flight! Jeans on, she grabbed her boots and fumbled with the laces, her mind spinning. She had to get back to her room, change into clean clothes, and get her bags. Call the airline, arrange another flight, which was probably going to be very expensive. Oh, God. Her mom was probably on her way to the airport now.

"Damn!" she cursed aloud, frustrated and angry at herself. What in the world had she been thinking? Getting drunk. Passing out. How had she gotten into such a mess? Shoes on, she hurried to the front door and yanked it open. A burst of sunlight hit her in the face and forced her to step back. She had no car. Keeney Hall was on the other side of town. How was she going to get there? With a sigh, she went back inside, slammed the door, and then sat down on Rod's sofa to wait for him to arrive and take her back to campus. She reached for his phone. Better call her mom and explain . . . but how? she wondered, chewing on her bottom lip.

CHAPTER 15

"Where *is* Jaiden?" Camille muttered impatiently, inching her car toward the passenger pickup exit for the fourth time. She'd been circling the airport for close to fifteen minutes and traffic was horrendous due to holiday travel and the extensive security measures now in place at Bush International in the wake of the terrorist attacks. She and Jaiden had agreed that they would meet at passenger pickup twenty minutes after her plane had landed. Frustrated, Camille pressed redial and put another call into Jaiden's cell phone, but was greeted by her voice mail—again. Irritated, she slammed the phone back into her purse and smiled grimly at the impatient policeman who was waving her on her way. The moment she started to ease back into the flow of traffic, preparing to make the tedious circle again, her cell phone rang.

"Hi, Mom. It's me," Jaiden said.

"Finally. What is taking you so long?" Camille asked, slowing down, determined to stall the policeman who was approaching her, a frown on his ruddy face. She rolled down her window and called out to him, "My passenger is on her way out. I'll be gone in a minute."

The officer squinted his displeasure, but backed off, shaking a finger in the air to emphasize his desire that Camille get on her way.

"Mom," Jaiden started. "I'm not at the airport."

"What? Where are you?"

"Still in Providence."

Camille swallowed hard, nostrils flaring as she took a deep

breath and steeled herself for an explanation that she knew she did not want to hear. "What is going on? Why aren't you in Houston?"

"I overslept. Missed the flight. Sorry."

Now, the policeman was really angry. He stepped in front of Camille's car and slapped the hood, hard, then glared at her through the windshield. "Move it!" he shouted, gesturing emphatically with both arms. "Gotta go, lady!"

"Shit." Camille muttered, more at Jaiden than at the policeman whom she barely missed as she swung angrily back into traffic. "Hold on. I've got to get out of here." She placed the phone in her lap in order to concentrate on merging into the flow of heavy traffic that was exiting the airport. Once she was back on the freeway, she grabbed the phone and resumed her conversation, though she hated to drive and talk. "You said you overslept? What in the world were you doing last night?"

"Nothing."

"Nothing? Well, for your information, I called you last night to remind you to bring your suede jacket home so I could have it altered. Mona said you were out. I called again this morning and she said you were still out. Where were you all night, huh?"

"With a friend. And I was not out *all* night."

"How could you be so irresponsible? You knew you had to get up and catch a plane. I don't believe I'm hearing this."

"I don't know what happened. I was tired, Mom. Anyway, I called the airline and there's another flight at four. I went ahead and booked it."

"And how much extra is that going to cost? Your ticket was non-refundable—the cheapest fare we could get . . . and now, I guess I've got to pay full price to get you home?"

"An extra two-fifty," Jaiden told her. "They charged it to your credit card."

Camille gritted her teeth to keep from screaming, then paused for a second and then told Jaiden, "I had hoped being away at college would make you more responsible, but obviously it hasn't. You had better get yourself together, young lady. This kind of behavior is totally unacceptable. Your father and I did not send you to Brown to party and stay out all night. Two-hundred and fifty dollars! I can't believe it."

"I said, I'm sorry! Really. What do you want me to do? Stay here?"

"No. Get your butt to the airport right now and stay there. What time will you get in?"

"Nine-ten tonight. I have an hour layover in Newark."

"Fine, your *father* and I will pick you up. We have a lot to discuss."

Jaiden sat up front with Max while Camille simmered in silence in the backseat, still too upset to trust herself not to blow up and say something she might regret. She had spent the day shopping for groceries and getting a head start on preparations for Thanksgiving dinner, anything to keep her mind off her disappointment with Jaiden. As a professional in the travel business, Camille had never missed a flight in her life, and had drilled Jaiden on how important it was to prepare carefully the night before an early flight: Set more than one alarm clock, pack everything, even your toothbrush, the night before and arrange for transportation, too. Jaiden knew the drill. This never should have happened.

She was too busy having a good time to get herself together, Camille concluded, disappointed that the short holiday with her daughter was starting off under a cloud of tension. She had thought that she and Jaiden would be chattering away about what they were going to do over the holiday, her new life on campus, her course load, her classes, and her new friends. Camille wanted to know what Jaiden's professors were like, how demanding they were, and how life on campus unfolded.

Unable to afford college for herself, Camille had looked forward to vicariously experiencing life at one of the most prestigious universities in the country through her daughter. When Camille had arrived in Houston at the age of seventeen, her first venture from the backwater town on the Florida coast where she had grown up, she had never dreamed that one day her daughter would attend college, let alone Brown University. Jaiden's letter of acceptance to the university had been one of the high points of Camille's life, and all of her expectations for her daughter had come true. So, why didn't the present situation resemble any scenario she had pictured it in her head about the mother-daughter relationship she had dreamt of experiencing one day? Why did she sense that Jaiden was deliberately going out of her way to exclude her from this new life away from home? In a pensive gesture, Camille scooted to the middle of the backseat and studied Jaiden's profile, trying to discern what was fueling the rebellious attitude that now separated them.

Once Max had cleared the airport, Camille caught his eye in the rearview mirror and held his gaze for a moment, hoping he could read her thoughts. She had told him before they left home that she was not going to say a word to Jaiden, and it would be up to him to come down hard on her for pulling a stunt like this. If she wanted her parents to treat her like an adult, then she had better start acting like one. They were not going to bail her out forever.

A few uncomfortable minutes passed before Max spoke, expressing his disappointment over what had happened in a rather lighthearted manner. "And I am not asking where you were all night or who you were with," he went on. "That's your business. All I'm saying is that your actions have consequences, and often those consequences have a great impact on other people. Like your mother and me."

"If you *have* to know . . . I spent the night with a friend. A student," Jaiden admitted to Max in a short, sarcastic tone. "Missing a flight is not the worst thing that I could have done. You know?"

Max blew out a short breath. "All right. Let's drop it. But the two-hundred-fifty dollars will be deducted from your monthly spending money, and you ought to be grateful that you have parents who love you and have high expectations of you. Understand?"

Without looking over at her father, Jaiden said, "I know. I love you both, too, and I promise to do better. I'll *never* stay out all night again. Okay? *Never.*"

Camille rolled her eyes and waited for Jaiden's dramatic declaration to have its usual effect on Max. When he reached over and punched Jaiden playfully on the shoulder, Camille had to clamp her lips together to keep from speaking.

"Now, you don't have to go *that* far," Max told Jaiden. "I want you to go out with your friends . . . have fun. Parties are a part of college life. I know that much. But try to be careful, all right? I've pulled off a few doozies myself. Partying can be fun, but it can become addictive, too. Once you get into the routine of hanging out with a group of friends on a regular basis, it's hard to stop. The pressure is on. You've got to pace yourself. Know when to stop."

"Oh, perfect," Camille remarked, exasperated by Max's comments.

"Sure," Jaiden answered, then leaned her head back and closed her eyes, clearly no longer interested in talking.

Max switched on the radio and tuned it to the news. For the rest of the ride home, no one spoke.

Thanksgiving dinner was a quiet affair, and Camille was glad that she had not invited anyone other than Rochelle to join her and Max and Jaiden for dinner. In past years, Camille and Max had celebrated the holiday at Vendora, enjoying the meal in the company of family, friends, loyal customers, and their guests, usually numbering close to fifty. The festive buffet had always signaled the launch of the hectic holiday season, a time when Vendora's reservation list stayed full, champagne flowed, and everyone, especially Max, concentrated on enjoying the season. The private parties, gay laughter, couples dancing, champagne flowing. It had been a wonderfully crazy time, and getting through the season had meant long hours for Max and his staff, but he had never complained. The money he made during the six-week period between Thanksgiving and New Year's made the brutal work schedule worth it.

Now, with the meal complete, Camille got up from the table and went into the kitchen to get the pie and coffee, while Max shared Vendora's renovation plans with Jaiden and Rochelle. Even though the work was well under way and the grand reopening was scheduled for New Year's Eve, Camille was not as enthusiastic as she thought she ought to be. A subtle sense of emptiness that she could not shake had been with her for weeks, and the heavy malaise was beginning to wear her down.

She wondered if her depression might be connected somehow to the attacks on September 11. Conditions at the travel agency were awful, and the sudden downturn of business kept the tragic event in her thoughts every day. She had read online about the post-traumatic syndrome that was affecting a lot of people. Was she a victim, too? Jaiden's politely distant and less than communicative behavior didn't help her mood either. But whatever was wrong, Camille knew she needed to do something about it soon.

Pushing her somber thoughts aside, she returned to the dining room with dessert. Once the pumpkin pie and chocolate mousse had been served and the coffee poured, Rochelle told Camille, "You and Max go watch the game. Jaiden and I will clean up."

"That I will not protest," Camille told her sister, rising from the table. "Just be careful with . . ."

"Shoo," Rochelle interrupted. "Go on. You act like I've never cleaned your kitchen. I know exactly what to do. And," she paused, tilting her head toward Jaiden, "I'm sure she does, too."

In the kitchen, Rochelle tied a white apron over her ruby velour skirt, pulled on a pair of rubber gloves to protect her matching manicure and picked up a stack of dirty plates.

"How's school?" she asked, making small talk with Jaiden as they rinsed and scraped Camille's Wedgwood plates.

"Okay, I guess," Jaiden replied, leaning down to put a coffee cup into the dishwasher.

"You like your roommate?"

"Sure. She's fine."

"That's good," Rochelle replied, thinking that Jaiden was definitely in a blue mood today. They usually chatted nonstop about one thing or another whenever they were together, but after a half-hearted hug and a weak hello, when Rochelle first arrived for dinner, Jaiden had hardly spoken. "You've been awful quiet today," Rochelle stated, determined to get to the bottom of her niece's moodiness. "Anything wrong?"

Jaiden shrugged and shook her head. "No."

"Well, Camille told me about you missing the flight and all," Rochelle prompted, wondering if that was what her niece was pouting about. "You have to remember, your mother is a travel agent. To her, missing a flight is a sin." Rochelle clucked her tongue, trying to lighten the mood. "It happens. I've missed a few myself. One time, when I was in New York . . ."

"Forget about it," Jaiden said, curtly cutting Rochelle off. "It's over. Not a problem."

After a few strained moments of silence, Rochelle tried again. "How's Nici?"

"Okay, I guess. Haven't seen her. Haven't talked to her much, since I got home."

Rochelle thought that was an odd response. When Jaiden left for college the two girls had been nearly inseparable and now they were hardly speaking?

"I remember, this time last year . . . after the dinner party at Vendora. It had rained so hard all day . . . you and Nici were planning on going to a dance that night, and Camille didn't want you to drive. So you called Kevin and got him to pick you up. And he drove up in his daddy's dented Jeep. I remember how horrified you two were." Rochelle chuckled. "You guys were always up to somethin'."

"That was last year. A lot has changed," Jaiden replied in a dull tone as she put a plastic container of leftover collard greens into the refrigerator.

"Sure has," Rochelle agreed, pressing on. "I guess Nici is pretty busy with her wedding plans, huh? Isn't it set for sometime in December?" Rochelle stuck the good silverware, which she knew Camille wanted hand washed, into a sink of sudsy water, and then added, "Got your dress, yet? I'd love to see it."

Jaiden slammed the refrigerator door, went back to the dining room table and brought back the large turkey platter. She set it down on the granite countertop in front of Rochelle, and then narrowed her eyes at her aunt. "*Yes*, I have my dress. It's pale blue and it cost four hundred-seventy-five dollars. Only problem is, I won't be wearing it." Shaking her head, she began to jab at the turkey with the carving fork.

"What do you mean? You're not going to be in the wedding?" Rochelle asked, surprised. Had Jaiden and her best friend had a falling out? Was this the reason for her glum attitude?

"There isn't going to be a wedding, Aunt Rochelle. Nici broke off with DeJon."

"What? When did this happen and why?" Rochelle stopped what she was doing and focused on Jaiden, mouth slightly agape.

"He was tippin' on her. Creepin'." Jaiden jabbed the turkey again.

"You mean screwing around?" Rochelle clarified.

"Yeah, with Nici's cousin, Della Lee. Who is now pregnant with DeJon's baby. That's why she was gaining so much weight. It's a big mess."

"Sounds like a soap opera," Rochelle remarked, shaking her head in wonder.

"They had a fight. Nici went over to Della Lee's house and slapped her. Now her aunt and her mother aren't speaking. But Nici's keepin' the engagement ring. I didn't know about any of this until I got home. "

"You guys didn't talk about this?" Rochelle asked in amazement. "I thought you two talked every day . . . or at least e-mailed."

"She called me the day before I left school but I didn't have time to talk to her. So, she's mad at me. Not too interested in hangin' out. I guess I can understand why."

"My, my," Rochelle muttered under her breath. "And after all those big wedding plans. Her mother must be very upset."

"She said her mother returned the wedding dress to Bridal Mart. They gave her a full refund. The caterer wouldn't budge on the deposit, though, so they lost all of that five hundred dollars."

"Too bad. And where'd you get your dress, Jaiden?" Rochelle wanted to know.

"High Fashion. But they won't take it back because I had it altered. I already tried."

"Humph. You give it to me. I'll get your money. I know every salesperson in that store on a first name basis. I guarantee I'll get you a refund."

"Good," remarked Camille, who had walked into the kitchen and caught the end of the conversation. "So Nici's wedding is off?" she asked Jaiden.

"Yeah," Jaiden said.

"Well, if Rochelle can get a refund on your dress, Jaiden, that would be great."

"Right," Jaiden said, brightening. "I paid four hundred-seventy-five dollars in cash for that dress . . . money I earned at Pizza Palace last summer, remember?"

"I do," Camille confirmed. "You worked hard for that money and if you get the refund, maybe you'll be able to pay me the two-fifty that you owe me for missing your flight," Camille finished in a calm voice, pouring herself another cup of coffee.

"I owe *you*? Mom, you could let that slide!"

"Nope. Sorry, I can't. Don't be selfish. You ought to pay for your mistake."

"I don't believe this," Jaiden snapped. "I could use that money when I go back to school. It's real expensive up there."

Camille arched a brow, head tilted to the side. "I know. Your dad and I have to foot your bills."

"Whatever!" Jaiden threw back, her voice shrill with frustration. She tossed the carving fork on the counter and folded her arms on her chest, a grumpy frown on her face. "Okay. Aunt Rochelle can *have* the stupid dress and you can *have* your money. I'm outta here." She turned in a huff and walked out of the kitchen, stomping her way up the stairs. "I can't wait to get out of this house and back to Providence!" she shouted to no one in particular before slamming the door to her bedroom.

Camille let out an exasperated sigh.

Rochelle shook her head, wiped her hands on her apron, and then propped them on either side of her wide hips. "Girl, you and your daughter! You two need to calm things down."

Max stuck his head into the kitchen and asked Camille, "What was that all about?"

"What do you think?" she snapped. "Your daughter is mad at me because she can't have her way."

"I'll go up and talk to her. See if I can straighten this out." He started toward the staircase.

"Please don't," Camille stopped him. "Leave her alone, Max. Let her work this out by herself."

In her room, Jaiden threw herself, facedown, on the bed and squeezed her eyes shut, trying not to cry. Her mom could be so damn mean . . . really cold. What was two hundred fifty dollars to her? She spent that much on her hair and nails every month. Jaiden knew if she went to her dad right now and told him she wanted to keep the refund money, he'd make sure she got it. And even Aunt Rochelle would never have asked for that money. She'd have immediately gone shopping for another dress. Why couldn't her mom ease up?

And she has the nerve to call me selfish? Jaiden thought, brushing away a tear that was sliding down the side of her nose. *Does she think I've forgotten that she left me behind when she went to live with Aunt Rochelle when I was nine years old? How selfish was that?*

Jaiden turned over onto her back, wishing she could banish that vague hollow sensation that filled her up when she argued with her mother. It had been like that forever, it seemed, and she didn't know why. No matter how hard she tried, she could never please her mom, but no matter how many mistakes she made, her dad never made her feel as if she had let him down.

I wish Rod would call, she thought, mentally acknowledging that her foul mood was partly due to the fact that she had not spoken to him since arriving home. On the day of her departure, after dropping her off at her dorm, he had kissed her good-bye and promised to call—every day. The least he could have done was phone to wish her a happy Thanksgiving, or something, she fretted, glancing at the clock on her dresser. It was eight o'clock in Houston, nine o'clock in Pennsylvania. She did have Mona's home number, but not Rod's. Did she dare call Mona and fish around for a reason why Rod would do this to her?

Fresh tears welled in Jaiden's eyes. This was the worst Thanksgiving of her life. Her mom was mad at her. Nici was acting like a real bitch. And Rod had let her down. Only her dad, it seemed, understood what was happening.

CHAPTER 16

The water in the hot tub was a warm, bubbling steam of lavender scent that went straight to Davis's gut and immediately made him hard. He reached out, cupped Lara's left breast with one hand, and moved closer, then slid his other hand between her silky thighs as he inched his way slowly upward until she giggled, splashed water in his face and scooted beyond his reach. Groaning, he shook his fist at her in a playful challenge, then went to the side of the tub and picked up his champagne glass. After taking a sip, he dove under the water and emerged between Lara's long legs, which he quickly pinned with his. This time, she did not slip out of his grasp, but wrapped her smooth legs around his waist, and softened under the kiss he planted on her moist, pouty lips. Easily, he slipped inside her. Holding his breath, his need for her erupted, and he gripped her tightly and waited until Lara shuddered in a delightful moan and collapsed in breathless laughter.

"Davis!" She finally managed, gasping. "You can be so bad!"

"What's there to be good about?" he taunted. "And you didn't seem to mind too much." Turning back to his flute of champagne, he drained it, then jumped, naked, from the hot tub and went over to a nearby lounge chair on Lara's secluded patio. He grabbed his swim trunks and pulled them on, and then sat down at the edge of the padded reclining chair and studied Lara, who was catching bubbles with her fingers and pushing them across the surface of the water.

His return to L.A. had come at exactly the right time: Lara had truly missed him. Her desire for him was as strong and insistently palpable as before he left. Now that his deal with Max Granville was complete, Davis felt energized and whole, as if his former insecurities about his future had been healed. It had taken all of his cash, and most of his line of credit at Republic Bank to close the deal, but he was now owner of Vendora—in charge of his future and running a business he could truthfully call his own. He had Lara Stanton, one of the most beautiful black actresses in the business, begging him to make love to her, and not only for one night, but forever.

When he told Lara the details about his acquisition of the supper club, and how he had stood outside that very house when he was a boy and dreamt of owning it, he had seen the pride in her eyes, felt her approval. He had experienced such a strange combination of excitement and calm. Was this the way truly successful men felt when they achieved their goals? he wondered.

"You're coming to Houston for the grand opening on New Year's Eve," he now told Lara, more in the manner of an order than a request. He could not wait for the opportunity to show Lara off, and demonstrate to his partner, as well as his guests, exactly how important a man he was. Surely, Vendora's unveiling would receive a great deal of press coverage in the local papers, at least, and if Lara Stanton were there . . . well, he could see it now. The curious women, the envious men, the zealous reporters. It was going to be a magical evening, the likes of which Houstonians had never seen before.

Lara pressed her back against the side of the hot tub and placed her arms along the edge, letting the swirling water lap gently at her round dark nipples. "I'll try," she said coyly, wiping perspiration from her top lip with the fluffy towel around her neck. "I have six other invitations to parties that night. I haven't decided what I'm going to do."

"Forget those other parties. You *have* to be in Houston with me, Baby." He was not about to let her wiggle out of this; a major part of his grand opening plans included keeping her profile very high, cementing his reputation as a successful, well-connected, up-and-coming businessman from Los Angles who was going to have an impact on the social scene in Houston.

Lara frowned, clearly irritated by Davis's request. "I don't know if I ought to go out of town. Roberto scheduled post-production work on *Flashfire* to start January second. I'd have to be in and out of Houston so fast." Lara stepped haughtily out of the pool and paused, naked and wet, in front of Davis, taking her time pulling on a flimsy black wrap that hit her at mid-thigh. "I don't know about this, Davis." She walked over to a low table near the patio door, bent over to pull the champagne bottle out of its cooler—showing Davis a great deal of her perfectly shaped ass—then stood and refilled her glass.

Davis allowed his eyes to roam over the most beautiful woman he had ever been involved with, knowing he could get her to do whatever he wanted. She wanted marriage, he wanted her at his side to help him get ahead, and he would use their relationship to his advantage in any way he could. Right now, he had to concentrate on his business, and generate some serious cash. She was a significant part of the plan.

"How are you going to make it work . . . for us?" she pouted, heading toward him in a long-legged stride. "You in Houston, me here in L.A. I don't think I'm going to like this very much. How can we have fun? No trips to Vegas . . . and you said I was your good luck piece, remember? Every time we hit the casinos together, you cashed out. Now, you won't have time to do fun stuff like that with me. I'll never see you anymore."

"Don't worry. I got it all planned out. I've already hired a guy named Percy Cleary to manage Vendora. Used to run the Starr Club on the top of the America Building. He's first-rate. Once I get him trained to manage things exactly the way I want them done, I'll be free to come and go as I please. You didn't think I was gonna be in the kitchen watching the cooks, or dishing up food, or tending bar every night, did you? Let Max Granville deal with that hands-on stuff. I'm the owner. I make decisions and keep the staff in line; let them do the work they are hired to do, right? One day, I'll own three, maybe four supper clubs. I'll be a mogul, you know? All comes down to good management."

Lara sat down beside Davis and put her arm around his neck, kissed him on the temple, and then slid her red fingernails along his jaw. "You got big ideas, Davis. I like that. Ambition turns me on." She placed one hand on his thigh, very near his crotch, and pressed down hard. "I like a man who thinks beyond the moment. For you . . . of course, I'll come to Houston for your grand opening. Might be fun."

"Promise?" Davis asked her. The last thing he needed was Lara promising to come, then backing out on him and making him look dumb. He'd lose all credibility with the press, whom he knew would turn out in droves. It was going to be *the* party of the year on the Houston social scene. He had to nail this one down.

"Promise," she said, snuggling beneath his outstretched arm. "I'll come to the opening, even stay a few extra days. Roberto can work around me. But when you get a break, we've really got to be together. What about . . . if I do this for you, you go with me on the Afro All-Star Celebrity Cruise in April? Fair? I committed to doing that gig months ago and the press is already out. I can't get out of it. But who wants to cruise the Hawaiian Islands alone? Not me." Lara gave him a smoldering smile and a firm squeeze on his thigh, sending a jolt of need through Davis.

"Sure, Baby. That would be great," he murmured, his voice thick and rough. He took her hand from his thigh and eased it deep between his legs, then opened the front of her robe and nuzzled both breasts softly. He raised his head. "Now, give me the kind of welcome home that I been dreamin' about for weeks. I really missed you, Doll."

CHAPTER 17

December slipped by in a haze of cool, rainy days, during which Camille's unshakable sense of gloom increased. She rarely slept more than four hours a night, and a subtle sense of perpetual anxiety clung to her during the day. Names and dates and events that ought to have easily come to mind, eluded her all too frequently, and the idea of doing more than what was absolutely necessary to get through her workday, made her irritable and cross. Intimate moments with Max became rare, though she desperately missed his touch.

Camille stared into the bathroom mirror. There had been a time when she would have been thrilled to drop fifteen pounds in three months, but now that she had lost so much weight, she was not happy. Her doctor had prescribed Prozac, after determining that she was suffering from a mild case of post-traumatic syndrome in the wake of the terrorist attacks, but the medication only seemed to make things worse, so she stopped taking it after the first week.

She pulled on her robe, went into her dressing area and began to touch up her nail polish in preparation for the grand opening party at Vendora. She was looking forward to getting out and mixing with old friends tonight, hoping the event might help her find her way back to her old happy self. The opening gala started with a buffet dinner at eight o'clock and would last until well after midnight. There would be dancing, laughter, hats, horns, and endless glasses of champagne. Exactly what she needed to chase away her blues. Camille glanced at the porcelain clock with black cherubs on the sides that was sitting on her dressing table among an assortment of perfumes, lotions, and powders. Five-thirty. Rochelle ought to be arriving any minute with her dress.

As she finished her nails, Camille's thoughts went to Jaiden, and she was thankful that the two of them had been able to move past their Thanksgiving Day disagreement and were speaking civilly now. Jaiden had arrived home for Christmas break in a much-improved mood and had delved right into the holiday preparations with enthusiasm, both surprising and pleasing Camille. The tension that had permeated the house during Thanksgiving vacation disappeared, making for a pleasant visit, so far.

Camille and Jaiden had spent a full day Christmas shopping at the Galleria, and afterward had gone to lunch at the Mason Grill. Over their dessert of chocolate caramel cheesecake Camille finally learned why Jaiden had returned home in such a buoyant mood: She had met a young man in Providence and he *might* come to Houston for New Year's Eve to attend the grand opening party at Vendora with her. His name was Rod Henry, and he was Jaiden's roommate's cousin.

Good news, Camille had silently mused, taking note of the glow on her daughter's face. Hopefully, this friend would make New Year's Eve a special night for Jaiden. Camille had suggested that Rod stay in their house since they had two guest bedrooms that were empty; however, Jaiden quickly informed her that *if* Rod came, he would stay at the Hyatt Regency Hotel downtown and could not arrive until the day of the party.

The Hyatt? Pricey digs for a college student. And on New Year's Eve, too? thought Camille, though she was impressed with the fact that the young man had sufficient maturity and resources to take care of himself. She wondered how much time her daughter was spending with him in Providence.

A tap at her bedroom door broke into her thoughts, and she glanced around to see Jaiden standing in the doorway, wearing a burgundy velvet sheath with a matching shawl that was trimmed with tiny black beads. She looked so grown up and beautiful. Camille broke into a pride-filled smile. Her love for Jaiden flooded her heart, and she felt, at that moment, that their days of clashing over petty matters might be behind them. Jaiden had a boyfriend and was maturing into a woman. Her mind was on Rod, instead of her mother, and that was fine with Camille.

"I'm off to have Sue touch up my manicure, then I'm going to the Hyatt and pick up Rod."

"Come in here and let me see you. That dress is awesome," Camille remarked, shifting fully around on her vanity bench. "Fits you perfectly . . . and your hair looks great, honey."

"Thanks," Jaiden replied, posing for Camille so that she could inspect the elegant hairdo that had taken her stylist two hours to complete. Her thick brown hair had been smoothed back from her face and fastened into a loose, soft bundle on top of her head. Long twisted curls floated freely down her back. Chandelier earrings and a wide choker of garnet stones at her neck sparkled against her honey tan skin. "It's raining pretty hard, so I'm carrying my good shoes and wearing these." She stuck a foot out from beneath her floor-length dress and showed off a well-worn sneaker.

"Good idea," Camille laughed. "Well, tell your dad that I'll be there by eight. Not before. That is, if Rochelle ever gets here with this dress she swears I *must* wear tonight. I had planned on wearing my navy blue chiffon, but she called and said she has this perfect dress. We'll see."

"It'll be fine, Mom. Can't deny that she has good taste . . . and knows what looks good on you."

"I guess so," Camille agreed, hoping Jaiden was right.

"Gotta go. See you there." Jaiden said, cheerily. "Can't wait for you to meet Rod."

Camille accepted the impulsive kiss that Jaiden planted on her cheek, and then watched her daughter leave, smiling to see her so happy, and feeling better herself.

Thirty minutes after Jaiden left, the doorbell rang and Camille hurried to greet Rochelle, who was holding a plastic-draped dress.

"It's been pressed and it's ready to wear," Rochelle told Camille once they were upstairs in her bedroom.

Camille unzipped the plastic garment bag that Rochelle handed to her and removed a floor length black satin spaghetti strap dress with beaded trim on the bodice, as well as on the collar of the matching short, fitted jacket. She held the outfit high and fluttered the soft creation, admiring its fluid lines.

"Hmm . . . very nice, Rochelle. Rather sexy, but I like it. Where did you find this?" Camille asked as she examined the price tag, which Rochelle had conveniently pinned to the outside of the garment bag. She was not surprised to see that her bargain-hunting sister had come through with a designer dress for less than half its original price. Though Max had acquired a partner and their cash flow situation had eased, Camille was still cautious in her spending. It would take months for Vendora to provide the kind of income that she and Max had grown accustomed to, and the travel agency, though doing better, was still struggling to get passengers over their fear of flying. The agency was making a slow comeback and her boss had recalled all but one of her former coworkers.

Camille went to the peach satin slipper chair beside the bedroom window and picked up her purse, removed her checkbook and began writing a check to Rochelle. "Thanks for doing this, Rochelle. I didn't have the energy to get out there and deal with shopping for a new dress. You really came through."

"No problem. Picked it up at Tootsie's while I was shopping for Alberta Wilson's cruise wardrobe," Rochelle replied, crossing the room to accept the check that Camille handed her. She stuck it into the pocket of her ankle-length tan suede skirt.

"Oh? Where's Alberta cruising? The Bahamas?" Camille asked absently, engrossed in slipping out of her white silk blouse and black slacks and into the dress, hoping it would fit.

"No. Alberta and Tom are going on the Afro All-Star Celebrity Cruise to Hawaii. You know how they love to rub shoulders with celebrities and like to be seen in the right places. True jet-setters, or so they think."

Camille laughed, and then commented, "That's the cruise that is so expensive, and has to be booked directly with the promoters, isn't it?"

"That's it," Rochelle agreed.

"Sometime in the spring, right?" Camille turned her back to Rochelle, who stepped over and helped her with the zipper.

"First week in April. After most university spring breaks, so the airports are not so crowded. Not many students go on that cruise, though. It's an older crowd."

"A wealthier crowd," Camille clarified.

"You got that right, 'cause it sure ain't cheap." Rochelle agreed, giving the zipper a firm pull.

"And Alberta's got you shopping already?" Camille commented, adjusting the shoulder straps on the dress.

"Winter *is* the best time to shop for spring clothes, Camille. Great bargains. I bought a two hundred dollar Princess Tam Tam swimsuit for Alberta for fifty bucks."

"Good for you . . . or Alberta, I guess." The dress on, she turned around so that Rochelle could see her. "I love it. What do you think?"

"Well . . . it fits perfectly, but I gotta say . . . you're too damn thin," Rochelle flatly stated, one hand at her thick waist. She frowned. "And, I have to be honest . . . you look a little drained. I'm worried about you, Camille. Isn't your medication helping?"

Sighing, Camille sat down on the peach satin chair and considered how to answer. "Not really. In fact, I stopped taking it. Made me so sleepy and sluggish. I hate that kind of feeling. And the dreams! I had nightmares every night. I started to toss it down the toilet, but decided not to. I might *have* to take it one day."

"So, what are you supposed to do now?"

"My doctor wants me to exercise more, keep busy, and try not to dwell on negative things. I'm trying. Some days *are* good. He says this kind of depression will pass."

"Well," Rochelle started, her tone resonating with authority, "I think you ought to quit that job. How can you get better when you spend all day listening to people tell you how worried they are about flying? They bring up the attacks and how traumatized they are. That can't be good for you. Only makes things worse, if you ask me."

"I can't quit my job! The agency is finally bouncing back."

"Then get away for a while. You ought to go on the cruise I was telling you about . . . if you can still get a cabin. I went two years ago . . . had a blast. It usually sells out by Christmas, but there may be a few slots left. You and Max haven't been out of the city for nearly a year. Time for a vacation, girl, especially after all you've been through."

Camille sighed, thinking that she and Max, could use a break. Before the flood and the September 11th disaster, they had traveled quite often, with Camille making all the arrangements and getting very good deals. But recent circumstances had changed everything for them, and a vacation had been the last thing on their minds. But she knew she did need to do something . . . this malaise was not going away on its own.

"Might be something to think about," Camille commented. "But I doubt Max could get away." She went to her jewelry box and opened it, trying to decide which earrings to wear with the dress.

"Bull," Rochelle tossed back, waving a hand in dismissal. "He's as worried about you as I am. He could manage it, somehow.

Doesn't he have a partner now? Surely, his partner can hold things together for ten days." Rochelle sat down on the foot of Camille's bed and watched her sister. "And what's he like, anyway?"

"Who?"

"Max's partner."

"Oh. Davis," Camille replied, dangling a pair of heavy gold and diamond loops from two fingers as she assessed them. "All about business, though personable. Max brought him out to the house a few times. We've had drinks, business conversations. Talked mainly about Vendora. He seems totally focused on making Vendora successful. Has interesting plans to turn things around."

"Then he's exactly the kind of partner Max needs," Rochelle declared.

"Yes, I think he is," Camille agreed. "They complement each other. As you know, Max can be a bit too easygoing at times, and his staff took advantage of him, I think. Nothing major, but I think having Davis on board has tightened things up . . . created a more professional atmosphere. He keeps everyone on his or her toes. Hired a new manager, who is wonderful. His name is Percy Cleary and let me tell you, he is the real boss. Even Max takes orders from him."

"Good. That means Max can get away." Rochelle decided, pausing with a hand in the air. "So, what does Davis look like?"

Camille touched her tongue to her lip, knowing what Rochelle was after. "Handsome . . . in that suave, West Coast way, you know? Golden tan, well-dressed. Smooth, is the best way to describe him."

"Hmm. Yeah, I can imagine," Rochelle murmured, then prompted, "Single? Married? Divorced?"

Arching a brow, Camille grinned. "Girl, please. From what I've gleaned from our short conversations, he's a bachelor and happy to be one, but he's also heavily involved with Lara Stanton. Can you believe that?"

"Lara Stanton? The actress?"

"The same. And she's supposed to come to the grand reopening tonight. Davis asked me and Max not to tell anyone, in case she has to cancel, but as far as I know, she's coming. You'll get to meet her."

"Well, I hope so! I was reading the *Movie Monitor* while I was standing in line at Walgreens the other day, and I saw that Lara Stanton recently signed to do a thriller for Blue Crest Films—a multimillion dollar deal. *And*, she is going to be one of the celebrities on the Afro All-Star Celebrity Cruise. Maybe if you talk to her tonight, she can get you and Max an ocean-view stateroom, if you decide to go."

"Don't get ahead of yourself, Rochelle. I really doubt Max will be able to leave Houston right now," Camille cautioned, though she was considering broaching the subject with Max. It would be nice not to worry about anything but enjoying herself for a while. "What other celebrities are going to be on the cruise?"

"DeJay Junior; Chaka Kahn; Monica . . . she's so crazy, girl; and Erykah Badu, I love her stuff. Sinbad might be there, but he's not confirmed. Lots more." Rochelle went on, "Imagine, flying into Honolulu, boarding a luxury cruise ship to sail the islands for eight nights. Dancing under the moonlight, great music, partying with the stars, and eating all of that exotic food. There's a fabulous casino on board the ship, too. No limits on the bets. And you can believe those rich movie stars are gonna drop shiploads of cash at the tables. It'll be amazing."

At the mention of gambling, Camille placed the earrings on a mirrored dresser tray and turned to Rochelle. "Max *would* love that. Thank God, he's not a heavy better, but he likes to play the slots. A little blackjack, too. Did you know the Alabama-Coushatta Casino opened last month?"

"No, I had no idea," Rochelle commented, going over to Camille to inspect her choice of earrings. "The rubies look better with that dress," she advised, taking the gold loops from Camille, who picked up the delicate ruby sprays and clipped them on her ears.

"Yeah, you're right." Then Camille continued, "Davis told Max that he'd heard a lot about the casino and wanted to check it out, so Max took him out there last Saturday night. I didn't want to go. Apparently, Davis is pretty good at blackjack. He won five thousand dollars!"

"Get outta here!" Rochelle declared. "For real?"

"I'm telling you the truth. He told Max that he goes to Vegas all the time, and wins. Substantial amounts. Thousands at a time."

"Well, some people are lucky like that, I guess. But I wouldn't drop a dollar for a lotto ticket, let alone into a slot machine."

"Me neither," Camille agreed, finished with selecting her jewelry. She put the jewel box back into her dresser drawer, slipped off the dress and hung it on the back door of her closet. Over her shoulder, she told Rochelle, "I have to admit, I was worried about this partnership thing at first, but now I think selling an interest in

Vendora was the best thing Max could do. A lot less stress now that he has someone to share the workload and the risk."

"He was doing everything before, wasn't he?" Rochelle commented. "Managing the staff, paying the bills, ordering the liquor and food, doing the books."

"Yes, but Davis has brought in a bookkeeper as well as a manager, so all Max has to worry about now is keeping the customers happy. Can't wait for you to see the place. It's beautiful. Vibrant colors on the walls, new sleek furniture, and the window coverings . . . sheer lacy panels instead of those heavy green drapes. It's bright and modern, but it still has that historic feel that people love. Davis really had some great ideas and he's made Vendora so comfortable and attractive."

"I'm happy it's all worked out," Rochelle said. "Sooo, think about getting away and spending some time with Max, girl. I'd love to pull your cruise clothes together. Talk to him, okay?" Rochelle shouldered her gray Coach purse and gave Camille a quick hug. "Glad you like the dress." She checked her watch. "God, it's almost six. Gotta run. See you tonight. But not before ten. Got another party to glide through. "

After Rochelle left, Camille went back to her closet and began looking through her clothes, thinking about her sister's advice. A cruise might be exactly what she needed to pull herself out of these doldrums and back to enjoying life.

Silver streamers, huge white balloons, and lots of sparkly bunting festooned the reception area at the Hyatt Regency Hotel. Christmas carols played over the hotel sound system, extending the holiday mood while creating a cheerful ambiance in the bustling lobby.

Jaiden strode past two workmen on extension ladders who were busy adjusting a bright gold hat and a blue glitter horn to a huge sign at the top of the escalators. She headed to the elevators and squeezed in with the crush of party-ready passengers, feeling elegant in her burgundy gown and silver heels. She pressed Eighteen and stood off to one side, waiting for the elevator to come to a stop, thinking about Rod.

She was so glad he had decided to come to Houston for New Year's Eve and relieved that he had insisted on staying in a hotel. If he had come to her house . . . what a drag that would have been; her mom in their face all the time, her dad watching them every minute. No privacy at all. This was definitely a much better arrangement, and she couldn't wait to get upstairs and give him a serious welcome to Houston kiss.

They were as tight as ever, and Jaiden had been on target when she had decided not to charge him up for ignoring her over the Thanksgiving holiday break. After returning to school, they had talked and he had said he'd gone hunting in the Pennsylvania mountains with his dad and some friends, and then asked her out for Friday night, as if the matter was closed. Jaiden had been smart enough to keep their conversation about her holiday activities light, divulging few details about her miserable vacation.

Now, things were back to normal. They went to Twist, played pool and hung out with Rod's friends, and when the weather cooperated, they went for long rides on his bike, resuming their pattern of weekend dating. Jaiden was spending more and more time at his apartment, playing video games and watching TV, and had even spent the night a few times. They kissed, hugged and touched each other intimately when they were alone in his apartment, but so far, their sexual relationship remained on hold.

The elevator stopped at the eighteenth floor and Jaiden got out, having made up her mind that Rod's arrival in Houston gave her the perfect opportunity to move their relationship to a more serious level. And she planned to do so tonight.

When he opened the door to his room, she drew in a short breath and gave him a serious once-over. "Damn! You got it going on!" She walked past him, then turned around and stood in the middle of the room, taking in a Rod she had never known existed: He was wearing a tuxedo, ruffled shirt, shiny black shoes and a gold earring in his left ear. His glistening brown braids no longer brushed his shoulders as usual, but were tied back from his face with a thin black ribbon, giving him a male-model image.

He spun around once, laughing, "You like?"

Jaiden moved closer. "I love it!" she responded, taking him in from head to toe once more, more certain than ever that she was going to go through with her plan. In the trunk of her car, she had stashed a small overnight bag containing a skimpy Victoria's Secret black lace camisole and French-cut panties with matching bedroom slippers, jasmine scented candles, a tiny bottle of Only For Love body oil, and a package of Trojans. She knew exactly how this night was going to unfold and had carefully planned each detail. No alcohol at the party—except perhaps, a sip of champagne at midnight—she wanted to be totally aware of Rod's every move. They would come back to his room after the celebrating cooled down, and she would ask him to go into the bathroom while she lit the candles, slipped into her sexy outfit, and placed the condoms under his pillow. Then, she would tune the radio to KTSU-FM and fill the room with soft jazz music, creating a mood that would drive Rod straight into her arms. Tonight they were going to do more than kiss and hug and feel each other up, of that Jaiden was certain.

Rod grabbed both of Jaiden's hands, breaking into her thoughts, and held her at arm's length. His face was lit with approval. "And look at you," he beamed. "You clean up good, yourself." He pulled her close and kissed her lightly, respecting her carefully applied makeup.

"I knew you'd come," Jaiden whispered, although she hadn't known until two days ago that he was actually coming, and had begun to wonder if he had deliberately refused to commit in order to keep her guessing. He had a way of keeping to himself that was frustrating yet intriguing, and Jaiden was sure he worked hard on perfecting this elusive behavior.

"I'm here. So, let's have some fun," he finished, breaking away when the phone rang. He answered, nodded, then said, "Okay," and turned back to Jaiden. "The limo's downstairs," he told her, casually pocketing his wallet, his room key, and a pack of chewing gum before opening the door for Jaiden.

"You booked a limo for tonight?" she remarked, eyes wide as she passed him and entered the corridor.

"Of course. This is a special night, isn't it?" Rod replied.

"It sure is," Jaiden agreed, thinking, *If you only knew how special it is going to be.*

CHAPTER 18

Preparations for the grand reopening of Vendora had begun the moment Max had shaken hands with Davis and signed off on their deal, and tonight the unveiling of their creation was finally about to take place. The decision to enclose the deep wraparound porches that surrounded the house had added much needed floor space downstairs. Now, there were four main rooms on the first floor, in addition to the state-of the-art commercial kitchen and separate offices for Davis and Max. First, a spacious reception area with low couches and grouped seating for casual gatherings; the ballroom, with a stage and dance floor; the main dining room, which had an indoor open pit grill and a small alcove for private dining; and an Old World wine room for intimate dinners for eight.

Tonight, Vendora's elegant dining room had been transformed into a fairyland of white and silver, spiked with splashes of tropical green from well-placed exotic plants. Dark wood wainscoting, original to the house, gleamed with a warm patina, as did the crystal chandeliers, delicate goblets, and the glistening silverware placed on antique lace linens. At the far end of the room, a fire glowed in the rustic brick indoor barbecue pit, softening the formal ambiance. Tall cut crystal vases filled with delicate white orchids had been placed in the center of each silk-draped table for eight. Party favors—tiny silver hand mirrors for the ladies and leather card cases for the men—were hidden in small silver bags that had been placed on the seat of each chair. Fragrant sprays of ruffled green ferns nestled beside the silver place settings, which caught the light from the diamond cut spheres that were suspended above the tables.

In the ballroom, the highly polished dance floor was waiting for the guests. Heavy silk tiebacks held pristine white sheers away from the eight-foot-tall paneled windows, their luxurious sheen adding sparkle to the expansive room, which could accommodate two-hundred-and-fifty partyers. The men in the five-piece band, dressed in white tuxedos, were busy warming up their instruments, while the female singer—a petite, pecan-colored woman wearing a blonde wig and a slinky silver dress—exercised her vocals.

Satisfaction, relief, and anticipation swept through Max as he strolled to the rear of the supper club and peered out at the fully decorated and heated tent in the backyard, where food and drinks would be made available for the press and the limo drivers, and anyone who wanted to smoke.

The press. He shook his head in amazement at Davis's ability to create such a buzz. Lara Stanton's presence was worth the price of a full-page ad in the daily paper, and her endorsement—which Davis had assured Max he would secure—would be used in promotional material to entice visiting celebrities to drop by Vendora while in town.

Max worked his way through the elegant dining room, double-checking each detail of every table, finding little to correct. Percy Cleary swished along in front of him, feigning a huff, as if daring Max to make one negative remark about the room, the decorations, the staff, or the food. The staff was thrilled to have Percy over-seeing the restaurant and managing the kitchen, and Max knew that this manager was doing a much better job than he himself ever could have done. When Max gave Percy a big thumbs-up and sent him on his way, Percy rolled his eyes in a told-you-so manner, and then fled into the kitchen, leaving Max alone to assess his and Davis's accomplishment.

Once a gutted shambles, Vendora was now a showplace compa-rable to any luxury club he had ever visited. There was no resem-blance to the muddy, dank structure it had been only a few short months ago. It shone with a brightness that gave Max pause, and he knew it was due to Davis Kepler's insistence that the place be a first-class operation and that the work on the renovations be of the highest quality. He had insisted that the workers stay on the job twelve hours a day, seven days a week, no matter the cost. Yesterday, when the light fixture outside the double mahogany doors at the entry had been hoisted into place and lit for the first time, had Davis finally given the workers a thumbs-up and told them, "That's it, guys. Vendora is complete."

However, despite the drastic changes, for Max at least, the house seemed eerily the same. Yes, it appeared different—more hip, modern, and charmingly sophisticated. Max surveyed his precious supper club with eyes that brought back memories of its appearance when his father and his grandfather had lived here. Certainly, they would be proud of him: He had held onto their legacy, when by all rights, he could have easily lost it. So what if he was no longer the owner? That didn't matter much—he would regain full possession soon, because he planned to do everything in his power to make sure the business grew fast enough to meet the terms of the contract.

Satisfied that everything was ready for his guests, Max left the lower floor and ascended the grand staircase, crossed the upper hall and went into the bedroom where he and Camille had first started their marriage, and most recently, spent a few nights waiting out the flood. He went inside and closed the door, narrowing his eyes as he studied the room: the antique linen spread on the old four poster bed, the bouquet of pink roses he had placed on the Victorian table at the window, the clusters of fragrant candles carefully arranged on three silver trays, which he would light at midnight, after he kissed Camille. How many New Year's Eves had they rung in at Vendora? He thought back. Too many to count, but he did know that each year he had made a resolution to make sure Camille, his most precious blessing, was happy.

He sighed, memories of the bad parts of 2001 starting to crowd his heart. Last year, he had not done a very good job, but 2002 was definitely going to be different.

Leaving the bedroom, he went into the storage closet across the hall where small electrical appliances, oversized vases, and extra serving pieces were kept. He found the extension cord that the electric guitarist had asked for, and was turning to leave when he heard Davis's voice, clear and strong. It was coming through the ventilation shaft at his feet. Max overheard Davis checking with the limo service to make sure that Lara would be there before twelve o'clock.

Max glanced down and grinned. Davis's office was directly under the storage closet and shared a common air vent with the space. When Max was a child, he had loved to sit upstairs in the small room and listen to the grown-ups talking downstairs, and they always wondered how he knew so much about their affairs and why he was always two steps ahead of them when he was about to be punished for breaking some rule. Arching a brow, he thought, *Some things about this old house will never change.*

He stepped over to the tiny round window in the small space—which afforded a view of the well-lit curved driveway and entry. The valet service was already busy helping the first guests out of their cars. Among those arriving he saw Camille, and smiled to watch her mount the steps. She was so beautiful, so fragile, but too thin, he worried, silently praying that the surprise he had in store for her tonight would help chase away her blues. He stepped out of the closet, eager to go downstairs and get on with the party that he knew was going to be one to remember.

Throughout the evening, the party people arrived, chattering, laughing, and singing praises about Vendora's new look and new attitude. They loved it, and loved the fact that Houston now had a luxurious, much-needed, upscale black-owned establishment that was equal to any supper club in Vegas. All that was missing, they laughingly commented, were slot machines, roulette wheels, and blackjack tables.

Max and Davis met everyone at the door and welcomed them to Vendora. Max was thrilled to greet personal friends, loyal customers, society patrons, business associates, and the press. He gave each new arrival a warm handshake and introduced them to his partner, who handed them over to Percy Cleary's care. Percy escorted the guests to their tables, where the all-male waitstaff, dressed completely in white, hovered attentively nearby to fetch a fresh drink from the bar or refill a plate from the lavish buffet, which took up one side of the dining room and was anchored by an elaborate flamingo-shaped ice sculpture. Exquisite food arrangements, so beautiful they appeared artificial, spilled over on silver trays placed on the long banquet table.

Upon her arrival, Camille had only been able to give Max a quick peck on the cheek and a few words of good luck before getting swept up in conversation with several of Vendora's most loyal customers, many of whom she had not seen since before the flood—and all of them exclaiming over the supper club's gorgeous renovation.

Rochelle showed up at nine-fifteen, wearing a tight fitting red dress and red platform shoes, accompanied by her favorite ex-husband, Buzz Wyatt—the one who had given her the house she now lived in. They immediately hit the dance floor, causing quite a stir as they swung out to a raucous rendition of Aretha Franklin's "Respect," belted out by the petite blonde vocalist. Soon everyone was on their feet, cheering the couple on.

Camille shook her head in amused envy as she watched Rochelle shake her hips and jiggle her generous bosom, keeping one eye on the door as she waited for Jaiden and her friend. When they finally arrived, she hurried over, anxious to meet Rod Henry.

Max was shaking Rod's hand when Camille stepped up and extended hers.

"We're so glad you could come," she told Rod, thinking, *What a nice looking young man . . .* though the lightning bolt tattoo running up the side of his neck did give her pause. *Well, body art is popular among young people,* she conceded, glad that Jaiden had never gone in that direction. "Welcome to Houston, Rod. Have a good flight?"

"Fine," he answered, then added, looking around, "Very nice place you have, Mr. and Mrs. Granville."

"Thank you," Camille replied.

"We're very proud of this house," Max said. "Been in the family for a long time. Jaiden was born here. Did she tell you that?" Max boasted with pride. "Right upstairs. This used to be our home, and I spend so much time here now . . . it still feels like home." Sweeping an arm, he went on. "You'll get the grand tour before the night is over, I'm sure."

"Jaiden told me all about the flood and the damage. You must have had to make major renovations," Rod said, assessing the rich interior with interest.

"Right," Camille answered for Max. "We suffered a great deal of damage during a flood last August. Horrible ordeal, but we've pulled it together. Made the best of the situation. Sometimes an unfortunate event is needed to force us to change, and change is not always bad. But I'm sure you don't want to hear about that," she stated, glancing toward the dining room, which was bustling with people who were table hopping and chatting, drinks in hand. "We think it's lovelier than before and we're happy to have you here to enjoy this night with us,"

"Please," Max commented, edging out of the conversation, "You two go on in and have fun. Camille, I have to go over and greet Judge Tunney and his wife. I see they're already seated at our table." Max patted Rod on the back, and then strode into the dining room, stopping to speak to guests as he made his way to his and Camille's table near the stage.

Camille leaned over and gave Jaiden a quick hug, whispering in her ear, "Rod is gorgeous. Take good care of him!"

"Mom, please," Jaiden giggled. "Be real. He's just a friend."

"Okay, okay. I'll say no more." Camille said, a mischievous gleam in her dark gray eyes.

"Thanks," Jaiden said, taking obvious notice of her mother's dress. "Who is at our table?"

"Judge and Mrs. Tunney, Trent Young and his wife, Rochelle and Buzz . . ."

"I have to say, Aunt Rochelle really hooked you up, Mom," Jaiden interrupted. "That outfit is hot." Turning to Rod, she explained. "My Aunt Rochelle . . . the one in the red dress out there on the dance floor . . . is a personal shopper. Picked out my mom's dress."

Rod leveled his deep brown eyes on Camille's face, held her attention for a moment, and then swept his glance down to her shoes and back up. He shook his head slowly, up and down. "I agree. Your mom's hot, all right. Your aunt did a hell of a job."

Taken aback by his blunt but flattering comment, Camille lifted both hands and laughed. "Well, thank you, Rod. I appreciate the compliment. I can see why Jaiden keeps you around." Then turning to Jaiden, she told her, "Okay. Enough chitchat. You guys go . . . enjoy. Percy will show you where our table is." She ushered them over to Vendora's haughty manager, who was standing near the entrance to the ballroom where a few couples had congregated to make special requests of the band.

"Okay. Later," Jaiden called back to her mother as she and Rod headed into the dining room.

Camille continued greeting guests, stopping by tables to chat for a moment before moving on, eventually working her way to her and Max's table, where she found Rod seated by himself. He was watching Max and a sexy redhead, whom Camille had never seen in her life, get cozy on the dance floor. She tried not to stare, but was taken aback by the way he was holding her: eyes closed, snuggled up with a stranger as if he had known her forever.

My God, doesn't he realize how that looks? She silently groaned. Over the years, she had learned that Max simply was a big flirt, and his desire to impress the ladies was cemented in his genes. She was far beyond feeling threatened by nanosecond flirtations like this, and knew that nothing would be accomplished by mentioning it to him. It had taken time, but Camille had taught herself how to ignore his flirtatious behavior and not feel threatened. They were secure in their marriage and she loved him, flaws and all.

Deciding to take advantage of this moment alone with Rod, Camille settled down next to him, and then asked, "Where's Jaiden?"

"I think she went to the ladies' room with her aunt," Rod replied.

"Oh . . . I'll keep you company, then."

Rod smiled and lifted one hand in a sign of welcome, giving Camille the opening that she needed.

"So, Rod, what are you studying?"

"Software development."

"Really? Good for you. Brown has an excellent business college, and computer programming is a good field."

"I don't go to Brown," he declared, looking straight at her, as if making sure she got the message that he had nothing more to say about the school.

"Oh?" was all Camille was able to manage. Forging ahead, she clarified her comment. "When Jaiden told me you were a student . . . I assumed you went to Brown. Sorry. Where do you go?"

"East Tech Business College. It's in Providence."

"Really?" Camille remarked, wishing she could sound a bit more enthusiastic. "How nice. So, you don't live on campus, then?"

"No, I have an apartment. Not far from campus though."

"Roommates?" she prompted.

"No, I live alone."

"Oh . . . and I understand you're Mona's cousin?" she pressed, eager for additional information about this guy who obviously had more than a casual interest in her daughter. He had his own apartment, could afford to fly to Houston on short notice to spend New Year's Eve with Jaiden, and was staying at the Hyatt. Smooth operator, she mused.

"Yeah, Mona and I are cousins," he confirmed, giving Camille a quick nod.

"I see. And what are your plans after you finish your studies?"

"I'm going to work for my father. He owns several automotive repair shops in Essex . . . has four locations. My goal is to computerize my dad's operation . . . which is so outdated and unreliable. You see, he has no computer program in place to track what's happening with his company. I hope to streamline his operation."

"Good for you. I'm sure your dad will be happy to have you working with him in the family business. That's the way to do it, you know? Keep everything in the family." But as she said those words, the reality of Max's situation hit her—he no longer owned Vendora. Davis Kepler did.

But, that situation isn't going to last forever. Camille told herself, smiling at Jaiden, who had returned to the table after leaving Rochelle at the edge of the dance floor with Buzz, who draped his arm casually around his ex-wife's shoulders.

The music stopped. Camille excused herself and went to get Max, aware that the redhead was standing around, waiting for the band to strike up the next tune.

"Thanks for rescuing me," Max whispered, allowing Camille to ease him away from his dance partner.

"What was that about?" Camille wanted to know.

"The girlfriend of our major wine supplier. He gives us great deals." Max shrugged, as if to say—*What can I do*? "And she is a huge fan of Lara Stanton's. All she really wanted to know was if, and when, Lara Stanton would arrive."

"I doubt she's coming," Camille scoffed.

"I think *so*," Max countered. "Apparently she *is* in town. I heard Davis checking on her limo, and he told me he had spoken to her earlier this evening. Everyone's talking about getting her autograph."

"Yeah," Camille commented dryly. "Everyone? Especially the guys?"

Max shrugged. "Well . . . what can I say? She's famous . . . she's beautiful."

"I saw a cameraman from Channel Two outside when I arrived."

"I'm sure there's more press out there by now. Davis set up the tent so they'd have a comfortable place to sit, eat, and drink while they waited for her to make her appearance."

"She'll certainly add a touch of glamour and excitement to the evening, that's for sure."

"Right," Max replied. "When Davis first told me that she might come to our grand reopening, I thought he was kidding."

"Oh, she'll probably show up precisely at midnight," Camille commented cattily, "So she can make a grand entrance and cause a stir. Isn't that what celebrities do?"

"I guess so," Max laughingly agreed, smiling as he firmed his arm around Camille's waist. "Can't deny that it will be good publicity for Vendora. Can't fault Davis for that."

"No, you can't," she agreed, catching a glimpse of Jaiden and Rod, now on the dance floor, holding onto each other, eyes closed.

They were definitely into the music, as well as into each other. *More than friends*, Camille assessed, leaning closer to Max as she whispered for him to direct his attention to his daughter. "Jaiden's friend seems nice enough, though he's not much of a talker. However, I did get him to open up a bit while you and your redhead were dancing."

"And?"

"He does not go to Brown, attends a business college, and he lives off campus in his own apartment. Alone."

"Uh-uh," Max groaned. "I hear disapproval in your voice."

"Well, doesn't that worry you?"

"Not at all. Think back, Camille. I didn't go to college, I lived alone—in this huge old house . . . I didn't get girls into trouble, did I?"

Cocking her head, Camille grinned. "Depends on how you define trouble."

"You got me. So how much trouble was that?"

Laughing, Camille went on. "Rod is quite the charmer, too. He told me I looked hot!"

Max grinned. "So? Nothing wrong with that. Would you expect your daughter to go out with a guy who didn't enjoy paying a well-deserved compliment to a pretty woman?"

Camille squinted her dark gray eyes at her husband; lips pursed in a tease, and then said, "I guess not. Influenced by her father, I think."

"Exactly," Max replied with a wide smile, pulling her flush against his side. "You *do* look hot. And tonight, I plan to charm the hell out of you. What do you say? Let's dance?"

Camille lifted her chin and tossed her jet-black curls from her face, and then let him lead her onto the dance floor. It was a slow number, which suited Camille: She loved holding Max close, and he was so handsome in his tuxedo tonight. He had danced with many of his guests tonight, and she had felt proud to be his wife, not jealous to see him twirling other women on the dance floor, as she once would have been. Everyone knew that Max loved a party and he had done himself proud tonight.

Now, cocooned in his arms, the uneasy sense of gloom that had shrouded her for months began to fade, and with her cheek on his shoulder, she closed her eyes, let her mind drift, and lost herself in the music.

* * *

Davis knew exactly what time Lara's plane had arrived—7:27 P.M. He ought to know: He had made the reservation and paid for the ticket himself, though Lara certainly could have afforded to do so. However, *he* had asked her to decline her other New Year's Eve party invitations in order to come to Houston, so he wanted to treat her right. He had sprung for a first-class, round-trip ticket, shelling out close to two thousand dollars, and had booked her a suite at the Ritz Carlton—she had insisted on a suite, not a room, and it was costing him four-fifty a night. He had filled the room with flowers and arranged for a chilled bottle of Cristal champagne to be there when she arrived. A stretch limousine would bring Lara to Vendora and, later, take the two of them back to her hotel—after all, he was paying for the suite and he damn sure was going to sleep there tonight. Besides, the Galleria area condominium he had leased when he arrived in Houston was not yet fully furnished; he hadn't had time to even think about decorating it with all he had had on his mind. Maybe he could persuade Lara to take that on while she was in town.

He had spoken to her at 8:20 P.M., right after she arrived at the Ritz, and had been promptly informed that she needed time to rest and bathe before dressing, but would definitely be at Vendora to ring in the New Year with him and his guests.

So, where the hell is she? Davis fumed, furious at her for making him stall the press and pacify her fans, to whom he had made promises that Lara Stanton would not only appear, but make a few remarks and sign autographs, too. Davis was getting anxious. He had reporters from three local television stations, the society reporter from the *Houston Chronicle* and the editor of *Style Magazine* badgering him for information about Lara's whereabouts.

Who did she think she was dealing with? He wasn't the owner of some no-name rib joint in South Central L.A. The cream of Houston society had turned out for his grand reopening and he was going to impress the hell out of them. Tonight. He was much too busy overseeing the evening's festivities to track her down, and besides, he didn't want to give Lara the satisfaction of knowing how important her presence at Vendora really was. He checked his watch for the third time in ten minutes. 11:20 P.M. If Lara didn't get her ass over here soon, he was going to dump her. He knew the game she was playing: the pampered star who wanted to make a grand entrance, doing things her way. Well, he wasn't playing, and she'd find out soon enough who was in charge of this relationship.

* * *

Lara checked her reflection in the pull-down mirror in the back of the chauffeur-driven limousine and adjusted a wisp of auburn hair that had slipped over one eye. Tucking it firmly back into her elaborate up-do, she smiled, and then drew her white fur stole over her bare shoulders, glad she had decided to bring it along. Though she had been told that the weather in December in Houston could be warm one day and cool the next, tonight was rainy—with a definite chill in the air—perfect for her white fox wrap.

Here she was, in Houston, Texas, attending the grand reopening of Davis Kepler's luxurious supper club. He had insisted she be there, so naturally she had complied, and was pleased that he had wanted her at his side.

Like a dutiful wife, she thought, putting the tip of her tongue to her glistening mauve-colored lips. All that talk about other New Year's Eve parties and post-production work. Ha! She had nothing else to do but come here and be with Davis. She laughed under her breath. If only he knew how much she loved it when he begged.

She hadn't seen Davis since their Thanksgiving rendezvous, and had barely spoken to him on the phone for longer than ten minutes at a time. But that had been understandable—he was building the foundation of a successful business and needed to concentrate on his work. She had no problem giving him the space he needed to get everything perfect for tonight, but now that his showplace was finished, it was her turn. And she damn well deserved his full attention. She hoped he was fretting and pacing and desperate to see her walk through the door of his club. Arriving at exactly eleven-forty-five ought to do it.

She leaned forward and tapped on the glass window between herself and the handsome Hispanic chauffeur. "Go around the block one more time, please. Slowly."

"Yes, Miss Stanton," he replied, sweeping the long car around another corner.

Lara leaned back against the soft black leather and studied the brightly lit Houston skyline. She could hardly wait to see Davis's face when she arrived.

Jaiden nursed her second glass of Perrier and lime while Rod finished off his fourth rum and Coke, and then signaled to the waiter to bring him another. They had spent most of the evening on the dance floor, but had taken out time to fill their plates twice at the lavish buffet. She knew Rod was having a good time and he had told her more than once that this was one of the best New Year's Eve parties he had ever attended.

And it's far from over, Jaiden thought, checking the time on the huge countdown clock above the stage. It was shaped like an hourglass, and as each minute ticked down, the face of the dial changed colors. Eleven-forty-five. Only fifteen more minutes and they could get out of there and back to the hotel where, as far as Jaiden was concerned, the real celebration would begin. The waiters were already uncorking the champagne and had begun filling glasses at each table, preparing for the toast.

"Look," Rod tapped Jaiden on her shoulder and pointed toward the entry. "Lara Stanton's here."

Jaiden was amazed to see a crush of people surge forth, including many of the waiters. They crowded around Lara in a mass of chattering glee.

Davis brusquely pushed his way through the crowd, glaring at Lara as he created space for her to enter.

"Where the hell have you been?" he hissed into her ear, while smiling at the crowd as he hurried her through the dining room and across the ballroom floor, which was ringed with excited fans.

"Getting ready," she whispered, her nipples hardening at the sight of Davis's desperate expression.

"I needed you here an hour ago," he growled.

Lara took his hand and sensuously rubbed her thumb into his palm. "Didn't you want me to look good?"

"I wanted you *here*," Davis muttered, through thin lips, handing her up onto the stage, then taking his place beside her. He casually rested his hand low on her back, inches above her perfectly rounded butt. Adopting a glowingly possessive stance, he beamed at the expectant faces. When the partyers burst into applause, Lara lifted a swanlike arm, waved, and blew kisses at them.

She was wearing a sleek lavender-beaded dress that emphasized her hourglass figure, delicate stone-studded stiletto heels, and she had draped her white fox fur over one shoulder. She had a spray of tiny purple flowers tucked into her deep auburn hair, which cascaded in wispy curls that framed her famous face. Her eyes were smoky brown and huge; her bosom, unbelievably exposed; and all her bare skin glistened with a sparkling of pale gold powder, giving her an exotic, ethereal appearance.

Davis stood tall and proud as he introduced her to his guests.

Cameras flashed, reporters surged forth, cameramen hustled close to focus their huge lenses on the star. And when she took the microphone from Davis to express her delight at being in Houston, the room immediately fell silent.

"God, she is beautiful," Jaiden whispered, glancing back at Rod, catching him in the act of lifting a half-full bottle of champagne from the tray beside their table.

"What . . . ?" she started, but he quickly shushed her with a finger to his lips.

"Come on," he hissed, jerking his head toward the side door, which led out to the tented area and on to the parking lot. "Let's get some air."

"But I want to hear Lara."

"She's got nothing to say that interests me. Come on!" He lifted the champagne bottle high.

Giggling, Jaiden checked the room and realized that everyone was absorbed in listening to Lara Stanton. Besides, she was awfully tired of Perrier and lime. A glass or two of bubbly did seem like an excellent idea. No one would miss her, anyway. Taking Rod's advice, she slipped away with him as Lara continued to speak.

". . . and I want to wish every one of you a happy New Year," Lara finished in a delicate coo. She lifted her glass of champagne toward the clock and joined in as everyone began counting down the last two minutes of 2001.

Rod hurried toward the limo that he had hired for the night, opened the door and fell, laughing, inside, while Jaiden gathered her dress in one hand, climbed in and sank down beside him. He kissed her hard, and then poured champagne into two flutes he had retrieved from the minibar. After handing a glass to Jaiden, he pulled a joint from his jacket pocket, lit it, and inhaled deeply.

"Ahh . . ." he moaned, sinking back, propping his feet on the seat opposite him. "Nice in here, huh?"

Jaiden stared nervously at the darkened windows. "Rod. Maybe you better not smoke that. The driver might come back. We better not do this."

He calmly passed the joint to her and waved a dismissive hand. "I put a fresh fifty dollar bill in the driver's pocket. He ain't gonna show till I go get him."

"Oh. Great," was all Jaiden said, taking the joint from him. She drew on it, and then held her champagne glass high. "Happy New Year, Rod. This is the best."

"Right, the best. Happy New Year, Jaiden." They clinked glasses, and then sipped their bubbly, grinning mischievously.

A loud chorus of "Auld Lang Syne" burst from the ballroom, along with the clatter of noisemakers and blasts from the horns that every guest had been given to blow when the clock struck twelve.

Shouts of "Happy New Year" erupted as Rod leaned over and kissed Jaiden again, this time with a kind of urgency that she had never felt before. He set their glasses aside. She snuggled into his arms and kissed him back, dancing her tongue over his, thrilled to be alone with him, yet anxious to return to the hotel and carry out her plan. The sexy outfit, the candles, the music. The luxury of being at the Ritz Carlton Hotel in bed with Rod. Her heart began to race. He was going to love her surprise.

Suddenly, Rod slipped both hands under Jaiden's dress and gave her panties a firm tug.

She tensed. This was not supposed to be happening *here*. No way was she going to lose her virginity in the backseat of a car, even if it was a limo. "Don't do that, Rod," she purred, not shifting from his touch.

"Why not? Let's really celebrate, Jaiden," he whispered, maneuvering his fingers between her legs and into her soft mound of hair. "We've been together long enough. You know how I feel about you."

No, actually I don't, Jaiden thought, desperately hoping he might speak those three lovely words to her tonight. Anxious, she told him, "I feel the same way," then paused. "I love you, Rod." There, she had said it, but would he?

Rod cleared his throat, and pressed on, skirting her declaration of love. "So, don't you think it's time? Don't you think so?" he urged, massaging her damp, warm skin.

Jaiden melted when his fingers slipped inside her, creating a surge of need that forced her to draw in a sharp, short breath. "Well . . . uh . . . I've been thinking the same thing, but . . ."

"Good," he replied, easing her panties down, then over her ankles.

"I want to, Rod. I do, but not here," she weakly protested, making no effort to stop him from shifting her burgundy dress up and over her hips and pushing her legs apart.

"Good a place as any," he murmured, unzipping his tuxedo pants.

"I thought . . . later . . . at the hotel . . ." she sighed, sinking down under his weight.

"Why wait?" he asked in an important tone, as if everything had been decided. He was on top of her and inside her with one smooth, easy stroke, before she could give him an answer.

Jaiden gasped, then relaxed, and the initial pinch soon gave way to a flood of warmth that spread rapidly throughout her body. She wrapped her arms around his back and held on as if fearing he might be swept from her arms as he thrust into her with long, easy strokes—gentle movements that rocked her back and forth. After adjusting to the new and oddly comforting feel of him being inside of her, Jaiden set aside her disappointment at not going back to the hotel, and concentrated, with much abandon, on making love to Rod. She wanted to become a part of him. This joining had to be a sign that they had moved their relationship into a permanent union, and they would never be separated physically or emotionally again. Once she finally relaxed, she realized that Rod was patient, gentle, and thoughtful of her feelings. He even inquired, twice, if she was okay, but Jaiden was too overwhelmed with joy to answer: Having sex was much more pleasurable than she had ever dreamed it would be! She could do this forever.

While the band was playing "Auld Lang Syne" for the second time, and the guests were still making toasts, Max caressed Camille, whispered in her ear to come with him, and then led her to the grand staircase, their arms around each other's waists. They mounted the stairs together in silence.

It had been a perfect night for Max: His old customers were thrilled with the new and improved Vendora, the press coverage was going to give business a huge boost, and Davis's marketing ploy of inviting Lara Stanton had been brilliant. His guests had been thrilled to be included in such an exclusive event, and Lara was busy signing autographs and posing for pictures with them, while Davis chatted up the society reporter for the *Chronicle*, making sure his name was spelled correctly. Max had never felt so energized and confident about the future.

He followed Camille into the bedroom, and then stood back as she took in the glowing candles he had sneaked upstairs to light, the vase of pink roses on the table, and the sweet scent that perfumed the room. He motioned her to sit down in the chair by the window and then kneeled beside her, trying to hide his amusement at her puzzled expression.

"*Now* are you going to tell me what this is all about?" she asked, a twinkle in her dark gray eyes. "We really ought to be downstairs with our guests, Max. What are you up to?"

"I love you very much, Camille," he started, pausing to let his words take effect, realizing that he did not say those words often enough. "It's been a difficult year . . . for both of us . . . and I want to give you something to make up for all the stress I've caused and for time we've been apart." He reached into the drawer of the tiny Victorian table and took out a folded piece of paper. "Here," he said, handing it to her.

"What's this?" Camille opened what appeared to be a printout from an Internet Web site.

"Something we both need very much."

She unfolded the paper, read it, then laughed aloud. "How did you know about this?" she exclaimed, swatting playfully at Max.

"Rochelle called me this afternoon and we had a long talk . . . she convinced me that this is something we need to do. What she said made sense."

"But . . ." Camille started to protest.

"But what? You don't want to go on the Afro All-Star Celebrity Cruise with me?"

"Of course I do!" Camille planted a quick kiss on Max's lips, then held his chin with two fingers. "I am going to kill Rochelle. Jumping ahead of me like this. I was going to ask you about it, but wasn't sure if you could get away."

"I can, and I will," Max vowed. "Davis and Lara Stanton are going, too. She's one of the featured celebrities. Did you know that?"

"I did. Rochelle told me all about it."

"After she called, I spoke to Davis about the trip. We both agree that Percy can handle things for a week or so, and will most likely welcome the opportunity to play boss around here. So, there is no excuse, Mrs. Granville. We are going to cruise the Hawaiian Islands in style."

PART THREE

THE CRUISE

CHAPTER 19

April 2002
At Sea

The *Sea Wind* set sail from Honolulu on April 1st, slipping out into the incredibly blue water in the quiet hour before dawn while Camille and Max stood at the ship's rail, holding hands, and watched a spectacular sunrise break on the horizon. The sight of the vibrant yellow globe, shot with streaks of gray and orange, was a mesmerizing launch to what they both hoped was going to be a much-needed and exotic vacation.

"We're on our way," Camille commented, resting her head on Max's shoulder. "It's all so beautiful. Seems like a dream."

Max gave her a soft squeeze. "I've always heard that the Hawaiian Islands are a good place to dream, especially at sunrise."

Camille leaned back and studied Max, then playfully gave him a swat on the arm. "Where did you hear that?"

Max grinned. "I don't know. Somewhere. Maybe in a movie. Sounds good to me, though. Why not believe it?'

With a nod, Camille relented. "I can't think of anything I want to dream for right now. Everything seems perfect. At last."

"Pretty close," Max agreed. "The flood, the terrorist attacks, the drop in business at your travel agency. All behind us. Now, if Jaiden can pull up her grades . . ."

"Please, let's not go there," Camille stopped him. "I've put that issue out of my mind for the duration of our vacation, and I refuse to deal with that until we get home."

"I can understand," Max commented. "At least Vendora is fully restored and business is great. We're booking twice as many reservations as this time last year. The patrons love the new menu and décor. Davis is doing an amazing job with promotions, and to be absolutely honest, as much as I want to be here with you on this cruise, I can't stop thinking about getting back to work. I'm excited about the future and really miss the place."

"Well, forget about it for now. I doubt you'll be singing that tune in six months, when you're burned out and exhausted from putting in long hours of dealing with problems that are sure to come up."

"You're probably right. But we've made it through the worst," Max concluded, brushing a hand over Camille's unruly curls, which were being buffeted by the ocean breeze. "For now, I promise to put business matters out of my mind and do nothing but enjoy this vacation. For starters, how about breakfast?" he asked.

"Sounds good. I'm starved," Camille replied, as they broke away from the railing and headed to the elevator that would take them up to the Sky Deck, where the Bistro, a casual eating spot was located.

Emerging from the elevator, Camille focused on an elderly couple that strolled by. They were holding hands, and seemed serenely content simply to be together. *That's what I want for me and Max*, she mused, following Max into the cluster of small round tables that were crowded onto the open air deck. *A long lifetime together.*

"Over there," Max called over his shoulder to Camille, increasing his pace. "Davis and Lara, under that umbrella." Max lifted a hand in greeting and Davis waved them over.

"You guys all settled in?" Camille asked, smiling at Lara as she pulled up her chair. She had not been able to spend any private time with Lara during her short visit to Houston for Vendora's grand reopening, and during the long flight from Los Angeles to Honolulu, Camille had hoped to pass the time getting to know the sultry actress. However, once the foursome had settled into their seats in first class, Lara had immediately covered her eyes with a black sleeping mask, tilted back her seat and shut down for the duration of the flight. Upon arrival in Honolulu, they had gone their separate ways to different hotels and had not met up again until late yesterday afternoon when passengers had been permitted to board the ship in preparation for the early morning embarkation.

Once aboard the *Sea Wind*, Davis and Lara had disappeared into their stateroom, which was located on the Emerald Deck on the opposite side of the passageway from Camille and Max's, and had not emerged until this morning. Now, the two couples were captive on the ship, and Camille had made up her mind that Lara was not going to ignore her forever.

"Oh, yes. All settled in," Lara replied in a sugary sweet voice, turning her full attention to Camille for the first time. "All of my cruise clothes are hanging up, my shoes are lined up on the floor beneath each outfit, my lingerie is in the drawers, cosmetics in the bathroom. I'm ready to party. And I'm really excited. There is so much going on . . . and I love the shower in our bathroom. Huge!"

"Ours, too," Camille agreed, relieved to find Lara in a more chatty mood. "What's on your agenda today?" she went on, deciding to sit back and let the actress do the talking.

"First . . . the casino!" Davis laughingly cut in. "I hear the celebrities are gearing up for quite a show in there. I've got to be in on that action."

"Ugh. Go ahead without me! The pool is where I'll be," Lara chirped. "I bought six new swimsuits for this cruise, each with a matching sarong wrap and sandals, and I plan to wear every piece of clothing I brought along."

"Are you guys going ashore at Nawiliwii tomorrow?" Camille asked. "There are going to be tours into the rain forest. Ought to be interesting."

Lara frowned. "Please. Not me. I have no interest in trekking around in a damp muggy forest, ruining my hair and my Cole Haan sandals. Besides, I have heard that there are all kind of weird creatures living in the trees . . . frogs, huge lizards, snakes. Sorry, I'll pass."

"There are no snakes in Hawaii," Max commented bluntly.

"How do you know?" Lara tossed back, fingering a lock of auburn hair that brushed the side of her neck. "Anything could be living out there. No thanks."

"You should come, Lara," Camille urged. "There are beautiful flowers, rare orchids, and exotic plants that you'll never see again. The islands are beautiful. Great shopping, too. Don't you think it would be fun?"

"Nope, I don't. You nature lovers can have it."

"Well, Camille and I will be going ashore every time we can," Max offered, giving Camille a smile and a wink. "We want to take advantage of every opportunity to enjoy this exotic adventure. I can't wait to go ashore. We love to shop, and I want to hike into a volcano . . . snorkel, too. We're going to try it all."

"Have at it," Davis replied. "As long as I can stay on board, out of the sun, and at a blackjack table, I'll be fine."

Camille shot Max a puzzled glance, then shrugged. *Each to his own*, she thought, studying the menu that a tanned young man handed to her.

As they continued to make small talk while waiting for their food, the sun ascended higher into the sky, passengers began moving about the ship and the *Sea Wind's* cruise began.

They sailed all day under a clear blue sky, and when night fell everyone set out to enjoy the evening. Camille and Max attended a comedy show in the main lounge featuring DeJay Junior and a parade of new, hip comics who were launching their careers on the cruise. Davis settled down in front of a slot machine with a glass of Scotch and a handful of one-hundred-dollar bills, remaining in the casino while Lara table-hopped in the Crystal Room, chatting with other celebrities featured on the program.

The next morning, when they reached their first port of call, Nawiliwii on Kauai, Camille and Max ventured ashore to travel in a four-wheel-drive Jeep into the lush rain forest where they saw strange and beautiful foliage, orchids, hibiscus, and tall leafy ferns. Next, they kayaked down the Hulei River, an adventure Camille would never forget, and ate dinner in a grass thatched hut while native musicians and dancers performed.

The *Sea Wind* remained in port overnight, and the next day sailed on, serenaded good-bye by a chorus of scantily dressed Hawaiian girls dancing on the beach. The luxury liner floated on to Lahaina on Maui, where Camille and Max visited the enchanting whaling town and explored the nearby West Maui Mountains and its 10,000 foot volcano and crater; then on Hilo and Kailuna Kona, where more incredible adventures awaited.

While on board, Camille and Max dined with interesting people from all across the country, exchanged contact information with wealthy black professionals, and personally chatted with quite a few of the celebrities—most of whom were turning out to be very agreeable to posing for photos or joining them for drinks. They were royally serenaded, feted, and embraced by the sensuous Hawaiian people, making Camille fall in love with the islands.

However, Davis and Lara, who did not have an interest in learning about the Hawaiian culture, remained on the ship at each port of call. Davis was either glued to a stool in one of the subdued, well-appointed bars with a glass of Scotch in his hand, or at a blackjack table in the casino. Lara lounged on the sundeck day after day, in skimpy designer swimsuits, reveling in the attention that her adoring fans eagerly heaped upon her. Left alone every day, Lara smiled and chatted with the strangers who eagerly vied for her attention, rarely able to enjoy a meal without interruption or a stroll across the deck without a proposition.

Feeling sorry for Lara, who Camille felt deserved more attention from Davis, she finally convinced the actress to come along on a shore excursion to a pineapple plantation with her and Max—an overture she quickly regretted having made. First, Lara was late arriving at the appointed spot to leave the ship, forcing Max and Camille to lag behind and wait for her. Arriving at the tour bus, it was impossible for Camille and Max to get seats together, so Camille squeezed in between two retired schoolteachers in the back, while Max sat up front, with Lara sitting behind him. During the ride to the plantation, Lara leaned forward, her lips next to Max's ear and whispered to him the entire ride, leaving Camille fuming as she watched.

Once they got off the bus and began the walking tour, Lara boldly held onto Max's arm and flirted and cooed and teased him relentlessly, making a spectacle of herself while creating a great deal of commotion. The other tourists on the excursion loved her. She posed for photos, signed autographs, and generally became the highlight of the tour, taking the spotlight from the young male guide and his explicit commentary, which faded next to the actress' exuberant outbursts of appreciation for the attention from her zealous fans.

Throughout it all, Camille gritted her teeth and kept quiet, not wanting to embarrass herself by validating the insecurity that was creating an acidic churning sensation in her stomach. The afternoon turned out to be the most miserable day she spent on the cruise and Camille made up her mind that it would never happen again.

Back aboard the ship and alone in their stateroom, Camille let loose.

"I resent the way you tolerated, and even seemed to enjoy, Lara's blatant flirting."

"God, Camille, she wasn't flirting. *Acting* would be a better word."

"I don't care. She was shameless and embarrassing. As far as I'm concerned, Lara Stanton can fry in the sun by pool every day. She will never tag along on any of our outings again," Camille told Max as they dressed for dinner.

"Don't be so sensitive," Max laughed. "Lara's touchy-feely ways don't bother me. She's an actress. It's all about being seen. This is an all-star cruise, remember? The people want to get close to the stars. That's what this is all about, and her behavior today was nothing more than an attention-grabbing act. All celebrities are like that."

"Maybe so, but not with my husband," Camille tossed back, hating herself for having confirmed her jealousy to Max. "From now on, if Lara starts hanging all over you, you better not stand by in silence and let it happen, Max. That is disrespectful to me." She went over to the open door that led out to the veranda and gazed over the water, catching the ending of a spectacular sunset. She turned to face Max. "I do feel sorry for her . . . the way Davis ignores her, but that is not our problem. We are not responsible for making sure she has a good time. I don't want her tagging along with us anymore."

"Fine," Max grumbled, before entering the shower and slamming the door, leaving Camille flushed and anxious as she stared back out to sea.

CHAPTER 20

Camille took a chocolate-covered strawberry from the fruit plate on the small table between her and Max and bit into it, savoring the rich sweetness of the berry. The *Sea Wind*'s midnight buffet had beckoned to her and Max, encouraging them to taste many of the exotic offerings that had been spread out in an elaborate display, accompanied by a mind-boggling selection of wines and dessert liqueurs. They had started with lobster bisque and caviar and worked their way through dishes of chicken, fish, goat, lamb, and an array of side dishes with gusto, topping off the gastronomic feast with champagne and bittersweet chocolate-covered berries.

"Delicious," Camille murmured, easing forward, her low-cut dress revealing quite a bit of cleavage.

"It can't possibly be as delicious as you," Max whispered, leaning close, his eyes moving from her plunging neckline back up to her face.

Camille's breath caught in her throat when their eyes met, and after finishing off the strawberry, suggested, "Why don't we go back to the room? I think we're finished here."

"Exactly what I was thinking," he agreed, rising to lead the way.

Lighthearted and slightly high from having drunk so much champagne, they made their way along the open deck toward the passageway that led to their stateroom, giggling and enjoying the balmy, tropical night. After arriving at their cabin, Camille shed her party dress and slipped into a flowered wrap, then went to sit on the side of the bed. It had been a crazy, wonderful evening and the elaborate buffet had enhanced her feeling of euphoria. She lay down, waiting for Max to join her, and when he slipped in beside her, she opened her arms and drew him down, caressing the back of his head.

Max snuggled close, then kissed her face, neck, shoulders, and the soft place between her breasts. "You're beautiful tonight . . . every night for that matter." His voice was low, but steady. He untied the belt that held Camille's wrap in place and pushed the soft flowered fabric off her shoulders. After putting one hand at her waist and the other beneath her hips, he eased her to the middle of their king size bed, and then dimmed the stateroom lights. He shed his robe and reached for her with strong, familiar hands.

The weight of Max's body atop hers made Camille feel secure, safe, and newly fallen in love, despite the fact that they had been married so long. His slightly crooked smile still excited her, his large, but gentle dark brown hands still heated her up, and her heart still raced whenever he reached for her in bed. Tonight, the skin on Max's back felt warm and soft to Camille's touch, while the firm muscles of his arms created an excitement that underscored her desire for him tonight. Fused to Max, Camille's body moved with his in a practiced rhythm driven by the vow she made to him twenty-two years ago. And as he kissed her, stroked her, made love to her, Camille reminded herself that Max was the perfect man for her, and he gave her as much love as she could ever hope to receive. She and Max were lucky to be together, still in love and looking forward to the future. They had survived disappointments that had tested their marriage, but had not given up.

The next morning, Camille dropped her towel over the back of one of the *Sea Wind*'s colorful deck chairs and hurried into place as the aerobics instructor's voice boomed over the ship's deck, "Hustle up. Hustle back. Grapevine left, grapevine right." Stepping forward, then back, Camille slid her feet from side to side and swung her arms left and right, easily keeping up with the much younger participants in the aerobics class. Her mood was upbeat, her legs were strong, her back was straight, and she knew she looked good in her red and black Adidas workout shirt with matching spandex shorts, which Rochelle had picked out for her—along with a shameful number of new outfits for the cruise. Camille's jet-black curls bounced with each twist and turn, as she pushed her forty-two-year-old body to cooperate, hoping the effort would incinerate the horrendous number of calories she had consumed at the midnight buffet last night. Despite the faintest remains of a hangover, she had gotten up and struggled to make the 7 A.M. aerobics class, as she had done without fail since the second morning at sea. No way was she going to punk out now—not midway through the cruise.

Camille inhaled, exhaled, stepped and jumped, while the sports deck began to fill up with sunbathers hurrying to claim deck chairs and settle in to catch the morning rays. The huge Hawaiian sun was cooperating fully, shining round and bright above a flat sheen of blue water that stretched to the shores of Kailua Kona.

The warm breeze off the Pacific Ocean brushed Camille's buff-colored face and shoulders, making her wish that this was her first day at sea and not the middle of the cruise, wishing to prolong the sensuous adventure as long as possible. By this time next week, the Afro All-Star Celebrity Cruise would be over and the ship would be back in port at Honolulu. She and Max would be hurrying to get ashore, and on to the airport, and eventually back to Houston. The thought of leaving this exotic paradise to resume their daily grind made Camille worry a bit. What if the perpetual sadness that had lifted on New Year's Eve resurfaced?

So far, five days of sailing the Hawaiian Islands in luxury aboard the *Sea Wind* had banished her depression entirely. She had three more days of sunshine and leisure ahead of her in which to swim in the blue pool, take long walks along the ship's decks, eat romantic dinners with Max and make passionate love to him, making it difficult to give up this idyllic sojourn for the fast-paced routine facing her when she got home.

The cruise had been exactly what she and Max had needed: time alone to celebrate their love, talk about the future, and put their financial worries behind them. They were back on track and focused, with life moving along as she had hoped. If only she could say the same for Jaiden.

As Camille gathered her things and headed to her stateroom, Jaiden's latest outburst rang in her ears. The argument they had had the day before leaving for the cruise had been one of their worst. To calm things down Max had wanted to relent and let Jaiden go to Florida for spring break with her roommate, Mona, and her boyfriend, Rod, but only for a few days, not the entire vacation period. However, Camille had been adamant: Jaiden was to stay at home while they were gone and hit the books. Her first semester grades had been disastrous: Two Ds, one C and an incomplete in Art History. Not acceptable, in Camille's opinion, and she was worried that Jaiden was not taking college seriously.

She is spending too much time with Rod, Camille surmised, and she had to do better. With the house to herself, she ought to be able to put in some serious study time. Jaiden had exploded, acting as if the world would end if she did not go to Florida with Mona and Rod.

Too bad, Camille thought, clenching her jaw. First, she knew very little about Rod, and was beginning to sense that he was not the best influence on her daughter. Jaiden had sent Camille a photo of her and Rod sitting on his motorcycle, and Camille had been less than thrilled to see the intricate tattoos covering Rod's bare arms, which were crossed defiantly on his chest. He was cute, had a lot of attitude, but since her conversation with him on New Year's Eve, she had only spoken to him once—when he had answered Jaiden's cell phone with a short, "Hold on. I'll get her," when Camille had asked for Jaiden. Was he the reason Jaiden had cut her beautiful thick brown hair and had streaked it with blond highlights? What would be next? A tattoo? A ring in her nose?

Sighing, Camille lifted her black curls off her neck, adjusted the plastic clip holding her hair in place, and then headed toward the elevators leading back down to her stateroom to shower and dress before meeting Max for breakfast at the Bistro. Hopefully, he had gotten up and gone to the business center to take care of a fax that he wanted to get off today, but it wouldn't surprise her if she found him still buried under the covers where she had left him snoring loudly this morning. He'd certainly been the party boy last night, closing down the karaoke bar, then the midnight buffet.

Last night. Camille grinned. She and Max had enjoyed the buffet—without Davis and flashy Lara. They had dressed in their best evening clothes, with Max looking quite handsome in his dark pinstripe suit, the newly emerging streaks of gray at his temples underscoring his rugged sexuality, and not aging him at all. Camille had actually grinned back at the envious women in the dining room who had turned their heads to watch him when they entered, noting their obvious envy, making her proud to be Mrs. Maxwell Granville.

The sheets still smelled of Camille—of the rose-scented perfume he first bought for her in London years ago, and which she quickly adopted as her signature scent. Max turned over onto his stomach, pulled the pillow from the other side of the bed to his chest, and buried his face in the soft white cotton. He inhaled, and then smiled as the familiar scent of his wife brought him fully awake. After twenty years it was still all good, and as he lay there thinking about last night, he felt himself becoming aroused all over again.

They had acted like newlyweds last night, drinking too much champagne, making entirely too much noise in the corridor while returning to their stateroom, where they tumbled into bed and made love twice before falling asleep.

Camille was too good for him, Max knew, and he would never take her love for granted. He had messed up once—ten years ago, and he would never make that mistake again. The thought of losing her made his heart nearly stop. Getting away like this, had been a wise move, because he could concentrate on Camille and give her the attentions she deserved.

Running Vendora was demanding, but he was finally making money again. Since their grand reopening, customers had begun to make dinner reservations two weeks in advance, and the nightclub that they had created in the ballroom was standing room only from Thursday through Saturday nights. Max was willing to put in long hours and work his ass off to make his place successful, profitable, and special.

His place? he thought wryly. *Davis Kepler's* supper club, was a more accurate description, he realized, especially in the wake of the press coverage they had received on the grand reopening. Davis's connection to Lara Stanton and the actress' appearance had overshadowed Max's role in the operation, his family's legacy, and the historical significance of the house.

Davis. Max paused to think about his new partner. Too bad he and Davis didn't share more than their desire to make the business a success. They had enjoyed a few turns at the gaming tables at the new Indian casino, but other than that, they spent little time together. He was Hollywood. Max was Texas. Davis was flashy, brash, and determined to become a significant player in restaurant/nightclub circles. Max was conservative, understated, and more concerned with making a comfortable living for his family than a name for himself. His and Davis's personal worlds were light years apart.

The more time Max spent with Davis, the more he came to understand that, like many bachelors, Davis enjoyed risqué entertainment and flashy women—his girlfriend, Lara Stanton, for example, who had nothing in common with Camille. Davis's idea of a good time was a lap dance at a gentlemen's club, or a game of cards in a smoky club with a bunch of cigar-smoking guys, while exotic dancers in tight shirts waited on them. It boggled Max's mind the way Davis could spend money, of which he seemed to have an unlimited supply.

At Vendora, he often personally picked up the tab for parties of eight to ten at a time, after serving them four-course dinners with three kinds of wines, all to impress his guests—who, at least tipped the employees well. However, Max had no complaints, as long as Davis's lifestyle did not interfere with his management of Vendora.

Davis's innovative promotion was working. Vendora *was* attracting younger, upwardly mobile African-American professionals, and those who had already made a significant mark in the creative, social or business worlds. It was a totally different crowd than had frequented the supper club in years past, one that spent freely and demanded the best in food, drink, and entertainment. Money was flowing in, but it was also flowing out, and Max was certain that once they worked through the expenses of the initial rollout phase, profit margins would rise. On paper, it appeared as if he was right.

With a jerk, Max tossed back the bedcovers, raced into the shower and turned on the coldest water he could stand. He showered vigorously, anxious to clear away the fog of last night's overindulgence—he had to get dressed and up to the business center on the Sunset Deck and get a fax off to his insurance agent before meeting Camille for breakfast. Davis and Lara were supposed to join them, too.

He stepped out of the beige and gold marble shower, toweled off, and then walked through the stateroom, gathering up clothes he had tossed aside last evening. The suite was a luxurious 300-square-foot ocean view stateroom with a veranda that could accommodate eight people, an entertainment center with TV, VCR, and DVD players, and direct dial phones. Every day Paolo, their cabin steward, placed fresh flowers and fresh fruit in the suite, along with fluffy terry robes, fragrant bath oils, and an assortment of newspapers from around the world. Booking this opulent deluxe suite had cost him a bundle, but he had no regrets. In his way of thinking, he and Camille deserved the best. Moreover, he was willing to work as long and hard as he had to, to provide a first-class life for his wife and his daughter, and would give them everything they wanted as long as he could.

He had big plans for the next few months, and felt confident that his financial resources would be sufficient to make them happen.

First, he planned to add a grotto-style waterfall to his swimming pool; then a new BMW for Jaiden—if her grades improved. For Camille, a trip to Paris next fall. She deserved that, and more.

Max pulled on his tan khaki shorts and a brown knit shirt, and was reaching into the top drawer for his socks when he came across the red velvet box that he had tucked into a corner. He pulled it out, opened it, and then removed the three strands of large pearls intertwined with pale peach coral beads. Looking at it, he hoped his gift would help Jaiden get over the fact that things had not gone her way. It had been best for her to stay at home and study instead of flying off to Florida. He knew Jaiden was spoiled and somewhat demanding, and even though she would turn twenty in August and had nearly completed her first year in college, she was still his little girl. He glanced at the direct dial telephone on the desk, and thought about calling her. It would cost him, but why not? He picked up the phone and dialed his home number, needing to speak to her.

When she came on the line, he grinned to hear a lilt in her voice, thinking she was back to her old self.

"Hello. How's my girl?"

"Dad! Hi. This is a surprise . . . I'm fine. Well . . . not really fine, but okay, I guess."

"Come on, Jaiden. Don't start with that."

"But it's true. No one's here. This place is like a ghost town and there's nothing to do. Everyone I know went *somewhere* but me!"

"How can there be *nothing* to do? Don't you have some serious studying to do, anyway?"

"I can't study *all* the time. I'd rather be in Florida. I talk to Mona every day."

And Rod, too, I'm sure, Max thought, knowing that she most likely was using the home phone for daily updates, and not the long distance minutes on her cell.

"Her father rented the most fabulous beach house. Mona says all of our friends are there, too. Everyone but me."

Thank God, Max thought, but said instead, "I'm sure Nici's around. You two are speaking again, aren't you?"

"Yeah, but she's in Galveston."

"What about Kevin? Give him a call, go out. No one said you had to spend your entire spring break in the house."

"I'd rather do that than go out with Kevin," Jaiden muttered crossly.

A long pause gave Max time to think of another way to smooth things over. When Camille had insisted that Jaiden stay home during spring break while they were on the cruise, he had fully supported the decision, nixing Jaiden's plans to go to Florida with Mona and Rod. He did want Jaiden to have fun, and she deserved a break from books, exams, and the pressure of boosting her GPA, however, he couldn't sanction rewarding her with a vacation in the sun after bringing in such miserable grades.

"Your mother . . . and I did what we thought was best," he finally stated.

"Best for Mom, you mean," Jaiden threw back. "I know she did this because she's mad that I cut and bleached my hair. She's still mad about that."

"I don't think so. It's your hair. And, I kind of like it, myself."

"Dad, why didn't you make her change her mind about me going to Florida? Huh? If you had taken my side, she would have given in. I know it."

The phone was silent again, and when Max replied, he chose his words very carefully. "That's not fair, Jaiden. We both want you to have fun, but you knew the conditions when you went off to school. Do your best, and no fooling around. You have not done your best and your grades were awful. Get them up, and maybe you'll get more privileges. An incomplete in Art History. I don't understand."

"Well, I didn't need Art History anyway. I only took it because Mona did. We planned to visit art galleries, study together, you know? The non-credit wouldn't have hurt my GPA anyway, and I can take it over in summer school."

"From now on, young lady, try to put in more study time and don't spend so much time with your friends, including Rod."

"All right. Don't yell. You just don't like Rod, do you? That's what this is about?"

"I'm sure Rod is a decent young man, even though I've never had more than a two-sentence conversation with him. However, he shouldn't be the center of your college life. You've got to get serious about school, Jaiden. Now is a good time to start."

Jaiden mumbled an unintelligible reply, and Max knew it was time to change the subject, not wanting to be too harsh. He could sense that she was feeling somewhat under attack, and abandoned, too. "I bought something very special for you in Lahaina yesterday. The shopping was great. Your mother and I made a day of it. I think you're going to love what I found."

"What is it?" Jaiden asked.

"Can't tell you now. A surprise. You'll have to wait until I get home."

"Not fair, but I guess I can wait. Where's Mom?"

"Up on deck. Never misses her morning aerobics class."

"Aerobics? What time is it out there?" Jaiden asked.

"Seven . . . A.M."

"Wow. It's nearly noon here. And I've gotta go. I'm on my way to pick up my dry cleaning. Tell Mom hi."

"I will. See you next week. We'll be home on Wednesday," Max ended.

He hung up, went to the in-room safe inside the stateroom closet and punched in the combination to open the security box. He slipped Jaiden's pearls into the safe beside the velvet pouch containing Camille's diamond bracelet and matching earrings, closed it, and then went to the bed and sat down. He thought about his conversation with Jaiden, and was glad that he had called her, though sorry that she still seemed so angry. Usually, Jaiden did not remain mad at him for more than a few hours, but with Camille, it could be an entirely different story. Jaiden had been known to hold a grudge against her mother for weeks, sulking, pouting, and giving her the silent treatment. Max hated it when his two favorite women were not getting along, and if it had been up to him, he probably would have relented and let Jaiden go to Florida with her roommate's family, but only for a few days. She was a good girl. He trusted her, and had never put pressure on her to ace her classes, as she had done in high school. However, this first year away at college had not gone well. She had slacked off terribly, become distracted by a young man, he decided. Max sighed, recalling how distracted *he* had become when he first met Camille.

With the top of her mother's silver Audi convertible down and the sun shining on her face, Jaiden zipped in and out of traffic as she sped down the freeway, trying to guess what her father's surprise might be. He had good taste, always bought the best, and had never bought her anything that she didn't immediately love. Whatever it was, Jaiden knew it had to be classy, special, and of course, expensive.

She glanced up into her rearview mirror and caught her reflection, satisfied with her new ultra-short, spiked brown hair, now streaked with blonde highlights. She had lacquered it with hairspray so that the wind would not muss it up, once she decided to take her mom's jazzy new car, which she was seldom permitted to drive. But what the heck? She was stuck in Houston, and her mom was cruising around somewhere in the Pacific Ocean, having a blast—why not take advantage?

Thin gold hoop earrings swayed against Jaiden's honey-tan cheeks and her bronze-tinted sunglasses with 14 carat gold rims made her eyes look as if they had been sprinkled with flecks of gold. Momentarily taking her eyes off the road, she lifted the sleeve of her white tee shirt and checked her new tattoo—"Rod, Forever" encircled by tiny chain links on her upper right arm. It was perfectly drawn, but still very fresh, and hurt terribly. She had gone into the city yesterday, found a tattoo parlor on Montrose Boulevard that seemed clean and safe, and told the artist what she wanted. An hour later she had walked out with Rod's name inscribed on her arm. He was going to love it, she decided, reaching over to press the volume button on the CD player, sending Erykah Badu's smooth voice out into the wind.

Jaiden missed Rod terribly. Since New Year's Eve, they had become more like a real couple, and they spent most of their free time together. Rod had not told her that he loved her yet, and had made it clear that, though he liked having her around, he did not want her to move in with him. Occasionally, she spent the night, but still kept her clothes and personal things at her dorm, respecting his desire to protect his space. She never dropped by uninvited or asked him where he was going or what time he would return. She had learned that asking too many questions made him distant and moody. However, little by little, Jaiden was making progress. If only she had been able to go to Florida with him. That would have been the bomb!

Her thoughts returned to her dad, and despite the gloomy picture she had painted for him . . . mainly to make him feel sorry for her, being in Houston in April was not so bad. At least the weather was great, not yet stiflingly humid as it was going to be very soon, leaving her feeling as if she had been wrapped in a heavy blanket and rolled out to sea.

But, she thought, tightening her jaw, *this is not as nice as Florida, where I ought to be right now.*

After picking up her dry cleaning, Jaiden made another stop: Ray's Cash & Carry, where she bought two limes, a frozen pizza, a carton of Virginia Slims, and a six-pack of Coors—luckily her friend Tim was working today. He never asked for ID, and even though her dad had plenty of brew at the house, he had probably counted it and would notice if any was missing. Why court that kind of a hassle? After finishing her errands, Jaiden headed back home, parked the car in exactly the same spot where it had been, and went inside.

After stowing the beer and the pizza in the refrigerator, she took her cigarettes up to her room, pulled out her English Literature book and began to read. The silent house suddenly seemed eerie, and she realized that the absence of noise was distracting. Studying at home, all alone, was nothing like studying in the dorm, when on any given day music blared from the CD player, the TV ran non-stop, and a girlfriend or two might be lounging on the sofa, chatting on a cell phone or playing solitaire on the floor. Now, no one was yelling, "Hey, what's up?" No one was spilling gossip about a classmate. No one was chattering about plans for tonight. Jaiden suddenly grew angry, resentful, and depressed. Why did her mom have to spoil everything for her?

Unable to concentrate, she glanced at the digital clock on her dresser, tossed her English Lit book aside and headed back downstairs. It was twelve-thirty in the afternoon. *Not too early for a beer*, she decided, pulling a can from the refrigerator. She popped the top and downed half of it in one long gulp.

CHAPTER 21

Max signed his name beside Davis's at the bottom of the Riverview Security insurance policy, then leaned back in his chair and glanced around the *Sea Wind*'s sleek business center. He began tapping his pen on the desk, anxious to lock in the numbers today and save thousands of dollars in premiums. It had taken weeks to negotiate the terms of the policy, which included health, disability, dental, and life insurance for the employees of Vendora, including himself and Davis. He had personally overseen every detail, and since he had borrowed so heavily against his old life insurance policy, saw this as a way to start fresh.

Max got up, went to the fax machine on the other side of the room, and slipped the first page of the contract into the feeder tray. He punched in the insurance company's fax number, his mind already moving on to the meetings he needed to schedule with the sales representative from Golden Delight, a company that offered a variety of expensive luxury food items to restaurants, as soon as he returned to Houston. The new chef at Vendora used many of their products to create dishes for the restaurant's discriminating clientele.

The first page of the policy slipped through, but the second page jammed in the machine. Max went over to the attendant and asked for assistance.

"It's been acting up all morning," the young man apologetically informed Max. "The technician will be here in a minute. We'll have it back in order as soon as possible."

"How long do you think that will take?" Max worried. He had to get this to his agent before twelve o'clock today.

"Oh, about twenty . . . thirty minutes, I'd guess," the attendant replied.

Max scowled, not anxious to sit around the business center and wait for the technician. Camille was probably already at the Bistro waiting for him.

"Or," the young man added, "You can leave your folder with me and I will fax it for you. I can deliver your originals to your stateroom personally."

The tension in Max's jaw eased. He nodded, and then said, "Fine. Let me get the pages in order." He went back to the table and began sorting the pages, thinking that his new policy would be an attractive benefit in assisting him and Davis in securing highly-qualified employees. He was pleased with the changes he and Davis had made and was relieved that the supper club's gross earnings for the first quarter of the year had been the highest since he'd first opened.

Davis had decided to focus on the big spenders—people accustomed to luxury and exclusivity who didn't think twice about paying high prices for quality products and service. He had been adamant: If Vendora provided what the target clientele wanted, they would come to the supper club and spend their money, no matter the cost. Max now saw that Davis had been right.

At first, Camille had resisted this shift to a pricier menu and more extensive wine list, fearing no one would be willing to pay such high prices for food, beverage, and entertainment. However, Max had been steadfast in his support of his partner: Houston needed a unique entertainment and eating establishment targeted toward wealthy African Americans with discriminating taste. In addition, the grand reopening had served as the catalyst to spread the news throughout Houston, and even nationwide, that Vendora was an establishment that offered quality food and drink in a unique setting.

As Max arranged the pages of the contract, Davis's elaborate signature caught his eye, as well as the single word beside it— Owner. The word still annoyed him, and today it sent a chill of emptiness through Max, and for the first time, made him nervous. Davis was gambling too much, and his isolating behavior had begun to worry Max.

As soon as the *Sea Wind* had pulled out of the harbor, and the Grand Casino had opened, Davis had virtually disappeared, settling in at the roulette and blackjack tables, a glass of Scotch nearby.

Max had had no idea that Davis's love of gambling was so intense. Max had learned his lesson about taking risks with money at the blackjack table in Louisiana and knew better than go that route again. There was no need to take those kinds of risks now. However, Davis thrived on the excitement that came with taking risks, and he had made it clear on the first day of the cruise that he was going to take advantage of the gaming opportunities while at sea.

Now, Max wondered if such an appetite for gambling might lead to other problems. What was bothering Davis? What drove him to gamble so incessantly, and what else he did not know about his partner?

Shaking off a feeling of apprehension that he did not like, Max took his folder to the attendant and told him, "Be sure to get this off before twelve o'clock . . . noon. It's vital, understand?"

"Yes, sir," the man assured Max, accepting the folder with a smile.

Davis's hand trembled as he slid three short stacks of chips into the betting box printed on the green felt table. Nervously, he glanced up and locked eyes with the casino dealer, a stocky, dark-skinned man with wisps of thinning black hair slicked across the top of his head. With one eyebrow raised, the man opened his mouth slightly, as if poised to ask a question, but said nothing, and then began to deal the cards.

Davis refused another card and sat with both hands on his knees, his eyes flitting over the ace of clubs and the seven of hearts that the dealer placed in front of him. The dealer had drawn an eight of diamonds, faceup, while the second card remained hidden. A lump of excitement eased into Davis's throat as he grazed his palms along his thighs and waited, aware of the murmurs of interest coming from a small knot of onlookers who had gathered to watch the play. He stubbed out his cigar, blinked against the stream of smoke that drifted into his eyes, which were raw and burning from lack of sleep and too much Scotch, and calculated what might come next.

The dealer revealed his second card—an ace of clubs.

Davis bit down hard on his bottom lip and pushed back from the table. Enough. He could not take any more. It was seven-thirty in the morning. He had been at the tables since four A.M., outplaying and outlasting several serious gamblers. He had won many hands, but not nearly enough to make up for his losses.

Heading toward the exit, he thought about Lara, who was most likely up and dressed, her makeup perfectly applied, but fuming mad because he had not been there when she woke up. He thought about Max and Camille, too, recalling that he had promised to meet them for breakfast in the Bistro, having decided to try and spend more time with them. However, he certainly wasn't in the mood to eat anything right now. The thought of sitting down to bacon, eggs, and sausage made Davis's stomach turn over. His mouth was dry. His head ached. He had lost fifty-eight-thousand dollars. Every dime he had withdrawn from the Romero's bank account before he left Los Angeles.

No, he decided, turning around and heading back to the table. *I have to stay exactly where I am until I've recouped Reet's money.*

Lara Stanton's stateroom on the Emerald Deck smelled of lavender—a scent she swore could banish a migraine, chase away the blues, depress the appetite, and make any man within a twenty-foot radius lift his chin and turn her way. Inside the *Sea Wind* cabin she shared with Davis, she had tucked small silk sachets of the sweet-smelling herb among the folds of her sheer teddies, peignoirs, panties, and bras that were stowed in the cabin's dresser drawers. A large bowl of lavender-colored potpourri sat on her vanity beside a crystal atomizer filled with perfume. She had matching creams, lotions, gels, and powders, too.

A stream of warm water sluiced over her head and down her slim, straight back as she gathered her long auburn hair in one hand and doused it with a generous amount of shampoo. Inhaling her favorite scent, she let the shampoo bubbles slither through her fingers as she mentally calculated how much credit remained on her *Sea Wind* expense card, determined to use every dime of the shopping money Davis had given her before the end of the cruise.

She had gone to bed at twelve-thirty last night, exhausted after a riotous appearance on stage with Monique—her favorite female comic, and left Davis sitting on the sofa watching a western movie on the DVD player. She had slept like a bear in hibernation and when she awakened this morning, discovered that Davis was gone. Lara had a good idea where he was: the Grand Casino, where he seemed to have taken up residence. When had Davis decided to slip out? She knew he was a night owl, who never slept more than four hours a night, while she insisted on eight hours of beauty sleep to maintain her movie star complexion. Though Davis had promised to have breakfast in the Bistro on the Sky Deck, along with Max and Camille, Lara would not be surprised if he didn't show up.

She thought about her day. After breakfast, she planned to have a pedicure and a French manicure in the beauty salon, then make another foray into the Hibiscus Boutique where she was going to splurge on a pale aqua bikini that she had had her eye on since the first day of the cruise. It was terribly expensive, more than she usually spent on the tiny squares of fabric that barely covered her pubic hair and her breasts, but it was exotic and unique—shimmering blue-green silk. She simply had to have it for her upcoming photo shoot for *Guys & Girls* magazine next month—and she could write the purchase off as a business expense.

"And," Lara murmured to herself as she lathered suds into her hair, "that aqua bikini might be the catalyst to inspire the editor to put me on the cover." Smiling, she tilted back her head to rinse out the shampoo, added conditioner, and continued her task, wondering if Roberto Simona had forgiven her for not canceling her commitment to go on the cruise after he pushed up the start date for *Daddy's Baby Doll*, her highest paying role. The hefty advance on her seven-figure salary had come in handy to pay down on the mortgage of her new house in Brentwood. What a great feeling—to own a piece of property in one of the most exclusive neighborhoods in California. She might be cash poor right now, but that wouldn't last long. As soon as shooting started she would receive another fat check, and though she certainly didn't want any problems, she knew Roberto could shoot around her for ten days.

It took an hour for Lara to dry and curl her glossy auburn hair, thirty minutes to apply her makeup, and another fifteen to decide what to wear. She finally chose a pair of tiny white shorts with matching halter top, thin-strapped aqua Cole Haan sandals with a three-inch wedge, and six turquoise-studded silver bracelets with matching earrings. After applying a liberal amount of sun block to her shoulders, arms and legs, Lara tossed the aqua and red striped Fendi tote that she had bought in Honolulu over her shoulder, pulled on her Valentino sunglasses and left her cabin.

Camille waved Max over, watching him closely as he threaded his way past deck chairs, knots of passengers gathered around white metal tables, and children playing near the bright blue pool. He appeared to be more rested and relaxed than she had seen him in months. His face, arms and legs were tanned a deep brown and his standard shipboard dress of white tennis shoes, khaki shorts and a soft knit shirt, gave him a jaunty, carefree appearance—one that Camille rarely saw. At home, Max started every day in a suit, dress shirt and tie, wearing his business attire long into the evening due to the many formal functions and social events he hosted at Vendora. Even on the weekends when he should be free to play golf, go fishing, or simply do nothing—he spent far too much time on his cell phone, talking with Davis or straightening out some emergency with the club. Today, Camille thought he looked ten years younger and sexier than ever. Was there any wonder Lara Stanton couldn't keep her hands off him?

"Hey," he said, giving Camille a quick kiss on the lips before sliding into the chair beside hers. "How was your aerobics class?"

"Crowded," Camille replied. "Guess we're all trying to work off the calories we've packed away over the past few days." She pulled off her red and white sweater and draped it over the back of her chair, then signaled for the waiter.

Max sat back, stretched out his long brown legs and lifted his face to the sun. "Gorgeous day," he said, pulling his sunglasses over his eyes.

"Sure is," Camille replied, accepting a menu from the waiter.

"I spoke to Jaiden," Max remarked, his focus remaining on the clear blue sky.

"Oh? She called?"

"No, I called her before I went to the business center to take care of that insurance policy." He pulled back his legs and sat up straight. "She's not in a very good mood. Says she's bored. Feeling abandoned."

"Ah, too bad," Camille replied, her remark tinged with sarcasm. "Did she think spring break was going to be fun after the grades she brought home? How's her studying going?"

"Okay, I guess. She didn't say much about it, only complained about not being in Florida with Mona."

"And Rod, too, don't forget. I know Jaiden said that Mona's parents would be at the beach, but I don't know them . . . and I don't know Rod that well either. I don't regret holding my ground on this one," Camille stated, jerking open her menu. "She can be mad at me all she wants. I don't care."

Max lifted a shoulder in response. "Well, you know Jaiden is good at pouting."

"You're the one who spoils her. You give her anything she asks for, and she thinks she'll always get her way. I'm sorry Jaiden is upset with me, but I could not back down. I hope this experience has taught her a lesson."

"I think so," Max murmured, scrutinizing his menu.

Camille could tell that Max was unhappy about the friction between her and Jaiden and felt caught in the middle of their mother-daughter power play—one of many they had had since Jaiden went off to college. Jaiden had counted on her father to step in and take her side . . . something he had done far too often, fueling Jaiden's belief that she would eventually get her way if she worked on Max long enough. Early on, Camille had known that it would be up to her to draw the line on her daughter's demands because Max surely wouldn't. Camille sighed. She loved Jaiden very much and wanted her to be happy, but she was not about to let her daughter's foul mood ruin her day.

Camille studied the menu, suddenly very hungry, and decided to splurge one more time and eat whatever she wanted. After all, once they returned home, she was going to be busy at the travel agency, and her meals would most likely be whatever she could grab from a drive-thru on the run.

"I'm going to splurge," she told Max. "Think I'll go for the *Sea Wind* Champion . . . in the mood for waffles." Pausing to consider whether she ought to add a side order of sausage, she prompted, "What about you? Hungry?"

When Max did not answer, Camille glanced over at him and saw that he had not even opened his menu yet, and was paying no attention to her chattering. Frowning, she followed his gaze across the crowded deck and saw what was holding his attention: Lara—in tight white shorts and a halter top that barely covered her ample bosom, which jiggled provocatively with each long-legged step she took as she teetered precariously on four-inch wedges.

All across the deck, people gaped, their eyebrows raised onto sunburned foreheads, but Lara haughtily ignored their stares and crossed the deck in a runway model's strut, head high, her bronzed shoulders thrust back.

Camille had to admit—the woman was gorgeous, with long brownish-red hair that caught the sun and actually sparkled with glints of gold. She was tall and trim, with a complexion that was lightly tanned and incredibly smooth. Camille could not help staring either, thinking that Max had been right—Lara thrived on attention, and would get it any way that she could.

Lara approached the table where Camille and Max were sitting, bringing along an invisible cloud of lavender scent. She paused, lifted her sunglasses and pointedly stared at Max, then said in a whispery voice, "Hello, you guys. Where's Davis?"

"Haven't seen him this morning," Max replied, watching Lara wiggle into the chair next to his. "He'll probably be along."

"He better not be in the casino," Lara stated, her nostrils flaring as she picked up her menu. "If he is, I'm gonna be pissed. The other night, he promised to take me to do karaoke and never showed 'til way after midnight. I don't get it. He comes all the way to Hawaii and stays cooped up in that smoky casino. What a jerk. He's gonna be sorry for treating me this way," Lara finished in a whiny voice, and then rested her long fingers on Max's arm, as if turning to him for help.

Camille silently blew air through her parted lips and sneaked a glance at Max, who calmly removed Lara's hand, then gave her a sympathetic smile. "I have to agree with you, Lara. I had no idea Davis liked to gamble so much. What's going on with him?"

Lara made a short, dismissive laugh. "Going on? Davis *loves* to gamble. Surely you knew that, didn't you?"

"Well, no," Max replied, giving Camille a worried glance. "I didn't know how *much*. We went out to a casino near Houston a few times, but he never made any serious wagers."

Lara playfully punched Max on the arm. "Well, I've been to Vegas with him *more* than a few times. Can't get enough. Blocks out everything when he's rolling the dice, holding a handful of cards, or sitting in front of a roulette wheel. I'm telling you, I know from experience. Once, in Vegas, he won the big jackpot . . . seventy-five thousand, I think. Boy! We really lived it up that weekend. He spent six thousand in one night at Circus Circus. Set up everybody at the bar and let the tab roll. He likes to do crazy things like that. Davis is a pretty good guy . . . most of the time. He is generous with his winnings, I'll say that for him." She paused and giggled, then said, "I think it's so he can play the big spender . . . spread his money around. But, that's all good with me."

"Hmm," Max murmured, in obvious concern. "That explains a lot."

Lara picked up her menu as she continued speaking. "You see?

He's not here, and I am really ticked off. He's already warned me that tomorrow, he is going to be in some big blackjack tournament . . . lasts twenty-four hours. He'll be gone all day. And, he had promised to escort me to the All-Star Luncheon. I dread going alone." She touched the side of her mouth with her index finger. "Max. Would you go with me? Please." Turning to Camille, she smiled. "You wouldn't mind lending your husband to me for a few hours tomorrow afternoon, would you?"

"That's entirely up to him," Camille answered in a flat tone.

"Well . . ." Max started. "I guess I could . . . if you can't get Davis to . . ."

"He won't change his mind. I know that," Lara finished.

"Well, I don't know. If you don't mind?" Max started, turning to Camille.

"I'm sure Davis would appreciate his partner standing in for him," was all that she could manage.

"Okay, Lara. I'll do it," Max brashly replied, as if denying the request would be giving in to Camille's silent pressure to turn her down.

"Gee, thanks, Max. You're a doll," Lara said in a breathy stream of words.

Camille rolled her eyes and pretended to read her menu.

"You know, I feel like going into that casino and yanking Davis out," Lara went on, "but I couldn't cause a scene. The press would jump on that."

"If you want . . . I'll talk to him," Max offered.

"Would you?" Lara pleaded, her mascara-laden lashes fluttering at Max. She reached up and pulled him into a quick hug. "I really would appreciate that. He has paid no attention to me since we got on this ship. I want to go dancing, have some fun, and not sit in my cabin while he's at the tables. Would you tell him that for me, too?"

"Sure," Max replied, letting Lara's information about his partner sink in. Davis had a gambling problem, and Max had to figure out how to confront him about it. A compulsive gambler was not much different from a drug addict or an alcoholic. Davis needed help, but would Davis listen to him? Max wondered, suddenly losing his appetite.

Lara turned to Camille and pressed her large breasts onto the table, nearly popping them out of her halter. "Camille, you've got a real good guy, there. Better watch him. I might try to steal him away."

"I doubt you could," Camille said in a light, though level tone, hoping her retort effectively carried her message. With a jerk, she shifted her attention to an adorable baby girl seated between her parents at the table next to theirs. Anything to keep from looking at Lara. Or Max.

Toward the end of the meal, three of Lara's fans, two young men and a teenage girl, approached the table and asked for her autograph. She graciously agreed, signing her name with a flourish under her photo in their commemorative cruise program books. Then, the waiter asked for permission to film himself with her on his video camera. Max did the honors before he and Camille said good-bye and left Lara at the table talking excitedly about *Daddy's Baby Doll* and how eager she was to get back to L.A. to begin shooting.

Ten minutes later, Davis arrived at the Bistro, looking wired and disheveled, though he did have a glint of joy in his puffy, bloodshot eyes.

"Sorry," he mumbled, sliding into the chair next to Lara's. "Couldn't get away."

Lara shifted around and bored dagger-filled eyes into him. "Then why the hell did you bother to show at all? You don't think we waited, did you?"

"No. No, I ran into Max and Camille in the passageway on the Emerald Deck. They told me you were still here."

"Well, I'm finished with breakfast now, and I may as well be finished with you, too!" She gave her halter top a hard tug and pushed her sunglasses higher onto her nose, then jerked around and focused on the blue water beyond the ship's rail, her shoulder turned toward Davis. "I can't believe you stood me up for breakfast so you could stick around that stinky casino and gamble. That's disgusting, Davis."

"Gimme a break, Lara. I knew what I was doing, and I had to hang in there once I was on a roll. Is this worth missing breakfast with me?" He reached into his pocket and pulled out a roll of bills. "Here, go buy that bikini you been talking about, and whatever else you want."

Surprised, she studied his offering for a long moment, even lifting her sunshades to make sure the money was real. "That's for me? You mean it?"

"Sure. I apologize. I know I left you hanging, but somethin' in my gut made me stick it out at that table. I think it was the dealer. Snooty kinda guy. I knew I'd get my payback, and I did."

Lara let Davis press the thick fold of bills into her hand, then quickly slipped the money into her colorful Fendi bag. "Well, it wasn't very nice . . . standing your partner up like that, too. Max is worried about you, and I think he's kinda pissed."

"Forget about Max. He didn't say anything about being pissed when he stopped me in the hallway a minute ago. Anyway, what's he got to worry about? If it weren't for me, he'd be back in Houston singin' the blues about his washed-out supper club. Things are going great, Doll, and you and I are gonna spend the rest of the day together. I promise. Tonight we go to dinner at Club Tropica and have some fun. Okay? No more gambling. I promise."

"You better not be lying to me, Davis. I mean it. I've gotten more attention from strangers on board this ship than I have from you since the day we left Honolulu. It's kind of embarrassing, going everywhere alone, never being seen with my . . . boyfriend."

"That's gonna change, Doll. As of now, and for the rest of the cruise, I'm all yours," he told her, stroking her arm, his eyes fastened on her eye-popping cleavage.

CHAPTER 22

The Hawaiian moon hung in the sky like a huge pale disk, casting a silvery glow over the water, lighting the secluded veranda where Camille and Max were spending the evening. Inside their intimate retreat, Camille shifted in her chaise longue and extended her champagne glass for a refill, giggling when the bubbly that Max poured for her fizzed up and dripped onto her sheer flowered wrap. She brushed the spill away, then lifted her champagne flute to his, preparing to make a toast.

"To the *Sea Wind*," she said.

"To my wonderful, understanding wife," Max countered.

"A *most* understanding wife," Camille agreed, clinking the rim of her glass against his.

"I'll accept that," he tossed back, a satisfied smile touching his lips. He took a sip, and then kissed Camille quickly, yet seriously. "The luncheon with Lara was a bore. The food was great, but once we entered the dining room, she began flitting from table to table, giving air kisses to her 'friends,' and throughout the program all she did was high-side the other celebrities: Her catty remarks truly wore on my nerves. For all the *escorting* I did, I could have had lunch with you."

"Well, you did your good deed for the day," Camille replied in a tight voice, trying not to let her annoyance show.

Both were quiet, having no need to say more. They had spent the remainder of the afternoon playing shuffleboard and swimming in the pool, and Camille was glad to have Max all to herself this evening.

"God, this is so much better than dressing for dinner and going into the dining room," Max commented, resting his head on the edge of his high-backed chair as he turned to look at Camille. "Not sorry are you?"

"Sorry?" she gave a short, curt laugh. "Not at all. I don't think I could've pushed my feet into a pair of shoes tonight."

A comfortable lull followed as they continued to sip champagne and watch the water—a rippling sheet of black that shimmered like fluid satin—until Max broke the silence with a serious tone.

"I'm worried about Davis," he said. "I checked the casino while you were showering, and he wasn't there, but I don't know what he might be up to now. I've got to talk to him."

"Hopefully, he's spending the evening with Lara," Camille replied rather sharply, suddenly tired of all this talk about Davis and Lara. To Camille, they both seemed vain, self-centered, and overly impressed with themselves. It would suit her fine if she did not see or speak to either one until they boarded the plane in Honolulu.

"I can't stop thinking about what Lara said about Davis at breakfast yesterday. Do you think he could be a compulsive gambler?" Max wondered. "I never would have thought so, not from what I know about him."

"I think Lara was exaggerating," Camille suggested. "She can be a bit dramatic, as you know. I wouldn't spend too much time worrying about what she said. She was pissed at Davis, wanted to make him look bad in your eyes. Probably made everything up."

"Maybe . . . but she made me think about something," Max replied. "Davis has been going back to the West Coast about once every three weeks. Could be he stops in Vegas . . . or someplace else, and gambles. I don't know what he does when he's not at Vendora. Never thought much about it . . . but if his gambling is more than an occasional bet for fun, then I've got to watch out. I'm not feeling too comfortable about what's going on, and if he has a *real* problem . . . it could affect Vendora." Max got up, walked over to the veranda's rail and stared out to sea as if penetrating the future. "Think I'm off base?" he asked, glancing back at Camille.

"Off base? I don't know, but you know what? Davis is on *vacation* and if he wants to spend his time in the casino, so what?" Camille suddenly snapped. "You know what else, Max? I'm tired of hearing you talk about Davis . . . and Lara. Forget about them. I don't care what they do as long as they don't ruin *my* cruise."

Max pursed his lips and stared at Camille. "That's a pretty selfish thing to say."

"Selfish? Please. So, you don't think I should be upset because Lara Stanton has the hots for you and is brassy enough to tell me to my face? You know you enjoy being around her. She flatters you, and you love it. Admit it, Max. All her sweet cooing and helplessness turns you on."

"Stop it, Camille. That's not true."

"It is. You let her use you . . . and rob us of time together. This is our cruise, Max. Why let Davis's recreational vices get you so upset that you can't enjoy spending time with me? If I'm being selfish, so be it."

"You're wrong, Camille, about everything. Lara means nothing. She's a bit lonely, and I guess I felt sorry for her."

"She could have gone to that stupid luncheon with anyone. Any man on this ship would have jumped at the chance to be seen with her and you know it!"

"Damn. I wish you had said all of this earlier. I wouldn't have gone."

"Forget it," Camille said, folding her arms in disgust.

"All that may be true, but I'm still going to talk to Davis about this gambling business, and his heavy drinking," Max decided. He got up and started back into their stateroom. "I have to get some answers."

"Tonight?" Camille spat out, shocked. "Max. It's one o'clock in the morning. What can you possibly accomplish by charging him up tonight? Don't you dare leave this cabin. You'd better not let Davis ruin our evening," she ordered, though she knew he already had.

Turning back to look at Camille, Max paused, then relented and returned to the veranda and sat down. "First thing tomorrow morning, I'm going to have it out with him and find out what's going on."

"Whatever," Camille grumbled, furious that the romantic mood she had wanted to create had been shattered. After a few minutes of sitting beside Max in strained silence, she got up, went into the bathroom and rummaged through her toiletry case until she found the bottle of antidepressants that she had brought along—just in case. The pills would put her to sleep, and that was what she wanted. No tossing, turning, or worrying about anything tonight. All she wanted to do was forget about Lara and Davis and the friction they were causing. She swallowed the pill and climbed into bed, leaving Max sitting on the veranda, staring out to sea.

* * *

Inside her luxury stateroom on the Emerald Deck, Lara stubbed out a cigarette and blew smoke through her nose, mentally chastising herself for chain smoking five cigarettes in less than an hour. She had given up smoking so many times, and had even undergone hypnosis two years ago. However, the stress she was enduring tonight had brought the habit back full force.

Davis could have sent me a bottle of champagne to let me know he is thinking about me while he's gambling his ass off, Lara silently grumbled, fidgeting with the amethyst pendant at her neck. She was dressed in a pale pink blouse of soft silk and matching slacks that hugged her curvy hips, with four-inch high stiletto heels on her feet. She had thought she would be dancing at Club Tropica right now, instead of cooped up in her stateroom, puffing cigarettes. Davis had turned out to be a true disappointment.

Davis. He was handsome, great in bed, and quite the businessman, but his gambling had gotten out of control. *If I had known he planned to spend our Hawaiian cruise in the casino, I would have stayed in Los Angeles. Once the ship docks, I'm breaking off with him. He'll be sorry he's treated me like an afterthought.*

Lara angrily ripped off her blouse, yanked off her slacks, and threw on a short negligee. Even if Davis showed up and begged her to go dancing, she wouldn't be seen with him in public. She poured a double Scotch and water into a glass and picked up another cigarette.

Inside the Grand Casino, Davis checked his watch. Two-thirty-six in the morning. Lara was either cursing him to hell or fast asleep, he decided, disgusted with himself for letting her down again. He had planned to play the slots only for an hour, then take her dancing at Club Tropica, but things had not gone as he'd hoped. He should have quit hours ago, while he had been up ten thousand dollars, but he hadn't . . . and now his luck had run out.

He growled at the bartender, "Chivas on ice," ordering his fourth drink in the past hour. He knew he was drinking too much, too fast, but did not care, and had no plans on slowing down. He stared morosely at his reflection in the mirror behind the bar. He was a stranger to himself. Too much Scotch and too little sleep had flushed his complexion reddish-brown. Dark shallow half-moons had settled under his eyes and bristly stubble covered his chin. Davis let out a dispirited sigh as the gravity of what had just happened set in, and in a moment of panic, fleetingly considered going to the ATM to withdraw more money from the Romero's account. Thank God, Reet had not changed the PIN for the business account, leaving Davis with access to company funds. However, he knew he owed Reet too much already. He could not get another dime on his American Express card, and didn't dare use Vendora's company credit card—Max tracked each transaction with zealous scrutiny. Somehow, he had to undo this mess.

He could not move. His shoes felt as if they had been weighted down with sand. He swallowed back a surge of nausea, trying hard not to get sick right there in the casino. How was he going to handle this? He had to get the money to replenish Romero's account before Reet got wind of what he'd done. If he didn't, he might as well jump ship.

Disappointment and self-disgust rushed through Davis. Buying into Max's supper club had taken every cent he'd been able to scrape together, and now he had exhausted his line of credit at his bank, too. Flexing tired fingers, Davis drew in a deep breath, tilted back his head and tossed down his drink in one quick swallow. When he lowered his chin, he caught Max staring back at him.

"What's going on, Davis? Why are you still here? If you've got a problem, we'd better talk."

"I got no problems," Davis said, his gruff tone thick with Scotch. "You're not in this, so butt out."

"Sorry," Max countered. "As long as we're in business together, your gambling problem *is* my concern."

"Problem?" Davis laughed aloud. "You've been listening to Lara, haven't you? The bitch. What's she doin' talking to you about me and what I do?"

"Don't blame Lara. Anyone can see you're in trouble."

Davis laughed again, narrowing bloodshot eyes at Max, "Well, buddy, you can't even begin to imagine the troubles I have."

"Then maybe you should tell me," Max offered, assessing Davis, who looked as if someone had slapped him around and roughed him up. Clearly, he was out of control and close to being very drunk. His face was red, his eyes were puffy, and his hair was matted with perspiration.

"I don't need a lecture, from you," Davis snapped. "You may be my business partner, but not my keeper. I need cash, not advice. If you don't have cash to hand out, then get the hell out of my face."

Stunned by Davis's nasty remark, Max held his tongue, turning to the bartender to order a beer. Davis was desperate, that was clear. The only thing he wanted was money, and all that Max wanted, at that moment, was to get Davis Kepler out of his business and out of his life. He had made a big mistake partnering with him and now he had to straighten it out. But how? His mind reeled with disappointment, while a seed of hope began to grow. He accepted his beer from the bartender, and then gave Davis a sympathetic once-over. "How much cash do you need?"

"How much?" Davis threw back. "More than you can get your hands on tonight, I'm sure."

"Maybe not. How much would it take for you to get back in the game . . . to play long enough to cover your losses?"

Hearing that, Davis perked up and began studying Max with bleary brown eyes. Quickly, he blurted out, "Twenty-five thousand. If I had twenty-five thousand, I know I could recoup my loss in three or four hands."

Max turned to face the blackjack tables, bracing his back against the bar. He twirled his drink in the palm of his hand as he watched the dealer tossing cards to the players. He spoke to Davis as he watched the action. "And what would I get for helping you out of your jam? What's in it for me?"

"What do you want?" Davis said, now clearly interested in hearing what Max had to say.

Max did not hesitate to answer. "Full ownership of Vendora."

The ringing of bells that signaled another win at a slot machine filled the space of time it took for Davis to reply. "You're crazy!"

"You're in trouble. I don't know what is going on, but I think you'd better take this risk. That *is* what you are best at, isn't it, Davis? Taking risks and coming out a winner?" Max deliberately taunted Davis, hoping his partner's desperate mind-set and dispirited condition would work in Max's favor.

"You're saying that you'll stake me the $25,000?"

"Yeah, and if you can increase that stake by as much as a dollar, you win the bet."

Davis squinted suspiciously at Max. "If I win, I keep my share of Vendora plus all the cash?"

"Yes, and if you lose, full ownership of Vendora reverts to me and you walk away. Our partnership is finished."

"Four hands of blackjack," Davis decided.

"Three," Max easily countered.

Davis rubbed the stubble on his chin, considered the wager, then said, "You're on."

Max smiled as Davis rushed back to the blackjack table and reclaimed his former seat. He went to the cashier and, using his American Express card, secured the chips and asked for a sheet of *Sea Wind* stationery. He quickly drafted the terms of their agreement, signed it, and took it over to Davis.

"Fine," Davis said, glancing it over, then quickly scribbling his signature to the bottom of the document as he placed his bet on the green felt table.

Holding the signed wager, Max moved to stand behind Davis, his heart pounding, his fingers crossed. If this worked out as he hoped, he'd be free of Davis and back in control of his company. If he lost, he'd be out $25,000—but that, he could live with. He thought about Camille, fast asleep in their stateroom. He had remained on the veranda until he was certain she was asleep, then he had come inside, locked the veranda doors, and pulled the blackout curtains over the glass doors, shutting out the bright silver moonlight. He had not been able to stop thinking about how best to approach Davis, and after realizing that he could not wait until morning, he had dressed and slipped out of the stateroom, leaving quietly as Camille still slept. He hated that they had argued, and was going to make up for it tomorrow, hopefully, with the good news that Davis and his flashy girlfriend were no longer a part of their lives.

Davis gave an involuntary shiver, squinted down at the cards, and jerked himself more fully erect. He pulled back his shoulders and attempted to smooth his rumpled dress shirt, then scooted closer to the table. He zeroed in on the two cards before him: A queen of hearts and a six of diamonds, then placed his right hand over the cards and motioned that he would stand. *This has to be the one,* he prayed. *It just has to.* He had everything riding on this wager with Max and he had to win if he wanted to survive. Losing Vendora did not loom as much of a worry in his mind as dealing with Reet once he learned that Davis had stolen fifty-eight grand from him.

Davis stuck his tongue between his teeth and bit down hard, steeling himself for what would come next. His heart raced and his mouth grew dry as he waited for the mandatory hit the dealer had to take. Quickly, the dealer placed a king of hearts next to his eight of hearts. Eighteen! The dealer had eighteen! Onlookers gasped in disappointment. Davis groaned and shut his eyes. The first hand had been a bust. Max smiled, his heartbeat quickening to see the cards fall in favor of the house, and continued to smile as he watched the next two hands play out, silently congratulating himself for having had the guts to take the biggest risk of his life.

Davis cursed each card that the dealer revealed, and when it was over, he had lost the entire amount that Max had advanced him, as well as his stake in Vendora.

Neither man spoke as the dealer cleared the table. Davis stood, brusquely pushed past Max, and strode out of the casino in a huff. Max went to the bar and calmly ordered champagne to celebrate his good fortune. He reread the terms of the agreement, flooded with satisfaction. His most risky wager had paid off for him and he was back in control—Davis Kepler was history.

Max left the casino, got into the elevator and descended to the Emerald Deck, his mind buzzing with the ramifications of what had transpired. He had regained his company, and was returning to Houston as his own boss. What a grand feeling, he thought, hurrying along the corridor, trying to decide if he should wake Camille up and give her the good news or wait and spring it on her in the morning . . . maybe with a surprise breakfast in bed. As he turned the corner and entered the passageway leading to his stateroom, he saw Lara coming out of hers. She was wearing a long embroidered silk robe that hung open, revealing a see-through pink lace negligee underneath. A huge amethyst on a gold chain was hanging around her neck. Her feet were bare, her hair was loose and wild, and her strained expression betrayed her anger.

"Lara! What's wrong?" Max asked, stopping outside her stateroom. "Where are you going?"

Her bottom lip quivered as she focused on Max. "Into that Goddamn casino to drag Davis out." She slurred her words together in a mushy whine. "We were supposed to go dancing tonight. Spend the evening together. He promised. No one treats me . . . Lara Stanton . . . like this! I'm gonna go in there and embarrass the hell out of him and I don't care who sees me do it."

"Hold on, Lara. He's not in the casino." Max hesitated, wondering if he ought to tell Lara what had gone down. Davis was upset, and was most likely drinking his blues away somewhere, and it would not be a good idea for Lara to go traipsing around the ship, looking for him. Not in this condition. It was clear that she had been crying, and drinking.

"If he's not in the casino, then where is he?" Lara demanded.

"Let's step inside . . . out of the hallway," Max urged, helping her open her stateroom door. "I'll tell you what I know."

Once inside, Lara paced her luxury suite in frustration while Max told her what had happened in the Grand Casino.

"Serves him right," she spat out, going to the bar to fix a drink. "Have one?" she offered Max.

He shrugged. "Why not? It's been a hell of a night. Vodka, neat, if you have it."

"Are you kidding? This bar is as stocked as Vendora's. Davis made sure of that," she remarked, pouring a hefty shot of vodka into a glass, and then handing it to Max. "I am so through with Davis Kepler. He's an ungrateful user." Reaching across the bar, she grabbed the slick Afro All-Star Celebrity Cruise souvenir program and flipped it open to her full-page photograph. "See this?" She stabbed the page with a pink lacquered fingernail, and then read aloud from the blurb beneath her picture. "Lara Stanton, *accompanied* by Davis Kepler, owner of Vendora, the hot new supper club in Houston, Texas." She threw the magazine to the floor and glared at Max. "Do you know how much that kind of publicity is worth? I didn't have to do that. And I didn't have to come to Houston for his grand reopening and pose for pictures and meet with the press and sign autographs until I had cramps in my fingers. But I did it for Davis. And what has he done for me? Fly out to L.A. to spend two days a month with me? Desert me aboard this lousy ship? I'm through. If he's smart, he won't *even* come sneaking back here tonight."

Max wiped his fingers across his lips, unsure if there was anything he could say, or do, to calm her down. After all, what she said made sense. Davis had used her, all right, and Max was glad he was no longer involved with him. "I understand what you're saying," Max sympathized. "And now that I have *this* . . ." he tapped the folded piece of *Sea Wind* stationery on the bar, "I don't care if I ever see or speak to him again. I want to go home, run my supper club, and be my own boss. I don't need Davis to make it now."

"Good for you." She lifted her drink in salute, and then said, "Let me see that." She took the agreement from Max, and then picked up a pen from the desk. "I'll even sign my name as a witness to this to make sure you don't get screwed."

*   *   *

A stiff ocean breeze hit Davis in the face as soon as he stepped onto the Sky Deck, however, instead of cooling him down, the blast of wind seemed to increase the sense of suffocation that had come over him inside the elevator. He struggled to breathe, heaving convulsively as he rushed to the ship's rail. Numb with fear and disappointment, he glanced around and was glad to see that he was alone. He leaned far over the rail and pressed his face into the black night, a wide beam of moonlight providing enough illumination for him to distinguish the inky sky from the dark deep water that lapped against the side of the ship.

What have I done? I've lost everything. Vendora. Reet Collins's money. And probably Lara, too, he thought, knowing she must be raving mad at him. If only he had kept his promise to Lara and stayed out of the casino tonight. If only he had stopped gambling while he had been ahead. If only he had not used Reet's money. That was the worst of it. Reet Collins would not give him a chance to explain what had happened or why. He'd send one of his "boys" around to make sure Davis got what was coming to him. Tomorrow the *Sea Wind* would sail on, eventually docking once again at the port in Honolulu. Too soon, he'd be back in L.A.

I have to convince Max to tear up that agreement, he decided. Surely, they could work something out.

CHAPTER 23

Inside the darkened stateroom, Camille awakened from a restless sleep that had been crowded with disjointed images. She turned over onto her stomach, vaguely aware of a bell ringing in the distance and voices in the corridor outside her door. Groggily, she pushed her face deeper into her pillow, shut her eyes tightly, and tried to force the voices away, determined not to allow the late night partyers who were stumbling through the hallway to disturb her. However, the voices grew louder, a pounding noise started up, and she heard someone yelling words that she could not understand.

Camille struggled to sit up, but gave up and lay back down, her body too heavy and her mind too fuzzy to deal with whatever she thought she'd heard. Was it a part of her dream? Brought on by the antidepressant she had taken before turning in? Probably so, she decided, burrowing back into her pillow, anxious to fall back asleep. However, the persistent noises continued outside her door. Eyes open, she blinked into the pitch-black room, which was so dark she could not even make out the form of Max beside her in the inky darkness.

"Open up!" A man's voice boomed outside, then the pounding began in earnest, on her cabin door.

Weakly, Camille tried to pull the bedsheet back but her arms felt like pieces of wood. What was going on? How long had she been asleep? It seemed as if she had barely closed her eyes before this racket began.

A dizzy spell hit her and she could feel herself spiraling down into that safe dark place where everything would be nice and quiet. However, her descent was interrupted when her stateroom door burst open and the shadowy outline of a man appeared at the cabin entrance. He was framed by a ghostly gray light . . . or was it light? she worried, now recognizing the pungent smell of smoke.

The man ran to the bed, grabbed her by the arm and yanked her to her feet.

"Get out! Get out!" he ordered.

"What's going on?" Camille mumbled, struggling against this stranger's pull.

"Fire! Fire! Get out!"

Her mind was a muddle, her nose was stinging from the smoke that the man had brought with him into the room, and her eyes began to water. *"Fire?"* she repeated hoarsely, then turned and screamed, "Max!" She groped blindly into the bed, desperate to awaken him, but her hands slid over cool empty sheets. *Where was he? Still on the veranda where she had left him when she had turned in? In the bathroom?* "Max," she yelled once more. "Max!"

The man pushed her roughly toward the door. "Go, please!" he shouted. "I will get Mr. Granville."

In that instant, Camille recognized the man's voice—it was Paolo, their Filipino cabin steward, the politely quiet man who had been so attentive to them during the entire cruise. "Paolo. Is it you?"

"Yes. Yes. Please hurry!"

"My husband. Get my husband! Check the bathroom. The veranda." Camille screamed, trying to remain in the doorway to see what Paolo was doing.

"I will get him. You go on to the lifeboats," the steward called out to her, giving her a brusque shove into the corridor.

A wave of panic rose inside Camille as she stumbled backward and looked up and down the passageway. *I have to move quickly,* she told herself. *Speed is all that matters.*

In the corridor, a stampede of frantic passengers were scrambling toward the stairwells, pushing and shoving against Camille, who was eventually pulled into their throng. She followed the crowd through the smoky passageway, down a narrow inside stairwell, and on to the staging area for evacuation into lifeboats. Fire alarms were ringing, people were screaming, children crying. Her mind whirled. Where was Max? Had Paolo gotten him out? This could not be happening, and she could not leave without Max.

In a panic, she turned around and pressed into the oncoming crowd that was determined to get to the lifeboats. The smoke was much less thick in the evacuation area and she could see the faces of the people she as tried to shove them out of her way. Frantically, she searched each one. Max was not among them.

"Please. Let me through," she shouted, urging people to give her room to go back to her stateroom. "Please! Let me pass." She groped and pressed and cursed, until a man in a white uniform with gold braid on his jacket grasped her firmly by the wrist.

"Get to the front! Please!" he ordered. "You must keep moving forward. You cannot go back in there!"

"I have to. My husband! My husband is still in our cabin," she shouted at the officer.

"He'll be along. Don't worry. Our staff will evacuate all of the passengers. This way," the officer ordered, brusquely spinning Camille around. Holding her arm very tightly, he marched her to the evacuation area and handed her a lifejacket. How did she put it on? She had forgotten everything that the crew member had explained to her during the mandatory practice evacuation on the first day at sea. Tears streamed down her face as she thought about the drill that she and Max had completed, and how they had joked that everyone resembled stuffed penguins in their bulky jackets, never dreaming they would actually have to wear them!

Horrified, Camille shrugged her arms through the straps and moved into line to get into a boat, her heart pounding, her face wet with tears. A frightened child was crying. Camille swung her attention toward the noise and found herself looking into the face of a terrified little boy who was clinging to his mother's hand. She pressed a hand over her own mouth and swallowed hard, desperate to get control.

Max will be fine. Paolo woke him up and got him out, just as he did for me.

She accepted a helping hand that someone thrust at her and somehow managed to climb into the lifeboat.

Max is right behind me, watching me, trying to catch up with me.

She sat down beside the mother with the crying child and watched the ramp, searching the frightened people waiting for their turn to disembark. She saw a woman with her hair still tied up in the satin hair wrap that she had worn to bed that night, and behind her, a young girl who reminded Camille of Jaiden. The girl was dazed and blank-faced, as if she had no idea where she was or what was going on.

"Where is he? Where is he? Why doesn't he come out? Camille worried. She curled her fingers into a hard ball, focused on the ramp, and willed her body to stop shaking.

Davis hurried to an elevator on the Sky Deck and pushed the "down" button. Nothing happened. He could smell smoke drifting from the elevator shaft and hear fire alarms sounding below. In a panic, he headed to the stairs and made his way down until he eventually emerged on the Emerald Deck. He pushed against the crowd until he came to his and Lara's cabin. The door was open, he ran inside.

"Lara! Lara!" he checked the bathroom, the balcony, even the closet. "Damn! Where is she?" he cursed, swinging around, racing across the hall and into Max and Camille's stateroom, which was also standing wide open.

A thin veil of smoke billowed up and into his eyes, and he shielded them with one raised arm, while frantically waving the other to clear the gray haze that was quickly filling the room. He inched deeper into the cabin, and was both relieved and surprised when he stumbled over Max, who was kneeling on the floor in front of the in-room safe.

Max shot to his feet. "Davis! We've got to get out of here!" he shouted.

"Max! Have you seen Lara? Where is Camille?"

"Camille has gone ahead. I saw her go down the corridor. But Lara, I don't know where she is now. Didn't you see her in the corridor?"

"Shit! No! What the fuck is happening?" Davis cursed, wiping his eyes, starting back toward the door. Suddenly, he stopped and abruptly turned around. He glared pointedly at Max, then down at the safe. "You put it in there, didn't you? Get it out," he ordered. "Tear it up, Max. We can settle this at home."

Max stared at Davis in disbelief, and then pushed him roughly out of his way. "What the fuck are you talking about? I have to find my wife! Get out of my way, Davis!"

Davis remained rigid, blocking the doorway. "You've got to give me that paper. I'll pay back your money. That wager was a big mistake."

"Move out of my way!" Max repeated, slamming both hands against Davis's chest, hurtling him aside.

Davis's hand shot out and he gripped Max by the shirtsleeve, spun him around, and then forced him, face first, against the bathroom door, pinning him down with one arm across his back. "I won't leave without it. Give it to me." He jammed his free hand into Max's coat pockets, fumbled around, then yelled. "It's not on you. It's in the safe, isn't it?"

"Let go of me!" Max demanded, coughing through the smoke.

Davis slammed his body hard against Max's, crashing both of them into the bathroom and into the glass shower door. Shards of broken glass scattered about the room as Max fell forward and cracked his head against the bathtub faucet, creating a huge gash across his temple. Davis stumbled back, stared in horror as Max's blood spurted up and splattered the shower walls, then he fled the room.

Lara had no idea where she was or which way she ought to go. The lower deck was sheer pandemonium, and she had managed to escape it by climbing through an inside cabin window to emerge on the next higher deck. Here, the smoke was heavier than it had been in the narrow passageway below, and she paused to get her bearings, trying to recall the layout of the ship. Which way to the lifeboats? Why was no one else around? What was she going to do?

From below, she could hear the ringing alarms, the passengers screaming, and the shrieks of horror that told her that the fire was raging through the Emerald Deck. So far, she was safe, but she had to keep moving. Higher. Higher. She had to go up. She ran up a flight of stairs and emerged on a deserted section of the deck that was a jumble of old poolside tables, umbrellas, and deck chairs in various states of disrepair. Lara raced, barefoot, to the end of the deck, and into a dark corridor that branched off to the left. Without hesitating, she turned the corner and walked straight into a raging wall of fire. She heard a thunderous cracking sound, followed by a sinister hiss, and before she could flee, the wall in front of her exploded in a tower of flames. Lara lifted one arm to cover her face as a shower of red-hot debris rained down.

CHAPTER 24

Camille climbed out of the lifeboat and onto the walkway that the crew of the *Festa Brava* lowered to accept passengers from the *Sea Wind*. The wooden boards cut into her bare feet, and her nightgown—damp from the sea mist that had sprayed everyone in the lifeboat during their ride to safety—stuck to her body like a sheet of plastic. A man threw a blanket around her shoulders as soon as she stepped aboard the *Festa Brava,* and then escorted her and the other blanket-draped evacuees into the four-story Grand Plaza of the Greek liner that had come to their aid.

The evacuated passengers were agitated and frightened, yet surprisingly calm. They followed the officer's directions and soon settled onto the banquettes, sofas, and comfortable chairs scattered around the lobby to wait for the captain to arrive with news about their fate, and that of those they had left behind.

Camille found a comfortable chair in a secluded corner of the brightly lit lobby and sank into it, then tilted her head back and closed her eyes. Despite her anxiety over Max's absence and her current situation, the lingering effects of the sleeping pill dulled her apprehension.

Please let Max be okay, she prayed. *Bring him out of this horror. Bring him to me.* She chanted those words over and over, wishing she had never taken the damn antidepressant. If she hadn't swallowed that pill, she might have been more alert, more help in getting Max to safety. Had he fallen asleep on the veranda, where she had left him when she went to bed? Had Paolo even searched out there? Her mind whirled with worry until she fell into a kind of

twilight, neither asleep nor awake, but somewhere beyond the un-
bearable pain of not knowing what had happened to Max.

At daybreak, a drizzly, gray morning steeped in gloom, the captain of the *Festa Brava*, a tall black-haired man with a prominent
nose and very stiff posture, arrived with news. A distraught teenager,
who had slumped down beside Camille, gently nudged her. Blinking
her eyes, Camille slowly came to, and immediately remembered
where she was and what had happened. She held her body very
still, as if making a move might bring the horrible images back: The
pounding on the doors. The ringing fire alarms. The thick smoke.
The unforgettable screams. She struggled to focus on the captain,
who had quieted the group and was preparing to speak.

"Welcome to the *Festa Brava*," he started, "though I am saddened
that your visit to my ship is made under such distressing circumstances. I am Gregorio Nevares, captain of the *Festa Brava*. The *Sea
Wind* has been completely evacuated, and its passengers placed
aboard three rescue ships: The *Festa Brava*, the *Caribe*, and the *Grand
Riviera*. I have prepared copies of a list that has the names and locations of the remainder of the evacuees, so that you may locate your
friends and loved ones. All three rescue ships are now headed to
Honolulu where you will be reunited." He paused, then handed a
stack of papers to one of his officers who began passing them out to
eager hands.

"As for the personal property you left behind," he continued,
"your cruise line will make arrangements to get any salvageable
items to you as soon as possible, but I suggest that you be patient.
The in-room safes are fireproof, so anything you put in them will
most likely be intact. As I get additional information, I will pass it
to you immediately. Also . . . if you do not see the name of the person you are looking for on the list . . . please come to see me in my
cabin." With that, he gave the evacuees a solemn nod, and left the
room, his hat under his arm.

When Camille got her hands on a copy of the passenger list, she
scanned it quickly. Lara Stanton, the *Caribe*. Davis Kepler, the *Grand
Riviera*. She read the list three more times as her heart raced, her
stomach sank, and the tears in her eyes blurred her vision. Max's
name was not there.

Jumping up, she raced across the Grand Plaza, stepping over
sleeping bodies as she hurried into the corridor where Captain
Nevares had disappeared. Her heart was pounding so hard she

could feel it hitting the inside of her chest and her throat was tight with fear. "Captain! Captain!" she called out to him, waving the sheet of paper she had crushed in her fist. "What does this mean?" Sobbing, she slumped against the wall, then slid to the floor, where she huddled as the captain turned around and came back to her.

He stopped and looked down at Camille. "Who are you looking for?"

"My husband," she whispered, shaking the piece of paper at him, her eyes asking the question she could not articulate.

"Come with me," Captain Nevares said in a gentle tone, extending his hand. Camille was too frightened to move. When she did not reach up to take the captain's hand, he bent down and helped her to her feet. "Come with me," he told her again, ushering her into a brightly lit room at the end of the corridor.

Camille refused his offer to sit down in the chair positioned in front of his desk, and remained just inside the door, clutching her blanket tightly around her quaking body.

"What is your name?" he asked.

"Camille Granville. Mrs. Maxwell Granville. My husband . . . where is he?"

"Granville," the captain muttered, as he picked up a legal-size piece of paper and ran a finger down it as he read a list of names. When he looked up at Camille, he slowly shook his head. "I'm sorry, Mrs. Granville. Your husband did not make it out."

"What do you mean? He got out. He was behind me. Where *is* he?"

"His body is on its way to Honolulu . . . where the medical examiner . . ."

"No!" Camille shouted. She snatched the piece of paper out of the captain's hand and scanned the list herself, "Not Max! Not Max!" she cried in disbelief, her mind too numb to comprehend the enormity of what was happening.

CHAPTER 25

Jaiden felt trapped. Her head throbbed, her eyes burned, and though the air conditioning unit whirred quietly as it pumped cool air into her sun-splashed bedroom, the space felt stiflingly warm and claustrophobic. With little attention to what she was doing, Jaiden shoved panties, bras, a tie-dyed tank top and several pairs of ripped jeans into her multi-zippered duffel bag, which lay among the tangle of sheets on her rumpled bed. With a pair of white socks clutched in her fist, Jaiden's eyes traveled slowly toward the green digital numbers flashing on the clock on her bedside nightstand. It was eleven-fifty-two in the morning. One hour since her Aunt Rochelle had called to tell her to pack a bag: She was coming to get her. Two hours since her mother had called and initiated this hellish nightmare.

Blinking at the clock, she placed two fingers to her lips and pressed down hard, as if trying to repress the rage and disbelief that rumbled around inside her head and threatened to spill out. Her head felt cloudy, every breath she drew took a great deal of effort, and simply thinking about the news her mother had delivered made her want to crawl into bed and sleep forever. Perspiration and tears wet the front of her red cotton sleep shirt, which she had not yet removed, and her hair was still a mess of tangled spikes, waiting to be combed. If only she could restart her day, awaken all over again and erase her mother's phone call. If only she could forget that her world had been torn apart by the four short words that her mother had barely managed to say: Your father is dead.

Tears slipped down the side of Jaiden's nose, but she did not bother to wipe them away. She knew her face was blotched, bloated and creased with pain, and the wetness of the tears suddenly felt oddly comforting and cool. Moving in a fog, Jaiden threw the white socks into the duffel bag, zipped it up and shoved it off the bed, then lay down among the tangle of geometric printed sheets that were still damp with her tears. She curled onto her side, drew her knees to her chest, and pressed her fist so hard against her teeth that she felt the skin break on her middle finger.

How could such a thing have happened? How did the fire start? How many others died? Thank God, her mother had managed to escape, but why hadn't she been able to wake her father up? Jaiden's thoughts fastened on her mother's words, initiating a fresh wave of pain. It must have been a horrendous ordeal, Jaiden thought, her mind shifting over images of what it must have been like aboard the ship when the fire broke out. The panic. The screams of the passengers. Thick dark smoke. Her father struggling to escape. Her mother's scramble to get into a lifeboat. As soon as the officials in Honolulu released her father's body, her mother would bring him home. The thought of her mother having to fly back to Houston alone, with her dad in a body bag in the baggage compartment of an airplane, made Jaiden begin to tremble.

She squeezed her eyes tightly shut, unable to fathom her mother's pain. She was alone—a widow now—and forced to accompany her husband home in a box. Sobs tore through Jaiden, spilling out in groans that she tried to muffle with the sheet, exhausting her once more. She could not imagine her mother, her home, or her future without her father in it. He had filled up their lives with his exuberant presence. He had been generous, fun loving, and the center of their lives. A loving father who had been so young-at-heart and energetic.

Jaiden's thoughts swung to her mother. How in the world was *she* going to recover from this? Jaiden wondered, aware that her mother had loved her father very much. Even though they had had their share of disagreements, they always made up.

Sitting up, Jaiden wiped her eyes with the edge of her sheet and forced her sobs into submission. Gaining control, she pushed herself off the bed and went into the shower, where she turned on the coolest water she could stand and stood stoically beneath it. She had to be strong for her mother, who was going to need a lot of help. Everything had changed, and there was nothing to do but accept it. Nothing would be as it had been before the telephone rang this morning.

* * *

Two things struck Reet Collins as soon as his banker, Sammy Lee, asked the question, "Who, in addition to you, has access to the PIN to Romero's primary account?" First, Davis Kepler had the number; and second, the report Reet had seen on CNN television this morning about the fire aboard the cruise ship, *Sea Wind.*

He had been stunned to hear that hip-hop rapper, DeJay Junior was dead; the comedienne, Monica, had been trampled by the crush of passengers and had suffered a broken leg and a concussion. She was on her way to Cedars Sinai in L.A. in critical condition now. Actress, Lara Stanton remained hospitalized in Honolulu with third degree burns to her face and neck, but her boyfriend, Davis Kepler, had managed to escape unharmed.

Reet groped for a cigarette and turned his banker's question over in his mind.

"Why do you ask?" his words rumbled out as he tensed his finger around the handset to his phone.

"Several pretty hefty withdrawals were made from three different Republic branches and one ATM machine several days ago. As I was looking over the transactions, it didn't seem to me that you would have gone to those locations to get cash."

"How much are we talking about?"

"A total of fifty-eight thousand dollars."

"What the fuck?" Reet shot to his feet, thrown by the size of the withdrawal. He began to walk back and forth in front of the huge window at the back of his high-rise apartment with its view of the Hollywood hills. He had thought Sammy was talking about a few hundred bucks. But fifty-eight thousand? Had to be someone from the inside. "Davis Kepler," he finally growled. "Got to be him. No one else. I was stupid not to change that PIN when we parted ways."

"Yeah, well, I agree with that. You left him an opening and it seems he's taken advantage of it." Sammy paused. "Do you know where he is?"

Reet filled his lungs to bursting with cigarette smoke, then blew it out in an angry whoosh. "Shit, yeah. He better be on his way back from Honolulu right now. He was on that cruise ship that caught fire."

"But he's okay?" Sammy inquired.

"Yeah, from what I've heard, he got out fine, but he's gonna wish he died in that fire when I get through with him."

"You want me to take care of this?" Sammy offered. "I can call him up . . . have a friendly chat . . . see what I can get out of him. Or do you want to bring in the authorities?"

"No, no police. I'll handle Davis. Thanks for keepin' an eye out for me, Sammy."

"That's my job," Sammy told Reet, before hanging up.

Davis is a stupid fuck, Reet thought, fuming over the idea that his longtime friend would steal money from him. Reet was well aware that Davis had used money from Romero's before—to fund those impulsive jaunts to Vegas, but he had never borrowed more than a few thousand and had always put the money back. It had amused Reet to watch Davis squirm when questioned about the missing funds, and keeping him under the threat of being found out had kept Davis in his place. He didn't deserve a classy chick like Lara Stanton, either.

Lara. Poor Lara. Reet could not imagine how desperate she must be. In the hospital! With burns to her face? What a tragedy! He wondered how serious her injuries were and if she would recover in time to start shooting *Daddy's Baby Doll*, her first big salary picture. He thought back to the last time he had seen her, two weeks before she was to leave on the cruise.

Reet had invited her to lunch with him at Spago—wanting her to be the first to know about his plans to open Romero's II in Las Vegas, and give her an opportunity to get in on the deal. She had arrived in a cloud of her signature lavender scent, wearing a deep rose-colored pantsuit that complemented her auburn hair, which shimmered in a red-gold cloud around her flawless face. He had never seen her look more radiant or relaxed. When he commented on her vibrant appearance, she had told him in a sassy tone, "And why shouldn't I be happy, Reet? Everything is going exactly as I had hoped. I received a huge advance on my next picture, I bought my dream house, and Davis and I are about to head off to Hawaii for the Afro All-Star Celebrity Cruise. How romantic is that?"

"You two are really tight," Reet had commented, thinking Davis must have a whole lot going on between the sheets to keep Lara so satisfied. "Be careful, though. You might wind up falling in love, getting married . . . you'd break the hearts of all those men who dream about you at night."

"Might fall in love?" Lara had laughed. "Honey, I am already. And I plan to marry Davis. He just doesn't know it."

Reet had been surprised to hear Lara talk that way. What was so damn special about Davis Kepler? He was good-looking, but he was also a two-bit, power-hungry hustler who was chasing some goddamn dream of becoming a wealthy mogul one day. He never could do things right. Too impulsive. Too independent. Too impatient. That was why he had been caught pushing the little white pills and had gone to jail, while Reet had walked away and had never done prison time. In the streets, Davis simply did not know how to calculate his odds, though Reet had to admit, the guy could play some mean blackjack, and win.

"Don't move too fast, where Davis is concerned," he had cautioned Lara in a fatherly way, fully aware that he had been the one to introduce them. However, hooking up with Davis might mean taking more of a risk than Lara understood. "Davis can be a bit . . . how do you say? Impulsive?" Reet had finished. "He likes to do his own thing . . . doesn't like to take advice. Could be, he might not be the marrying kind."

"Oh, I know that, and it doesn't worry me," Lara had blithely tossed back. "Once I get him alone—in the middle of the Pacific under the spell of a full Hawaiian moon, he'll do anything I say. Watch. By the time we get back, I'll be engaged to Davis."

"Maybe," Reet had hedged. "But while you're cruising, don't let Davis spend too much time in the casino. The guy gambles way too much . . . and sometimes with other people's money."

"Oh? Really?" Lara paused. "Well, he has never asked me for a dime. Don't worry. If he gambles aboard the *Sea Wind*, he'll be using his own money."

Reet had let out a sigh of relief to hear that Lara was not financing Davis's expensive hobby. "Speaking of money," Reet had gone on, "What do you think of my plan to open Romero's II in Vegas?"

"Fabulous," she had told him, pulling out her checkbook. "Count me in." She had written him a check for one-hundred-fifty thousand dollars without another word.

Now, Reet felt sick to his stomach to think of her so far away, all alone, and in pain. He liked Lara; she was not like most actresses— phony broads only out for themselves. She was a real original, and one of the best investments he had ever made. When he had been seeking capital, she had jumped right in with start-up money to invest in Romero's. He wondered how long it would be before she came home, and when she did, he planned to be there for her.

CHAPTER 26

"Sorry, Buck. We're not releasing the names of the deceased at this time," Neil Windman told the insistent reporter from KBXX-FM in Houston, well aware that Buck Boudreaux expected more from him than this standard no-comment reply.

"What about the cause of the fire? Has that been determined?" Buck pressed.

"Not yet. The investigation is under way, but it'll take some time to pin that down." Neil sucked back a yawn and leaned over his desk, supporting his forehead with one hand. He had been at it since six-thirty yesterday morning, soon after the call from his boss had come in, informing him of the *Sea Wind* disaster.

The news had jolted Neil awake and he had pulled on a pair of khaki Dockers and a tan short-sleeved shirt, while talking on his cell phone as he made his way to his car. Skimming along the deserted Galveston beachfront road in his white Land Rover, the drive from his townhouse on West Beach Road to the Tropica Cruise Lines headquarters had taken Neil exactly twelve minutes, and once he entered his office, he had either been on the phone or on his computer, managing the deluge of press inquiries and instructions from his superiors.

E-mails flooded his Tropica Cruise Lines mailbox, and details of the *Sea Wind's* disaster were steadily unfolding. The international press had already descended, demanding information about passengers from Europe, Asia, and South America—many of whom were now stranded or hospitalized in Honolulu. Neil dreaded the next wave—inquiries from family members of the deceased—and he was waiting for the final list of the names of those who would not be coming home.

After massaging his forehead, he sighed and took a quick sip of the cold coffee in his Tropica Cruise Lines mug. Frowning, he forced himself to concentrate on Buck's next question.

"Can you at least verify that four Houstonians are among the fatalities?" Buck asked. "Come on, Neil. Give your buddy a break. I won't use your name as my source on the air."

"I know you wouldn't, Buck, but I can't verify anything right now. I've given you all I can. Be patient," Neil stated in a firm tone, wishing he could tell Buck everything he knew.

Neil and Buck Boudreaux had been friends since their high school days at Surfside High, which stood on a shady street only two miles from the Port of Galveston where Neil now sat in his office overlooking the bay. They had played football together in high school, double-dated while attending the University of Houston, and Neil had been Buck's best man when his friend had married his college sweetheart. A bachelor at forty, Neil held onto the hope that one day, after he found and wooed the right woman, that Buck would return the favor at his wedding.

During the early days of his seventeen-year career with Tropica Cruise Lines, Neil had traveled from one international port to another, learning every phase of the cruise line industry. Sailing from the Caribbean to the Mediterranean and throughout the Pacific Ocean had fulfilled his desire to see the world, introduced him to places that had captured his imagination as a child, and allowed him to romance beautiful women in each port of call. However, none of the exotic beauties had been able to hold him in her country one day longer than his assignment required, or entice him to return once he was ready to move on. As the years slipped past, Neil matured and eventually settled into his assignment at the Port of Galveston, finding satisfaction in staying put in familiar surroundings. However, he had never given up on his belief that one day he would find the woman with whom he was meant to share his life, in Texas, where he belonged.

Now, Neil was anxious to get off the phone and back to his e-mails where minute-by-minute updates were being fed to him from the investigative team in Honolulu. He lifted his head from his hand, brushed a damp lock of black hair from his forehead and swiveled in his chair, turning his back to his office door. Finally, he told Buck, "As soon as I get the okay to release additional information, I'll give you an exclusive."

"Call me first?" Buck verified.

"Promise," Neil confirmed, already removing the phone from his ear.

As he clicked off, he absently scanned the activity at the busy Port of Galveston where the *Trade Wind*, the largest cruise ship in Tropica's fleet, was now docking at Pier 23. He could have told Buck that the body count from the *Sea Wind* fire was sixteen, that one-hundred-thirty-one passengers had been injured, three of them in critical condition, and were now hospitalized in Honolulu; and that the bodies of four Houstonians were, indeed, on a plane headed for Bush Intercontinental Airport right now. However, all of that would be released in time, as soon as he received clearance from his boss.

Neil Windman had worked for Tropica Cruise Lines for seventeen years, starting as a data entry technician when he was fresh out of college. Eventually, he worked his way up to customer relations specialist and had traveled the world while learning the intricacies of the industry. Back at home, his days had been filled with tracking down lost baggage, negotiating itinerary disputes, and processing refunds for cancelled excursions, nothing as exciting as he had imagined. But six months ago, when his job description had been expanded to include media relations, he had been eager to accept the added responsibilities and the pay increase that went with it. He had thought that interacting with reporters from around the world, scripting press releases, and making personal appearances on behalf of Tropica would be a welcome change from the routine aspects of his job. However, now that he had to deal with the darker, more serious side of his work, he wasn't so sure.

Neil gazed out his window at returning passengers who disembarked from the *Trade Wind* and waved at the family and friends who had come to meet them. They carried brightly colored hats and straw bags from their Caribbean vacation. They cheered, shouted greetings of hello, hugged and kissed their loved ones. He narrowed his brown eyes and focused on the chaotic scene that always unfolded when a cruise ship returned to port—a scene that usually made him grin with satisfaction. But, not today. His thoughts stayed on the *Sea Wind* and the horrible tragedy that had occurred. His chest tightened as he thought about the passengers who would never come home, and those who would be scarred or severely disabled for the rest of their lives. Many would be too traumatized to ever cruise again.

The fax machine rang, jolting Neil back to work, and looking over, he watched three pages slip through. He removed the document that he'd been waiting for, quickly scanned the names of the deceased and those who had been so seriously injured that they remained hospitalized in Honolulu, searching for names he recognized: Many of his relatives, friends, and neighbors on the island often cruised with Tropica, and he knew the names of every Tropica Cruise Line employee who had set sail from Honolulu on the *Sea Wind* eight days ago.

Neil studied the pages closely, and was relieved that the document did not contain the names of anyone he knew. *Not yet, at least,* he thought, fully aware that this was only the beginning of an extensive, complicated disaster investigation that was going to take time to unravel and settle. It was the first cruise ship accident with fatalities that he had worked, and most likely, it would not be the last. However, when Neil stopped reading the pages he had gripped in his hand and returned his gaze to the calm waters of the bay, he felt a strong premonition that there was something definitely different about this fire and the people whose lives it had touched.

Honolulu

Lara adjusted the pillows that the nurse had propped behind her back and shifted her eyes from the bright lights of the Honolulu skyline to the large mirror hanging above the dresser in her hospital room. She stared in disbelief at the swath of bandages covering her face and thought about what the doctor had told her when she had awakened in this strange, sterile room three hours ago. He had said that she had been through four hours of delicate surgery after suffering third-degree burns on the right side of her face, a deep gash to her right jaw, and a fractured arm. A burning wall had fallen on her while she had been trying to escape the fire aboard the *Sea Wind,* and she had been unconscious when the rescue team found her and brought her into the emergency room of Hilo Hospital. However, the doctor had assured her that they had done everything they could for her at this point, and that plastic surgery would be needed at a later date to restore her appearance. However, there were no guarantees, and facial reconstruction was a long way down the road. For now, she needed to rest, remain calm, and allow the doctors and nurses at Hilo to make her as comfortable as possible until she was strong enough to return to Los Angeles.

The longer Lara stared at her mummified image, the more intensely acute her fear became, finally inching into a kind of nausea that actually made her sick. She had no eyelashes, no eyebrows, and no hair on her head, though the nurse had promised it would all return in time. She tried to swallow back her fear, but her mouth was dry and the back of her throat was raw from having had tubes in it for long hours during surgery. She wanted to cry, scream, or curse at someone. But who? And what good would that do? The slightest facial movement, even a squint of her big brown eyes caused sharp, excruciating pain. Would she ever regain the use of her right arm, recover her photogenic face? How in the hell was she supposed to accept what had happened to her?

Clenching her fingers around a wad of thin hospital sheeting, she sucked in a long, slow breath and tried to calm down, struggling to remember . . . to tear through the black veil that claimed her mind. She remembered being pissed off at Davis for not taking her dancing, and drinking Scotch after Scotch . . . alone. In a fog of alcohol, she had left her room to go and find Davis, but after that, she drew a blank. Alarms began to ring. Loud whooping sounds that had forced her up to the Sky Deck and into the corridor where the burning wall had crashed down. After that, her memories were a blur of gray and black images, shot through by a huge streak of orange.

Where was Davis? What about Max and Camille? What had happened to them? Clutching the sheet, Lara forced her mind to clear, but the lingering anesthesia, as well as the dull throb of pain that pulsed beneath the surface of her skin, prevented her from catching onto any clear images. Shutting her eyes against the bandaged stranger facing her in the mirror, Lara slid down beneath the sheets and prayed for sleep to come and interrupt this terrible dream.

Camille moved closer to the window and placed one hand against the cool glass as she shifted her focus from the jumbo jets lining up for takeoff on the tarmac to the glittering night skyline of Honolulu. The buildings resembled lighted stacks of Lego blocks, arranged in various shapes and heights, and she imagined that the tallest structure in her view was the Hilton Honolulu, where she and Max had stayed before departing on the cruise. Their suite had been first class, with a whirlpool, a bar and a breathtaking view of Diamond Head in the distance, which they had admired from the private balcony of their suite. Those same lights had blinked on at dusk and created this dazzling skyline, she thought, and the memory flooding her eyes with tears. She blinked several times to clear them away, surprised that she had any tears left to shed. Tilting her head against the tiny window, she let her body go limp, too tired, too frightened, and too sad to do more than sit there like an empty shell and wait for takeoff.

All around her the airplane was buzzing with the usual sounds of noisy passengers moving toward their seats, stowing bags in the overhead bins, laughing and chatting about their Hawaiian vacations. Soon, everyone settled down and a flight attendant began the safety instructions while the plane revved up for takeoff. Camille wanted to go home, hold onto Jaiden and never let her go. She was all Camille had left of Max.

The airline personnel had been very sympathetic and helpful to Camille, working overtime to accommodate her, as well as the other displaced passengers from the *Sea Wind* who needed special arrangements to get out of Honolulu. Camille glumly studied the stub of her first-class ticket, to which the agent had attached a special baggage claim tag indicating that she was traveling with a casket. The local police and the Tropica Cruise Line representatives had treated her with great respect and made her as comfortable as possible for the past two days while processing Max's body. She had asked to see him one last time, but the chief of the morgue had advised against it; Max's body was so badly burned. Now, she was tired and anxious to get home to Jaiden, who was staying with Rochelle while dealing with this devastating news.

In a sudden blur of tears, Camille's grief surged to the surface, and she pressed her handkerchief to her mouth, struggling to keep her sobs from bursting forth. How in the world was she going to hold herself together for the seven and a half hours it would take to get home, let alone through the ordeal that lay ahead—planning his funeral, laying him to rest? A fresh sob rose in her throat, but she swallowed it back, determined not to break down. She had to conserve all of her energy for getting through this trip, for comforting Jaiden on her arrival, for taking care of the hundreds of details related to this strange and dreadful turn of events.

Rochelle had promised to break the sad news to Winston, Max's brother and only living relative, who had settled in San Diego to finish his military career. Camille was not close to Winston, but he and Max spoke on the phone a few times a year, and he had visited them twice in Houston. *Winston is going to need support, too,* Camille thought, hoping she would be able to carry the burdens coming her way.

A light touch on her right shoulder made Camille turn around. Davis had come up from his seat in coach. She removed her carry-on bag from the vacant seat beside her and made room for Davis to sit down. The flight attendant in first class gave him a weak, understanding smile, and then moved on down the aisle.

"How're you holding up?" he asked.

Camille shrugged, not really in the mood to talk, but knowing she couldn't brush him off. He had been through the horrible ordeal on the *Sea Wind*, too, and had helped her with the myriad of details related to taking Max home. "I'm here . . . functioning as best as I can."

He patted her on the arm.

She went weak, letting her shoulders slump as she sat back, and then asked, "Any news about Lara?"

"Yeah," Davis said with a sigh. "She's out of surgery and in her room. Her status is listed as fair, but the nurse on her floor assured me that she came through the operation with no problems."

"You couldn't speak to her?" Camille asked.

"No. They refused to put me through, and she's not allowed any visitors except family, which she doesn't have. They want her to remain quiet." Davis checked his watch. "I'll call again from Houston first thing. We ought to get in a little before ten."

"Davis, maybe you should have stayed. Leaving Lara alone in the hospital . . . are you sure you should have done that?"

Davis sat back and stared at the seat back in front of him. "I couldn't let you take Max home alone. I owe this to him. If I had stayed in Honolulu, what would I do? Hang around the hospital until the doctors gave the okay for me to see Lara? She's in good hands, and it will be weeks before they release her. I can fly back and be with her then . . . if she wants."

"Call her as soon as you can . . . tell her what's happened," Camille urged. "I doubt she's aware of Max's death."

Davis clasped both hands together between his knees and gazed at the floor. "I may not have known Max for very long, but I do know he was a really good guy. One of the best . . . better than most that I've dealt with. He and you . . . well, you deserve all the help I can give, so don't ever worry about imposing on me. Whatever you need. Just ask." Davis stretched out his legs and slumped back in the seat. "God. I'm sick about this. Why did this have to happen? And why to him?"

Camille tucked in her lips and concentrated on the lines in the fabric pattern on the seat. How many times had she asked herself that same question? Max's body had been found in the bathroom, where he must have been when Paolo entered their stateroom. Why hadn't the cabin steward gotten to Max? Did Paolo get out alive? She silently vowed to find out as soon as she got home.

A swell of sorrow cut off her breath when she glanced back over at Davis. Her last words to Max had been harsh ones—about Davis—and she had gone to bed angry, without kissing him good-night. How she regretted that now! But how could she take her anger out on Davis, who had been at her side since their reunion in Honolulu?

"Thanks, Davis, for all you've done. I'll need your help when we get home, too."

"I know, I know," he murmured. "Whatever I can do."

"Especially with Vendora," Camille went on. "You'll keep it going, won't you? It meant everything to Max."

"Of course, Camille." Davis reached over and took her hand, then squeezed her fingers firmly with his. "I wouldn't dream of burdening you with business matters. Don't worry. I'm not going anywhere."

CHAPTER 27

The sympathy counselor at Hilo Hospital filled Lara in on the fate of the other passengers from the *Sea Wind*, including the sad news that Max Granville was dead. Shocked and horrified, Lara shrieked her disbelief and thrashed around in her hospital bed, threatening to dislodge the intravenous tube in her arm. The doctor immediately sedated her, and ordered the nurse not to allow Lara to speak to anyone for the next twelve hours, not in person or on the phone.

All day yesterday, Lara had complied with her doctor's orders, though she had asked the nurse for more Vicodin to cut the god-awful pain that had not eased since coming out of surgery. Speaking those few words had been extremely painful.

However, today, she felt stronger and had made up her mind to talk to *someone* who could give her some answers. She knew Max was dead. But where was Davis? Had he left Honolulu without saying good-bye, or was he still around? How was Camille holding up? Lara worried. When could she go home? Though relieved that Davis had not been hurt in the fire, she was incensed that Max had been the one to die. Why? How had such a thing happened? Everything remained fuzzy and far off, as if that horrible night aboard the cruise ship had been a scene in a bad movie. What a tragic ending to what she had hoped was going to be a romantic getaway with the most important man in her life. *Davis,* she thought glumly. *Not half the man that Max Granville was.* Turning onto her side, she tucked her hand under her chin and willed herself back to sleep.

* * *

After solemnly greeting Rochelle and Jaiden, Davis headed to the baggage carousel to watch for his and Camille's luggage, while the women, arms linked supportively, headed to the Airport Bereavement Office to arrange to transfer Max's body to the funeral home.

Both he and Camille had slept through most of the long night flight back from Honolulu, and he had been glad for the rest, as well as the chance to ease the tightening thread of anxiety that had begun to pull at him the moment he raced from Max's stateroom that last night aboard the *Sea Wind.*

Watching the jumble of bags and boxes slide by, he sagged under the strain of the complicated situation: His arrival in Houston created an immediate sense of urgency. He did not want to initiate any unnecessary questions about what had happened on the ship that night. The coroner had ruled that Max died from smoke inhalation, not from a blow to the head, as Davis had thought might have happened. The news had sent a cold chill through Davis, who had assumed that the cabin steward would get Max out in time. All that blood spurting everywhere. The way Max's body had lain limp and still among the shards of glass. It *had* been an accident, Davis rationalized: He had not entered Max's stateroom with the intention of murdering him and if he had known that no one would get to Max in time, he never would have run out. Or would he?

Now, he had to handle Camille with care. As far as she knew, he was still the majority owner of Vendora. He could never allow her to find out that he'd lost his ownership in a frantic, ill-thought moment of panic. He would hold onto the supper club, while maintaining Camille's trust, because he was in too deep to do anything else.

Somehow, he had to get his hands on that wager and destroy it. Max must have put it in the safe because the Honolulu police had given Camille all of the personal property that had been on Max's body. If the wager had been among those items, she would have mentioned it to him by now. Wouldn't she? But what if she did not know she had it?

Their luggage appeared, interrupting his thoughts. Davis grabbed his green rolling duffel from the conveyor belt, and then reached for Camille's black garment bag. Taking both bags off to the side, he quickly went through Camille's, checking each pocket and zippered enclosure, pulling out every piece of paper to examine it closely. The wager was not there. After putting everything back in place, he started toward the exit where the town car that he had ordered was waiting.

Camille and Jaiden would ride with him. Rochelle had agreed to follow in her car with the hearse between the two vehicles. As Davis made his way through the crowded passenger pickup area, he mentally clicked through the list of things that needed to be taken care of right away, and number one on that list was a call to Lara. He would deal with Reet, who must have discovered by now that fifty-eight thousand dollars was missing from Romero's bank account, after things settled down.

After stowing their bags in the car's trunk, Davis slid inside, pulled out his cell phone and dialed the number of Lara's hospital room, relieved that the driver had respectfully decided to wait outside for the other passengers.

Lara answered on the first ring, her voice a shaky whisper.

"Lara. Davis here. How're you doing?"

"Finally. I've been wondering when you'd call."

"I'm back in Houston. You heard about Max?"

"Yes. Terrible. Terrible," she mumbled.

Davis pulled in a long, slow breath, then plunged ahead. "Sorry I had to leave you there, but I had to help Camille bring Max home. I couldn't . . ."

"I know . . . don't worry. You were right to do that. I'm so sorry." Lara breathed her regret. "God. It's awful . . . Camille . . . how is she?"

"Coping. Going through the motions. It's a real bad scene. Believe me, Lara. This is the worst."

"Tell me about it. I'm sitting here looking like a goddamn mummy. Can hardly talk," Lara whispered. "But you're both all right?"

"Yes. Camille managed to get into one of the first lifeboats. I was right behind her. Looking for you. Somehow, Max got trapped in the bathroom in his cabin. He never made it out." The line was silent for several seconds, then Davis went on. "What'd the doctor say about you?"

"I'll heal. I'll have scars, but I'll heal."

"Scars can be removed," Davis offered. "Don't worry about that. Concentrate on getting well." He paused, thinking about how horrible this situation must seem to Lara, whose face had been her most valuable commodity. Scars from serious burns never disappeared completely: A good plastic surgeon might make her face presentable and less likely to draw stares in public, but she would never recapture the flawless skin she had had before the accident. "Things are tough on this end, Lara. I'll try to get back out to see you, but I don't know when. There's a lot to take care of here. The business. Max's burial."

"Don't worry about me, Davis," Lara replied. "Tell Camille how sorry I am. It's a bum deal, Max dying. He was a real nice guy." She sighed, clearly distressed, and then added, "I'll be fine. You have to be there for Camille . . . and handle your business. I can take care of myself."

Davis was about to tell her that he'd call as soon as Max's funeral arrangements were settled, but she clicked off without another word. Davis sat back, the dead cell phone in his hand, wondering if he really ought to keep Lara Stanton around, considering what he had to do. He wanted no reminders of the *Sea Wind* disaster, and for now, Lara's life was going to revolve around her recovery. It would be easy, though cruel, to drop her while she was in Honolulu, but that was exactly what he had to do.

Davis tapped his cell phone on his knee, wondering when Tropica Cruise Lines would send Camille the contents of her in-room safe.

CHAPTER 28

Maxwell J. Granville, 46, died on Wednesday, April 4, while vacationing in Hawaii. He was the owner of a popular Houston supper club and a member of Alpha Phi Alpha Fraternity. He is survived by his wife, Camille; his daughter, Jaiden; his brother, Winston S. Granville of San Diego, California. Public visitation will be Thursday, April 12, 2002, from 1:00 P.M. to 3:00 P.M. at Linton Funeral Home. Funeral services will be conducted at 4:00 P.M. with interment following at Forest Park Cemetery.

Neil Windman folded the obituary section of the *Houston Chronicle*, stuck it into his briefcase, and then turned his attention back to his boss, Frank Bee, who had brought the item to Neil's attention.

"Sure, I'll attend the visitation on behalf of Tropica," Neil told Frank, nodding solemnly.

"Thanks. I think it would be proper to have a representative of the company stop by . . . express our sympathy and deepest regrets," Frank stated, taking a seat in front of Neil's desk. "The investigation into the cause of the fire is far from over, but it appears that it started in a stateroom on the Emerald Deck. The cabin suspected to be the source of the fire had been occupied by three young men from Columbia. Eighteen, nineteen years old. Who knows what was going on that night? Anyway, none of this is public knowledge, so keep a lid on it, okay?"

"Sure," Neil agreed. "So you want me to be the official liaison between Tropica and the Granville widow?"

"Right. For now, make contact with Mrs. Granville, assure her that we will make sure she has everything she needs and answer any questions she may have. As for specifics about compensation . . . I'm sure it will come up . . . I can't say how much the company will be willing to pay. We don't have enough information to speculate on that. After damages are determined, we will let her know what we can do."

"What about personal property?" Neil wanted to know. "Any progress there?"

"Yes," Frank said. "The contents of the in-room safe from the Granville's stateroom should arrive in a few days. I'll let you know when I get it. Mrs. Granville can pick it up." Frank stood, preparing to leave. "Do what you can, Neil. I'm counting on you to keep this situation as low key as possible, but because of the celebrities involved, the press has been relentless, and will continue to speculate about every detail of the accident. Keep in touch with Mrs. Granville and keep her calm. This is a horrible tragedy and Tropica *will* be fair. It's going to take some time to work out the details."

"I'm on it, Frank," Neil quickly volunteered. "I'll be at the visitation tomorrow."

In Los Angeles, the media attention given to the *Sea Wind* disaster was extensive, sensationalized, and relentless. Those who had returned to the mainland unharmed gave interviews to zealous reporters, describing their fear during the hellish evacuation, while praising the *Sea Wind*'s crew for the prompt and efficient manner in which they had guided passengers to safety. Monica, the comedienne, spoke from her hospital bed, vowing to sue Tropica Cruise Lines for seven million dollars; the funeral for DeJay Junior was a lavish affair that lasted an entire day and attracted throngs of hip-hop artists, who posed for pictures with curious fans and even sang a few lines into the cameras; actress Lara Stanton was still in seclusion in Hilo Hospital in Honolulu, and refused to give any interviews. Davis Kepler's brief association with the actress made him newsworthy, too.

As Reet Collins followed another segment on television about the fire, he learned that Davis's partner, Maxwell Granville, was among those who had died on the ship. The news made Reet pause: Without a partner, Davis was vulnerable. Reet was still in shock over Sammy Lee's phone call, informing him that *someone* had stolen fifty-eight thousand dollars from Romero's. *Davis* he thought, grimly.

After turning off his television, Reet opened his laptop computer and logged onto the Internet, and then clicked his way to the obituary section of the *Houston Chronicle*. There it was. All of the information he needed about Max Granville's funeral arrangements. After reading through the announcement, he went to Orbitz and booked a seat on the last flight that evening from Los Angeles to Houston.

When Davis had left Los Angeles, Reet had genuinely wished him well, understanding a man's need to make his own way, be his own boss and hold onto the power he created. Lara had told Reet about the grand reopening at Vendora, and how profitable the supper club was, and that a huge attraction for Davis was the arrival of casino gambling in the area. When Reet heard that, he had begun to think about possibilities for making money in Texas, and that perhaps, opening Romero's II in Las Vegas ought to be put on hold. He and Davis hadn't parted on bad terms—just parted, and Reet was more disappointed than angry that his childhood friend would steal from him.

"I'll give him a chance to return every dime, and then some," Reet decided, his approach to solving this problem slowly evolving in his mind. Houston was as good a place as any for his next investment, so why not pay his buddy, Davis, a visit to express his regrets about the loss of his partner?

Camille stood at the bottom of the stairs and listened to the sobs coming from Jaiden's room, her heart breaking for her daughter, who had been inconsolable for days. She had become distant and uncommunicative, often walking out of the room when Camille entered, and she refused to sit down with Camille to eat a decent meal, preferring to subsist on Ritz crackers washed down with diet colas and coffee. Camille worried that Jaiden was making herself sick and spending too much time shuttered away in her bedroom, where she would huddle on the bed, knees drawn up, her face tight against her pillow.

Rochelle had spent several nights at the house, and during that time had tried to get Jaiden to open up and talk about her feelings, thinking the effort might make her feel better, but Jaiden had not cooperated. Rochelle had advised Camille to step back and simply wait. Jaiden would come around in time.

Max's wake and funeral were scheduled for tomorrow, and Camille was still reeling from the revelation that Max had borrowed so much against his life insurance policy that there had barely been enough money left to give him the kind of funeral he deserved. The new insurance policy that he and Davis had taken out with Security Insurance was to have become effective the day after the fire. Upon hearing this news, Camille had become agitated and resentful, but after thinking about what this meant, she calmed down. Max would be given a proper burial. Jaiden's college fund remained intact. She was healthy and could keep working, but she might not be able to hold onto the house.

As she walked up the staircase, she suddenly felt okay about leaving her huge, custom-built home that had memories of Max stamped on every detail of every room. In time, it might be better if she started over somewhere else. Max had managed to keep them afloat financially during a very difficult time, and Camille had never questioned how he had been able to meet the overwhelming expenses that had hit him week after week. He had done the best that he could, and she would not fault his choices now.

She thought about tomorrow—the visitation, the funeral, the final good-bye. She was terrified of having to face the many friends and acquaintances expected to come by the funeral home to offer their condolences. It would be a hectic, sad, and emotional day; one that Camille prayed she and Jaiden would survive.

Classes had resumed last week at Brown, and Jaiden had been granted permission to remain at home an extra week, but if it were up to Camille, Jaiden would stay in Houston for the remainder of the spring semester, and return in the fall. However, Jaiden wanted to leave the day after tomorrow. How could she possibly catch up on the work she had missed and do well in her classes? Camille wondered. How could she go on as if nothing had happened? That, it seemed to Camille, was asking too much. However, Jaiden was adamant about leaving.

Probably because she wants to be with Rod, Camille speculated, certain that he had prodded her to have that gaudy tattoo inked into her arm, though Jaiden swore it had been her own idea. In the midst of the tragedy surrounding Max's death, it had not seemed important to Camille to express her displeasure with Jaiden's first piece—as far as she knew—of body art, so she had not even mentioned seeing it when Jaiden had greeted her at the airport. *Rod has captured her heart, but I don't think he is the right man for my daughter,* Camille decided, knocking softly on her daughter's door. She waited a few seconds, and then peeked in.

Jaiden was sitting on the side of the bed, her face in her hands, staring glumly at the floor. Camille sat down beside Jaiden and slipped an arm around her back, realizing it had been a long time since she had simply held her. The years between infancy and adulthood had flown by in the rush of day-to-day living, leaving behind the young woman that Jaiden had become. Camille knew Jaiden would always be her little girl, one who needed all the love, support, and understanding that a mother could give. With Max deceased, Camille was the only parent Jaiden could turn to as she moved into adulthood, and the subtle reminder that Max was gone forever, swept through Camille and brought fresh tears to her eyes.

Jaiden scrutinized her mother with eyes that were hollow, questioning, and filled with misery, then shuddered and tilted her head to the side. Letting it rest on Camille's shoulder, they sat without talking until Jaiden stopped trembling. "Tell me again how it happened," she asked.

Camille tensed slightly, but understood the request: Jaiden needed answers to the same questions that still haunted Camille, and believed that somewhere within the retelling of the events, a reasonable explanation for her father's death would emerge. Haltingly, Camille took Jaiden through the evening again, speaking with all the honesty and clarity she could summon. She started with the disagreement that she and Max had had over Davis's gambling, including the fact that she had been upset when she went to bed and had taken the sleep-inducing antidepressant in order to fall asleep quickly. She described her groggy awakening by the cabin steward, his rush to get her out of the stateroom, and her inability to get back into the cabin to look for Max.

"He must have been in the bathroom when I woke up. That's where they found his body," Camille finished.

"But you said there was no light in the room," Jaiden remarked, her voice betraying her grief. "Didn't you say it was pitch black? Wouldn't the light from the bathroom shine under the door? Why was there no light?" Her agitation forced her voice to rise and crack as she pressed Camille for answers.

"I don't know," Camille replied, wishing she could remember if there had been a tiny strip of light at the bottom of the bathroom door. All she could remember was blackness, the smell of smoke, and Paolo's frightful orders to get out.

"Mom," Jaiden started, stopping to blow her nose on a tissue and take a deep breath. "According to the autopsy, Dad died from smoke inhalation, but he also suffered a pretty bad blow to the head. How did that happen?"

"He had fallen into the shower, most likely because he had gotten confused or disoriented. I really don't have the answer."

"But wouldn't the cabin guy, Paolo, have heard Dad in there? *If* he was in there?" Jaiden pressed, wiping at her eyes with the sodden tissue.

"Oh, Jaiden, I've gone over the same scenario so many times I am sick. Sick of thinking about what might have happened, or what could have happened. All I know is that I could not save him!" Camille got up and went to Jaiden's dresser where she glared at her reflection. *Please stop asking me to remember. Let me bury that awful night so deeply it will fade away completely. Oh, God, I want my husband back!*

"You should have stayed, Mom," Jaiden broke into her mother's thoughts. "You should have checked the bathroom for yourself."

"I was still half-asleep. There was no time."

"If you hadn't taken that sleeping pill and if you hadn't been in such a hurry to get out, you might have saved Dad."

Shocked, Camille spun around, hands at her hips. "That is a cruel thing to say, Jaiden. You apologize for that!"

"I can't. I won't. It's all your fault."

A flash of rage shot through Camille, and she wanted to shout some nasty retort, but held her tongue and covered her face with both hands to keep from lashing out. How dare Jaiden accuse her of abandoning Max, the man she loved with all her heart? Raising her head, she snapped back, "You will not make me feel guilty! I trusted the cabin steward to get Max out. I did all that I could!"

"But it wasn't *enough*!" Jaiden shouted, getting up from the bed. "I hate you for running out on Dad. I hate you!" Quickly, she pushed her feet into a pair of thong sandals, wiped her face with the remainder of the wadded tissue, and then grabbed her purse from the closet doorknob and fixed Camille with a frigid stare. "You left Dad once before, remember? I sure do. And over some silly argument about money, you said. You didn't care about anybody but yourself then and you didn't think of saving anyone but yourself on that ship. I'll never forgive you for letting him die." Then she left the room, ran down the stairs, out the back door, and into the garage.

When Camille heard the engine of Jaiden's car come to life, all she could do was pray that her daughter would not do something foolish and wind up getting hurt. She wished she could tell Jaiden the truth: Your father was unfaithful to me, and his infidelity forced me to leave. *Now is not the time to dredge up that painful period. Doing so will only destroy Jaiden's respect for Max and her perception of him as a good husband and father. Why add to her suffering now?*

Jaiden will come home. We will work through this, though it won't be easy or without a lot of pain. But we will survive, Camille vowed, breaking down in bitter tears.

She missed Max so damn much. Her anger at losing the only man she had ever loved, despite his imperfections, filled her with rage. Yes, they had argued that last night of his life. Yes, she had taken medication that made her groggy, but she had not abandoned him—she would never have left him to die alone. *What else could I have done?* she fretted, exhausted from hours of internal questioning. Had she been thinking of her own survival, as she had done when Max cheated on her and she walked out? Had she focused too much on escaping the danger, instead of finding her husband? Moreover, if that were true, how could she fault Jaiden for thinking that she hadn't done enough to make sure Max survived?

The farther Jaiden drove down Deep Piney Lane, the darker and more isolated the country road became. Her headlights created two narrow yellow strips of light on the winding asphalt, guiding her into the thick forest of pines. It had been nearly a year since she had last been at the family cabin on the lake, and she had never driven up there alone. Nervously proceeding, she tried not to second-guess her decision to escape from her mother at their summer cabin on the lake.

She was wrong, Jaiden kept telling herself. *Mom was wrong to think only of herself, and I am not sorry I told her so. She ought to be the one apologizing. How could she run off and leave Dad?*

Jaiden's vision became blurry with tears, but she swiped at them with the back of her hand and kept driving, watching for the turn-off that she knew was marked with a red wooden sign with their last name stenciled in black paint. She had come up to the lake on impulse, after deciding that she did not want to go to her aunt's house, where she'd surely be pressured to talk about her mother; or to Nici's to listen to her rave about her new love interest, a Hispanic musician she recently met at a club. That would only make Jaiden lonelier for Rod. She could not wait to get back to Providence and back into his arms, but until then, all she wanted was to be left alone.

When the familiar turnoff sign appeared, Jaiden took a right turn. The road, banked on both sides with bushy shrubs, narrowed even more, but after a short drive, the path suddenly opened up and she emerged inside the sandy clearing in front of the cabin.

The house was square, low, and built of dark brown logs chinked with white plaster, giving it the look of a real old-fashioned log house. It consisted of two bedrooms, a kitchen, and a bath, and had a large covered patio at the back. Now, with its dark windows and abandoned presence, the place looked as desolate as Jaiden felt.

She stopped the car, but left the headlights shining onto the front door as her thoughts shifted to memories of the summer days she had spent there with her father during her parents' separation. He had brought her up to the lake to distract her from missing her mother and had taught her how to swim in the cold blue water, shown her how to build a fire, and had taken her fishing with him in the early morning hours while the sky was still dark and the stars still shone. That time alone with him had been filled with a sense of adventure, and she treasured the stories he had told her while walking along the lakeshore or waiting for a fish to nibble at their bait. She knew he had exaggerated his tales to entertain her, and to keep her from asking too many questions about why her mother was not around, but Jaiden hadn't cared that he was stretching the truth. She was with him, had his full attention, and knew that he would never desert her—as her mother had.

Now, how in the world was she going to go on without him?

After entering the cabin, Jaiden made a cup of tea and curled up on the red and gold plaid sofa, content to be left alone with memories of her father.

CHAPTER 29

Earlier in the day, a soft spring rain had watered the lush green foliage and expansive lawns of Linton Funeral Home, bringing the cool April temperature down ten more degrees. The line of limos and sleek black cars that were parked in the curved driveway trailed out into the street.

The wake for Maxwell Granville was a somber, yet oddly fulfilling affair, and at times Camille felt less like the rage-filled widow that she was, and more like someone who had lost a best friend. The attendees, who included personal friends, business associates, fraternity brothers, and longtime customers who had been coming to Vendora since the day the doors opened, approached Camille and Jaiden with sincere warmth and sorrow. Many, while expressing their condolences, included in their words of sympathy an anecdotal story about a memorable experience with Max, most often revolving around a party. Oh, how he had loved to throw a party, they all said. He had been the consummate host, as well as the guest who never failed to have the most fun. More than once, Camille found herself laughing through her tears as she patiently listened to recollections of fun-filled nights and unforgettable parties that she and Max had hosted. Even Jaiden—who had returned home early that morning to inform Camille, in a sullen tone, that she had spent the night at their cabin—warmed to the genuine love she received from those who hugged her, patted her shoulder, and wished her the best.

Davis insisted on standing directly behind Camille—to lend his support if needed, he had said. Rochelle was busy circulating among those who had come to pay their respects and monitoring the guest book to make sure everyone signed their names. The crowd was overwhelming, the reception line never slowed, and by three o'clock in the afternoon Camille was totally exhausted.

Where will I find the energy to make it to the end of this long, sorrowful day? she silently wondered, sending Jaiden off to a private room to rest until the funeral service began. She turned to Davis. "Thanks for standing with me," she told him.

"The least I could do since Max's brother couldn't be here."

"I didn't know he was ill, but we hardly kept in touch. I know he would have come if he had been able to travel," Camille remarked.

"If you want, I'll make sure he gets a copy of the funeral program," Davis offered.

"He'd like that. Thanks."

"No problem," Davis assured her. "That's what I'm here for . . . to take some of the pressure off you." He took her by the elbow. "Why don't you go and see how Jaiden is doing? I'll stay here and greet any late arrivals. Get off your feet for a while."

"I think I will," Camille agreed. "You've been such a help, Davis. I've had so much to do, to think about. I don't think I could have managed without you taking care of things I had not even thought of. No wonder Max trusted you with his precious Vendora."

Davis answered her compliment by giving her a warm hug.

Over Davis's shoulder, Camille saw a man standing patiently off to the side, as if waiting to speak to her. She blinked back the sudden rush of tears that filled her eyes and gave the man a timid smile, acknowledging his presence. Breaking away from Davis, she waited as the man approached.

"My name is Neil Windman," the man said. "I am the public relations manager for Tropica Cruise Lines."

"Oh?" she remarked, not sure what else she should say.

He went on. "I want to express my personal regrets and offer condolences from my company. We are deeply saddened by this tragedy."

"Thank you," Camille replied, shaking his hand.

He reached into his coat pocket, pulled out a card and handed it to her. "I am available to answer your questions and be of any assistance as we work through this tragic situation. Nothing is more important to Tropica than your satisfaction and future well-being. Call me any time. I am your personal link to the company."

"That is very nice of you," Camille said, studying the man's face, liking him instantly. He was soft-spoken, respectful, and seemed to genuinely want to help her. He had olive-tone skin, with a reddish undertone, dark hair with a slightly wavy texture, and chiseled cheekbones that gave him a strong, yet distinguished appearance. She glanced down at his card, then remarked in surprise, "Oh, you're based in Galveston, I see."

"Yes, our pleasure cruise department is housed in the Rockport Building at the port. Near Pier 23."

"I'll keep your card handy and most likely will give you a call very soon," Camille promised, then turned and introduced Davis.

"You were on the *Sea Wind*, too, weren't you?" Neil responded, after shaking Davis's hand.

"Yes. Luckily I wasn't injured . . . my companion, Lara Stanton, was."

"Ah, yes. The actress." Neil paused, a frown of concern touching his features. "A shame. Such a beautiful woman."

"Yes, she was. My hope is for a fast and complete recovery. She is very dear to me."

"I understand," Neil replied.

"Mr. Windman," Davis went on, "will you personally handle Mrs. Granville's case?"

"Yes. I am her link to the company."

"Good. Good," Davis replied, going on to tell him that he was Max Granville's business partner. "I'm determined to help Mrs. Granville get through this sorrowful time, so I am available if there is anything I need to do for her."

"That's good to know," Neil went on. "When the contents of the in-stateroom safes arrive in Galveston, I will give you both a call. The packages must be picked up in person . . . sorry for the inconvenience, but for security reasons . . . I'm sure you understand."

"Absolutely," Camille said, relieved to hear that her and Max's passports, which they never traveled without; her diamond earrings and bracelet; and Jaiden's pearl and coral necklace were safe. "I wouldn't think that you would do anything less. I'll try to come as soon as the package is available. How soon . . ."

"But," Davis interrupted. "That's such a long drive. Camille, let me take care of it for you." He looked to Neil before continuing. "With Mrs. Granville's permission . . ." he glanced back at Camille, ". . . I'd be happy to pick up her package, since I have to make the trip, anyway."

Not looking forward to the long drive, or the usually heavy traffic on the Gulf Freeway, Camille eagerly agreed. "Oh, would you,

Davis? I don't want to make that drive. Would it be all right, Mr. Windman? For Davis to pick up my things?"

Neil lifted his hands in acceptance. "Of course, if you like, Mrs. Granville. Be sure to send along written authorization to release the package to him."

"I will," Camille agreed, shaking Neil's hand again. "Thank you so much for coming."

"Nice enough guy," Davis remarked after Neil had left.

"Very nice," Camille agreed, linking her arm through Davis's as he escorted her out of the reception area to prepare for the second stage of saying good-bye to Max.

The funeral ceremony lasted forty minutes and ended with a stirring solo delivered by Lora Green, a local singer who had entertained at parties at Vendora many times. Six pallbearers, all members of Max's fraternity, picked up their brother's flower-covered coffin and began the slow walk toward the hearse that would take him to his final resting place.

Under a shady canopy of pin oak trees, Max was laid to rest. Camille gripped Jaiden's hand and briefly rested her head on Rochelle's shoulder, drawing comfort from the closeness of the two most important people left in her life. Then, she turned and headed toward the glistening black limousine that would take her home.

Davis watched the limo carrying Camille, Jaiden, and Rochelle depart, a heavy sense of dread descending. Now that Max had been laid to rest, it was time to go on with the business of running Vendora and put this god-awful incident behind him. He went to the town car that would take him home and stepped aside as the driver opened the door for him. He bent to enter, and then suddenly backed up.

"What the hell?" he muttered, shocked to see Reet Collins sitting inside, waiting for him. "What the hell are you doing here?"

"Paying my respects, of course," Reet calmly answered, motioning for Davis to get in.

Davis turned to the driver. "Wait outside for a moment, please."

"Yes, sir," the man replied, moving away from the car.

Once inside, Davis repeated his question. "Why are you here? This is neither the time nor the place to conduct the business I know we need to settle."

Reet laughed. "Well, at least you've got the good sense to acknowledge that we have business to discuss." He raked a frigid glance over Davis's face. "Like fifty-eight thousand dollars worth?"

"I can explain," Davis started.

Reet shook his head. "I don't want your explanations. Nothing you have to say has any importance. You are going to listen to me and do exactly what I tell you to do. You don't have any choice in this, Davis. Let's go someplace quiet and work it all out."

Davis and Reet sat across from each other at a table in the empty dining room at Vendora—shuttered out of respect for Max. Many of his customers and all of his employees had attended the funeral, and were grief-stricken over the loss of a man they had respected and loved.

Davis poured brandy into two bulb-shaped glasses, watching Reet with interest. He had been puzzlingly silent during the short ride from the cemetery to the supper club, infuriating Davis, who was anxious to get on with whatever Reet had come for.

"Spill it, Reet. What's on your mind? I don't deny that I borrowed a few thousand from Romero's to take with me on the cruise. But you know I'm good for it. I'll pay you back in a few months. Just gotta get my bearings, understand? I've been through a pretty traumatic experience . . . the fire, Lara getting hurt, my partner's dead. Surely, you can give me a break."

Reet studied his fingernails, no expression on his face, and then he picked up his glass of brandy and tossed it down in one gulp.

Davis swallowed hard, steeling himself for the kind of tongue-lashing that he knew Reet was capable of delivering, and one that he deserved. What had he been thinking? That this day would never come? That he would get away with stealing from his childhood friend, who had never let a wrong against him go unrighted?

"You got a nice place, here," Reet finally said, getting up to wander around the room, his hands thrust deep into his pants pockets. He pointedly assessed the furnishings, the rich oil paintings on the walls, the thick rugs on the floor, even going to the bar where he picked up a heavy crystal vase filled with antique silk roses and held it up to admire. "Real classy, Davis." He moved behind the bar and began examining the stock. "Vintage wines, premium liquors, all high-end stuff."

"We serve a high-end clientele," Davis ventured, more nervous than ever.

"Making any money?"

"Enough," Davis replied.

"But not enough to keep you from stealing fifty-eight thousand from me," Reet finished, returning to the table.

Clearing his throat, Davis hunched over the table. "That was a mistake. I got caught up in a few high stakes games of blackjack on the cruise. Can't play cheap with celebrities. You know that. They wager big, I had to stay in the game and to match them, I needed cash. Things spiraled out of control, that's all. An isolated incident, and a huge mistake. I really am sorry."

Reet remained stone-faced, though his upper lip curled slightly in feigned sympathy. "I accept your apology, Davis. In fact, I don't even want you to repay the money you gambled away on the *Sea Wind*."

"Then what do you want?"

"Your help. I'm thinking about making an investment here in Texas."

"Really? Where?" Davis asked, praying that Reet was not going to ask for a part of Vendora, which in reality was not his to sell. However, no one knew that . . . no one except Max, and he was dead.

"Before I go into that, let me ask you a question."

"Shoot."

"Now that your partner is dead, you gonna buy out the widow? Get the control you need to make some real money?"

Clenching his hands together under the table, Davis thought carefully before answering. "I'd like to do that, but it's a little soon to bring that subject up with Camille. Maybe in a few months . . ."

"Too long," Reet snapped. "Move on it now, while she's grieving. She probably wants to get rid of this place . . . too many memories, and all that."

"I don't know . . ." Davis stammered. "There's more to this place. She used to live here. It's been in her husband's family forever. Plus, right now my funds are not very liquid."

"Don't worry about the cash. Get the widow to agree to sell. I want you to have full ownership of *this* place, Davis, and then we'll talk again. For now, you owe me nothing."

Not at all sure that he could do as Reet asked, or what his friend intended to do to him if Camille refused to sell, Davis decided to play along. "I'll get right on it," he promised, "Give me a week or so."

"Fine. Now, tell me what you know about the Indian casino

north of here," Reet abruptly changed the subject. "I've been doing some checking and I think there're significant gaming opportunities in this area."

"I don't know too much about the casino. It's only been open since last November, and the state is already trying to shut it down."

"So I've heard," Reet interjected.

"Right. The Indians' argument is . . . the state of Texas has a lottery, which is a form of legalized gambling, so they ought to be allowed to run their casino. However, the attorney general comes back with the fact that casino gambling and a lottery are two different things. I've been out there a few times. It's a pretty big operation . . . four hundred or so employees, good jobs for the Indians. It's a hit around here. Nobody wants to see it shut down. People come from all over and Texans don't have to drive to Louisiana to gamble now. Has a few sharp dealers, too. I've done more than okay at the tables."

"That's what I thought," Reet remarked, his voice suddenly bright with interest. "Let's take a drive out there tonight. I'd like to try my luck."

"Sure," Davis agreed, standing up and going to the bar where he poured himself another shot of brandy. His mind was not on a pleasure trip to the casino, but on Camille. How was he going to convince her to sell him her forty percent share of Vendora?

It took fifty-five minutes of freeway driving to reach the casino, which was nestled in a heavily wooded section of the Alabama-Coushatta Indian Reservation. Tall pine trees towered over the rustic lodge; an A-frame structure built of heavy logs with a wide overhang porch, sturdy log railings and generous multipaned windows on either side of the front door. The number of cars, pickup trucks, and recreational vehicles crammed into the parking lot and scattered over the grounds was staggering, causing Reet to whistle softly under his breath when he saw how popular a place it was.

Inside the casino, a dark aqua, Indian-motif carpet muffled the noise of three hundred slot machines as well as the clatter that comes from crowding twice as many gamblers as the place could service into the busy rooms. People were standing two and three deep, either waiting for a turn at a slot machine or in anticipation of grabbing an opening at one of the five blackjack tables where dealers spread their cards. Servers drifted by with trays of nonalcoholic drinks and gave encouraging smiles to those who were either trying their luck, or impatiently waiting their turn.

"A million dollars a month," Reet excitedly informed Davis as they walked around and checked out the action. "That's the official estimate, and I got it from a reliable source. Can you believe that? Imagine how much money this place is losing because it's too damn small."

PART FOUR

THE WAGER

CHAPTER 30

Lara's facial burns were healing, but she remained badly scarred and in constant pain. She had a steel pin in her jaw, her right arm was in a sling, and after Doctor Johansen, a famed plastic surgeon in L.A., reviewed her case, he strongly suggested she undergo facial reconstruction by a skilled surgeon in Phoenix who specialized in the kind of operation that she needed. The procedure would cost $220,000, with one-half payable at the time of the surgery, and recovery could take as long as six months.

Whenever Lara looked at herself in the mirror, she sobbed. Who was that disfigured woman who had once been called one of the most beautiful women in the world? Now, all she saw was a monster. With no money, no income, and no word from her lawyer about the three million dollar settlement she was seeking from Tropica Cruise Lines, her future looked grim. If Tropica refused to settle out of court, she would have to file a lawsuit, which might drag on for months.

Upon her arrival at LAX, her agent, Artie Perlman, had helped her avoid the inquisitive reporters and aggressive photographers waiting for her in the terminal. He had met her at the gate, hustled her down a back stairwell and into a nondescript black Jeep, whisking her directly to her house in Brentwood, where she had remained in seclusion for the past seven days.

When the phone on her nightstand rang, Lara's first thought was that it might be Davis, but remembered it couldn't be him. Only Reet and Artie knew that she was back in Los Angeles, and she had sworn them to secrecy about her return. She had telephoned Reet as soon as she had settled into her bedroom to discreetly inquire about Davis; not that she wanted to speak to him after the way he had treated her. His phone call to her at Hilo Hospital had been his last, and she certainly didn't want or need his long overdue sympathy now. However, she was curious about where he was and what he was doing. Reet had told Lara that Davis was living permanently in Houston now and managing his supper club, which he planned to expand.

Forget him, Lara had silently grumbled. She had toughed it out alone for four weeks in a Honolulu hospital, and could certainly get on with her life without Davis Kepler in it.

The phone rang six more times before Lara relented and picked it up, mumbling a barely audible hello.

"Lara. Thank God, you answered. I was getting worried," Artie rushed ahead. "Did ya get my flowers? They better be beautiful. Are they purple lilacs, like I asked for?"

Lara blinked, recalling that an oversized bouquet had arrived yesterday afternoon and she had placed it on the dining room table. "Yeah, they're here, Artie. Lilacs. Thanks a lot."

"You hang in there, okay?" Artie rattled on. "Just wanted to send along something to cheer you up. Let you know I'm thinking about you."

"I really appreciate that, Artie," Lara told him, struggling to focus.

"You concentrate on getting well. That's all you need to do."

"I plan to," Lara told him, wincing from the pain that flashed into her jaw. Every day, she began her regime of pain pills immediately after breakfast, in order to take the edge off the incessant throbbing that never left one side of her face. By midday, she was usually so lethargic that she had to climb into bed and sleep the afternoon away. When evening rolled around, she often could not remember much of what had happened during large portions of her day. The pills were highly addictive, she knew, but didn't care. She'd do anything to get relief from the excruciating pain. "That's what I intend to do from now on, Artie. Concentrate on me."

"Right. Don't worry about a thing . . ."

"But what about the picture?" Lara asked, determined to get all the information she could from her agent while she was alert.

"The picture? We can talk about that later . . . when you're . . . ah . . . feeling b-better," Artie stuttered his reply.

Lara caught the hesitation in his voice and tensed. He sounded evasive and unsure, and that was not the Artie she liked to hear. He was naturally a fast talker, a busy deal maker who had been her friend and agent for nine years. She knew him well enough to know that when he had bad news to break, he sometimes stuttered—and he was certainly stuttering now. He had not called simply to inquire about her health or find out if her flowers had arrived. He had more on his mind. Holding her breath, she braced for the pain that cut across her cheek and ripped its way into her temple, and then asked in a wispy voice, "Roberto *can* shoot around me for a while longer, can't he?" Lara listened to Artie's breathing whir like a ceiling fan as he wheezed into the mouthpiece of his phone.

"We'll see," he offered, his voice a tad stronger, but still devoid of its initial enthusiasm.

"What the hell does 'we'll see' mean?" Lara shot back, sitting up straighter, ignoring her pain. "If something's going on with Roberto, tell me now, Artie."

"Ah, don't get yourself all keyed up, Lara. I just got off the phone with him. Sends his get-well wishes. Said he plans to drop by to see you soon."

"I told you I don't want any visitors!" Lara yelled, convinced that there was more to their conversation than Artie was divulging. "What else did he say?"

"Ah, you know how Roberto can get c-crazy when there's any l-little wrinkle in his m-micro-managed shooting schedule," he stuttered.

"So? What'd he say?"

Artie's pause was longer and his stuttering much more evident when he told her, "He's . . . c-canceling your contract. *Daddy's Baby Doll* has to stay on schedule. It's been a month since the accident and Roberto c-can't hold up production any longer. Roberto says he's sorry to let you go, but he can't wait around for your face to heal. I see his point. What guarantee does he have that your f-face is gonna look as beautiful as before the accident?"

Lara went limp, her shoulders sagging forward while a slow burn rose in her chest. So, Roberto was dumping her. Just like that. The bastard! What kind of chickenshit was that? And after all the money she'd made for him over the years. "And what about my $225,000 advance?" she asked Artie, unable to begin to think about the nonperformance and other clauses in the contract, which she had hurriedly signed, not wanting some unforeseen glitch to appear and prevent her from playing the most important role of her career.

"I'm trying to negotiate that. Leave it to me. I'll work something out, I promise."

"You'd better," Lara replied, using every bit of focus she could muster to block out the pain brought on by the awful conversation. "I'm broke, out of work, and in a hell of a lot of pain, Artie." Summoning all of her strength, she shouted into the phone, "*Do* something, you hear?"

"I'm on it, Lara. Don't worry."

Lara clicked off before he could say more, reached for the crystal tumbler on her nightstand, and threw it across the room, shattering the glass, as well as her bandaged reflection in the mirror. *Roberto can't do this to me. I've made him a fortune and I've got a name in Hollywood now. He'd better not mess over me or he'll be a sorry son of a bitch.*

As Camille placed her bag of groceries on the kitchen counter, she noticed the red message light blinking on the answering machine and pressed the button to listen to her voice mail.

Neil Windman's voice came on: *Mrs. Granville, Neil Windman. I got your message, and yes—you certainly may speak to Paolo Homers, the cabin steward who assisted you during the Sea Wind evacuation. He is presently working aboard the Trade Wind, in the Mediterranean, but he should be back in port here in Galveston at the end of the month. I'll arrange a meeting for you. Also, the contents of your in-stateroom safe are here in my office. You may pick them up at your convenience. If you have any questions, please give me a call.*

"At last," Camille murmured, thinking how nice it was of Neil to arrange this meeting between her and the cabin steward who had helped her escape. She had prepared a list of questions to ask Paolo and was anxious to meet with him. She also hoped that the return of her personal property was a sign that the company was moving closer toward a settlement. Neil had called her twice since Max's funeral, assuring her that Tropica was making progress on the death and injury cases, though quite a few issues still needed to be settled. Paul Cotter, Camille's attorney, who stood ready to negotiate the best possible settlement, had advised her to be patient. According to him, her financial situation was stable, but without any money from Max's life insurance policy or income from her job at the travel agency, she ought to spend conservatively.

Paul had conducted a cursory audit of Vendora's books and learned that the supper club was doing better than similar establishments in the area, generating an acceptable amount of revenue. However, overhead was enormous. Paul had warned Camille that unless Davis made serious cuts in spending, or was able to significantly increase revenue, the supper club might run into trouble down the road. For now, he could not guarantee that Camille could depend on a steady income from Max's forty-percent share of the business. His advice: Consider selling out to Davis and invest her money elsewhere.

That news had shaken Camille, who until then had been fine with leaving Davis to handle her interest in Vendora, but now she was concerned. She and Max had lived a luxurious lifestyle, but had carried a great deal of debt, too. Their mortgage was a killer, property taxes on the cabin at the lake had increased fifteen percent, the balance on Jaiden's dorm fees was currently overdue, and there was a pile of bills on Max's desk that she had not had the heart to examine. Sell her share of Vendora to Davis? Never, she decided.

It had been three weeks since the funeral and Camille still hardly slept and had not returned to her job at the travel agency. She rarely left her house other than to purchase groceries at the nearby Krogers, not trusting herself to drive very far since her doctor had insisted she resume her antidepressant medication. So, she took the pills and was happy to give herself over to the sleepy, floating feeling that eased the pain of missing Max, if only for a while.

Her days slipped by in a fog, and at night, she crawled into the king-size bed she had shared with Max, fretful and irritated, often crying to recall the intimate moments they had shared in the bedroom. Somehow, she had to find closure and move on, but how? Not only did she miss him so much that thinking of him brought on physical pain, but she was also weighed down with guilt from Jaiden's accusations.

Jaiden had returned to school the day after Max's funeral, still angry with Camille and openly blaming her for Max's death. Camille prayed that Jaiden would be able to settle back into her studies and was worried about her daughter's emotional state. Camille had expected Jaiden to exert her independence after leaving home, but had never dreamed her daughter would get a tattoo, receive low grades, and fall into the heavy partying that she seemed to be enjoying.

It is up to me to pull myself together and salvage my relationship with Jaiden, she admonished, heartsick over the situation. *A strained relationship with Jaiden is too high a price to pay for not getting the answers we both deserve. Somehow, I must resolve this and get to the truth, even if I have to talk to every crew member who had been aboard the Sea Wind that night. Someone knows something about what had happened and why my husband was found dead in our cabin on the bathroom floor.*

Giving herself a mental shake, she dialed the number to Davis's private line at Vendora.

"Davis. Neil Windman called," she started right in. "Our property from the in-room safes has arrived. Can you possibly pick up my package when you go down to get yours?"

"No problem, Camille. I told you I would. Fax over a release for me to take along, and I'll drive down in the morning."

Camille sighed, Paul's concerns about the future of Vendora lingering in her mind. Perhaps allowing Davis to assume the burden of managing her business interests at the supper club was not such a good idea after all. Vendora was her daughter's legacy, and Camille had a responsibility to hang onto it, protect it at all costs, even if she lost money for a while. Maybe it was time to get involved. "I'll send the fax right away," she told Davis, beginning to feel more in control of her affairs than she had in weeks.

The one-hour drive to the port at Galveston gave Davis plenty of time to think about several things: First, how had the cruise line packaged his and Camille's property? Second, would he be able to open her box without her knowing he had done it? And if the wager was not included, had it been destroyed in the fire? Would it ever surface and interfere with his plans?

Reet, who was due back in Houston tonight, had called Davis late yesterday evening to tell him to pick him up at the airport at eight o'clock. He had hinted at the fact that he was ready to unveil his newest venture, which Davis assumed would somehow involve him. How? he wondered. What was Reet up to and why was he being so secretive about it? When Reet had inquired about Camille's willingness to divest her share of Vendora, Davis had asked him outright if he planned to buy Camille's share. Reet had laughed at him and told him that owning a supper club in Houston was not on his agenda, but he would be willing to advance Davis the cash to close the deal.

"Why?" Davis had asked, suspicious of this generous offer in light of the fact that it was Davis who owed fifty-eight thousand dollars to Reet.

"Because it's important to you," Reet had cagily replied. "Just persuade the widow to sell her share to you."

Davis had lied to Reet, ensuring him that he was working on Camille, knowing he had to move forward with an offer soon.

I'll talk to her this afternoon, he decided, turning in to the graveled parking lot outside the Tropica Cruise Lines building.

Inside, a wispy, simply dressed woman wearing glasses and a light blue sweater greeted Davis and escorted him into a large room that contained three long tables and rows of folding chairs.

"Mr. Windman is out of his office today, but he told me to expect you," she told him, indicating that Davis take a seat at one of the tables. "Now, I understand you have written permission to take the Granville property?"

"Yes, I do," Davis told her, handing her the statement that Camille had faxed to him.

The woman read the paper quickly, glanced at Davis over the top of her glasses, asked to see his identification, and then told him, "I'll be right back." And then she disappeared through a door at the back of the room.

Davis fidgeted nervously with his car keys, hoping the woman would not take too long. His mind retraced his encounter with Max on that last night aboard the *Sea Wind*, and for the thousandth time, he tried to imagine what Max might have done with the piece of paper so hastily drafted and signed in the casino. From the time they had parted after the losing bet, until the fire alarms sounded, there had not been enough time for him to do much more than return to his cabin and tell Camille what had happened. However, if he had done that, why hadn't Camille ever mentioned the wager? No, Max must have put the document into the safe the moment he returned to his stateroom, and before Camille awakened. He had been trying to retrieve it when Davis interrupted him. That was the only way it could have gone down.

The door opened, and the woman reappeared, interrupting his speculation.

"Here we are," she said, placing two square gray metal boxes on the table. Davis immediately saw that keyed locks secured the lids. One was marked GRANVILLE/EMERALD DECK. The other was marked KEPLER/STANTON/EMERALD DECK.

"This," she said, handing Davis a small brown envelope that was clearly sealed, "is for Mrs. Granville's box." She placed a hand on the top of the second steel chest, while assessing Davis with concern. "Do you also have a release from Lara Stanton? Apparently, you shared your stateroom with her?"

The question took Davis by surprise, as he had not thought about Lara in some time. As far as he knew, she was still in the hospital in Honolulu; there had been no reports in the media about her leaving the island to return home.

"No, I don't have a release from her," Davis admitted, not caring if he was permitted to take the box or not. He recalled that she had put some of her jewelry and a few hundred dollars into the safe when they first unpacked, but he had never used it.

"Then I'm very sorry, but I can't let this go. Is there any way you could contact her? Perhaps she could fax us a release?"

All Davis wanted to do was take Camille's security box and get out of there. He didn't have the inclination or the time to deal with this complication. "Tell you what," he offered. "I'll give you Miss Stanton's phone number. You contact her and make arrangements to ship her property to California. There is nothing of mine inside that box that I care about. Okay?"

"Fine, if that is what you want to do," the woman answered vaguely.

"It is," Davis snapped, going on to give the woman Lara's home number and permission to relinquish his claim on the box. "She may still be in the hospital in Honolulu. If so, someone within your company can locate her, I'm sure."

As soon as he was back inside his car, Davis carefully pried open the flap of the small brown envelope, removed the key, and opened Camille's box. Two passports, a blue silk pouch containing a diamond bracelet and matching earrings, a red velvet box with a coral and pearl necklace, five hundred dollars in cash, and a small digital camera that fit into the palm of his hand. That was it.

Perspiration beaded on Davis's forehead as he searched through the items a second time. The wager was not there! Slumping back against the seat, he went weak with relief. Camille knew nothing and would never find out what had happened. This had to be the end of his problems. He was free to bury his mistake and move on.

The drive back into Houston zipped by in a flash, with Davis silently congratulating himself on the way he had handled things so far. No drama. No casual slips of the tongue. No issues had raised Camille's suspicions. She trusted him and the confidence she had in him would serve him well when he moved forward with his offer to buy her out.

Once Camille greeted Davis, she led him into her living room and sat down beside him on the large suede sofa. Davis remained silent while Camille removed the key from the small brown envelope which he handed to her. A surge of relief swept through Davis when Camille made no comment about the obviously broken seal, and he knew that, if she had said anything about it, he had been prepared to swear that the woman who had given him the box must have taken out the key to inventory its contents. He watched as Camille examined the passports and the red velvet box and pulled out the blue silk pouch, which she lovingly untied, and then fondled the diamond jewelry for a moment. She put it back and pulled the drawstring tight, and with her fingers closed around it, allowed tears to brim in her eyes.

"I am so happy to have these back," she told Davis. "Not because they're valuable, but because these are the first pieces of real jewelry that Max bought for me. I remember the expression on his face the night he gave them to me . . . on our tenth wedding anniversary. We had had a pretty rough year, but we had recommitted ourselves to our marriage and this gift meant so much to him . . . and to me. Thanks for picking up the package, Davis."

"I had to get my things, anyway," he replied, thinking that Camille appeared more rested than he had seen her in weeks. Her hair was freshly styled; she was wearing full makeup and a stylish jogging suit that showed off her trim figure. She was an extremely attractive woman who did not look her age, and it suddenly hit Davis that it would not surprise him if, after a time, she became romantically involved with another man. The prospect of a complication like that pushed him into the discussion he had put off too long.

"You're looking well, Camille," he started. "How are you doing? Really?"

"Much better," she replied, with a tone of satisfaction. "For the first time since the funeral, I have not needed medication to get through the day and I think I've turned a corner. Maybe I've cried all of the tears that I can . . . grieved enough, you know? I still miss the hell out of Max, but I have decided it's time to get on with what needs to be done, and the first thing I am going to do is talk to that cabin steward who helped me escape."

This news brought a flicker of a frown to Davis's brow. "The cabin steward? Why dredge up that awful night again? Isn't it best to let it all go?"

"No, not as long as my daughter remains convinced that I could have done more to save Max."

"Camille, I don't believe Jaiden feels that way, and you can't go around weighed down with guilt because you survived and Max didn't. You don't need to prove anything. Max was in the bathroom, he became disoriented and fell. That is it. Forget about it."

"I can't. And I won't be satisfied until I am sure there was absolutely nothing more that I could have done." She paused. "If you had a child, you would understand why I have to do this. I am emotionally drained from worrying about Jaiden. I want her to be happy. I want her to have advantages. I need her back in my life, and she wants nothing to do with me!" Camille burst into tears, and then moved to the window overlooking the front lawn, keeping her back to Davis. "From now on, I'm going to focus on repairing my relationship with my daughter."

Davis hated that she was crying—weeping women made him nervous—and she had been in such an upbeat mood when he arrived. He paused before speaking—no words of comfort now—he had to press on with the business he had come prepared to finish.

"I agree. You should devote yourself to Jaiden . . . spend more time with her. You two ought to go on an extended trip and enjoy yourselves. After Jaiden comes home for the summer you two ought to go shopping in Paris, London, Rome. Travel through the Swiss Alps. Get out of this town and the sad memories that are here. A change of environment would do you both good."

Camille turned around, head tilted to one side. "That would be nice, but international travel is expensive, and I can't spare the money right now. You know the situation, Davis. My income from Vendora is all that I have, and I have to be careful."

"Exactly," Davis agreed, grasping the opening that she had provided. "I'd like to talk about the future of Vendora, specifically about your plans."

"Mine? I haven't any. For now, you can continue to manage the business, as you did when Max was alive. His share belongs to me now, and eventually I might like to be more involved."

Clearing his throat with a cough, Davis said, "I think you ought to sell your share of Vendora and move on. Sell it to me, Camille. I'll pay you a quarter of a million in cash. More than the market value, and quite fair."

Camille simply stared, a puzzled expression on her face. "Where would you get that kind of money?"

"I have sources," he answered vaguely. "And with that kind of cash, along with the settlement I know you are going to get from Tropica, you could secure your and Jaiden's futures. You could get out from under all this financial pressure and enjoy life with your daughter."

"I can't believe what you are proposing. I am shocked! I guess I don't know you . . . or you don't know me. Sell Jaiden's legacy? I'd never do that!" Camille stated with finality. "If you respected Max as much as you've been telling everyone you did, then you would do everything possible to ensure that his daughter's legacy remained in her mother's control." She shook her head in amazement. "I'll never sell what Max created."

"You're taking this all wrong, Camille. I'm looking at the situation purely from a business perspective, not an emotional one. You need security for yourself and your daughter. You want the best for Jaiden, best education, a comfortable lifestyle, and time to spend together. Selling out can give you that freedom and the lifestyle you deserve. Why bother with waiting around for a return on Max's share? Running a supper club will always be an up and down kind of situation. It's the nature of the business. Take the money I am offering and open your own business . . . a travel agency, perhaps. And don't you think it would be wise to sever your ties with a place that has so many painful memories for you . . . and Jaiden?"

"Painful memories? Obviously, you know nothing at all about me, my family or what is important to us. That house is the heart and soul of my existence and any memories I created there are precious. In fact, I had been thinking that I ought to leave the travel industry altogether . . . move into Max's office and put my energy into helping you make Vendora a more profitable venture."

"What are you implying?" Davis asked, skeptically.

"Paul Cotter thinks that your overhead is too high. If it continues to grow . . . if you continue to spend the way you are doing now, the business could collapse."

"Bullshit!" Davis threw back. "Paul Cotter doesn't know what the hell he is talking about. You have to spend money to make money."

"Maybe so, and I'd like to learn more about how the money is being spent."

"I advise you not to do anything drastic, Camille. As controlling owner, I make the decisions about what goes on at Vendora and I have a handle on all areas of the business, including those that had been under Max's control. Your accountant and your lawyer are free to review the books whenever you want, so they can see for themselves that I am running a well-managed, cost-effective operation. There is no reason for you to be at Vendora . . . ever."

"We'll see about that," Camille told Davis.

"Yes, we will," Davis challenged, then he left.

Shocked at how adamant Davis had become over her refusal to sell her shares, Camille began to speculate about what might be going on. Why had he seemed frightened at the prospect of her getting involved? He had been upbeat, though edgy when he arrived, and had nervously fidgeted with his car keys while she was opening her security box. When he handed her the envelope containing the key, she had noticed that the paper seal had been compromised. Had he looked inside her metal box? Why would he do that? Shrugging, she headed upstairs to put away her jewelry, mulling Davis's odd behavior.

Paul Cotter *had* suggested that she sell her interest in the business, and she trusted his judgment. It would be months before Tropica Cruise Lines settled her claim. Accepting Davis's offer would ease her financial situation.

But I was right to turn him down, she decided. *Keeping my commitment to hold onto the legacy that Max left for Jaiden is more important than any amount of money Davis could have offered.*

CHAPTER 31

While waiting for Reet to emerge from the airport, Davis silently mulled over his conversation with Camille. Things had not gone as he had hoped. *She plans to move into Max's office?* he thought, now wishing he had been more forceful in his approach. Maybe if he had intimidated her, made her understand that he had no intention of including her in the day-to-day operations and did not want her around, she might have realized that she would be wasting her time coming to Vendora every day. He had to make her back off. *If she thinks she is going to tell me how to run Vendora, she had better think again. I can make her life so miserable she'll beg me to buy her out.*

While considering his options to keep her at a distance, Reet appeared and tapped on the passenger side window. Quickly, Davis flipped the switch to unlock the door. Reet tossed his single bag onto the backseat and got in.

"Good to see you again," he told Davis, fastening his seat belt. "How's it going?"

Knowing that Reet would get to the subject of acquiring Camille Granville's share of Vendora eventually, Davis launched directly into the conversation he had had with her this afternoon as he headed toward the freeway.

"So, what are you going to do about her?" Reet shot back, impatiently.

"Let her move in. Then I'll make her life so miserable she'll beg me to buy her out. I know what will drive her crazy, and what she does not want to happen. A few changes to the operation, some renovations . . . it won't take long for her to pack up and leave."

Without saying a word, Reet reached into the backseat and retrieved his bag, unzipped it and removed a brown leather check-book. He placed it on his lap and quickly scribbled his signature.

"Offer her this." He handed the check to Davis, who glanced at it briefly and saw that it was blank.

"I don't get it, Reet. Why should you do this?"

Reet straightened his coat sleeves, and smoothed the front of his dark gray jacket before answering, as if taking time to phrase his words with caution. "I'm going into business in Texas . . . a short-term operation, in which you are going to be a major player. And everything hinges on you having complete control of Vendora. No partners. No nosy widow. No one involved but you and me." He reached back into his bag and pulled out a map. "So get rid of the Granville woman. Be reasonable. Be fair. And get her out. Okay? Now . . . we got someplace to go." He flipped on the overhead light to read the map. "When you get to Interstate 59, head north . . . to-ward Lake Livingston. There's something I want to show you that will explain everything."

Davis did as Reet requested and followed his directions, which Reet read from his map as they sped along. Soon he was heading deep into the Piney Woods that bordered the eastern edge of the county. The Big Thicket, the name given to this heavily forested area of the state, contained a network of dark narrow roads that wound through the dense woods, twisting and turning for miles. The eerie drive unnerved Davis, who began to fear that he might not be able to find his way back to the main highway. After twenty minutes on the sinister road, he emerged into a clearing and swung to a stop in front of a nondescript cement-block building. A black pickup truck was parked outside and weather-beaten lettering on the front door read WELCOME TO HORSESHOE PINES.

"Get out. Come on," Reet ordered, already out of the car and crossing the dark clearing before Davis had opened his door. Once outside, Davis took a moment to look around. What the fuck was Reet going to do with a rundown beer joint in the middle of no-where? Arching a brow, he followed Reet through the battered door and into a brightly lit room filled with gaming tables, slot machines, arcade games, and lots of blinking lights A man in denim overalls with his long hair pulled back into a ponytail, got up from the floor where he was assembling one of the slot machines and hurried over to extend his hand.

"Mr. Collins?" he asked.

Reet moved closer and took the man's hand. "Yes. You must be Clyde Yancy?"

"That's me," Clyde said, nodding at Davis, who simply nodded back.

"Things are looking good, Clyde," Reet remarked, walking over to one of the blackjack tables to run his hand over the soft green felt while studying the ambiance of the windowless room. "I like what you've got here. Real western feel. How much more to do?"

"Not much," Clyde said, stopping to assess his handiwork. "Once this machine is finished, I gotta get the safe installed upstairs and run a line down to the back of the bar so I can hook up that electric sign you ordered." He stuck his unlit cigar back between his lips. "Be done by tomorrow afternoon."

Davis walked around, inspecting what was obviously Reet's version of a casino. A full bar, complete with leather-topped stools and a staggering supply of glasses and liquor, took up one end of the room. A cozy sitting area with western style chairs and oversized oak tables had been arranged in front of a stone fireplace fitted with electric logs. The great room had been divided into separate areas for each type of play, with horseshoe-shaped light fixtures hanging above each one. Looking up, Davis saw that one end of the second floor had been glassed in, creating an observation area that provided a clear view of everything going on downstairs. The cement block walls were painted deep red, the carpeting on the floor was dark brown with a tiny horseshoe design, and the furniture was rustic cowboy, making Davis feel as if he had stepped into a tavern somewhere in the wild, wild West.

"What do you think?" Reet asked, coming over to where Davis was preparing to try out one of the slot machines.

Davis slipped in a quarter, pulled on the lever, then laughed aloud when a rattle of change dropped down into the tray. "I think it's innovative. Risky, but not impossible to pull off . . . for a while," Davis said, retrieving his winnings.

"I thought you might feel that way," Reet said, motioning for Davis to follow him. "Come on upstairs to the office so we can discuss the arrangement I have in mind."

Upstairs in the partially furnished office, Reet laid out his plan:

"The nearby Alabama-Coushatta Indian Casino is drawing high stakes gamblers into Texas—many from Louisiana, Oklahoma, and even farther away," he started. "As any real gambler knows, after playing for a time in one location, it's a good idea to move on to some place new and try your luck there."

With a nod, Davis agreed. "And currently, there is no other gambling casino around, unless you drive to New Mexico or cross into Louisiana."

"Right," Reet agreed. "And that is not an attractive option. Horseshoe Pines can fill that gap. It will be a membership only facility, with a carefully selected clientele. Located in this secluded area, in an understated building, we ought to be able to keep a low profile and discourage curious tourists long enough to make some real money."

"For how long?" Davis interjected.

"The odds are on my side, even if I only stay open for six months. That's all the time I'd need to clear a very hefty profit," Reet said, going on to tell Davis that the illicit casino would generate a lot of cash that had to be laundered through a legitimate business. "That's where Vendora comes in," he continued. "You will deposit the cash receipts from Horseshoe Pines into an account along with your receipts from Vendora. Then you will transfer my money back to me as a payment on a business consulting contract we will draw up. On the books, it's all very legitimate. You see?" Reet was pumped with excitement after explaining his proposition. "You in?"

Davis pursed his lips in thought and didn't answer right away, thinking of how complicated this situation had become. Camille had to be dealt with. Would she take the cash Reet had given him to buy her out? If not, did he dare commit to something as chancy as this if she remained in the picture?

"Let me make this easy for you," Reet cut in. "You go along with me on this and I wipe away the debt you owe me. You don't go along, and I go to the authorities and tell them you stole fifty-eight thousand dollars from my business account." He scrutinized Davis with a gritty stare. "And if you tell the authorities that you had legitimate access to that account because you are my partner, they're going to ask for the paperwork on that . . . and as you know there isn't any. I'll tell them you are a disgruntled former employee who stole my PIN and stole my money. And I know you don't want me to tell them that, do you?"

"No," Davis sighed, shifting uneasily. "That is not the way I want this to go down." Tapping his fingers on the arm of the heavy oak chair, he answered," Okay. I'm in. When do we get started?"

"Right now. Clyde Yancy, the guy downstairs, might look like a country bumpkin, good old boy, but he's a sharp operator. He is a full-blood Coushatta Indian from Louisiana and he used to run a casino over there. He will manage Horseshoe Pines. He's already got a guy that he trusts working on our membership list. He'll decide who comes in and who doesn't. You are going to work with Clyde, learn the operation, and act as his backup if he needs you."

"Okay by me," Davis said, suddenly feeling as if he had fallen into a deep dark pit.

CHAPTER 32

After returning to campus after her father's funeral, Jaiden had gradually moved in with Rod, and he had neither protested nor encouraged her decision to ease more permanently into his life. Relieved, Jaiden took his noncommittal attitude to mean that he was fine with the arrangement, though he maintained an air of elusive independence that Jaiden, for some reason, found intriguing. He was his own man and did not answer to anyone. Jaiden never took him for granted.

When he had seen her tattoo—Rod, Forever—which she had acquired in Houston over spring break, he had examined it closely, and then simply muttered, "Pretty good work," and never mentioned her first piece of body art again. His less than enthusiastic reaction had disappointed Jaiden, who immediately dispensed with the hope that one day, they would have matching tattoos.

Jaiden rarely spent time at Keeney Hall, or with Mona and the other first year students in her dorm now that she was practically living with Rod. It had been difficult to return to class, with so much catch-up work to do and so much sorrow in her soul. She missed her father, was furious with her mother, and peeved with herself for not being able to accept the fact that her life was forever changed. There was nothing she could do to bring her father back, and this helplessness fueled a silent rage that she struggled to control. Being with Rod did help, because he could banish her morose moods with an impromptu party, an evening of billiards at Twist, or a spin along the coast on his motorcycle. Without Rod in her life, Jaiden knew that she would have been totally lost.

Now, while he was at his computer class at East Tech, Jaiden was preparing for final exams—scheduled to begin next week. When the doorbell rang, Jaiden hurried to get it, and was surprised, but happy, to see Mona standing outside, holding a white paper bag when she opened the door to Rod's apartment.

"Hey, girl," Mona smiled, giving Jaiden a firm hug, and then following her inside her cousin's apartment. "Brought you some mail . . . and your favorite latte from the Coffee Cat." She held up the bag and grinned, then pushed her sunglasses onto the top of her head. She was wearing pale blue denim Capri pants, a white short-sleeved cropped top that tied in the front and sporty navy canvas flats. Her long dark hair was swept to the side and anchored with a white scarf in a long ponytail that trailed over one shoulder.

"God, can I use this right now," Jaiden replied with genuine relief, eagerly opening the paper sack to remove one of the steaming drinks. She popped off the lid and took a quick sip. "Fabulous. Girl, this is exactly what I needed. I've had my head stuck in these books for the past thirty-six hours, and I am going freakin' nuts!"

"Been at it that long?" Mona remarked, sitting down on a chair opposite the sofa, where Jaiden had snuggled back down with her laptop, amid a jumble of textbooks, notebooks and papers. "Rod at school?"

"Yeah, he won't be back until about three. What are you up to? All dressed up. I love the outfit," Jaiden said, glancing down at her grungy, comfy sweat suit, which she had worn for the past two days.

"Shopping. Wanna go?"

"I can't. I fell so far behind when I was at home, and now I have to do catch-up reading before I can even begin to start studying. My French final is Monday. Wednesday, Geology. On Friday . . . well, don't even ask about my English term paper. Haven't begun to organize my notes, let alone start writing the damn thing."

Mona grimaced as she flipped her long hair off her neck and then kicked off her flat shoes and curled her feet beneath her hips. "I feel your pain, girl. My paper isn't much further along, either, but I do have my notes together. I plan to start writing on Sunday, bury myself in it and push straight through until it's done. So, I will not be leaving our room for about three days. That's why today is the only day I can hit the shops."

"I hear you," Jaiden remarked, glancing through the stack of mail that Mona had handed her. "I need some summer clothes. Don't have a decent thing in my closet, and I'm gonna burn this outfit immediately after finals." She tugged at the pants of her green sweat suit and mocked a frown.

"So, what's your term paper topic?" Mona asked, settling in for a chat.

"*The Social and Economic Impact of Free Blacks in New England in 1799.*" Jaiden absently replied, busy opening an envelope with her mother's return address. Once she had examined the contents, she smiled and shouted to Mona, "Money from home, and right on time!"

"We can all use mail like that," Mona agreed, going on to say, "You know I think Rod wrote his English I paper on a similar topic. I know it had to do with free blacks in New England . . . don't remember exactly. But he may have some material you can use."

Surprised by this revelation, Jaiden tilted her head to one side, curious. "Really? He never talks about his time at Brown, so I don't bring it up. And I don't think I ever told him what I was going to write about, but I sure will now."

"Right on. His notes might save you some serious research time."

"And I'm gonna need every bit of help I can get," Jaiden agreed, tucking Mona's suggestion into the back of her mind. As soon as Rod returned from his class this afternoon, she was damn sure going to see if he had any information to help her out of this time crunch.

"How's your mom doing?" Mona inquired.

Jaiden glanced up quickly, then lowered her eyes back to the $2,500 check that her mom had sent. Setting the check aside, Jaiden continued to read the short note that her mother had included: $2,300 was to cover the balance of her dorm fees, with two hundred for Jaiden's spending money for the next two weeks, until she finished her finals and came home.

"My mom? Okay, I guess. Haven't talked to her lately, but she's fine." Jaiden paused, then murmured, "Hmm . . . sounds like she is definitely moving on. She says here that she has quit her job at the travel agency and is going to move into my dad's office and work at the supper club."

"Well, that's a good thing, isn't it?" Mona remarked, blowing at the steam that was rising from her coffee. "I would think keeping busy and working in your dad's company would help her get over losing him. Kinda make her feel close to him even though he's gone, you know?"

"I guess," Jaiden grumbled, in resignation. "Whatever she wants to do is fine with me." She jammed the note back into the envelope and focused on the check. "Mona. Shopping suddenly sounds like a great idea. Let's get out of here. I can't take this studying anymore. You driving?"

"Yeah. Missy Charles, the third year student in my Theater Arts class, let me borrow her car."

"Great. Take me to the bank so I can cash this check. I could use some serious retail therapy before I dig into that term paper."

"Girl, you know I'm down for that," Mona whooped, quickly shoving her feet back into her shoes.

"Really," Jaiden called out, already off the sofa and into Rod's bedroom where she pulled off her sweats, threw on some jeans and a loose blouse, ran her fingers through her spiky hair and grabbed her purse. "I'm outta here," she said, following Mona out the door.

Jaiden and Mona spent the remainder of the day happily zipping in and out of the funky small shops on Thayer Street buying clothes, jewelry, cosmetics, and whatever caught their eye, before moving on to Providence Place Mall, downtown. Jaiden ran through her two-hundred-dollar allowance in record time, but kept on spending, cutting deeply into the money her mother had sent to pay for her room and board. Why pay dorm fees and buy meal tickets when she no longer stayed on campus? she rationalized, handing a cashier a one hundred dollar bill for a leather and suede Coach wallet. With only two weeks of school left, why bother?

It was dusk when Mona dropped Jaiden back at Rod's apartment. The two hugged quickly and parted, with Mona zooming off to meet her boyfriend, Damian, for dinner. Mona had confided to Jaiden that Damian had asked her to spend the night at his apartment tonight because he wanted to make it a very special evening. Mona was certain he planned to propose.

That relationship is really going strong, Jaiden mused as she let herself in with her key, wishing she felt as optimistic about her future with Rod.

The place was dark, except for the light that was on above the stove in the kitchen. After dropping her shopping bags on the bed, she saw that Rod had left a note on the kitchen table. She went over and picked it up.

Gone to Twist for a few rounds of pool with Sid.
Know you have to study.
Be back late, Rod.

Shrugging, Jaiden stared at the sofa, frowned at her laptop, and sighed, hardly in the mood to pick up a book.

But I have to, she told herself, filling the coffeemaker with water. While measuring out the coffee, she thought about Mona's suggestion that she ask Rod for his research notes. Setting the coffee aside, she picked up the phone and called Twist. Rod was there, and quickly came to the phone.

"Hey," she greeted him. "I'm back at the apartment, about to hit the books again."

"Where were you?" he asked.

"Shopping with Mona. Had to take a break."

"I can dig that," he replied. "I'm gonna hang here for a while. Call me later if you want."

Setting the coffeepot down, she asked Rod about his term paper for English I and if he had any notes.

"God, it's been so long." He paused, and then told Jaiden. "If I still have the notes they would be in a box in the back of my closet. It's a white box. Marked *School Stuff.* If you feel like looking, go ahead."

"Think I might. I'm really under the gun on this one."

"Okay. See you later."

After the coffee was on, Jaiden went into the bedroom, found the box and began to dig through the papers until she found what she was looking for: Rod's term paper titled, *The Free Black in 1800 New England: A Social Analysis;* a stack of note cards secured with a rubber band; and a bunch of computer printouts held together with a big metal clip.

Exactly what I need, Jaiden decided, relief sweeping through her as she flipped through the Internet research that Rod had done. She remained on the bedroom floor while reading his paper, and was pleasantly surprised at how well it was written.

He should have stayed at Brown, she thought, thankful for the resource. *But he seems happy with his classes at Tech. That's what matters.*

She began to pick up the papers and books that she had scattered around while unpacking his box. The last thing she picked up from the floor was a bright yellow Walgreens photo packet, and though she knew she shouldn't do it, she removed the photos to take a quick peek. Most had been taken with a 35 mm camera, but a few were Polaroid shots. She smiled to see Rod standing on the beach in a pair of super tight swim trunks, showing off his tattoos while holding a can of beer. *God, he has a body,* she mused, thinking that the tattoos did more to enhance his attractiveness than detract from it. She studied another photo: Mona and Damian posing with their lips together in a staged kiss, on the porch of an ultramodern beach house. Thinking that the photo must have been taken recently, Jaiden turned it over and saw that indeed, it had been taken during this past spring break, when she had been stuck in Houston. The next photo she slipped out of the packet made her pause. Rod was sitting on a jet ski, and an attractive, dark-skinned girl in a tiny red bikini was sitting behind him, her arms around his waist. A slow burn began to rise inside of Jaiden, but she took a deep breath, telling herself that the girl most likely was a relative; a cousin he had taken for a spin on his jet ski. Mona had said that a lot of her family would be at the beach house for the vacation. Of course, that was who the girl was: Family.

However, the next photo shattered Jaiden's seed of hope that the girl might be related to Rod: He was standing between her and a fair-skinned beauty whose smile was as big as her bare, sun-bronzed breasts, and he was smiling as if he had just won the lottery. Slumping down to the floor, Jaiden began to tremble, afraid to go on, yet unable to stop. The fourth photo was even more detailed and hurtful, leaving no doubt about what Rod had been doing to entertain himself during spring break in Florida. Jaiden cringed to see Mona, Damian, Rod, and the red bikini-clad girl holding drinks, sitting on a blanket on the sand, big smiles on their faces, clearly having a grand old time!

Unexpectedly, Jaiden teared up. This would not have happened if she had been there with Rod. And it was all her mother's fault!

Frantically, she shuffled through the Polaroid photos and saw Rod in various poses while frolicking with the two mystery girls on a bed inside the beach house. All three were naked, sweaty, and tangled into positions that were so explicit, they verged on pornography. In one photo Rod was puffing on a joint while one of the girls rubbed his bulging erection. Disgusted by the sickening images, Jaiden flung them back into the closet, ran into the bathroom and threw up. As her stomach wrenched and sobs shook her body, all she wanted to do was get out of the apartment and out of Rod's life.

How could he have done this to me? How could Mona keep this from me? She was there during spring break. She never told me that Rod had fooled around with two women while he was there. Mona knew exactly what he was doing. The bitch. And she acts like she's my friend. Fuck 'em all, Jaiden silently raged, pushing herself up off the floor. She splashed water on her face and rinsed her mouth, then stomped into the kitchen and grabbed a large trash bag. Tears blurred her eyes as she swept through the apartment and gathered up everything that belonged to her: clothes, books, shoes, toiletries, and CDs, tossing everything into the plastic bag. *And I gave up my virginity to him! In the back of a damn limo, too! Even had his fuckin' name tattooed on my arm!* With a jerk, she yanked open the pantry door, snatched her special blend coffee off the shelf, along with two jars of creamer, and the box of Godiva chocolates she had purchased for Rod last Saturday.

Once she had claimed all of her possessions, she went back into the bedroom, retrieved the disgusting photographs and spread them out on the kitchen table.

"A welcome home you won't forget, you bastard," she muttered. Then she pulled out her cell phone and called for a taxi to take her back to Keeney Hall. Thank God, Mona would not be there. She was the last person Jaiden wanted to see tonight. All she wanted to do was pack her things, get on the next plane to Houston, and put Rod, his two-faced cousin, and Brown University behind her forever.

CHAPTER 33

"I don't think it's a good idea," Camille told Davis, calmly continuing to doodle on her notepad, focusing on the interlocking circles she was drawing instead of the wild plan that Davis was describing.

"You don't hear me," he snapped. "It will work."

"I doubt it," she tossed back, thinking, *You called this stupid meeting, at nine o'clock at night. If you don't want my opinion, why am I here?*

"Why not?" he said, obviously irritated by Camille's lack of interest in his idea.

Camille sagged. When he had asked her to stay late to get her opinion on something important, she had been surprised, yet curious to hear what he had to say. Now, she was beginning to see that he was simply going through the motions of including her, with no real intention of taking her advice. He wasn't fooling her: If he thought this kind of deliberate hassle would get her to sell out, he was mistaken.

"Converting the upstairs into a cigar bar and game room will only lower our standards and attract a different crowd," she finally answered. "And it would be a clientele that wouldn't appreciate Vendora's trademark, elegant atmosphere."

"Different? People who smoke cigars and enjoy playing non-betting games spend money, too, and on more than food and wine. We'd sell premium drinks, imported cigars, book more private parties. It's the rage in Los Angeles."

"This is Houston," she said dryly. "Our tastes in entertainment might be a little less exotic."

Davis snorted his disagreement. "Expanding this place to attract cigar aficionados is the way to go. It can give us a boost and increase our revenue substantially. At Romero's, Reet and I took in a minimum of . . ."

Camille groaned and lifted a hand toward him in protest. "I don't care what you and your partner in Los Angeles did, Davis, so please stop trying to compare Vendora to Romero's. They are two different operations with very different target markets. To convert the upstairs of Vendora into a game room with pool tables, poker tables, and arcade games is a terrible idea. Sounds to me as if you are catering to men . . . men whom I doubt would be accompanied by women."

"Women smoke cigars, too," Davis threw back in a challenge.

"Not the class of women who make up a large part of Vendora's loyal customers," Camille said, sighing as she thought, *I guess lap dances will be next.*

"That's what's wrong with this place, Camille. Too much goddamn tradition! I'm going to shake things up, and adding a gaming component to our offering is the way to go. People who like to spend money, also like to take risks. I want to give them something to get excited about, even if it's only non-betting poker and arcade games. Customers will stay around longer, eat more food, and bring their friends. Get with it, Camille."

"I think the idea stinks," Camille stated flatly, getting up from behind what used to be Max's desk to go stand near the bookcase where she had placed a framed picture of him. "And this place will literally stink, too, with all that cigar smoke filling up the place. You are courting disaster. Besides, our cash flow situation can't support that kind of investment right now. You act as if someone has given you a blank check. How are you planning to pay for this?"

"Don't worry about that," Davis barked.

"Max would have hated the idea of a game room at Vendora," Camille lamented.

Davis grunted, dismissing her concerns. "No money changes hands. Customers can smoke cigars, drink wine or whiskey; have fun. What's the big deal?"

With a quizzical expression, she studied Davis, and then told him, "Your interest in gambling puzzles me. I would have thought that after your experience on the *Sea Wind,* you would have lost your desire to be involved in any form of gaming."

Davis suddenly shifted in his chair and scooted to the edge of his seat, where he posed stiffly, his shoulders pulled back in indignation. "What the hell are you talking about?" His voice was louder than normal. "The *Sea Wind*? What does that have to do with anything remotely related to my plans for Vendora?"

In a leisurely manner, Camille picked up Max's photograph, gazed at it for a moment, then set it back on the bookshelf. "Davis, I had thought that I would never say this to you, but I think now is the right time to tell you something."

"What?" he said curtly, now standing.

"In my opinion, your behavior on the cruise ship may have contributed to Max's death."

"You can't be serious!" He crossed the room in two long strides and stopped in front of Camille, his golden-tan face reddening in anger. "You had better clarify that remark! I don't like what you are implying."

"The last words that Max and I exchanged were about you, your fawning girlfriend, and your out-of-control gambling. I was sick of Lara hanging onto Max, using him to fill your role because you were never sober . . . or willing to get out of the casino long enough to spend time with her. Max was worried that your gambling was out of control and that it might affect your ability to perform as his partner. I told him that he was being paranoid. He wanted to leave me in our stateroom at one o'clock in the morning and go talk to you. I asked him not to leave, so he stayed. I went to bed angry, and left him sulking on the veranda, with no idea that I would never speak to him again." She bored her dark gray eyes into Davis, hoping he felt her rage and her sorrow. "I can't express how sorry I am that my last conversation with my husband was an argument about you!"

Davis's breathing had become audible and rapid. He swiped a nervous hand over his lips before he spoke. "Don't you dare blame me for Max's death. That is a cheap shot, Camille. I never would have expected this from you."

Camille shrugged. "And I never would have expected to say that I regret the day I encouraged Max to sell his business to you. You have no integrity. No class. It's all show and shine with you, isn't it, Mr. Hollywood? No real substance." Her voice cracked as she probed, desperate for closure. "You know what happened to Max the night of the fire, don't you?"

"I don't know anything."

"Did he come to see you in the casino?"

"No! I told you before that I never saw Max."

"Are you sure?" she taunted, wishing she could break him.

"Damn sure," he countered. "Be careful, Camille. Making accusations you can't prove, could be dangerous."

"I'm not worried. I wish I didn't have to work here with you, but that is too damn bad. I will stay and I plan to do everything possible to regain full ownership of Vendora."

"We'll see about that," Davis threw back before flinging open the door to Camille's office. The familiar noise of the busy restaurant swept into the room, along with the final notes of a ballad by Anita Baker drifting out of the sound system. Without another word, Davis walked out, went into his office next door, and slammed the door shut with a loud crack.

Shaken by the long overdue confrontation, Camille sank weakly into Max's high-back leather chair, put her head into her hands and struggled to collect herself, realizing that she had begun to cry.

She had moved into Max's office at Vendora two Monday mornings ago, and had immediately realized that Davis had no plans to make her feel welcome or help her learn the business. They were not getting along at all. She had turned to Percy, who had been eager to show Camille the ropes and help her take over the day-to-day functions for which Max had been responsible: managing food and liquor supplies, and paperwork related to the staffing, except the actual hiring and firing of employees: That was Davis's area.

Nearly every day, Davis got a phone call from his business partner in Los Angeles, a snippy man named Reet Collins who had little to say to Camille whenever she answered the phone. With her, he was brisk, businesslike and cold, and she had a feeling that he had a lot to do with these crazy changes that Davis was determined to initiate at Vendora.

Davis left her alone in the restaurant during the day, and she managed to avoid him as much as possible by arriving early and leaving by six in the evening, before Davis arrived to oversee the bar, the nightclub, and close the place down. He often remained at Vendora until three or four o'clock in the morning.

Now, she wondered if there was anything she could actually do to stop him from moving forward with his plan. The class of people his changes would draw would be awful, Camille concluded, and there would be arguments, fights, tension and attitude in a game room such as he proposed.

If only I could buy Davis out, she wished, her mind turning to the meeting that was scheduled for tomorrow morning at Paul Cotter's office with Neil Windman of Tropica Cruise Lines. The terms of her settlement were about to be finalized and with that money, she might possibly get control of Vendora again.

When the phone on her desk rang, she took a deep breath, wiped her eyes, and then answered.

"Hi, Mom."

"Jaiden. This is a surprise." Camille said as she glanced at the clock. 10:15 P.M. 11:15 in Providence. "What's up? You get the check?"

"Ah, yes. I got it today. Thanks."

Camille could detect that familiar tone of need in her daughter's voice: She wanted something . . . or something was wrong. "Studying hard? Ready for your exams?" she probed, holding her breath.

"I'm coming home," Jaiden blurted out in a shaky voice.

Tensing, Camille fought to remain calm, aware that Jaiden was struggling to keep from crying. "After your finals, sure."

"No. I mean now. I can't stay here anymore."

"Jaiden. Calm down. I can hear it in your voice. What's wrong? Did something happen? Are you worried about your final exams? If so, maybe I can get you a tutor, or extra help. I'll do whatever you need me to do so you can hang in there."

"It not about my exams, Mom. But I can't talk about it now. I'm packed and I'm coming home. I wanted to know if you can pick me up tomorrow morning. I get in at nine and I'll have too much stuff with me to take the shuttle."

Making a fist, Camille pressed her fingernails into her flesh, knowing it would do no good to push for more information now. She had cautioned Jaiden about returning to school so quickly after Max's death, and now it seemed as if her concerns had been legitimate. Jaiden had been traumatized by the sudden loss of her father, and it was not surprising that she wanted, and needed, to come home and be with her mother now.

"Of course, I'll pick you up," she said. "Don't worry. Everything is going to be fine."

CHAPTER 34

"I'm sorry Mrs. Granville couldn't make it," Neil told Paul Cotter, taking a seat in the conference room of the attorney's office. He spoke the truth; Neil had been looking forward to seeing Camille again. Over the past month, he had spoken to her on the phone several times and had been impressed with her tenacious attitude and determination to come to grips with her husband's death. He knew that she was in a great deal of pain and he wanted to do all that he could to help her through this difficult period.

"An emergency with her daughter," Paul told Neil, going on to explain that Jaiden, who was having a hard time dealing with her father's death, had unexpectedly returned home from school.

"I understand completely," Neil said, opening his briefcase and removing a slim file folder. He took out three sheets of paper and laid them side by side on the table in front of him, in preparation for his discussion about the *Sea Wind* fire. He was ready to divulge what Tropica Cruise Lines planned to do to compensate Camille Granville for her loss.

"The investigation of the *Sea Wind* disaster is complete," Neil started. "The National Transportation Safety Board (NTSB) and Marine Underwriters Insurance investigators have concluded that the fire was not the result of any mechanical failure or negligence on the part of the cruise line. The *Sea Wind* is fitted with security cameras throughout its interior, in passageways, public rooms, open decks, and above all outside activity areas of the ship. Security is a very high priority for Tropica and we take extensive measures to keep our passengers and employees safe."

"Are passengers aware of these security cameras?" Paul asked.

"In most cases, yes. We don't try to hide them, and all of the literature promoting our cruises contains clear statements that cameras are in public areas for their safety, and they are plainly visible. Anyone in a monitored area ought to be aware that they are under surveillance."

"And did the cameras capture some activity related to the fire?" Paul prompted.

Neil cleared his throat and picked up one of the pieces of paper in front of him. "Yes. Security cameras positioned on the upper decks beam down and monitor the outside of the ship. They caught two teenage passengers throwing ignited firecrackers from their Emerald Deck veranda. Apparently, a fire broke out on their balcony and their efforts to extinguish it failed. The fire spread quickly, consumed their stateroom, and eventually migrated along the starboard side of Emerald Deck. Investigators have traced the source of the fire to one particular cabin and evidence indicates that the kids had smuggled quite a cache of fireworks aboard."

"How is that possible? Aren't bags thoroughly checked before embarking?" Paul asked.

"Of course. But you would be surprised how ingenious people have become at getting around security checks. Somehow, these boys managed. Or, they might have purchased the fireworks while the ship was in port at Lahaina or Hilo and simply brought the devices back in shopping bags. We don't routinely check parcels brought aboard after onshore excursions once the ship has sailed. In any case, NTSB has absolved Tropica Cruise Lines of negligence."

"Will Tropica file a lawsuit against the boys' parents?"

"Most likely, but they are not wealthy people and I doubt that a judgment against them would result in any significant remuneration for us. However, in light of the damages suffered by many passengers, Marine Underwriters, as an act of good faith, is prepared to offer compensation." He paused, picked up the second piece of paper and then went on. "Tropica Cruise Lines has put together a settlement proposal for Mrs. Granville that we feel is fair."

"Let's hear what you have to offer," Paul said, settling back in his chair to let Neil proceed.

"We are offering Mrs. Granville an annuity in the amount of $500,000, to be paid out over ten years. Maxwell Granville was forty-six years old when he died, and this award represents an estimate of reasonable future earnings of which Mrs. Granville has been deprived. The calculations were done by Marine Mutual and conform to standard policy in cases like these where no negligence has been determined."

"I see," Paul replied, busy making notes on his legal pad. "Your offer sounds reasonable, but of course, my client will make the final decision. Would the videotapes that captured activity on the ship that night be available for her to view?"

"I think so," Neil replied. "If you make the request on behalf of your client in the appropriate legal manner, and I am sure Tropica would have no problem sending over copies for your review."

"Good. I'll do that," Paul replied. After referring to his notes, he asked, "What about the cabin steward, Paolo Homers? Camille would like to talk to him."

"Right. I'll arrange it . . . the *Trade Wind* docks at Galveston at the end of the week. Paolo will be in port for ten days. I'll call Mrs. Granville and set up a time for her to speak to him."

Jaiden cried all the way home from the airport, sniffling into the wadded handkerchief that Camille handed to her at baggage claim. She refused to answer any of Camille's questions, and once they arrived at the house, she ran inside, leaving Camille to lug her suitcases, boxes, bags, and sacks into the house and up to her room. When she slammed her door shut, Camille knew it was best to leave her alone.

"This child is not grieving over her father's death," Camille later told Rochelle, while sipping a glass of iced tea at her kitchen table and talking on the phone. "The only reaction of any significance that I got out of her was when I asked her if this sudden return home had anything to do with Rod."

"And?" Rochelle prompted.

"She told me never to mention his name again, and then burst into tears," Camille replied.

"Then that's it," Rochelle concluded. "A broken heart. The boy is history. A lover's spat. You ought to be happy."

"Happy?" Camille nearly shouted. "Do you have any idea how much it cost me and Max to send Jaiden to Brown? And she has the nerve to walk away without officially withdrawing, or taking a single final exam? Over a spat with her boyfriend?" Camille had to stop and collect herself, she was so furious she wanted to break something. "I knew there was something about that boy that did not sit right. She became too involved, too fast, and now he has done something to hurt her."

"Well, she'll get over it. Most women do," Rochelle commented, in a been-there-done-that manner. "When a man breaks a woman's heart, the best thing she can do is kick him to the curb and move on."

"Rochelle, please. This is not funny. Jaiden has been very irresponsible. If she had decided not to return to school after the funeral, I could have accepted that . . . her professors might have been willing to give her an incomplete so she could make up the class work in summer school. Who knows? But to go back to school, then simply leave and refuse to tell me why? No, she can forget about me being understanding. Obviously, she has her priorities confused."

"What's she doing now?"

"Shut off in her room, crying. And she can stay there with her miserable self."

"What are you going to do?"

"Me? Nothing."

"Want me to come over and try to get her to open up?"

Camille sighed in exasperation. "No, Rochelle. Let it go. If she wants to talk to you, she'll call. I am going to go about my business as if she were not here. I am through playing games with Jaiden. Let's leave her alone, let *her* tell us what the hell she plans to do with the rest of her life."

On Friday, Camille got into her silver Audi, lowered the convertible top and headed down the Gulf Freeway, looking forward to her visit with Paolo Homers. As she sped along, the wind brushed her face, and the sun warmed her back. She recalled a time when she had dreaded making the drive to Galveston to pick up her property from Tropica Cruise Lines and how grateful she had been to have Davis help her out. Davis. What a disappointment he was turning out to be. Right now, he had space planners and contractors working out the details to convert the upstairs of Vendora into his mini-game room. Her stomach tightened in revulsion when she thought about him and the way he was treating her. In his opinion, she was no more than a pesky annoyance that he was determined to remove.

For the last week of June, the weather was warm, but dry—a perfect day to escape the city and clear her mind of troubles at Vendora, as well as at home. Jaiden continued to mope around with a long, sad face and wallow in self-pity, refusing to discuss what had compelled her to impulsively abandon the university and flee home. However, Camille had overheard sufficient snippets of telephone conversations between Jaiden and Nici to arrive at the conclusion that Rod's activities during spring break in Florida were the root cause of her daughter's misery.

Exactly why I held firm and did not let her go to Florida, Camille thought, curious about what had gone on.

Her anger at Jaiden for her irresponsible reaction to whatever Rod had done had lessened over the past seven days, making Camille feel a bit sorry for her daughter, who was struggling with her first romantic breakup. *She will have to ride this out. The pain will pass. All it takes is time,* Camille reminded herself, thinking that she and Jaiden ought to go away together and work on finding a way to make peace.

The cabin, Camille decided. Next Wednesday would be the Fourth of July and the celebrations at the lake started this weekend. There would be fireworks, boat races, picnics, and families enjoying the outdoor festivities. *That's where we'll go. A week at the lake will do both of us some good. And I am sure Davis will not object to my being away.*

The trip into Galveston went smoothly, though traffic on the island was much heavier than usual now that school was out and Houstonians were flooding the beaches to sit on the sand and work on their tans. After locating the Tropica Cruise Lines building, she made her way to Neil Windman's office, where he welcomed her with a warm handshake and introduced her to the wiry, darkly tanned man who was seated in a chair at a square table near the window overlooking the bay.

"Paolo Homers," Neil started, "I think you remember Mrs. Granville?"

Paolo rose to shake Camille's hand. "Most certainly. I am very sorry about your husband," he said, sympathetically.

"Thank you," Camille murmured, taking the chair next to his. "I appreciate you making the time to speak with me."

"I am happy to tell you what I can remember." He turned to Neil. "It all happened so quickly. A lot of confusion. And it was so dark!"

"Yes," Neil agreed. "The electricity went out in all of the staterooms on the starboard side of the Emerald Deck, where we suspect the fire originated. The Granville stateroom was only three cabins away from the source of the fire, on the same circuit breaker, which blew out from the heat."

"That's why I did not see any light coming from the bathroom," Camille commented, her thoughts going back to Jaiden's remark about why a strip of light had not shone under the door. "Mr. Windman . . ."

"Oh, please, call me Neil," he told her smiling. "We don't have to be so formal here."

Camille let out a long sigh. "Neil . . . what you said about the lights being out . . . it explains so much. I simply could not understand why I did not notice that my husband was in the bathroom."

"But he wasn't," Paolo stated with conviction. "I remember that clearly. After I got you out, I did go into the bathroom. Used this very same light . . ." he paused and removed a small flashlight the size of a pen from his shirt pocket. "I checked thoroughly, the shower, behind the door. I looked everywhere, then I left."

"What about the veranda?" Camille suggested, feeling very confused.

"Only to see if the door was securely locked from the inside. It was."

"And you did not open it?"

"No."

"So, you didn't go out onto the veranda and check for him out there?"

"No, I didn't."

Camille's mind raced with possibilities. She had not locked the door to the veranda, and even if she had . . . and if Max had fallen asleep out there, how could he have reentered the stateroom to wind up dead in the bathroom?

"I want to believe you, Paolo, but what you say does not make sense. The shipboard firefighting team found my husband on the bathroom floor. He had fallen. Hit his head. Glass was everywhere."

"I know," Paolo replied, shaking his head. "The NTSB men told me the same thing. They questioned me so much about it and I told them the same thing I am telling you. I am absolutely certain that you were the only person in your stateroom when I entered."

Neil, who had been glancing through a file on his desk, referred to one of the papers. "What Paolo says is confirmed here in this report."

Biting her lip, Camille thought about what this meant: Max must not have been in their stateroom when the fire broke out. Had he gone to the casino? Had he been arguing with Davis, perhaps?

Opening her purse, Camille pulled out a photograph of her,

Max, Davis, and Lara that had been taken aboard the ship during a dinner cruise. She had brought it along in case Paolo had forgotten what Max looked like: Anything to jog his memory and get more specific information. "Do you recognize this man?" she tapped on Davis's image.

"Oh, yes. Mr. Kepler. He was on the Emerald Deck, too. I serviced his cabin. Very nice fellow."

"Did you see him the night of the fire?"

Slowly, Paolo shook his head, "No. And not the lady with him either. When I got to their cabin, it was empty."

Realizing she had gotten all the information she was likely to get from Paolo, she told him, "Well, this conversation has certainly shed *some* light on what happened. Thank you."

Paolo stood, bowed slightly, and told Camille. "My condolences, again, on the death of your husband. I wish I could be more help."

"You have been helpful, Paolo," she shook his hand. "And thank you for saving my life."

After Paolo left, Neil fastened a puzzled expression on Camille, sensing that she was not completely satisfied with the information that Paolo had provided, yet seemed resigned to accepting it. He wished he had the power to give her the peace of mind that she needed to find closure with this incident. He wondered what, or who, was fueling her obvious guilt over having survived while her husband had not. "Do you have any more questions?" he asked.

Startled from her thoughts, Camille shook her head. "Oh? No. Paolo was helpful, but I still don't understand what happened to Max. However, I'd better get started back to Houston."

Neil closed the file on his desk. "I received a message from Marine Underwriters. They will send over copies of the videotapes in a few days."

"Good. I really want to see them," Camille said vaguely, as if her mind had already moved on to another worry.

"I can tell that you still have something on your mind," Neil acknowledged, sensing that Camille was not quite ready to leave. "Is there anything I can get you? Coffee? A glass of water? A soft drink?"

With a slight nod, Camille relented. "Yes. A glass of water would be nice."

"Be right back." Neil went into the break room across the hall from his office, removed a small bottle of water from the refrigerator, and returned to hand it to Camille.

"I do appreciate everything you are doing to help me understand what happened to my husband during his final hours," she commented, uncapping the water to take a sip. She got up and moved to the window to gaze out over the bay. "Speaking with Paolo has clarified a few things."

"The least I can do," Neil replied. Watching her from behind, he felt sorry for her and could tell that she was under a great deal of strain. "Did your attorney fill you in on our meeting?"

She turned to face Neil. "Oh, yes, and I'm sorry I couldn't be there."

"I understand you had a family emergency?" he said, in an expression of concern.

"My daughter came home from college . . . a little earlier than I had expected. I had to pick her up at the airport . . ." Camille's words drifted off without further explanation as she set the bottle of water on the table and picked up her purse. "I really do have to go. The construction on the inbound side of Interstate 45 has traffic backed up for miles."

"That's one reason why I decided to move onto the island," Neil told her as he walked her to the door. "Five minutes, and I'm home."

Camille chuckled. "Good for you."

Neil went on, "I would be glad to deliver the videotapes to you next week, as soon as they come in, so you won't have to make that drive down here again."

"Well . . . I may not be at home," Camille replied, going on to tell him about her cabin at Lake Livingston and her plans to take a short vacation with Jaiden.

"Your cabin is at Lake Livingston, near the Big Thicket?" Neil commented with curiosity.

"Yes. We are on the southern edge of the lake, not too far from the Alabama-Coushatta Indian Reservation."

Neil shook his head, eyes glinting in recognition. "How nice! You see, I am one-fourth Alabama-Coushatta, three-fourths African-American. My grandmother still lives on the reservation and I have a few cousins and a nephew in the area. I go up there several times a year to visit. So I know the area well."

"That is interesting," Camille agreed, now connecting Neil's reddish-tan complexion, dark hair, and high cheekbones to his Native American ancestry.

"Ever go to the Dance Expositions?" he inquired.

"Oh, yes. My husband and I used to take Jaiden, my daughter, every year. The costumes, the music, the drama. Wonderful. It's been years since I've attended."

"They start next weekend and run through the summer. I had planned on going. If you decide to go up to your cabin, I have no problem dropping the videos off to you there. And, if you want to attend the dances, I'd be glad to accompany you and your daughter as your official guide. I can provide authentic insight into what is going on," he finished, hands palms up in a gesture of welcome. "It would be my pleasure to introduce you to a more personal side of the Native American experience. There is a lot more to the dances than the costumes."

Camille suddenly warmed to the idea, but took her time answering. "I can't commit now, but give me a call when the tapes are in. Leave me a message on my home number. I'll be checking it from the cabin. We'll see how it goes. I'm sure having you as a guide would be very nice."

"I'll give you a call, then," Neil agreed, escorting Camille to the door.

After Camille left, Neil went to the window overlooking the port, his thoughts still on the beautiful widow. She was an extremely attractive woman who had loved her husband very much, and had raised valid points about his death. He wished he had been more help. Even Paolo had not seemed to be able to help her shake the obvious guilt she was feeling for having survived—not an uncommon reaction for those who escape a major disaster. He hoped she would allow him to escort her and her daughter to the dances on the reservation. He definitely wanted to be Camille's friend.

Lara felt as if someone had punched her in the stomach, and for the few seconds it took for the news to sink in, thought she might be sick. She pushed aside the Caesar salad she had been picking at before answering the phone, her appetite definitely gone.

"Absolutely not," she screamed at her attorney after recovering her voice. "I do *not* accept Tropica Cruise Lines' offer of a half million dollar annuity. Over fifteen years? They must be fucking crazy. I want a three-million-dollar lump sum settlement for the loss of my good looks and future earnings and I will take them to court to get it." With that, she slammed down the phone, tossed her white linen napkin over her unfinished lunch and lit a cigarette.

What don't the bastards understand? My acting career is finished, she silently raged, her hands shaking as she put the cigarette between trembling lips. *Roberto Simona is suing me for repayment of that quarter million dollar advance, which I sank into this house, and I do not even have the money for the facial reconstruction that would allow me to go out and try to earn some kind of a living.*

Too angry to cry, she exhaled the cigarette smoke in a long, loud whoosh, staring defiantly across the table. She chewed the inside of her cheek, desperate for an end to the nightmare that had begun the moment she stepped aboard the *Sea Wind*. However, she knew this was just the beginning of a long, drawn-out process that her lawyer had warned her to expect: First, a tentative offer from Tropica far below what she would expect; next, her counteroffer in the maximum amount she thought she could get; finally the haggling back and forth, like a married couple splitting up community property, until they reached common ground. It could take months. Maybe years. How was she going to survive?

CHAPTER 35

Davis arrived at Horseshoe Pines at midnight, hurried inside, went straight upstairs and into Clyde Yancy's office. The two men made eye contact immediately, with Clyde quickly glancing up from the pile of cash he was fingering to nod briefly at his visitor, before resuming his count of the stack of bills.

Without speaking, Davis stepped over to the expanse of one-way glass behind Clyde and watched the action below in the casino. About one hundred people, mostly men, were seated in front of slot machines or at blackjack tables, totally absorbed in their games. Some wore business suits, others wore blue jeans, and a few wore big Stetson hats and pointed-toed boots. Two blondes in white spandex pants and matching pink tube tops were seated at the bar sipping margaritas and chatting up two men in expensive silk suits. The new neon sign—a red horseshoe with a green pine tree in the center—blinked gaily on the wall above the fireplace, and a country tune sung by an artist whom Davis did not recognize was playing on the jukebox, adding soulful ambiance to the rustic, cowboy theme.

A real moneymaker, Davis thought, a tweak of envy pricking his mind. Horseshoe Pines had been open for only three weeks and it was already raking in more money in a single night than Vendora took in, in a month. The approaching Fourth of July weekend ought to be a good one for the members-only club, Davis thought, acknowledging that Reet certainly had the golden touch where making money was concerned.

What am I doing wrong? he fretted, scowling down at the happy customers below.

Vendora had opened with a bang on New Year's Eve, impressing the crowd with its new management, innovative menu, and updated décor, but lately business had begun to slack off. Last week's receipts had been down fifteen percent, and as much as he did not want to admit it, he worried that Max's death might have something to do with this unanticipated decline. It had been *Max's* Vendora. *Max's* family home. *Max's* legacy to his wife and child.

Bullshit, Davis grumbled to himself. *I'm fuckin' sick and tired of all this talk about what Max would or would not have wanted. He's like a fucking ghost, haunting me, watching me, judging me. I can't seem to shake the man.*

Whether Camille Granville liked it or not, Davis was moving forward with his plans to install a game room upstairs at Vendora—the closest he could come to having a joint like this. The blank check that Reet had given him to pay off Camille had come at precisely the right time, providing sufficient funds to launch the renovation. And once the wine bar and game room generated the kind of cash that he knew it would, he'd have the dough to buy Camille out. Who was Reet Collins to tell him how to handle his affairs? He knew how to proceed with Camille; handle her firmly and keep her in her place. Show her who was boss. With limited access to his set of books, he could keep her in the dark until he was ready to deal with her—and on his terms.

"Congratulate Reet on another successful night," Clyde broke into Davis's thoughts, snapping a black leather satchel closed with his thumb. "It's ready to go. You be careful when you leave here, okay?"

"I always am," Davis told him, glancing at the numbers on the slip of paper that Clyde handed to him. Thirty-three thousand dollars. One night's take. The figure was staggering.

One eyebrow arched on his leathery face, Clyde commented with pride, "Impressive, huh? If we're doing this well in a small setup like this, think of what the Alabama-Coushatta are raking in. Millions. The best thing that ever happened to that tribe was opening a casino, but if Judge Hanna has his way, it'll be shut down by summer's end," Clyde finished, chewing on his fat, stubby cigar.

"What's happening with that?" Davis inquired, having followed the controversy over the legality of the Indian casino closely. Last December, the Texas attorney general asked the federal court to order the Alabama-Coushatta casino closed, on the basis that gaming activities prohibited in Texas were also prohibited on the Indian reservations. In spite of the fact that Texas had a lottery, casino-style gambling was still forbidden.

"Judge Hanna ruled that our tribe agreed a long time ago . . . under the Native American Restoration Act, that if it got federal recognition, it would never sponsor any gambling that was illegal in Texas."

"Doesn't sound good for the tribe," Davis commented, fingering his car keys, ready to get going.

"We are filing an appeal, but you're right. Things look bad," Clyde said, nodding thoughtfully. "However, on a brighter note . . . if the casino is closed down, somebody's gotta be around to pick up the slack." He grinned and winked at Davis.

I know who that will be, Davis concluded as he picked up the satchel and stuck the cash receipt into his pocket. "See you Friday night," he told Clyde, checking the hallway before exiting the room.

Back on the road, Davis drove with confidence, having memorized the twists and turns in the dark narrow lane that meandered through the heavily wooded acreage. In near-total darkness, his headlights created a dull yellow wedge of light that guided him to the interstate. For three weeks now, he had made the trip every other night to pick up Reet's money, preferring to come to Horseshoe Pines rather than allow Clyde to bring the cash to Vendora. That would be too risky, he had decided early on. The new bank account he had set up in Las Vegas was the perfect vehicle to transfer Reet's casino money into legitimate payments to get the money back to Reet. So far, their arrangement was working out extremely well.

Now, his mind drifted back to Clyde's remark about the Indian casino. If the courts did shut it down, where would the gamblers take their money? There was room for more than one private gaming club in the area, and who knew what opportunities might come his way if he played it right? This forced arrangement with Reet was turning out to be the perfect opportunity for him to learn all that he needed to know about running an illicit gaming house.

The UPS deliveryman accepted his clipboard through the crack in the door, checked the signature line, and saw that Lara Stanton, indeed, had signed for the box, which he left outside her front door as instructed.

Once Lara heard the roar of his truck as he sped away from her house, she stepped outside, picked up the small square box and hurried back inside. The return address read, Tropica Cruise Lines. A smile touched her lips. A representative had telephoned earlier in the week and advised her that the contents of her stateroom safe were available. When Lara told the woman that, due to her injuries, she would not be able to pick up her property, the representative from Tropica had reluctantly agreed to send it to Lara via UPS, but she would have to personally sign for the package.

The only items Lara recalled having put into the safe were her amethyst pendant and earrings. She hurried upstairs, went into her bedroom, and placed the package on her dresser. Quickly, she cut away the packing tape and tore away the wrapping. Inside, she found a small amount of cash, her Movado watch with the single diamond, and a round suede box containing her amethyst drop earrings. However, the necklace was missing.

Where is my pendant? she worried, thinking back. She recalled having worn it to the All-Star Luncheon, and to dinner the first night at sea, when she and Davis had dined with Camille and Max. She frantically searched through the box again. It simply was not there. What had happened to it?

Lara sat on the bed and remained quiet for a moment, allowing her mind to clear as she concentrated on her activities during the cruise. Day by day, night by night, she retraced her steps until she was back to the night of the fire, and remembered that she had put on the pendant that night, but not the earrings, preparing to go dancing with Davis. He had not shown up. She had changed into a sheer pink lace gown, donned her Chinese embroidered robe, but must not have removed the pendant. Had she been wearing it when the wall crashed down on her? Had she lost it on the ship? Had she been wearing it when she arrived at the hospital?

Focus. Focus, she told herself. With a start, she jumped up, pulled back the mirrored bi-fold door to her closet and reached for a heavy brown envelope from the top shelf. Black block lettering on the outside read: Hilo Hospital—given to her when she had been discharged.

"These are the items that were on your person when you were admitted," the discharge nurse had told Lara before handing her the parcel and then wishing her good luck.

Lara, not eager to look at the clothing she had been wearing that night, had shoved the envelope into her closet as soon as she returned home.

Now, she ripped back the flap and turned the envelope upside down. Her amethyst pendant tumbled to the carpet, along with her Chinese robe and a badly scorched pink lace nightgown.

"Thank God," she murmured, picking up the jewel. She caressed it in her palm for a moment, and then placed it, along with the matching earrings, into her jewelry box. Bending down, she picked up the Chinese robe, and immediately felt a surge of memories cascade into her mind. Shaking out the heavy silk garment, she saw where the fire had burned the cuff of the right sleeve, and there were bloodstains on the collar. She had purchased the robe in Honolulu, with the intention of bringing it home as a souvenir that she would enjoy wearing for years, and had worn it with joy during the cruise.

"It was so beautiful, but it's ruined now. Might as well get rid of it," Lara decided, balling up the robe, ready to discard it. The crackle of paper made her stop. Curious, she searched the pockets and discovered a folded piece of *Sea Wind* stationery. Puzzled, she swallowed hard. The handwriting seemed vaguely familiar, but she was not sure whose it was. Curious, she read:

April 4, 2002. I, Davis Kepler, divest myself of any and all ownership interest in the supper club known as Vendora, in Houston, Texas, for the amount of $25,000 in the form of a loan from Max Granville. I reserve the right to regain my ownership if I am successful in winning at least $25,001 in three hands of blackjack here in the Grand Casino of the cruise ship Sea Wind. If I am not successful, Max Granville becomes full and complete owner of Vendora.

The contract contained both Max Granville's and Davis Kepler's signatures, with her own, scribbled in a disjointed scrawl beneath it. The document was dated April 4th—the night of the fire, over twelve weeks ago. Lara's mind began to whirl with memories that had eluded her since the fire. Two o'clock in the morning. She had been drinking heavily, and chain-smoking, too. Furious with Davis, she had left her stateroom to go to the casino and confront him, but had run into Max in the passageway. He escorted her back inside her stateroom and told her about the wager he had made with Davis, and won. She had drunkenly volunteered to witness his and Davis's signatures, and then the fire alarms had sounded. Max panicked and pulled her into the corridor with him. Lara stuck the paper into the pocket of her Chinese robe for safekeeping, intending to return it to Max. He had pulled her with him toward his stateroom to look for Camille, but she had not been there. Lara fled. She never saw Max again.

Lara stared at the smudged piece of *Sea Wind* stationery, sorting through the implications:

Davis does not own Vendora. It belongs to Max's widow, Camille. From Lara's most recent conversation with Reet, it had seemed clear to her that Davis was still in charge of the supper club. How could that be? *Because Camille does not know that this silent wager exists,* she mused, answering her own question. Could this be the solution to her financial worries? Did she dare confront Davis— suggest that he compensate her for the return of his document? Was she prepared to make such a dangerous move?

Not right now, she decided rather quickly. *I won't do anything until I have more information about what Davis is up to,* thinking a chat with Reet Collins would be the best place to start.

CHAPTER 36

"No, Nici can't go with us," Camille told Jaiden as she cleared away the dinner dishes, forcing herself to ignore Jaiden's sharp retort to her suggestion that the two of them go up to the cabin at the lake.

"Then you can go alone. I don't ever want to go there again. Ever!" Jaiden glared at Camille, got up from the table, and stalked out of the kitchen.

Camille knew that returning to the cabin meant returning to a place where happier days had been spent when Max had been alive, and being alone with her mother at the lake meant dealing with their loss together, a frightening but necessary process that hung unfinished between them. Memories of the intimate weekends she and Max used to spend at the cabin rushed back and brought a lump to Camille's throat, but she knew she had to do this, too. Max was gone forever, but hopefully, once there, she and Jaiden could begin to rebuild bonds of trust.

Oh, why does every conversation have to turn into an argument? Camille worried, leaving the dirty dishes in the sink to calmly follow Jaiden into the entertainment room. She sat down next to Jaiden on the sofa, determined to finish making her point.

Ignoring Camille, Jaiden zapped the remote control to power up the television, and then flipped through the channels until finally deciding to settle on a raucous music video.

Camille sighed in frustration, not surprised by Jaiden's less than positive reception of her plan—a week together at the cabin might not be Jaiden's idea of fun, but they had to start somewhere.

"Please turn the volume down," Camille stated firmly. "We are not through talking."

"All right. But I don't understand why Nici can't come," Jaiden pouted, lowering the volume, then switching channels to the local news where the weatherman was predicting scattered showers over the next three days. "At least I'd have somebody to talk to."

"You can talk to me."

"About what?"

"Anything you want."

"Whatever," Jaiden grumbled with a dismissive shrug. "Anyway, it's going to be rainy and cold over the holiday. See the weather report?" She gestured at the TV screen with the remote control. "Probably be stuck inside the whole time."

"So, we can still find things to do."

"For a whole week?"

"Yes, a whole week. We can leave tomorrow—Friday—stay through the Fourth of July and come back next Friday. Only you and me." Camille replied, before racing on to intercept any possible protest. "I'll make you a deal. If you go with me," she bargained, "I'll let you use the cabin on Labor Day. You can invite whomever you want and I will not come up. It will be your party—for you and your friends—as long as everyone is over eighteen. How's that for a compromise?"

"Really?" Jaiden remarked, perking up as she tore her attention from the television and focused on Camille. "Just me and my friends?"

"Really. I promise. You want it in writing?" Camille joked, relieved to finally see a glimmer of enthusiasm on her daughter's face. "Jaiden, I trust you to be responsible," she continued in a gentler tone. "I know things have been rough, for both of us. We've made mistakes, but let's move on. Okay? I think we'll enjoy being at the lake together, and even though I know going there will bring back memories that perhaps we are both afraid of facing, we have to find ways to move on together without him . . . as hard as it may be. Come with me to the lake. Do this for me."

Looking over at Camille for a long moment, Jaiden finally whispered, "Okay. Okay. I'll go."

"Great. We'll leave tomorrow afternoon. I'll pack my things tonight, because I have to go into the office in the morning and take

care of a few loose ends . . . let Davis know I'll be away for a week."
Not that he will care, she thought.

"What about the food? What do you want to take?" Jaiden asked,
her interest in the trip increasing.

"You go to the grocery store while I'm at the office. Get whatever you want to eat. You are in charge of the food. If you want hot
dogs and barbecue every day, that's fine with me." Excited that
they were finally communicating in a positive manner, Camille
reached over and gently rubbed Jaiden's back. "We'll have fun.
We'll eat outside on the patio, water ski. Sit in the sun and read.
And if it does rain, we can rent some movies or play Scrabble."

"Pray for good weather, Mom. Please?" Jaiden tossed back, getting up from the sofa and leaving the room. Camille sighed in relief. That was the most lighthearted remark that Camille had heard
in months.

Jaiden was bored. To the point of screaming. She had fled home
to spurn Rod, to spite Mona, and to punish her mom, but the only
person she seemed to be hurting was herself: Not one phone call
from Rod, begging her to come back, asking what he could do to
make up for his unfortunate romp at the beach. No e-mails from
Mona expressing her regret for not informing Jaiden about what
Rod had been doing while they were in Florida (surely she had
spoken to her cousin by now). And her mother? She was so wrapped
up in her work at Vendora, she had not raised her voice with a single critical remark after their blowout the first day at home. Now,
Jaiden was tired of being stuck in the house all day, with nothing to
do but watch television or sleep. Shopping was out. She had no
money and her mom had taken back her Visa credit card.

Dressed in cutoff jeans and a faded baggy shirt, she flung herself
across the foot of her bed and attempted to concentrate on the latest
issue of *Black Women on the Go*, but soon tossed it aside, not really
interested in reading about career opportunities for black women
who were determined to take on white corporate America. She
couldn't stay in the house forever. Maybe a week at the lake with
her mom wouldn't be so bad, especially if it got her a chance to
party with her friends without her mom around. The next morning, Camille arrived at Vendora at eight o'clock and finished working up the food order for two weeks' worth of menus, which she
reviewed with Percy when he arrived at nine-thirty. When she told
him that she and Jaiden were going away for a week to Lake Living-

ston, he expressed his joy and assured her that he would take care of everything in her absence.

"Go. Enjoy." Percy told her, throwing up his hands as if shooing her away. "Don't worry about a thing. I know you need relief from all the pressure around here, and from all that pounding and stomping around upstairs. Right above your office, too. I don't see how you stand it."

"Progress is not always an easy thing to live with," she replied, blinking in silent understanding. The workmen who had begun renovating the upstairs to convert it into Davis's game room, were a noisy lot who came early and stayed late, making quite a mess. She had accepted the fact that Davis was going ahead with his plan, but would never give it her blessing.

"I think Mr. Kepler's money would be much better spent if he expanded the gardens and installed that outdoor dining area with the waterfall that Mr. Granville used to talk about," Percy told Camille in a conspiratorial whisper. "A cigar bar and game room? Really!"

Pleased that Percy felt comfortable enough to share his disapproval with her, Camille replied with a weary sigh, "Who knows? We may still get that *al fresco* dining room one day."

With a wink, Percy turned and strutted back into the kitchen while Camille went into Davis's office to leave him an update on a disputed wine supplier's invoice that she had finally settled, and to leave the phone number at the cabin in case he needed to get in touch with her.

Circling his desk, she placed the two items in the center of his calendar blotter to make certain that he would see them when he came in. Turning away, her eyes flitted over other papers on his desk, and came to rest on a bank statement for a Vendora account at Western Ridge Bank in Las Vegas, Nevada.

"Hmm," she murmured, puzzled. Neither she nor Max had ever used that bank and she was not aware of the account. Curious, she picked up the statement, to which a deposit slip had been paper clipped, and scrutinized the documents: A thirty-three thousand dollar deposit had been made last Monday. Into an account she knew nothing about. Fingering the deposit slip, she wondered what was going on. Davis had never discussed this with her.

"What are you doing at my desk?" Davis asked, entering the room.

"Leaving you a message," Camille answered tightly, still holding the papers. "I resolved that matter with Speck's Spirits and I'm going up to the lake with Jaiden for a week." She tapped her note. "If you need me, here's the number."

Davis approached, suspicion clouding his face, as if her news about leaving bothered him. But when he held out his hand, as if to take what she was holding, Camille realized he was concerned about the bank deposit slip, not her impromptu vacation.

"What's that in your hand?" he questioned.

Lifting the bank statement high, she asked. "You tell me. It looks like a statement and a deposit slip from a bank in Las Vegas. What is this about?"

Davis leaned across his desk and snatched the documents from her. "That is exactly what it is . . . a bank statement." His tone was cold and sarcastic.

"When did we start banking in Las Vegas?"

"When I decided to set up an account to get better interest on payroll and federal tax money."

"This is a huge deposit. More than I think we need to set aside for taxes right now. We need operating cash. I wish you had discussed this matter with me."

"I don't have to. As controlling owner I don't need your approval on every move I make. And if you do not like the way I operate, too bad."

Cutting her eyes at Davis, Camille shook her head and backed off. "Have it your way . . . for now," she replied through tight lips. "But don't think that you can do as you please where Vendora is concerned. I am going to be watching you closely, Davis. And if I find any misappropriation of money or bad business decisions that affect me—as a partner—I will call you on them."

Leaving him staring after her, she went into her office, snatched her purse off her desk and left.

In her car, driving away from Vendora, she fumed, realizing that Davis was deliberately making her life miserable. How could she start her vacation with Jaiden when she was so upset? Maybe now was not the time to leave town. Davis needed watching. Who knew what he was really up to?

Holding onto the steering wheel tightly, Camille felt the strain of the confrontation building in her chest. This kind of stress, she did not need. *Maybe Paul Cotter was right,* she thought glumly. *Maybe I should have taken Davis's offer and sold my shares to him because I don't know how much longer I can stand being around him.*

At home, she found Jaiden packed and ready to go. As they were loading the car, Neil Windman called to tell Camille that he had the surveillance tapes that she wanted to view. After giving him the phone number and address of the cabin at Lake Livingston, she and Jaiden started off on what Camille hoped would be a breakthrough week with her daughter.

"How does that feel?" Doctor Johansen asked Lara as he massaged her right arm after freeing it from the sling, where it had been cradled since having its cast removed.

"It feels fine," Lara replied cautiously, straightening her arm and flexing her wrist.

"Any pain?"

"None."

"Excellent," the doctor remarked with satisfaction, making a notation on her chart. Looking up at his patient, he went on. "We're all finished here, Miss Stanton. Your arm is healed, as are your facial burns and lacerations. The next step is for you to see Dr. Fulton in Phoenix and arrange for the reconstructive surgery on your jaw. He has all of your X-rays and your case file, and we have consulted on the procedure. He is ready to do this, and I recommend you make an appointment right away."

Lara slipped down from the examining table and reached for her purse, preparing to leave. "It's all arranged," she said. "My surgery is scheduled for July 3. I leave on Monday. Dr. Fulton's nurse called me yesterday afternoon and said that the doctor had had a cancellation and could work me in if I could be there on short notice. He wants to squeeze me in before he takes off on holiday for the rest of the week."

"Good. I'm glad he could fit you in. His clinic is booked months in advance, but I asked him to treat your case as a priority. It's been close to three months since the accident and we have to take care of that damage in your jaw before it becomes impossible to correct. Dr. Fulton is the best in his field. He'll do a good job for you."

"I hope so. I want so much to get my face back to normal . . . return to acting."

Dr. Johansen inclined his head in a brief show of sympathy. "I think you will. You are an excellent candidate for a full recovery. It will take time, and it will be a bit painful, but you are going to do very well."

"I'm ready," Lara replied with a brave smile of certainty. "I can't wait to go out to dinner again . . . attend parties . . . be among peo-ple. I've been in hiding for months . . . not the way I want to live my life."

"And you shouldn't have to," the doctor assured Lara, leading her to the door. "Doctor Fulton and I will be in close contact, so please call me if you have any questions about his recommenda-tions." He shook Lara's hand. "Good luck."

"Thank you, Doctor Johansen. For all that you have done."

In the lobby of the medical building, Lara pulled on her oval sunglasses and adjusted the sheer white scarf that she had tied around her head to hide the choppy mass of auburn curls that had recently grown in, as well as the purple-red scar on the side of her face. She took a deep breath. Doctor Johansen's prognosis was en-couraging, and she was ready to face the surgery, however, she had one more step to take before her full recovery could become a real-ity.

After exiting the building through a revolving glass door, she slipped into a waiting taxi and told the driver, "Fifty-Nine-Twenty, Hillshire Lane," satisfied with her decision to meet Reet at his apart-ment instead of at her house.

Her surgery was all arranged. Her bags were packed and her plane ticket to Phoenix was in her purse. All she needed was the cash to pay for the operation that would give her back her life. She lifted her sunshades, opened her purse, and peered inside to make sure that her bargaining chip was still there, praying that the smudged piece of folded *Sea Wind* stationery was going to pay off.

Reet was saddened and shocked to see the damage on Lara's once-beautiful face when she voluntarily removed her scarf to let him see how scarred and disfigured she was. As she re-covered her head, he averted his eyes, understanding why she had rebuffed his visits and had remained out of sight for so long. He could not imagine how much she must be suffering and knew that he would do whatever she asked of him, if he could help her cope with this horrendous situation.

"Have a seat over here," Reet suggested, ushering Lara toward a white suede love seat in a sunny alcove jutting off at an angle from his expansive living room. With its modern furnishings and dra-matic view of the mountains surrounding the city, the setting re-sembled a photograph from an upscale home décor magazine. "Can

I get you a drink?" he offered, trying not to appear too solicitous, though genuinely shocked at Lara's appearance. She was thinner than he had ever seen her. Dark half-circles hung beneath her large brown eyes, which had lost their luminous sparkle, and her right arm hung limply at her side.

A broken woman, he observed sadly, as he went to the bar on the other side of the room.

"A Perrier and lime would be great, Reet," Lara replied in a wispy voice.

"You got it," Reet tossed back, struggling to sound lighthearted. "I'll have the same."

After fixing their drinks, he sat down across from Lara and focused on her, curious about her request to visit him at home, which was something she had never done, and this was clearly not a social call.

"It's been a rough few months for you, hasn't it, Lara?" he started, hoping to ease into the conversation, curious about her mission.

"Rough does not begin to describe what I have been through," Lara replied with a grimace, going on to fill Reet in on the status of her condition and her doctor's prognosis. "I have to believe that I'm fixable," she laughed nervously. "Otherwise why get up every day and deal with this pain? I've never even had a toothache in my life . . . this pain has been so debilitating. Some days I'm too weak to do more than sit on my patio and stare at the garden. I can't even hold a book open long enough to read." She brushed away a tear at the corner of her eye and took a deep breath. "But enough about me. I want to talk about Davis."

"Davis?" Reet repeated in surprise, thinking that his old friend would have been the last person she would want to talk about. "Why? You thinking of getting back together with him?"

"No, not at all," she said, seriously defiant. "I'm curious about what he is up to now. Still in Houston? Still running his supper club?"

"Sure. That's all he's doing, as far as I know," Reet answered, glancing away. "He's staying busy, making tons of money. I heard he's expanding the place . . . adding a wine bar upstairs. Pretty much a Texan now. I haven't seen him in months."

"What about Camille?" Lara inquired.

"His partner's widow?" Reet clarified, as if he knew nothing about her.

"Yeah. Max Granville's widow. She must be involved in the business, too. Does she help Davis with day-to-day operations? Like a partner?"

Reet drained the last of his Perrier, shrugged, and then abruptly stood. He went back to the bar where he poured a splash of vodka over the ice and lime in his glass. Turning, he studied Lara quietly, trying to discern where she was headed with her questions, knowing he had to be careful. He could not give her the impression that he and Davis had had any contact since Max's death.

"I don't know for certain," he finally answered, "but from my last phone conversation with Davis, I got the impression that Camille Granville has little say in what goes on. Davis is the owner, so he pretty much runs the place the way he wants, though I'm sure Camille gets her share of the profits."

"H'mm. I doubt that she does," Lara remarked with sudden finality, one eyebrow arched.

"How would you know?"

"Because I know Davis. He is a greedy, self-centered son-of-a-bitch. He literally abandoned me on that cruise ship. Who knows how things might have turned out if he had been with me that night, instead of gambling in the casino? He dumped me in the hospital in Honolulu and only telephoned one time. Never heard from him again. Davis Kepler has never played fair. I know he was using me for publicity when he invited me to that grand reopening affair, and I was fine with that. Publicity works both ways. But to dump someone you supposedly care about when she's at her lowest point? A real shitty thing to do. He's doing the same thing to Camille Granville, you know?"

"You talk as if you have something on your mind that I ought to know about, Lara." He paused to give her time to explain. When she remained quiet, he pressed ahead. "You came to see me because you trust me, right?"

Lara's brown eyes widened as she murmured, "Of course."

"Haven't I always treated you right? Been fair? Watched out for your best interest?"

She inclined her head in a short nod.

"Okay, then. Tell me what's on your mind. If I can help, you know I will."

Lara reached into her purse and removed the folded piece of *Sea Wind* stationery. "Read this, and then tell me that Davis plays fair."

She extended the paper to Reet, who crossed the room to take it, and then sat back down in the alcove opposite Lara.

Reet forced himself to read the wager three times before he dared trust his voice to speak. "How did you get this?" he asked in amazement, tilting his body toward her.

"Quite by accident," Lara assured Reet, taking him through the events of that night, explaining how she had met Max in the hallway, and what he had told her about Davis losing the bet. She had taken the paper from him to witness it, and then stuck it into the pocket of her Chinese robe where it had remained hidden away until a few days ago.

"What do you plan to do with it?" Reet inquired, two fingers on his chin. "And why bring it to me?"

"I guess I want your reassurance that this paper has value. I could have gone directly to Davis, but I hoped you might be willing to guide me in how best to approach him. You see, I need money, Reet. I'm flying to Phoenix on Monday to have extensive reconstructive and cosmetic surgery on Tuesday, and I have no way to pay for it. I convinced the doctor's nurse to secure my appointment with my credit card. I am Lara Stanton, after all. Of course, she accommodated me. But I don't have the cash to go through with the procedure, Reet. I am dead broke. Look at my face! This face made you and me a lot of money. I need at least one hundred thousand dollars to begin to repair this damage. Don't you think that Davis ought to pay me for that piece of paper? It's proof that he does not own any part of Vendora. He is ripping Camille Granville off, Reet. And any judge in the world would agree that that piece of paper is a legitimate contract transferring total ownership of Vendora back to Max. Davis has no right to that supper club, or the profit he so easily pockets."

"He won't pay you for this," Reet immediately decided. "But I will," he said in a softer tone.

Lara studied Reet, head to one side. "You will? How much?"

"Sufficient money to cover your surgery and your living expenses until you resume your career."

"You'd do that for me, Reet?"

"Yes. I'll transfer funds into your bank account on a regular basis," Reet agreed, stunned to learn that Davis had no ownership at all in Vendora. He shifted uncomfortably in his seat, tensed his shoulders and tapped the wager with two fingers. "You were smart to bring this to me. I could never abandon you. All I want is a promise that you will keep your mouth shut about this. Forget you were ever on that cruise ship. Okay? Let me take care of Davis."

"No problem. I have already forgotten everything."

"Good, because if you ever speak to Camille Granville again or tell *anyone* about the existence of this wager, my deposits into your bank account will stop."

After putting Lara into a taxi and sending her on her way, Reet studied the wager and thought about the disastrous situation he was in. He had too much riding on Horseshoe Pines to pack up and run, besides, it was making more money than he had anticipated it would. He needed Davis to continue running the receipts through Vendora's bank account for at least six months, then he would be happy to shut the place down and get out of Texas.

Reet opened his wall safe and put the document inside, then placed a call to Davis.

"I'll be back in Houston next Wednesday night," he told Davis.

"On the Fourth of July?"

"Right. I'll get in around midnight."

"Want me to pick you up?"

"No, I'll get a car. The holiday action ought to be heavy at the Pines and Clyde wants the night off to take his kids to see fireworks. Some traditional Native American gathering at a lake near the reservation. Can you cover for him?"

"Sure. Percy will be working at Vendora, and he can close up."

"Fine. Shut the Pines down at midnight. Bring the night's take to Vendora and I'll meet you there at 1:00 A.M. We need to talk."

CHAPTER 37

It was hot at Lake Livingston; the lake was dotted with jet skis, kayaks, and sailboats, while residents who owned homes on the lake were busy settling in for the long holiday weekend. The perfect summer weather added to the bustling, festive atmosphere that Camille hoped would last the entire week.

After arriving late Friday afternoon, Camille and Jaiden jumped into the dirty work of cleaning and opening the cabin for their weeklong vacation. Jaiden loaded her boom box with her favorite music, placed it on the kitchen table and turned up the volume, telling Camille that doing housework to music was the only way she could survive.

Camille smiled, encouraged: Fixing up the cabin together was a good way to kick off what she hoped was going to be a week with no arguing, pouting, or sullen moods.

As Sade's smooth voice filled the small house, they cleaned windows, made up beds, swept floors, and stocked the kitchen with the groceries that Jaiden had selected: steaks, chops, tiger shrimp, salad greens, and fruit. Camille had been amazed by Jaiden's purchases, expecting her to pack chips, burgers, hot dogs and pizza, as she had done in the past, and when Jaiden volunteered to prepare dinner, Camille had sent up a silent prayer of thanks: This vacation might turn out to be a surprisingly pleasant experience after all.

While Jaiden was busy in the kitchen, Camille went into her bedroom, opened her overnight bag and removed the red velvet box that contained the coral and pearl necklace that Max had purchased for Jaiden in Hawaii. She had brought it along in hopes that this time alone with Jaiden might provide the opportunity for her to give it to her daughter. Camille sensed that tonight was going to be the perfect time.

The sun had slipped low over the lake when they finished their meal of shrimp kabobs, Creole rice, and salad. Seated under the huge umbrella on the patio at the back of the cabin, Camille and Jaiden finished off two generous slices of caramel cheese cake, and then sat quietly, gazing out over the shadowy water as they watched the last of the boaters head home.

"Dinner was delicious, Jaiden. Thanks. Tomorrow I'll cook. Okay?"

"Fine by me . . . I'm exhausted," Jaiden quickly agreed.

"Yeah, we really did accomplish a lot," Camille replied. "The place needed a good spring cleaning. It's been a year since I was here." Her voice fell as her thoughts swung back to the last time she had sat on this same patio, watching the sun sink over the lake with Max at her side. Afraid that her emotions might get out of control before she accomplished her mission, Camille reached into the straw bag she had placed next to her chair and pulled out the red velvet box.

"Jaiden," she started. "I know what you are thinking . . . that the last time we were here together, Max was with us." She paused and swallowed back her sorrow. "He was a good father and I know how hard it is going to be for you to go on without him. When we were cruising in Hawaii, he talked about you, worried about you at home studying, and shopped more for you than for me. You were never out of his thoughts. Always wondering what he could do to surprise you." She laughed dryly, recalling how picky he had been with the salesperson while selecting the perfect jewels for Jaiden.

Nodding, Jaiden used her napkin to wipe away a tear, and then said, "Did you know he called me from the ship?"

"Yes, he told me."

"He said that he bought me a present in Lahaina. Guess it got burned up in the fire."

"No, it didn't," Camille said quietly. "I have it. Right here."

Jaiden sucked in a breath of surprise as she stared at the red velvet box that Camille placed between them on the table. "How long have you had it?" she asked in a small voice.

"Not long. Max put it into our stateroom safe. The cruise lines recently returned it to me, along with my diamond jewelry. I've been waiting for a good time to give it to you." She picked up the box and held it out. "Here. It's for you. Open it."

Jaiden pushed her dessert plate to one side, placed the box in its place, and lifted the lid. She gazed at the three strands of pearls spaced with vibrant coral beads shaking her head. "This is gorgeous. Really unusual."

"Let me put it on you," Camille volunteered, getting up to go around the table and fasten the necklace around her daughter's neck. Stepping back, she admired the luminous strands of perfect pearls against Jaiden's rich brown skin. "He knew they would look lovely on you, and they do."

Jaiden touched the jewels gently, gave her mother a haunting smile, and wiping her eyes, stood. With a sob, she wrapped her arms around Camille and buried her face in her mother's neck. "I miss him so much. Why can't he be here with us? Why is he gone, Mom. Why?"

Camille stroked Jaiden's back, her muffled words spilling forth. "I can't give you that answer, Jaiden, Just remember how much your father loved you, and how good a man he was. We aren't the only ones who miss him. He had so many good friends. Let go of your worries about why he died and fill your heart with memories of the happy days we had together as a family. Can you do that? For him?"

With a whimper, Jaiden murmured, "I'll try."

"Good. Because if you don't, you'll never be able to get on with your life, and Max would not want you to mope around and cry for him forever. Can't you just hear him now? Shouting at you to get over it, please. Lighten up!"

Jaiden let out a soft chuckle. "Yeah. He'd say something like that, all right."

"He wanted you to have a good life and to be happy. You're all grown up now, so it's up to you to find your own happiness. Even in the face of this tragedy," Camille comforted.

A rough sob tore through Jaiden and her grief exploded in a fierce torrent of tears. Weeping uncontrollably, she held onto Camille as her body shook and her sorrow spilled out into the warm night air. Finally, she allowed her mother to comfort her.

"Cry all you want," Camille advised, softly caressing her daughter. "And I will cry right along with you."

After a few long moments, Jaiden pulled away, wiped her eyes with her napkin, and then told Camille, "Think I'll walk down to the water." In a trembling voice, she asked, "Want to come?"

"No, you go along," Camille replied, sensing that Jaiden really needed to be alone. "I'll start the dishes."

"Okay. Be back in a bit," Jaiden managed before striking off toward the water, which had become a shimmering silver disk under a bluish-white half-moon.

Camille watched Jaiden walk away, and was filled with a surge of relief and gratitude. Jaiden was on her way to healing and had matured before her eyes. She was going to be fine. She was going to become the young woman Camille had always known lay beneath the surface of her rebelliousness, and though Jaiden was not yet free of the heartache and pain caused by Max's death . . . and Rod's betrayal . . . at least she seemed willing to give Camille a chance to reshape their relationship to fit their new future.

The rain held off for the next two days and slowly, Jaiden grew closer to Camille as they shopped in the nearby touristy gift shops, went for Jet Ski rides on the lake, and sunned themselves on the patio behind the cabin. In the evenings, they watched game shows together on television, played Scrabble, or sat quietly and read the books they had both brought along. Finally, Camille began to think that hers and Jaiden's lives might get back to normal, though it would be a new kind of normal without Max.

Early Monday afternoon, Neil Windman arrived with four boxes of security videotapes, which Camille placed inside a locked, glass-front bookcase to view later that evening. The sight of the tapes made her nervously expectant, and she knew that she would have to be mentally prepared for a return to that disastrous night. After securing the tapes, Camille asked Neil, "Would you like some iced tea? Freshly made."

"Yes, that would be nice," Neil replied, glancing around the attractive interior of the cabin. "You have a very nice place. In a very good location, too. You've got beautiful shade trees and quite a bit of privacy."

Camille smiled. "We were one of the first to buy in this area, so we got first dibs on our lot. We wanted to be close to the water, but not too close. It can be noisy out there when the lake is crowded. Would you like to sit outside?"

"Definitely," Neil agreed.

Soon after taking seats at the patio table, Jaiden stuck out her head to see who had arrived and Camille introduced them.

"What's for lunch?" Jaiden asked Camille after greeting Neil.

"Thought we might drive over to Lugo's for barbecue," she told

Jaiden, and then spontaneously turned to Neil and asked, "Would you like to join us?"

"I'd love to," he replied, setting down his glass. "But I'm on my way to meet my nephew. We're going to the Indian Ceremonial Dance Exposition."

"Right," Camille replied. "I recall you mentioning that when I was at your office." She turned her face to the cloudless blue sky. "A beautiful day for the dances."

"Why don't you and Jaiden come along? There'll be food, music, a great crowd."

"Well . . ." Camille stalled, glancing back at Jaiden, who was standing at the door, a magazine in her hand. "I haven't been to the dances in years. It's always beautiful. What do you think, Jaiden? Want to go?"

Jaiden lifted one shoulder in a whatever-you-want-to-do gesture, and gave her mother a tentative smile. "Might be fun. Get us out of the house for a while."

"Fine." Camille grinned at Neil. "We'll go."

The Tribal Dance Square at the Alabama-Coushatta Indian Reservation vibrated with the sounds of drums, flutes, and rattles, as championship dancers from several states competed in a colorful explosion of authentic costumes, feathered headdresses, and beaded finery. They hopped and twirled in frenetic interpretations of their individual tribe's history, while spectators sat on long wooden benches, rising four tiers high, under wood-shingle roofing that surrounded the sandy performance area. The covered seating provided much needed shade for the visitors and a cool place for the dancers to rest between performances.

A flash of yellow ruffles. A swirl of red and white feathers. A parade of children in elaborate headdresses that trailed to the ground. One after another, the various tribes entered the square to great applause, doing their best to woo the favor of the five judges, who sat stone-faced at a table near the entrance to the arena.

The spectators' area was packed with local residents, tourists, and family members who had come to see their relatives dance. Neil and Camille sat together on a lower bench, with Jaiden one row higher, directly behind them.

"There he is!" Neil said to Camille in an excited voice, waving at a dark-haired young man who had entered the gate and was looking for a seat in the spectators' stands.

Jaiden turned to look in the direction of Neil's wave, one brow arched in interest. The young man was tall, tan, and slim, with long black hair tucked back behind his ears. He was wearing faded jeans, dusty cowboy boots, a blue-and-white checked short-sleeved shirt, and aviator sunglasses over his eyes. The oversize, silver belt buckle at his waist glinted when struck by the sun.

"Corey! Over here," Neil called out, waving his nephew over.

Corey signaled his recognition with a wide grin, showing off a beautiful set of white teeth, and then headed their way, climbing over the wooden benches to greet Neil with a handshake and a one-armed hug.

"Corey, I want you to meet my guests, Camille Granville and her daughter, Jaiden. They're spending some time at the lake."

"Nice to meet you," Corey replied, shaking Camille's hand, and then reaching up to shake Jaiden's. "How's it going?" he asked to no one in particular. He sat down next to Neil and studied the dancers twirling in the middle of the sandy arena.

"Couldn't be better," Neil replied. "Roaring River clan is going to win the grand trophy, I'd bet."

"Don't put money on it. The Turtles always come through," Corey laughingly replied, leaning forward to concentrate on the elaborately costumed performers.

Jaiden studied the back of Corey's head, trying to guess his age. At least twenty-five, she decided, scrutinizing his suntanned arms and slim brown hands, which he had rested on his knees. Clean short nails. No rings on his fingers. Nice hair. If he was single, she wondered what he did for fun since he obviously lived in the area. She'd go crazy living in the woods with no quick access to a mall, a movie theater or a Starbucks coffee shop. With an imperceptible shrug, she turned her attention back to the last dance of the second round, realizing that she had become genuinely interested in finding out which tribe was going to win.

The outing had been a good idea, and though she and her mom were getting along much better, spending twenty-four-seven with her was straining this togetherness thing. Before the dance competition had started, she and her mom and Neil, who was really a very nice man, had eaten lunch in the Twelve Clans Restaurant, and then taken the obligatory train ride around the Indian reservation and into the surrounding forest, which was referred to as the Big Thicket. Jaiden had ridden the authentic 1800s shiny red train many times as a child, yet this excursion into the cool dim woods had been the first one she had taken without her father at her side, pointing out the various trees, plants, and authentic Native American structures that were scattered across the area.

At first, she had felt sad to be on the train without him, and had almost slipped into that angry, sullen mood that she had promised herself was not going to happen. However, as the train wound its way through the sun-dappled forest, she deliberately put thoughts of her father away and forced herself to concentrate on today.

Mom was right. I cannot dwell on the past, she had told herself. *If I do, I will never enjoy anything again.*

Applause broke into her thoughts as the dancers left the arena. Neil stood and stretched. "Hardest darn benches in the world," he grumbled. Camille laughed as she watched him rub his backside.

"Think I'll go inside, cool off, and get a Coke," Neil decided. "What about you, Camille?"

"I agree," Camille replied, standing and stretching, too. "Would you mind if we sat out the last round inside? I think we can see the final dances from the windows across the back of the restaurant." Camille fanned her face and neck with her program.

"Good idea. Yes, that's fine with me. I was thinking the same thing," Neil agreed, and then asked, "You two want anything from the restaurant?"

Both Jaiden and Corey said, "No, thanks," in unison, then burst into laughter at their in-tune remark.

Once Neil and Camille had left, Corey eased up one tier and sat down on the bench beside Jaiden.

"Well, you enjoying the exposition?"

"Surprisingly, yes. Very much. I'm really kind of getting into the competition. From your remarks, I gather the Roaring River clan from Oklahoma usually wins."

Corey rubbed his thumb along the side of his nose, a crooked smile easing over his lips. "My maternal grandmother was Alabama-Coushatta—the Turtle clan. My paternal grandfather—Uncle Neil's father, was Creek—the Roaring River clan. So, it's kind of a running family joke around here about the two clans—Neil always sides with the male ancestry—the strongest, according to him, and therefore the one that absolutely must prevail."

"A bit chauvinistic, don't you think?" Jaiden teased.

Corey flashed Jaiden a knowing smile. "Oh yeah. I agree completely, but that's an old family theory. I am not responsible for initiating it."

"You live on the reservation?" Jaiden prompted, digging for a bit of personal information.

"No. Got an apartment in town. Small, but big enough for my dog, Brick, and me. An Irish setter. Real spoiled." He leaned back, stretched out his legs, and crossed his booted feet at the ankles in a comfortable, relaxed move. "How long are you gonna be at the lake?"

"Until Friday, I guess. Unless . . . my mom wants to stay longer."

"Good weather for the Fourth of July crush."

"That's what you call it?"

"Sure. When the holiday is over and the tourists leave, the traffic crush goes away."

Jaiden chuckled, and then asked, "What do you do for fun around here?"

"Nothing special. The casino is the biggest attraction. If you like to gamble."

"Do you?"

"No, I can't. I work for the casino. Employees are not supposed to play."

"Really? You a professional dealer, or something?"

"No, nothing glamorous like that."

"What do you do?"

"Repair slot machines, and they break down quite often."

"H'mm. Interesting," Jaiden commented, listening as Corey launched into an explanation of the state's determination to close the casino and the tribe's protest against the government.

"We've appealed the Texas state attorney general's ruling that Texas Indians have no right to operate casinos because casino gambling is illegal in Texas," he said with pride. "The state is wrong to try to squash the best source of income for the tribe. We need the money, and the jobs."

Jaiden, impressed with Corey, voiced her agreement and soon found herself involved in an intense conversation about Indian rights and government oppression. He was easy to talk to, intelligent, passionate about his Indian heritage, and to-die-for handsome. Jaiden hoped he would never stop talking to her or looking into her eyes.

The final round of dancers flew past in a blur while Jaiden told Corey as much as she wanted to reveal about herself, and listened to him describe his second job—making neon signs. After the closing ceremonial dances, Neil and Camille reappeared, ready to leave.

Corey turned to Jaiden. "Want to go see some of my neon work? I'd love to show you a sign I'm working on."

Jaiden threw a please-don't-mess-this-up look at Camille, who lifted both hands and said, "Go right ahead. I'm sure Corey will bring you home?"

"No problem, Mrs. Granville. We won't be long. Be back in an hour or so."

"I'll vouch for him, Camille," Neil added in a fatherly tone.

Happy to see Jaiden smiling again, Camille considered her daughter's acceptance of Corey's invitation a major step toward shedding her disappointment with Rod.

Neil drove Camille back to the cabin, walked her to the door and thanked her for attending the dance exposition with him.

"No. Thank *you*," Camille told him. "For inviting me *and* Jaiden along. It's exactly what we both needed. She has taken her father's death so hard, and being here again . . . at the lake, brought back a lot of memories. I think this afternoon's outing got her mind off her problems for a while and it's nice that she had a good time with someone her age. She was getting a little bored with my company."

"It was my pleasure. And don't worry about her being with Corey. He really is a responsible kid. Sometimes I wish he would loosen up. He's a very stable, predictable young man."

"Nothing wrong with that," Camille decided, relieved by Neil's assessment of his nephew. "Well, thanks again. For the afternoon, and the tapes. I plan to watch them tonight. And I guess you'll be in touch with me about the settlement? Perhaps when I get back to town?"

Neil cleared his throat and paused. "Well, not me. But someone from Tropica will get in touch with you and your attorney to finalize everything. You see, I'm leaving for Honolulu on Thursday. Have to wrap up some loose ends with the hospital that treated the victims of the *Sea Wind* fire. I'll be gone for three, maybe four weeks."

"Oh? I see. Uh . . . I hope it goes well."

"I'm sure it will. This trip should finalize the investigation." He turned to leave, but hesitated, and then said, "Would you have dinner with me when I return?"

Bumble bees buzzed in the rose bushes at the cabin entry as Camille considered Neil's invitation. *Three months have passed since the accident. Neil is my only ally in my quest to get to the truth about Max's death. He has been kind and understanding, a real friend, and I need a friend right now to help me accomplish my goal.*

Camille extended her hand, took his, and then shook it. "I'd like that very much."

Inside the cabin, after Neil had driven off, Camille realized that not only had the afternoon outing been good for her and Jaiden, but it had also left her feeling hopeful and less stressed than she had felt in weeks. As Camille walked through the cabin, she realized that she liked being alone in the house, and silently thanked Neil for having introduced his nephew to Jaiden. Corey was a nice looking, well-mannered young man, and Camille was not worried about Jaiden spending time with him. After all, when Jaiden had been at Brown, Camille had had no idea what her daughter had been doing or with whom. At nineteen, going on twenty, Jaiden could take care of herself.

Deciding that a long hot shower was in order, Camille stood under the warm relaxing spray of water for ten minutes and washed away the grit and grime of her day in the sun. Wearing a cool, cotton multi-print caftan, she poured herself a glass of white wine.

Now is the perfect time to view the videotapes, she concluded, going to the bookcase. She unlocked it and assessed the boxes of security tapes that had been labeled according to areas of the cruise ship. Her eyes moved from one boldly printed label to another: Promenade Deck, Atrium Lounge, Grand Plaza, Grand Casino, Emerald Deck, etc. She reached in and touched the three tapes marked Emerald Deck, as if afraid to actually pick them up and hold them in her hands; it would mean a return to the scene of a horrible crime and she knew what they contained: Panic. Fire. Smoke. Tragedy. Death. Her mouth grew dry and her heart began pumping fast.

Not tonight, she resolved. *Why put a sad ending on such a lovely day? I can do this tomorrow.* Relocking the cabinet, she poured herself a second glass of wine, and then stepped outside, where she sat on the patio and watched the fiery red globe of a sun sink down into the lake.

Corey's neon sign workshop was an eight-by-ten-foot metal shed on a corner lot at the edge of town, where the only other building in sight was a brightly lit truck stop that housed a taco stand and two gas pumps. His shop had a barnlike double door that was secured with a big padlock, and after Corey opened it up, he pulled on a long chain that was hanging from the ceiling and turned on an overhead fluorescent light.

Instantly, Jaiden's eyes widened at the dazzling display of brightly colored glass tubes in various stages of completion. Their fluid lines, intricate details, and bold hues resembled brash jewels that had morphed into signage on their own. There were geometric designs, floral arrangements, figures of dogs, cats, horses, and even a humpy armadillo. His clean, creative artistry raised Jaiden's interest in and respect for her new friend and his unusual talent.

"This is my biggest job, so far," Corey told Jaiden after giving her a tour of his workshop. He leaned over a messy worktable to pick up a huge piece from the floor, which he plugged in to illuminate. Holding it high, he struck the pose of a proud artist and flashed a dimpled cheek at Jaiden. "Like it?" he asked, waiting expectantly for her answer.

Jaiden studied the sign with amazement. It was a huge red horseshoe with a bright green pine tree in the center, so lifelike that she could count the pine needles on its branches. The words Horseshoe Pines floated across the two symbols, blinking golden yellow and black. "Wow," Jaiden remarked, stepping close enough to feel the heat coming from the elaborately molded tubes. "That sign is the bomb! You are too good!"

"Thanks." Leaving it lit, Corey hung the sign on a pegboard alongside a smaller sign designed like a martini glass with an olive sticking out of it. "This is the second sign like this that I've done for a guy who recently opened a private club down the highway. He commissioned me to make two of them and paid me a grand each. Can you believe it? That's the most I ever got paid for a sign. If the Alabama-Coushatta casino is shut down, and it probably will, I'll be out of a job. So, I want to get my neon sign business up and running right away. There's an empty building over on Highway 190 that I'd like to buy . . . if I can get the owner to come down a few thousand. He ought to . . . it needs a hell of a lot of repairs."

"Hey, if you can get paid for doing what you love, what's better than that?" Jaiden replied enthusiastically, silently admiring Corey's ambition.

"That's the way I look at it, too." Corey agreed, unplugging the horseshoe-shaped sign. He leaned over his worktable and carefully set it back down on the floor. When he straightened up and turned around, he was only inches from Jaiden, who did not step back. She held his eyes with hers, thinking they were the darkest eyes she had ever seen, and disturbingly attractive, too.

"Ready to go home?" he asked, lips moving, eyes steady.

"Hmm . . . not really," Jaiden murmured. "I'm in no hurry to get back."

"Great," Corey said in a breathy voice. "Want to go do something?"

"Like what?" Jaiden said, her voice as breezy as his, her stomach tight with anticipation.

"How about going over to the casino with me?" Corey suggested, moving closer, his expression serious. "I can get you in. Ever been to a casino?"

Jaiden giggled and stepped back. "No."

"So, it's time you went. What do you think?" Corey prompted.

Jaiden grinned, a glint of mischief in her eyes. At last, she was going to have some real fun, and with a guy who knew what he wanted, had real ambition, and who definitely turned her on in a way that Rod certainly never had. "Sounds good to me," she said, trailing a finger down the side of her face.

CHAPTER 38

Lara had not expected to be afraid, but when Nurse Paul, who had been at her side since her arrival at the Fulton Clinic, entered her room and said, "Ready to go, Miss Stanton?" she panicked.

"It's time already?" Lara asked, placing a hand to her chest. She had arrived yesterday morning and immediately undergone the battery of preoperative tests that were required before she could have surgery. Blood, urine, heart, lungs. Every part of her anatomy, it seemed had been poked, prodded or put under an X-ray machine.

Doctor Fulton had come to her bedside last night to assure her that all of her tests were fine and she was set to go. He had encouraged her to get a good night's sleep and not to worry about anything. Exhausted from the long, intensely demanding day, she had fallen asleep right away, and for the first time in years, had dreamed of her mother—whom she had abandoned long ago in the desert of Nevada.

In the dream, her mother had been standing at her bedside, holding her hand, and gazing at Lara with a loving expression. However, when Lara had attempted to communicate with her mother, no words had come out of her mouth. Frustrated, she had begun to cry, and had awakened with a start. Sitting up, she had searched the shadows in her private room for the woman she had neither spoken to nor seen in eighteen years. Feeling alone, abandoned and frightened, she had slumped back down under her sheet and remained motionless until Nurse Paul had burst in with her cheery announcement.

"The doctor is in the operating room, ready to begin," the nurse told Lara as two male attendants in white hospital scrubs wheeled a gurney into the room.

Once they wheel me into that operating room, my life . . . my future will be in the hands of Doctor Fulton, Lara thought as she allowed the two men to shift her from her bed to the gurney. *The operation will be a success and he will make me beautiful again,* she chanted in her mind, repeatedly as the solemn-faced attendants pushed her bed down the bright white hallway.

Inside the operating room, Dr. Fulton patted her on the arm and turned to his anesthesiologist, who peered down at Lara and said, "Can you count backwards for me . . . starting at one hundred, please?"

As Lara began to count, ethereal violin music filled the room and pulled her into unconsciousness.

It rained on the Fourth of July: A pounding, relentless rain that cancelled the traditional, festive parade of boats and forced frustrated vacationers inside to grill their hot dogs and hamburgers at their stoves. Corey arrived after breakfast to invite Jaiden to spend the day with him at a friend's ranch nearby. Camille had sent them off with a wave, thankful that she would not have to spend the day inside with a moody, grumpy daughter who had already told her, "I knew it was going to rain on the Fourth of July."

Alone in the cabin, Camille finally summoned the courage to watch the security tapes of the *Sea Wind* disaster, which she had put off for two days. Yesterday, she, Jaiden, and Corey had spent the day water-skiing on the lake, and that evening had enjoyed a cookout with the family in the cabin next to theirs. At midnight, Camille had fallen into bed, and quickly to sleep, leaving Jaiden and Corey sitting at the end of the pier that jutted out over the lake. *How quickly young people can rebound,* she had thought, watching the two laughing about some private joke.

Now, she set aside her second cup of coffee and pushed eject on the VCR to remove the movie that Jaiden and Corey had been watching last night: an action flick starring Jackie Chan that Corey had brought along. With a mix of anticipation and dread, she slipped in one of three tapes marked Emerald Deck and pushed Play.

The grainy image of a near empty corridor filled the screen, with passengers walking up and down. Toward the end of the tape she saw Max as he came around a corner and into view. He stopped to greet Lara, who was wearing a flowing robe and was walking unsteadily toward him. They exchanged words. He touched her cheek, then took her by the arm and led her back to her stateroom. The two disappeared inside.

Camille froze. Certainly not! Max with Lara . . . willingly? And in her stateroom, too? The sick feeling that swept through Camille made her dizzy. Quickly, she rewound the tape and viewed it a second time. She pressed her hand over her mouth and sucked back a deep breath. How could Max do this to her? How! With trembling fingers she struggled to insert the second tape.

She saw Paolo rushing down the passageway, knocking on doors, shouting for people to get out of their staterooms. Pandemonium followed. Camille pressed her fingernails hard into her palms as the vivid memories rushed back. She saw doors fling open, dazed passengers emerge in their bedclothes, rubbing their eyes as the smoke grew dark and thick. And then she recognized herself, stumbling from her cabin, alone. Camille gasped and cried out, struck anew by the intensity of the situation, which rushed back with alarming clarity.

With one hand still pressed to her lips, Camille continued to watch the video: She was turning back to go and look for Max. Paolo appeared in the doorway and gave her a quick shove, propelling her into the wave of people desperate for escape. She disappeared into the mob, and out of camera range.

It happened so quickly, she thought, rewinding the tape to play it two more times. *What else is there?* she worried, pushing the final Emerald Deck tape into the VCR. This one had been taken from a different angle, and on it Camille saw a door across from her stateroom open and a devastating image emerge: Max with Lara Stanton.

She was still wearing her flowing robe over a sheer pink lace negligee. "Oh, my God," Camille moaned, her jaw dropping open as she watched the scene unfold. Max was holding a drink in one hand and Lara was leaning on him in a desperately possessive clutch as they moved forward together, hands entwined, bodies close. When they reached the door to Max's stateroom, they paused, and for a split second, Camille could see their faces very clearly. Then everything went dark, as if someone had knocked down the surveillance camera. Stunned, she pressed rewind and played it again.

"That's why Paolo couldn't find him." Camille flung the words into the empty room, her heart racing, her mouth dry. "Max was having drinks with Lara in her stateroom when the fire broke out.

The bitch finally got her hands on my husband. But how could Max do this to me?" she prattled on, stunned, shocked, disappointed, and embarrassed. Hadn't she warned Max that Lara wanted him for more than a cordial escort? And he had mocked her concern! Well, he let that woman use him as a replacement for her inattentive boyfriend, and look at the mess he got himself into . . . and all because he could not resist the attentions of a pretty woman. Lara Stanton had literally been his final conquest.

Camille jettisoned the remote control across the room, smashing the vase of yellow daisies she had placed on the coffee table. Water drained onto the floor, petals scattered over the braided rug, shards of glass glistened among the debris.

"It's all very clear, now," she muttered through her tears, getting up to jerk the video out of the VCR. Jaiden's dogged questions made perfect sense, and it would be easy for Camille to simply hand the tape over to Jaiden and give her the answers she sought. However, Camille knew she could not do that.

Jaiden knows nothing about Max's earlier infidelity. Viewing this tape will only confuse and disappoint her, and at a time when Jaiden and I are finally beginning to repair our relationship. Seeing her father in a compromising situation will not help. It will only destroy her respect for Max. Why should Jaiden have to live with the truth: Her father was a philanderer?

Frustrated, Camille paced the room, struggling to make a decision. *I buried my husband's mistakes when I buried him and I will not place this burdensome memory on Jaiden. But I am going to talk to Lara about this. She was the last person to see Max alive and I want to know how he managed to wind up dead on the bathroom floor of our stateroom. She knows what happened and she is going to tell me.*

It took several phone calls for Camille to locate Lara's agent through Bright Light Productions, but eventually she reached Artie Perlman and told him who she was.

"I think Lara would like to talk to you," Artie told Camille. "I've been worried about her. She has not seen or talked to anyone except me . . . and her old friend, Reet Collins . . . since she got back from Honolulu."

"Reet Collins? Davis Kepler's partner?"

"Former partner," Artie clarified. "They went their separate ways some time ago. But anyway, Lara's situation is not so good. She needs somebody to talk to, especially now."

"Why? I supposed she was back in Los Angeles and recovering. Has something happened?"

"Lara is in a private hospital in Phoenix. Had reconstructive facial surgery yesterday. Hate to think of her all alone out there. You know? She ought to have a friend with her."

"Where is she?" Camille asked.

"The Fulton Clinic. On Sandford Drive. I'll get you the number."

When Artie came back on the line, Camille jotted down the information. "Thank you, Mr. Perlman. I appreciate your help."

"Anything for Lara. She's had a pretty rough time."

"We all have," Camille replied, dryly before saying good-bye.

Too agitated to think about what to do next, she cleaned up the broken glass and put the spilled daisies in fresh water, then paced the house while speculating about what might have been going on between Lara and Max. Reet Collins and Lara were friends? Davis had never mentioned that to her. Reet Collins called Vendora all the time, asking for Davis in his unmistakable baritone voice without ever speaking to her. What else did she not know about Lara and Davis, the two people whose activities had obviously affected Max's last night aboard the *Sea Wind*? There was only one way to find out.

Camille grabbed the phone book, called Continental Airlines, and booked a seat on the 3 P.M., one-hour-forty-five-minute flight from Houston Hobby Airport to Phoenix. Next, she called Jaiden on her cell phone.

"I have to leave for a while," she told Jaiden, not wanting to get into an involved conversation about why she was making an impromptu trip to Phoenix.

"Trouble at Vendora?" Jaiden asked.

"An emergency that only I can take care of," she hedged, not lying outright. "I'll be late finishing up what I have to do, so I'll probably stay in town tonight and come back up to the cabin tomorrow afternoon. You'll be okay?"

"Mom. Of course, I'll be fine," Jaiden groaned. "I'm not a child, please!"

"I know. I hate to leave you at the cabin. Leaving you at home alone is different." She paused, then stated firmly, "Let me speak with Corey."

"Oh, Mom! No."

"Please," she repeated in a firm voice. When he came on the line, she told him, "Corey. I have to leave to take care of an emergency.

Your uncle assured me that you are a responsible young man and I trust his word . . . and I trust you to watch out for Jaiden while I'm gone."

"No problem," Corey replied with level seriousness. "You have nothing to worry about, Mrs. Granville. I'll make sure she's fine."

"Don't disappoint me. Or her. Jaiden has had some problems . . ."

"Right," he interrupted. "She told me all about it."

"Okay. Jaiden has my cell phone number, but I want you to have it, too. Call me anytime. I'll be back tomorrow afternoon." After giving him her number, she clicked off, thinking, *That is all I can do. Trust them.*

CHAPTER 39

When Nurse Paul brought in Lara's breakfast, her first meal since surgery yesterday morning, Lara stared at the tray with blank disinterest, and then turned her face away. Still groggy from the anesthesia and in substantial pain, despite the strong pain medication she was on, the last thing she wanted to do was eat. Bandaged from chin to forehead, she looked like a mummy and felt as if she had been beaten about the face and head by a professional boxer. All she wanted to do was sleep. Forever.

"A soft-boiled egg, juice, and oatmeal," the nurse said brightly as she swiveled the food tray into position in front of Lara and began unwrapping the plastic utensils. "Must get your strength up, Miss Stanton. So eat it all. Okay?" She fluffed up the pillows behind Lara's back and helped her patient sit up.

"And after breakfast, a walk around the floor. We want to get your circulation going. After that, I'll help you bathe, and you may dress in your own clothes now," she chatted away, "You may talk on the phone and have visitors today, but don't tire yourself. You do need rest, but you can't sleep all day. You have a TV, VCR, a radio, and a CD player in your room, and we have an extensive music and video library on the third floor. If you'd like to watch a movie or listen to a CD this afternoon simply go up and check out whatever you want." After giving Lara a daunting grin, she walked over to the gigantic bouquets of purple lilacs, roses, Star Gazer Lilies, and a festive red, white, and blue patriotic arrangement of carnations that were sitting on the dresser. She buried her nose in each arrangement, sucking in deep appreciative breaths. "Lovely. All of them. What a nice thought . . . a Fourth of July bouquet! Just beautiful. I expect the lilacs are your favorite, aren't they? I read that about you in *People* magazine, I think." She crinkled her eyes at Lara in a conspiratorial manner. "I'll bet you get tons of flowers like these from admirers all the time, huh? Must be nice being famous."

Lara blinked and attempted a polite smile. *If it were not for Reet and my agent, there would not be flowers in my room. If you only knew how alone I am. Here I am, on the Fourth of July, stuck in a hospital room. No celebrating for me.*

"I'll be back to get you up for your walk," Nurse Paul chirped, sweeping out of the room in a crisp rustle of white uniform, stockings, and shoes.

Camille's plane touched down at Sky Harbor International Airport ten minutes early. After securing her rental car and checking her map, she took the 202 Loop east, through Paradise Valley on to Chaparral Road, which she followed out into the desert. Fulton Clinic, which she now realized was nearly to Scottsdale, was in a remote area on the outskirts of town. However, the drive did give Camille plenty of time to think about her face-to-face meeting with Lara. The closer she came to her destination, the more anxious she became. What if Lara refused to see her? What if Lara openly admitted to having had a liaison with Max? And if she did, would Camille believe her?

Do I really want the truth? Camille fretted, as she made a hard right turn, swung off the main road and onto a winding cactus-lined driveway. She stared into the hills in the distance, her jaw tight with determination, her hands firm on the steering wheel as she headed toward a cluster of white and pink stucco buildings squatted on the horizon.

A young man in khaki slacks and a burgundy shirt greeted Camille as soon as she stopped at the main building at the clinic: a four story, square, flat-roofed structure with tiny windows and an arched red door.

"Checking in?" he asked in a chipper manner.

"No," Camille informed him in an equally spirited tone. "Visiting . . . my sister. Lara Stanton."

"Really? You're Miss Stanton's sister?"

"Um-hm," Camille murmured, watching him closely. "I was here yesterday. I didn't see you."

"I was off. Supposed to be off today, but I traded with Joey so he could go see the fireworks tonight."

"Nice of you," Camille remarked, opening her purse to fold a twenty-dollar bill into her palm. She glanced around, as if she were puzzled. "Let's see. I think Lara's bungalow was that one," she pointed to the nearest white stucco, red-tile roof building, frowning. "It was dark when I left."

"Oh, no," the young man hurriedly corrected. "Miss Stanton is in Bungalow Six. The pink one over there."

"Right," she agreed, handing the boy the twenty-dollar bill. "I won't be long, so don't park the car too far away, okay?"

"No problem," he said, grinning as he slipped the money into his pants pocket and got behind the wheel of Camille's rental car.

Once he had driven away, Camille hurried inside. The receptionist, a striking blonde with sky blue eyes and a dangerously dark tan, checked Camille's ID and asked her to have a seat. While waiting to learn if Lara would see her, Camille absently flipped through a copy of *Perfection* magazine.

"Who?" Lara inquired of the receptionist. "Did you say Camille Granville?"

"Yes, Miss Stanton. Do you wish to see her?"

Lara's stomach knotted in panic. "Absolutely not," she tossed back. Camille Granville had found her in Arizona? How? Why? Surely, Reet would not have told Camille where she was. Would Artie? Of course. He knew nothing about the wager or her arrangement with Reet. But what did Camille want from her?

"Miss Stanton?" the girl questioned. "Should I tell her that you are not able to see her?"

"Yes! Tell Mrs. Granville that I am not up to having visitors. Tell her to go away!" Lara slammed down the phone. Breathing hard, her mind racing, she lay down, rigid with apprehension. As lonely as she was, and as much as she craved company, no way was she going to visit with Camille. First, she had promised Reet that she would never speak to Camille again, and second, they had no reason to talk. Clasping her hands together, Lara curled her knees to her chest and squeezed her eyes shut, as if willing Camille to go away.

When Lara's door opened, she rose up on both elbows and faced Camille, who stepped inside her room as if she had been invited, and then came directly toward the bed.

"Get out," Lara managed, touching one side of her bandaged face. "I told the receptionist I did not want any visitors."

"I know," Camille confirmed, ignoring Lara as she pulled a side chair close to the bed. She sat down and focused pointedly on Lara. "But you *have* to speak to me, Lara. You're the only one who can help me."

"Help *you*? How?" Lara snapped, glaring at Camille.

"I know that you were the last person to see Max alive and I have to know what was going on."

"Nothing was going on," Lara snipped. "Why do you think I was the last person to see him alive? Wasn't he with you?"

"You know he wasn't," Camille tossed back. "And the surveillance tapes from the cruise ship prove that you and he were together."

"I don't know anything about that!" Lara grumbled, pressing her lips together in a hard line.

"You were wearing a Chinese robe, a pink lace gown underneath, and I saw you and Max come out of your stateroom together while the evacuation was in progress. He was holding a drink. You were holding onto him. What did you say to him to make him go inside with you? Was this the first time that you and Max got together?"

"Ha!" Lara burst into a curt laugh. "That's what you want to talk about? Honey, please! You think I was seducing your husband?" Her remarks were laced with cynicism. "The last thing on my mind that night was having sex with Max . . . though I'll bet it would have been wonderful."

"Then why did he go into your cabin with you?" Camille countered.

"Because he was a damn good man. Didn't I tell you that more than once? Max was solid, true to you and decent. I invited him in for a drink. That's all. He never made a pass at me, though I sure as hell wish he had."

"What were you doing besides drinking? What did you talk about?"

Lara sighed with deep resignation. "That, I cannot tell you."

"Why not?"

"Let's just say it would be a costly mistake."

Camille placed one hand on the edge of Lara's bed and shifted closer. "The surveillance tape of the Emerald Deck caught you and Max at the door to my stateroom. Did you follow him inside? Argue with him? Push him? Leave him there to die?" Camille glared at

Lara. "I have proof that you were the last person with him. You must have some idea about what happened."

"No, I don't know anything. Please go away."

"What *happened*, Lara? How did my husband wind up dead in our cabin?"

The direct question, coupled with the tears streaming down Camille's face, initiated a flood of regret and shame in Lara for not having had the courage or the decency to tell Camille the truth. But what could she do about it now? If she had not drunk so much Scotch or returned to her cabin with Max, who knows how the night might have ended? Max might still be alive. But, he wasn't, and she had promised Reet not to reveal what she and Max had discussed. She needed his financial support now, and for a long time to come. However, she could set Camille on the right path without breaking her promise to Reet.

"Talk to Davis," Lara finally replied.

"I already have."

"Then talk to him again," Lara advised with more force. "And leave me the hell out of the whole mess."

Lying alone in the dark after Camille had left, Lara closed her eyes and burrowed into her pillow, wishing she could have told Camille the truth: Your husband was never remotely unfaithful to you and you are the rightful owner of Vendora. Davis is ripping you off.

But I can't tell her, Lara silently lamented. *Right now, I need Reet's money more than I need a clear conscience.*

"Have a good time?" Corey asked Jaiden as his truck bounced over the dirt road leading from his friend's ranch, back to the highway.

"Sure," Jaiden replied, touching her waist with both hands. "That barbecue was the best."

"Yeah, Willy's secret family recipe. Been eating it for years."

"His wife was real nice, too."

"Yeah. I've been friends with both of them since we were kids. Never thought he'd turn out to be such a family man. Three kids and another on the way. Whew!" Corey chuckled, shaking his head.

Jaiden shifted her eyes to sneak a peek at Corey, wishing that the day was not coming to an end. They had spent the holiday inside

Willy's huge barn playing horseshoes, Bid Whist, darts, and pool; eating barbecue and drinking beer. Close to thirty people had been there and they had been . . . well . . . normal people—no tattoos, scruffy motorcycle jackets, or body piercing. And definitely no drugs in sight. Most had been dressed in jeans, cotton shirts, and straw cowboy boots, and they had told corny jokes and played country music in an ambiance warmed by their easy camaraderie. The children had had as much fun as the adults, making Jaiden feel as if she had just been included in a big family reunion.

"Guess I better take care of getting you home before midnight . . . like I told your mom I would," Corey broke into her thoughts.

"It's still early," Jaiden protested, checking the clock on the dashboard, not looking forward to spending the rest of her evening alone at the empty cabin. "It's not quite eleven."

"I know, but I better keep my promise to your mother. Get you safely home, and not too late. Anyway, after I drop you off, I gotta go make a delivery . . . that sign I showed you at my shop . . . well . . . the guy wants it tonight. I'll give you a call when I finish over there . . . make sure you're okay," he promised. "I sure don't want your mom on my case."

Jaiden groaned. "Oh, she's all right. A bit overprotective, though."

"She's cool. I like your mom. Can't blame her for worrying about you. My mother died when I was six years old. Don't really remember her. All my life I've wished I had a mom who worried about me, you know? Nothing wrong with that."

The remark gave Jaiden pause and made her realize how sensitive and natural Corey was, and how much more comfortable she felt with Corey than she had ever felt with Rod. Corey talked a lot, never held back, and was always thinking of her. As soon as she got home, she was going to check out the cost of tattoo removal and erase Rod's name from her arm.

Soon after emerging onto the main road, an explosion of fireworks filled the night sky, spilling out in a glittering umbrella of color.

"How beautiful," Jaiden gasped, leaning forward in her seat, gazing into the distance.

"They're coming from the other side of the lake. Want to pull over and watch?" Corey suggested.

"Yeah. Let's stop for a while."

Corey easily maneuvered his truck into a clearing at the side of the road, turned it around so that the truck bed faced the fireworks display, and then cut the engine. "Come on," he said, getting out. "Let's sit in the back and watch."

Corey climbed in first, then helped Jaiden in, and they settled down together as the dramatic light show unfolded. Jaiden leaned against Corey, who wrapped his arms around her in a relaxed, natural manner, and then rested his chin on her shoulder.

"Comfortable?" he asked, nuzzling her ear.

"Yeah," Jaiden breathed, focusing on the sky, though increasingly aware of how much she enjoyed the sensation of feeling Corey so close to her.

A spectacular burst of bright pink and yellow lights, shaped in the form of three blooming roses, spread out above them and then slowly showered down. "Oh! Look!" Jaiden exclaimed, turning around to catch Corey's reaction to the dramatic display. Her lips brushed his. She jerked her head back, but he touched her chin and turned her face to his again, and then gently kissed her on the lips.

"Really beautiful," he murmured, his intonation making it clear that he was referring to more than the fireworks.

Jaiden smiled, studying Corey's shadowed image under the glimmer of light coming from the sky, and sighed. "Yeah. Beautiful." Turning around, she lifted her chin skyward, her mind whirling with the realization of what had just happened.

They sat together in easy silence, holding hands, their bodies close, until the final splashy display erupted, then faded into a smoky veil.

Back inside the truck, Jaiden groped for an excuse to prolong the evening. "Mind if I ride along while you deliver the sign?" she suggested.

Corey's glance in her direction let her know that he was not ready to part, either. He nodded as he started the engine. "Sure. If you want."

"I do," Jaiden eagerly replied.

"Besides, if I go to my workshop first, it'll save me some time," Corey added, taking a sharp curve, then making a left turn at the intersection in the empty country road.

Thirty minutes later, after retrieving the sign, Jaiden and Corey were traveling over a twisting, two-lane road that ended at a clearing where a concrete block building sat in a wooded area of the Piney Woods. From the outside, the building appeared dark and silent, as if no one were inside, but Jaiden knew the place had to be packed because cars were parked everywhere.

Corey got out and removed the sign, which he had secured in protective packaging, then crossed the gravel driveway and went over to a man who was standing outside the door—a security guard, Jaiden supposed. Corey spoke to him briefly, and then returned to the truck.

"He's Roy Rives, a member of the Alabama-Coushatta. I know him from way back. Clyde's not here but Roy says it's okay for you to come in with me," Corey said through the open passenger side window. "Might as well come on. I don't feel too good about leaving you sitting outside like this. I won't be but a minute. I've got to put the sign in the back room until Clyde gets time to hang it."

Grinning, Jaiden hopped out. Things were looking up.

The inside of the nondescript building was alive with men and women who were laughing, drinking, playing cards and dropping coins into slot machines. Roulette wheels made whirring sounds and winners' bells jangled every few seconds. The bright lights and noisy atmosphere captivated Jaiden, who latched onto Corey's arm as he made his way through the crowd.

"Here," he said shoving a handful of quarters at her. "Play the slots until I get back." Then he disappeared.

Jaiden plopped down on a stool and dropped in her first quarter, excited to be in her second casino in as many days. Looking over at the fireplace, she recognized the blinking neon Horseshoe Pines sign as a twin to the one that Corey was delivering. She was very proud of him and his gaudy, slick creations.

From his one-way window high above the action, Davis surveyed the floor of Reet's illegal gambling casino. When he saw Jaiden sitting at a slot machine, he grabbed his walkie-talkie and pressed speed dial to get his security guard on his two-way radio. "Get that girl at number twenty-seven out of here," he ordered.

"She's with the guy delivering Clyde's sign. He's cool. Clyde gave me the okay to let him in."

"Shut the fuck up and do as I tell you," Davis shouted. "Get both of them outta here. Now!"

"Okay. Okay," the guard grumbled into his two-way communicator as he made his way toward Jaiden, who was excitedly scooping handfuls of quarters out of the tray. He tapped her lightly on the shoulder.

"Sorry, miss. This is a private, members-only club. You have to leave."

"What?" She jerked around and blinked at the guard.

"Out. Now."

"But I'm with . . ."

"Hey, Roy," Corey called out, hurrying up from the back of the casino. "What's going on?"

"You two gotta go. Boss' orders."

"Clyde said that?"

"No, I told you, he's not here. Mr. Davis said you gotta leave."

"Who's he?" Corey questioned, suspiciously. "Clyde was the one who told me to deliver his sign tonight, and you know he gave me the okay to stick around."

"Not tonight. Sign's delivered. Now, you gotta leave." Roy positioned himself behind Corey and Jaiden, spread out his arms as if corralling them, and ushered them toward the door.

"Okay. We're leaving," Corey fumed, taking Jaiden by the arm. He hurried her out to his truck, cursing under his breath, his head down. "Who the hell is this guy Davis? Toss me out? I don't think so."

Jaiden sat quietly, watching Corey, whom she could tell was embarrassed and angry at having been ejected in her presence. "It doesn't really matter," she started.

"It does to me!" Corey threw back. "I ought to go back in there and charge this guy, Davis, up. Who the fuck is he to toss me out? I have every right to be in there. Clyde told me to come by anytime."

Jaiden placed a hand of caution on Corey's knee. "Just let it go. Okay?"

Sighing, Corey yanked his seat belt across his chest, snapped it into place and stuck the key in the ignition. "Only because you're with me," he muttered, starting the engine, and then switching on his headlights. "Otherwise . . ."

"Look!" Jaiden called out, pointing to a man who had emerged from the building and was hurrying across the parking area carrying a black duffel bag. "That's Davis Kepler!" she told Corey.

"Davis? You know that guy?"

"Yeah . . . he's my mother's business partner. Damn. I hope he didn't see me in there."

"Your mom's business partner knows Clyde?" Corey frowned. "Strange, don't you think?"

"Yeah. Really strange. But I don't know much about him, except that he is driving my mom crazy and she wishes she didn't have to work with him. He must have seen me, that's why he told Roy to throw us out."

"Well, I don't care. You were with me. That's all that should have mattered. When Clyde gets back, I'm going to find out what's going on," Corey vowed. "Something isn't right. That guy, Davis, has no say about who gets into the Pines."

Jaiden tried to piece it all together during the ride back to the cabin. If Davis had seen her, would he tell her mom? Would her mother start nagging? Make her stop seeing Corey because he had taken her to an illegal gambling casino? She'd better not interfere, Jaiden decided, having made up her mind that she was going to spend quite a bit of time with Corey Windman.

Exhausted after her whirlwind and disappointing trip to Phoenix, Camille headed to the airport parking garage to retrieve her car. During the short plane ride back to Houston, she had turned Lara's parting advice over in her mind, and now that she was back, that was exactly what she planned to do: Talk to Davis again. It was too late to call him now, but she would spend the night at Vendora, instead of driving back to the lake, and then go to see Davis at his condominium first thing in the morning. She was not going to stop until he clarified quite a few things.

Vendora was dark and empty when she arrived, and after putting her car inside the garage, she made her way upstairs and into the bedroom, which thankfully, had escaped demolition. Seeing that the bed had been stripped, she went to the storage closet to get fresh sheets, and while there, heard a car pull up in front of the building. Camille peered out the window and down at the circular driveway, where she saw a slim, dark-skinned man with a bald head get out of a town car. Frowning, she continued to watch as another car pulled in behind him. When it stopped, Davis stepped out, shook hands with the man, and together they entered the front door.

What is he doing here so late? And who is that with him? Camille wondered, quietly stepping closer to the air circulation vent in the floor above Davis's office, knowing she would be able to hear everything said downstairs.

As soon as the two men entered Davis's office, the stranger spoke, and Camille immediately knew who he was: Reet Collins. There was no mistaking his deep baritone voice and his brusque manner of speaking which she had heard many times. The rattle of glasses, the clink of ice, and the splash of whiskey being poured into glasses drifted up to her.

"You bring the money?" Reet demanded in a rather testy voice.

"Yeah. You were right. The holiday take has been good. But something came up and I thought it best to get out of there early. Didn't have time to close up. Roy said he'd keep everything under control until I got back."

"Don't bother. I'll go out and take care of that later. First, give me the cash," Reet stated in a firm tone.

"You don't want me to run it through the Vegas account as usual?"

"Naw. Not this time."

"Fine. It's in the bag over there. All yours."

There was a lull in conversation, during which Camille heard footsteps, a clasp click open, and a muffled comment about the bag's contents. She held her breath, terrified of making a noise that would alert them to the fact that she was standing above them, listening.

"Looks good," Reet said. "However, you've got big problems, Davis. There are some things we gotta straighten out."

"What?"

"What? How about the fact that you don't own this joint? I know all about your wager . . . you lost your interest in this place in the casino on that cruise ship, didn't you?"

Davis laughed nervously. "Where is this coming from?"

"From this." Another long pause. "Take it. Read it, Davis. Read it aloud so I can hear you say the words."

As Camille listened to what Davis read, a chill cut through her body and she began to tremble. He had bet his interest in Vendora and lost it to Max for $25,000? On the night of the fire? What a bastard! He had kept this from her all this time?

"Where did you get this?" Davis demanded.

"From Lara, and she told me everything. Max met her in the hallway. She was drunk, mad at you, and on her way to the casino. He didn't want her to embarrass herself so he made her go back inside her stateroom to cool off. That's when he showed her the wager and told her about the bet. She even witnessed it, as you can see. When the fire broke out, she left with the note . . . she's had it all this time. You don't own any share whatsoever of Vendora, and it wouldn't surprise me if you made sure Max never got out of that fire alive, so you could protect your interest."

"No way. Don't lay that on me. I confess that I ran into Max's stateroom that night because I was looking for Lara. It was hell on the ship. People screaming. Smoke everywhere. I saw Max closing his safe, and I tried to get him to set things straight. All I wanted was for him to get rid of the damn wager. He refused . . . got rough with me. We argued. I asked him to open the safe, get the wager and tear it up. I was sure he had put it in there, but later I found out that he hadn't. Anyway, it was not supposed to be a real bet . . . we were just having a friendly game in the casino."

"But you let him draw up a valid contract. Both of you signed it. Lara witnessed it. Now, I have to send Lara a steady stream of cash to keep her quiet about the whole nasty affair."

"Listen, Max grabbed me. I twisted his arm and he fell . . . hit his head. He was not dead. I could tell he wasn't, so I got outta there. I figured a cabin steward would come along and get him out in time."

"But that never happened, did it? You left Max to die."

"Hell, I had nothing to do with him falling. And I did not know that Lara had the document. But why are you so upset? Max is dead and Lara has what she wants. We're safe."

Camille was shocked to hear Davis admit that he had confronted Max. They had argued . . . struggled! He left Max unconscious on the bathroom floor! And he stole her inheritance, too!

He must have been looking for the document when he went through my luggage, she thought, recalling that her bag had been partially unzipped when she returned home from Hawaii. She had dismissed it as the result of a routine airport security inspection. And the broken seal on the envelope that had contained the safety box key! He had searched her box before delivering it to her. How awful! She bit her lip to keep from crying.

"Get rid of Camille Granville," Reet ordered. "Our operation is running smoothly and I need Vendora to keep the cash moving. Can't afford to have that woman snooping around. You gonna take care of her, or you want me to do it?"

"I'll take care of her," Davis shouted, in a shaky voice. "She's up at her house at Lake Livingston . . ."

"Well. I'm going out to the Pines to close up," Reet snapped. "I'll be nearby. I can easily get to her."

"No, I'll do it!" Davis repeated, his voice rising shrilly.

"You sure as hell better do it tonight," Reet threatened. "I'm gonna call you on your cell phone in two hours. I want good news. Got it?"

"Sure. Sure."

Camille heard the front door open, then a pause.

"And burn that goddamned piece of paper, too," Reet yelled back to Davis.

The front door slammed shut. A car engine turned over. Camille listened to the car drive away, thinking back: Davis set up the bank account in Las Vegas to move Reet's money around. Their illicit gambling joint must be somewhere near the lake. Probably in the vicinity of the Indian reservation. Slipping out of the closet and down the back stairs, she crept down the center hall and peered into the dining room. Davis was standing at the indoor barbecue pit and had lit a blazing fire. With a snap, he tossed a piece of paper into the flames.

He's burned it, Camille realized, discouraged. *Lara is getting money from Reet—that's why she refused to talk to me. Without that signed document, how can I prove anything?*

CHAPTER 40

The strange episode at Horseshoe Pines disturbed Jaiden, who had heard her mother complain more than once about Davis Kepler's gambling habits. Was he in charge of the place? Did he own it? Did her mother know?

Those thoughts tumbled around in her head while Corey, having arrived at the cabin, parked the truck.

"Safely home," Corey joked, seeming to have pushed the incident out of his mind.

"Can you come in? Stay for a while? We could finish watching the Jackie Chan movie we started last night," she suggested, not wanting to be alone.

"Sure. I'll stay . . . for as long as you want," Corey agreed, walking with Jaiden into the dark house. "And I'll be good. I promise," he added, winking at Jaiden.

Inside, Jaiden switched on the lights and turned on the television, then went to the refrigerator and opened the door.

"Want a beer? A Coke? Water? I'm dying of thirst." She removed a small bottle of water, uncapped it and took a long swig.

"Nope, I'm fine," Corey answered, removing his baseball cap to settle on the couch. He propped one booted foot on his knee, rested his head on the back of the sofa, and closed his eyes.

Jaiden eased down beside him. Corey stretched one arm along the top of the sofa, resting his hand lightly on her shoulder. Clicking the remote, Jaiden powered up the VCR, and then pushed Play.

"Oh, my God!" she exclaimed, jerking forward, eyes wide. The lively action film she had expected to see had not come on, and in its place was a grainy black and white image of her father coming out of a cruise ship stateroom with a gorgeous, scantily dressed— Lara Stanton.

"What in the world?" Jaiden muttered, shocked and embarrassed. She quickly pushed rewind and watched it again. "Damn. This is one of the security tapes from the cruise ship. How'd this happen?"

Corey glanced around and went to pick up the action movie from a side chair next to the sofa. "Your mom must have taken our tape out."

Mouth agape, Jaiden continued to stare at the upsetting footage. "That's my dad. Why is he with that woman?"

Corey simply shrugged.

"Damn! I think I know exactly what was going down," Jaiden whispered, tucking her feet beneath her hips as she crouched on the sofa.

Mom couldn't save my father from the fire because he was not with her, Jaiden realized. *He was with that bitch, Lara Stanton, all the time. What the hell was he doing?*

"There has to be an explanation for this!" Quickly, she dropped to her knees on the floor and yanked out the box of *Sea Wind* surveillance tapes that Camille had shoved under the coffee table. She pulled it out, rifled through the videos, and grabbed another, determined to explore this bizarre revelation. She was about to slip another tape into the VCR when the phone rang. Jaiden jumped up and snatched it on the second ring.

"It's me," Camille whispered in a raspy voice. "Jaiden, please do as I tell you and do not ask any questions. This is very important."

"Well, I'm glad you called because I was . . ."

"Please, Jaiden. Listen to me. Don't interrupt. Go through the security tapes under the coffee table."

"Exactly what I was doing," Jaiden threw back rather sarcastically.

"Pull out any tape that is marked Grand Casino. Got it?"

"Okay. Sure. Grand Casino. Why are you whispering?"

"Is Corey with you?"

"Yes, he's right here."

"Good. I want him to drive you into town . . . to Vendora . . . right now. Bring the tapes. But first, call the police and tell them that the place is being robbed."

"Robbed! Mom! Are you okay?" Jaiden shouted.

The line clicked off. Jaiden hurried to follow her mother's instructions.

Camille stepped into the shadows of a tall potted palm at the entrance to the cavernous dining room, now lit by the glow of flames rising in the circular barbecue pit. She watched Davis take the fire poker and stab at a piece of burning paper, then rip open a bulky envelope.

"I wouldn't do that if I were you," she hurled across the room, her voice hard and flat as it echoed in the empty space.

Davis spun around and dropped the envelope, shocked to realize that he was not alone. Pieces of paper fluttered to the floor, but he was too absorbed in watching Camille to notice. "Why are you here?" he spat out, glaring.

"I have more right to be here than you do," she replied with authority, stepping from her hiding place. She slowly walked toward him. "You're the intruder, not me."

"Intruder? I don't think so. I own this place, remember?"

"Own? Ha! I know for a fact that you have no claim to Vendora. You don't own this place. I do," Camille declared with steely calm. "I heard everything you and Reet Collins discussed tonight. You killed my husband! Stole Max's business! And you and your buddy are up to some very dirty business at my expense. I want you out of here . . . out of my life."

"You're talking crazy!" Davis accused, a glint of anger lighting his eyes. "You're groping for an excuse to get rid of me, but it's not going to work, Camille. You have no proof that I have done anything wrong."

Praying that the security tapes of the *Sea Wind* casino would prove her right, she plunged ahead. "You may have burned the evidence that proves that Max won back his rightful ownership of Vendora, but the entire transaction is on tape. I have it, and that is all the proof I need to reclaim what you have stolen."

"You're lying!" Davis shouted, baring his bright white teeth as he tapped the fire poker against the side of the brick pit. "It's dangerous to go around making nasty accusations like that. You'll find yourself in a whole lot of trouble."

"Don't threaten me. It's all over, Davis. The police are on their way, and I have the tapes. So, I wouldn't do anything stupid right now."

Slowly, he walked toward her. Camille stepped back, but never took her eyes from his face, hoping she appeared more courageous than she felt. Her heart pounded, her legs trembled, and she clenched both hands into hard, small fists.

Suddenly, Davis rushed forward, swinging the poker from side to side. Camille dodged the heavy iron pole and quickly circled him, forcing Davis to spin around and face her, the fire pit now to her back.

Caught off balance by her swift movement, Davis's hesitation gave her time to grab the envelope from the floor and tilt it upside down. Calculator tapes and bank deposit slips from Western Ridge Bank in Las Vegas tumbled out—evidence of the paper trail of Reet's dirty money. When Camille glanced up, Davis was on her, flailing the poker in sharp jerky stabs. He struck her shoulder, forcing her back. She stumbled, but regained her footing and ran for the door. However, he rushed her, caught her by the arm, and sent her crashing to the floor.

"I should have gotten rid of you a long time ago," Davis muttered through clenched teeth, as he stood over her, breathing hard. "Reet warned me that you would be a problem, but I thought I could handle you without resorting to violence. You brought this on yourself, Camille. All you had to do was take my money and sell me your shares . . . get on with your life. This did not have to happen, and really, I do hate to hurt you, but you are not going to ruin my plans. Vendora is mine."

An image of Max lying unconscious, still alive and alone on the floor of their stateroom shower, flashed into Camille's mind, giving her the courage to push herself onto her hands and knees. Enraged, she pinned Davis with eyes full of hate. Gathering all of her courage and strength, she suddenly shot to her feet, let out a scream and extended both arms, palms toward Davis. In one swift movement, she drove her hands into his chest and shoved him backwards, into the flame-filled pit.

Immediately, his shirt caught on fire. A cloud of black smoke shot up and the smell of burning fabric filled the air. His body jerked forward, he righted himself, and frantically managed to swat out the flames.

"You fool!" he screamed, rushing at Camille. He knocked her down and pinned her to the floor, one arm at her throat. "You are not going to ruin this for me," he yelled, increasing the pressure on her neck. "I made this place what it is. Without me all you'd have is a muddy, moldy pile of bricks, so don't act like you never needed me."

"Let . . . go of me!" Camille grunted, struggling to pry his body off hers. She dug her fingernails into his bare arm and scraped at his flesh until he cursed and let her go. "I'll see you in hell for killing my husband!"

"Oh, no you won't," he threw back, jumping up to retrieve the poker. Holding it tightly, he approached, the flames from the barbecue pit turning his golden-tan face a fiery red. Camille held her body very still as he came closer, and the moment he prepared to strike her, she fell to her knees and grabbed both of his legs, sending him backwards, into the fire again. His terrified screams mingled with the high-pitched sound of a police siren as a patrol car pulled up outside.

Camille tried to stand, but her knees were too weak. She collapsed just as two police officers burst through the front door and rushed to Davis, whose entire upper body was engulfed in flames. The officers yanked him from the red brick pit, smothered the fire, and then laid him on the carpet next to her.

"Call for an ambulance," one of the policemen shouted to his partner, before turning to her. "Are you hurt, ma'am?"

"No," Camille managed. "Not physically, at least." Her eyelids fluttered closed.

By the time she had given the officer her statement and the ambulance had arrived to take Davis away, Jaiden and Corey rushed in. Camille opened her eyes in relief, and taking Jaiden's arm, she struggled to stand.

"Mom! What in the world is going on?" Tears streamed over Jaiden's cheeks. "Davis was robbing you?"

Not knowing where to start, Camille simply nodded, thinking, *That's exactly what he's been doing.* "Thank God, you followed my instructions."

Jaiden rushed on. "I thought he must have been up to something illegal. Corey and I saw him tonight . . . coming out of this . . . this . . ."

"Illegal casino," Corey finished, going over to stand next to Jaiden. "You wanted these," he said to Camille, handing her the tapes.

"Yes. Exactly what I need to put Davis away for a long time and reclaim what is mine."

One of the officers approached. "Can you show us where the illegal gambling casino is?" he asked Corey.

"Sure. I can take you there," Corey assured him. "Let me know when you're ready to go."

"I saw the videotape," Jaiden was saying to Camille. "Mom . . . I know about Dad and Lara. I'm so sorry . . . I should never have accused you of abandoning him. But with Lara Stanton. That woman? How could he . . . ?"

"Shush," Camille whispered in a quieting murmur, linking one arm with Jaiden's. "There's a lot more to this. I'll tell you everything, when we get home."

CHAPTER 41

Six weeks later inside a Harris County courtroom

When the jailer wheeled Davis into the courtroom and left him sitting in his wheelchair facing her, Camille tried to ignore his presence, but her curiosity won out. She glanced over at him from her seat at a table in the front of the courtroom and flinched: The face of the once-handsome golden boy from Hollywood was lined with ridges and discoloration from the burns he had suffered at Vendora. How ironic that both he and Lara would suffer this fate!

With his eyes cast downward and his hands folded in his lap, Davis resembled an old man, dozing in his wheelchair—an old man who had resigned himself to living with his punishment. All of his boasting, overconfident brashness was gone, and in its place was a broken, beaten man. Camille found no pleasure in seeing him this way, but was relieved that he was out of her life and would pay for the wrong he had done to her family.

Lara Stanton, wearing a sheer black veil to shield her newly sculpted face from photographers, sat three rows behind Camille, her latest love interest at her side. At the back of the room, Rochelle was sitting with Jaiden, where they had sat together and listened to the proceedings for the past three days.

When the judge entered the courtroom, everyone stood, and then quickly quieted down, preparing to hear the judge render her decision. After giving Davis permission to remain seated in his wheelchair, she read the verdict.

"I have reviewed all of the evidence," the judge started, "including the Grand Casino security tapes from the cruise ship *Sea Wind*, and I have heard testimony from Lara Stanton, the *Sea Wind* pit boss on duty that fateful night, and Neil Windman of Tropica Cruise Lines, who has validated the authenticity of the surveillance tapes. In my opinion, the contract that Davis Kepler and Maxwell Granville drew up aboard the *Sea Wind*, as captured on the surveillance tape, is a valid contract, executed in good faith. My conclusion is that Camille Granville, the widow of Maxwell Granville, is the true and sole owner of the supper club, Vendora. I am ordering Davis Kepler to pay Camille Granville three hundred thousand dollars in restitution, and serve thirty-six months in state prison, excluding time already served."

Camille had to bite her tongue to keep from shouting with joy. Her mind was so full of relief; she paid little attention to the rest of the judge's verdict, which related to the punishment Davis was to receive for engaging in illegal gambling activities. There had not been enough evidence to bring charges of attempted murder, though Camille would forever believe that Davis had wanted Max dead and had left him to die in the fire. Reet, who had already been prosecuted two weeks earlier, was currently serving ten years in state prison for racketeering and extortion.

At the conclusion of the hearing, Camille gave Paul Cotter a big hug of thanks for his work as her attorney. Excited conversation erupted in the courtroom, forcing Davis to finally look up. He shot a nasty scowl at Camille, who averted her eyes as the jail guard wheeled him out of the courtroom and back to his holding cell.

Lara sauntered over, sat down in Paul Cotter's empty chair next to Camille, and adjusted her veil, which barely concealed the actress' big brown eyes, now brimming with tears.

"I am so sorry I couldn't tell you the truth when you came to see me at the clinic. There was no way for me to go back on my word to Reet. I couldn't take the chance," Lara apologized. "I never dreamed that Davis would try to hurt you. I was so involved in solving my own problems, I just shut your troubles out."

"I understand the pressure you were under, Lara," Camille conceded. "You were in a difficult position. However, I must believe that, if you had known that Davis deliberately left Max to die, you would have told me."

"That's true." She paused, thoughtfully. "I would have. Max was a good guy. He deserved better. You did, too."

"Thank you for testifying, Lara. I wish you the best."

Lara placed a delicate hand over Camille's. "You too," she murmured, and then straightening her back, cast a glance up at the handsome man standing at her side and touched his arm. "Guy, I'd like you to meet Camille. Camille, this is . . ."

"Guy Fernandes," Camille finished, reaching over to shake the actor's hand. "You starred in *Flashfire* with Lara, right?"

"Absolutely," Guy tossed back, a gleam of appreciation in his startling amber eyes. "A very exciting movie and my best work, so far."

"I'll have to catch it on video," Camille replied with amusement. "What's next for you?"

Lara tore her concentration from the television news reporters lingering in the hallway and answered for Guy. "*Jungle Flower*. Guy plays a wealthy coffee planter, and I play his mistress. We start shooting in three weeks. In Rio de Janiero. Can you believe that?"

"You? The mistress of a handsome, young Brazilian millionaire?" Camille laughed and stood. "Yes, I most certainly can believe it, and I'm sure you'll both be perfect in the parts."

Lara giggled and fluttered her fingers at the reporters. "Now, I must go and unveil my new face to the press . . . and fill them in on my upcoming picture." She squeezed Camille's hand, and then rose and linked her arm through Guy's.

With a combination of admiration and mirth, Camille watched as Lara tossed back her head and strutted toward the reporters who had covered her daily courtroom entrances with zeal.

When Neil came over and touched Camille's arm, she turned and gave him a gentle smile of acknowledgment. It was nice to see him again. She had not heard from him since that wonderful afternoon they had spent at the Indian dance exposition and his return to Texas was comforting. When she had seen him walk into the courtroom today, she had felt a jolt of satisfaction, confident that his testimony about the authenticity of the security tapes would be key to nailing Davis.

"Neil. It's good to see you again." Camille shook Neil's hand and held onto it longer than she should have, grateful for his friendship and his convincing testimony. "Thanks for not giving up on me or my search for answers about Max's death."

"You're very welcome," he replied. "I promised to do all that I could to help you, but I never dreamed things would turn out like this. You are very brave. It was dangerous for you to go after Davis alone. I wish I could have done more to help."

"No," Camille protested. "This was *my* fight and I had to go it alone, though at times I was tempted to give up and walk away from all that my husband worked so hard to build."

"You are not the 'giving-up kind'," Neil commented with seriousness. "I recognized that, the first time I met you."

When Jaiden and Rochelle caught Camille's attention and motioned from the back of the room for her to come over, she told Neil, "Don't forget. You promised me dinner."

"I haven't forgotten," he reassured her. "I'll be in touch . . . soon."

With a satisfied smile, Camille linked arms with Jaiden and Rochelle and started down the courthouse steps, secure in the knowledge that she and her daughter had finally moved beyond the mistakes of the past and were on their way to creating a wonderful future together.

SILENT WAGER

ANITA BUNKLEY

ABOUT THIS GUIDE

The suggested questions are intended to enhance
your group's reading of SILENT WAGER by Anita Bunkley.

DISCUSSION QUESTIONS

1. How would you describe Camille and Max Granville's marriage?

2. If your husband (not your boyfriend) committed adultery, would you forgive him? If so, why? If not, why not?

3. Why do you think Nici and Jaiden's friendship deteriorated after high school? Do you still have a best friend from your high school days? If so, how have you managed to keep the friendship strong?

4. If you had been Rochelle, would you have told Camille about Jaiden's drug use? If so, why? If not, why not?

5. Do you think Jaiden expected too much from her relationship with Rod? What do you think about the way she left him?

6. How do you think both Lara Stanton and Davis Kepler benefited from their relationship?

7. Which do you think was more important for Camille, to repair her relationship with Jaiden or to discover the truth about Max's death?

8. Was Tropica Cruise Lines fair with Camille? With Lara? Would you have sued the cruise line for more money?

9. Do you believe that compulsive gambling is a disease? Do you know anyone who suffers from this problem?

10. Do you think Indian tribes in Texas should be allowed to own and operate casinos? What would be beneficial? What would be harmful?

11. Mother/daughter relationships often go through difficult periods. Did Camille try hard enough to understand Jaiden? Did Jaiden try hard enough to understand her mother?

12. Max was a risk-taker. Are you?